The Secret Watcher of Summit Avenue

a novel

by

Mark J. Morlock

ISBN: 978-0692790328

Edited by Tara Grover Smith
Front cover painting by Cindy Maderos and used with permission.
Cartoons drawn by Mike Swann

Table of Contents

Epistle

If old houses would only talk, what stories they could tell of all that's gone on inside their closed doors and sometimes shaded windows. Often enough, I suppose, these stories would be what most people would call unexceptional: of day-to-day life interspersed with the commonplace periods of joy and disappointment, of comfort and heartache that are the human's lot. But that old Winkler house across the street, the stories that house could tell would take a long time in the telling.

Now, at the beginning of the new century, it's over one hundred years old. Built in the Victorian style that was popular at the time, it sits on the top of a long rise overlooking the city below, and has housed, on and off, four generations of Winklers. And though you would never know it, it has over those long years witnessed many times over seasons of great joy and terrible grief, and has weathered through periods of madness and delusion, of deceit bordering on treachery, and of well-disguised crime. And it remembers all these stories, I'm sure of that. Oh, yes, it remembers.

We first met—that house and I—in the years just before World War II, when I was young and it was already middle-aged. I was attracted to it, and the people in it, right from the start. From my bedroom window across the street I could look down the block and see its tall roofline and part of that long porch. That would be a comfort to me later, after the war started and things turned bad for everybody. Well, almost everybody.

We were happy back then—at first, anyway. I was in love, and so, I think, was that house. The long, low, welcoming porch shone with a warm blush, and especially, it seemed to me, when Henry Winkler was sitting there in his old wicker rocker, puffing on his pipe. Back then I swear that its long, high porch literally smiled out at the world, its corners pointing up, its picket railing offering a toothy, contented grin.

Yes, that old house loved Henry Winkler, as, in the years to come, would I. But our story doesn't start here. It starts years earlier, in 1894, on a warm Sunday in mid-summer, when Wilhelm Winkler, Henry's father, had a secret to reveal.

Chapter One

In 1894, America was reveling in a new-found industrial affluence. It was a time of growth and marvelous change, of forward-looking optimism. In the cities of the nation, steel was replacing wood, underground waterworks were providing running water at the turn of a tap, electricity was lighting homes and buildings and propelling trolleys, and rutted, dusty streets were giving way to wide avenues of cobblestone and smooth brick. Summit Avenue, in the newest part of a city in the heart of America, was one of these new streets. Situated on the extreme north of the expanding city and removed from the noisy industry to the south, it ran along the crest of a hill for six blocks between Centennial Drive and Market.

Immigrants and sons of immigrants were rapidly filling the high avenue with large and beautiful homes. In style and design, these new houses reflected the diversity of their owners. There were stately Gothic Revivals with steeply pitched roofs; high dormer windows and board and batten siding; tall Italianates with low-hipped roofs, towers and cupolas; rectangular Second Empires with colored-tile patterns on their mansard roofs; and exotic Queen Annes with long porches and gaily decorated turrets and bay windows. And in 1894 their cornices and cupolas, parapets and porticos were all sparkling and new.

Now, on this particular mid-summer Sunday, the morning service at St. Paul's Lutheran Church was finally over, and after the obligatory punch and light conversation, Wilhelm Winkler had loaded his wife Sophie and seven-year-old daughter Ellen onto the old delivery wagon and turned the wagon north to begin the long, slow climb up Centennial Drive. Wilhelm had a secret, and they were on their way to a surprise.

He was a small man, short—five feet-eight in his Sunday shoes—and wiry, with dark straight hair and deep brown eyes that sparkled with energy and humor, and a thin mustache that turned up at the ends. He was a first-generation American, coming to this country with his widowed father when he was two.

As they made their way up the half-mile grade, Wilhelm took it easy on the old horse, allowing it to set its own slow pace for the climb. But Wilhelm would never be a man who would relish a slow pace, not when there were things that needed fixing and jobs that needed doing. And at the Winkler Sausage Factory, taken over by Wilhelm at his father's death, there were always these things.

Sophie sat on the right side of the hard bench on the swaying wagon, waiting patiently for Wilhelm to unveil his surprise. She was a gentle and sympathetic woman, with a forbearance that matched and restrained the impetuous and sometimes brash energy of her husband. She was slim like her husband and almost as tall, and had long, naturally wavy light-brown hair and soft, intelligent blue eyes under thin arching eyebrows. Her hands were small, with long, nimble fingers that rested calmly in her lap.

Swaying easily in the warm, bright sunshine, she half listened as Wilhelm lambasted St. Paul's pastor, Reverend Schneider. It wasn't that Wilhelm had anything against religion. He considered himself to be a Christian man with a readily admitted appreciation for what he saw to be the major points of the Bible. But if Reverend Schneider was the shepherd of his flock, Wilhelm Winkler was his black sheep, and Wilhelm's litany of complaints against the old German was growing.

"And where's that pompous old coot get off telling me what I oughta be doing in the privacy of my own home?" Wilhelm offered to the street.

"It's his business, darling," Sophie said absent-mindedly, responding for the street. "He's a preacher."

"He's an idiot," Wilhelm grunted.

"He's an idiot!" Ellen repeated enthusiastically.

Wilhelm and Sophie, on opposite sides of the little girl, looked down to her with surprise, then to each other.

"You shouldn't talk that way about the Reverend, honey," Sophie offered weakly.

"Papa did," Ellen countered.

For a second Sophie was stymied. "Then Papa shouldn't talk that way either," she said finally.

"Idiot!" Ellen said again, liking the word.

"Stop it now, missy," Wilhelm snapped down to her.

Ellen knew she could challenge her mother but knew better than to challenge her father. After stealing a quick glance up to him, she turned her face forward and shut her mouth. Idiot! She mentally yelled to herself. Idiot! Idiot! Idiot!

When they reached the top of the hill, Wilhelm turned the wagon west onto Summit Avenue. Stopping the wagon, he turned to his two passengers. "Now I want you to close your eyes, and keep them closed until I tell you to open them. Promise?"

Sophie nodded playfully, and for emphasis placed her hands over her eyes.

"I don't want to," Ellen complained.

"You have to," Wilhelm said.

"I don't *want* to," she said again, staring him down. She liked this little game.

7

"Now if you don't close your eyes, there'll be no surprise," Wilhelm said sternly.

Trumped, Ellen closed her eyes and clamped her hands over them, imitating her mother.

"Good!" Wilhelm said, getting the horse moving again.

As the wagon lurched forward, Ellen turned her head towards her father, watching him through the slits in her fingers. Idiot! she screamed to herself. Idiot!

Halfway down the second block of Summit Avenue, Wilhelm pulled the wagon to a stop, then directed his gaze up and to the right, to the sparkling new home with its long, low porch and ornate bay window rising all the way to the rooftop. It's a beaut, he thought. To Wilhelm, the house represented the fruits of his labor, the result of ten years of hard work in the sausage factory, developing it into an enterprise profitable enough to propel him and his family into a new home on Summit Avenue.

"Can we look now?" Sophie asked.

"You sure can," Wilhelm replied.

Squinting from the shock of the bright spring sun, she looked for the first time on what was to be their new home.

"Is it for us?" Ellen asked.

"If your mother agrees," Wilhelm answered softly. He looked past Ellen to Sophie, who sat quietly, her gaze moving slowly up, down and around the gleaming new home, her mouth open, as if she wanted to laugh. "Did you guess it?" he asked.

Finally Sophie forced her eyes away from the house, to her husband. "I was hoping," she said.

"Now if it's not exactly what you want, I'll keep looking," Wilhelm said, knowing that the words were wasted.

"Can we afford it?" Sophie asked.

"We can," Wilhelm answered, the ends of his mustache tipping up at the edges of a toothy grin. "As long as people keep eating our sausages. Let's go in," he said. "I have a key."

At the door, Wilhelm turned the key in the lock, the big oak door swung soundlessly inward, and they entered into the foyer. The house smelled of freshly cut wood and new paint, bright and glossy in the strong light of the late morning. Immediately in front of them a stairway climbed up to the second floor, bending to the left at a stairwell halfway up. Light from a round stained-glass window at the stairwell danced on the hard wood of the floor and the dark wood of the heavy banister. Sophie caressed the smooth surface of the wood.

"Walnut," Wilhelm said. "And there's more in the dining room."

8

"It's beautiful," Sophie said. It was all there was to say.

"And look," he said excitedly, his eyes shining. He moved to a button on the wall by the front door, and when he turned the button, a chandelier hanging from the ceiling became bright with light.

"What makes it do that?" Ellen asked.

"Electricity," Wilhelm answered proudly. "The whole house's wired. No more gaslight and oil lanterns."

"Electricity," Ellen repeated.

To the left of the foyer, double doors opened into the parlor, where a huge brick fireplace dominated the west wall. Two large front windows, bordered with stained glass, looked out onto the porch and beyond, down the hill to the city below. It was to be a bright and cheery room, especially on spring and summer mornings when the new sun, low in the sky, would sparkle against the stained glass, sending errant kaleidoscopic patterns dancing against the far wall.

Ahead, under the curving staircase, an arched doorway led into the dining room, with its recessed walnut china cabinets against the north and south walls, the intricate pattern of the leaded glass doors looking like stars set against a chocolate brown sky. Soon this room would be dominated by a huge walnut dinner table where the Winklers would take their meals, and where Wilhelm would read his morning newspaper when the weather was too cold for the porch.

To the left, off the dining room, sliding doors opened into what was to be Wilhelm's study. Wilhelm's great oak roll-top desk would sit against the north wall, his leather chair and ottoman in the corner facing west, where he could look out through a wall of windows to a young sugar maple tree, and, in the early evening, to the setting sun.

Like a master of ceremonies, Wilhelm led the two of them through each room, pointing out with pride and enthusiasm the conveniences and innovations offered by blooming technology: electric lighting in every room, and outlets low in the walls for table lamps; sliding, counterbalanced windows; steel heating radiators supplied with hot water from the coal-fired furnace in the cellar below.

Finally, Wilhelm led them through the dining room into the kitchen, attached as a single story to the rear of the house. A side door opened to a small, east-facing covered porch, and a line of small windows looked out to the north, past the boundaries of the back yard and down the long hill to the farms and pastures beyond, and to the blue-green line of the river far in the distance.

Wilhelm pulled Sophie to the sink sitting against the north wall. "Look here," he said, turning a spigot and watching the clear water bubble from the faucet. "Running water, both hot and cold."

Wilhelm shepherded them back through the house and up the winding stairway to the second floor. To the left from the top of the staircase were two doors, one opening to a small side bedroom, the other into the large front bedroom where Wilhelm and Sophie would sleep. At the end of the hallway to the right were two more doors opening to rear bedrooms. Ellen would reluctantly choose the east-facing room for her own, where on fine days the new sun would shine in through her side window.

Wilhelm's immediate concern, though, was in what lay straight ahead: the bathroom. "Come on honey, this you have to see," he said, grabbing Sophie's hand and pulling her into the small side room.

But Ellen didn't follow them in, her attention taken by a glimpse through a half-closed side door of a stairway leading up. Alone now in the hallway, she moved cautiously to the doorway. Looking in, she saw that the stairway led to the attic, empty, airy and now mid-day bright above her. And it was odd, because although the little girl was most often frightened by the new and the strange, she felt the attic to be welcoming and friendly, beckoning. And so, alone but without fear, she began her climb up the steep, narrow, curving steps.

In the bathroom, Wilhelm was excitedly pointing out the virtues of the state-of-the-art fixtures: the bathroom sink and huge claw-foot bathtub, both with hot and cold water, and the new-fangled water closet, its tank and chain at head-high level above the seat. Wilhelm guided Sophie to the water closet. "Look here now," he said. He pulled the chain and let the water, rushing down through the toilet, speak for itself.

Sophie watched the swirling water. "Miraculous," she said.

Wilhelm looked around. "Where's Ellen?" he asked. "She needs to see this too. Ellen!" he called out. "Ellie, honey!"

There was no answer, and after a moment Sophie walked to the doorway. "Ellen!" she called out into the empty hallway.

Up in the attic, Ellen sat in the middle of the rough wood floor, staring out at the long row of dormered windows to the west. She vaguely thought she heard her name being called, but her rapt concern was up here high, at the top of the house. The spacious attic was bright with light, for while most attics are sparsely windowed, this one was full of them. In the front was the large bay window rising all the way to the sides of the inverted V of the gabled roof, and in the back, another large window looked out and down onto the roof of the kitchen and the back yard. And to either side, long dormers opened the attic laterally, warm sunlight dancing off the rows of wide windows. This wasn't just an attic, Ellen thought. This was a room, for living.

And this was how Wilhelm and Sophie found her, as, climbing the narrow stairway, their heads cleared the level of the attic floor. "Ellie," Wilhelm complained a bit crossly. "What're you doing up here?"

"Can this be my room?" Ellen asked hopefully.

"It's the attic," Wilhelm said. "You've seen attics before. Now come on down. I've got something to show you."

"I don't want to," Ellen said firmly, tightening her hands into little fists and setting her jaw into a tight pout.

"Come on, honey," Sophie said soothingly. "You can choose your bedroom."

"I want *this* to be my bedroom," Ellen said defiantly, her eyes bright and hard.

"You come down these stairs right now, missy, before I go looking for a switch," he said sternly.

For a moment, Ellen and Wilhelm's steel eyes sparred, then Ellen's dulled, and she slowly, grudgingly rose from the floor.

"You'll want to see the bathtub, honey," Sophie said gaily, hoping to lighten the mood. "It's big as a lake!"

Wilhelm and Sophie started back down the stairs, and Ellen took one last long look around her new-found rough-wood sanctuary, out through the dormered windows looking east, the windows she would later appropriately call her windows to heaven.

* * * *

It was late afternoon in early June, ten months since the Winklers had taken up residence in their new home on Summit Avenue. Already the house looked well lived-in. The grass Wilhelm had planted was full and lush, and on this particular Saturday, newly-mowed. Sophie had planted two trees—a dogwood and a hornbeam—
on either side of the front yard, and her flower beds lining the perimeter of the house—roses and gladiolus, and beds of pansies and snapdragons—bordered the fresh white paint with bright dots of color.

Ellen played alone in the back yard. She was trying to catch a butterfly. Running in her bare feet in the warm grass, her light cotton dress dancing around her ankles, she chased behind the erratic flight of the gold and black insect. She followed the bobbing butterfly out of the sun and into the shade of the young sugar maple tree at the side of the house. It was just in front of her, and as she reached out to grab it, she stumbled and fell. Shaken by the fall but unhurt, she sat up on her knees and brushed bits of grass and dirt from her dress. Then she saw it: a bird's nest fallen from the tree, lying half-

11

hidden in a tuft of grass near the trunk. And inside the nest was a robin's egg, small and blue and unbroken. Cautiously, Ellen moved to the nest and carefully extracted the perfect egg. She examined it intently, her eyes bright with the excitement of the lucky find. She'd hide it, she thought, hide it in her secret spot in the attic.

Holding the egg gently in her cupped hand, Ellen scampered around to the front of the house and entered through the front door, then hurried up the wide stairway to the upstairs, her feet making soft tapping sounds on the polished wooden steps.

At the top of the stairs, she stopped for a second to catch her breath, her pink lips parted as she breathed heavily and quickly. Then she heard a sound coming from her parents' bedroom. It was the sound of laughter. Then the laughter stopped, and Ellen heard a long, low groan. "Ohhhh," the sound said. The sound, hinting of sickness and pain, confused and frightened the girl. "Mama?" she asked softly.

Now discomfited, she moved unsurely toward the door to her parents' bedroom. She forced her hand out to the brass doorknob, then turned it, and fearfully pushed open the door that Wilhelm had neglected to lock. What her untrained eye first saw on the big four-posted bed some twenty feet away was simply a mass of human flesh, surreal to her, like an impressionistic painting. Then quickly the body parts emerged: feet and legs, heads and arms, and her father's pink rump pointing back straight at her.

To Ellen's shocked mind it seemed clear that Wilhelm was hurting her mother, that he had gone mad. For a heartbeat, the little girl stood frozen in the doorway, the fragile blue egg falling unknowingly from her hand and breaking on the wooden floor at her feet. Then she screamed.

In the years to come, Wilhelm and Sophie would remember this moment with good humor, both surprised by the speed with which passion was transformed into mortification, and mortification into calculated damage control. But at the moment all they felt was wild confusion.

"Gott im Himmel!" Wilhelm exclaimed, reverting to the language of his father, his left hand frantically fumbling with the bedclothes as he tried to cover himself.

"It's okay, honey. Everything's okay," Sophie said soothingly to the little yellow-haired girl standing wide-eyed and frozen, like a portrait framed by the dark wood of the doorway. Then Ellen's mouth fell open, and she turned and ran from the room.

"Ellie, stop!" Sophie cried out in vain. But she was gone down the hallway, and Wilhelm and Sophie could only share a look of sick chagrin before scrambling from the rumpled bed and searching frantically for their clothes.

12

When Wilhelm managed to get his undershirt on and his pants pulled up around his middle, he left the bedroom for the hallway. "Ellie? Ellie honey?" he called out as he hastily buttoned his pants.

A moment later Sophie, a thin robe wrapped around her naked body, joined him in the hallway. "Where'd she go?" she asked.

Wilhelm could only shrug his shoulders. "Ellie?" he called out again. There was no answer.

Walking the length of the hallway, they entered Ellen's bedroom to find it deserted. After checking the closet and finding it empty, Wilhelm stood in the middle of the room, scratching his head and thinking.

"I know where she is," he said finally.

"Where?" Sophie asked.

In answer, Wilhelm pointed wryly to the ceiling.

And so the two of them slowly climbed the rough steps leading to the attic. The attic was almost empty and bright with the afternoon light shining in through the many dormered windows, so it didn't take them long to spot her.

She was sitting in the corner where the gabled roof began its rise toward its peak in the middle of the room. "You come out of there, missy," Wilhelm said sternly. Little Ellen shook her head from side to side; Wilhelm's voice of authority was a bad choice.

"Come on out," Sophie offered soothingly. "There's nothing for you to be afraid of."

Still, she wouldn't move.

"Come on. Let's go downstairs," Sophie said, smiling encouragingly to the round face peeking back from the corner of the attic. "You need a bath, and I need to start dinner."

Finally, Ellen rose from the corner and walked to them. Wilhelm and Sophie hugged her, and smoothed her hair and dress.

They walked down the attic steps together, Ellen in between the two adults.

"What were you doing to Mama?" Ellen asked when they'd reached the hallway.

Wilhelm was afraid of this; in the back of his mind, he'd known there would be this reckoning. He'd hoped that she'd be a bit older, and that Sophie would do the explaining, preferably with him safely away.

"Uh...well," Wilhelm stammered, smiling nervously down to the little girl. "You explain it, Mother," he said to Sophie.

Sophie flashed an exasperated "thank-you-very-much" look to her apologetic husband. "Well," she said, smiling awkwardly down into Ellen's probing eyes. "We were doing what married people do. To have a baby."

13

"What married people do to have a baby," Ellen repeated. She would remember that.

The three walked slowly down the hallway toward the front of the house. And unbeknownst to any of them, a solitary sperm—one of a hundred million competitors—was at that very moment doggedly swimming the treacherous, winding course up Sophie's fallopian tube, soon to implant itself in the waiting fertile ovum. The following spring Sophie would give birth to a baby boy who would live eighty-two years on this earth, far longer than either his parents or his sister. His name would be Henry Winkler, in honor of his grandfather.

Epistle

If you were to see *Summit Avenue* today, it would look much the same as it did over sixty years ago, when I first saw it. Miraculously, all of the original houses still stand: not one has burned. A hundred years of wear have, of course, taken their toll on the street. Like people, old houses wear down, and like people too, it seems, fall out of favor with age. In the sixties and seventies especially, Summit Avenue was abandoned by the well-off in favor of the newer suburbs sprouting like weeds in all directions. Dull and sunken, the once-grand houses became rentals and boarding houses. The single exception was the Winkler house, which Henry maintained with vigilant loving care right up to the very end of his life.

Now, though, virtually all of the houses have been restored. Wealthy young couples seem to have gotten the bug for the old architecture, and over the last dozen years or so have moved back, restoring the old houses inside and out. And so if you walked the length of Summit Avenue today, you'd see, once again, the big houses sparkling with new paint, the wide lawns thick with bright flowers and lush green grass, and the porches filled with playing children. Ironically, the solitary exception is again the old Winkler house, which now stands empty and abandoned, the paint peeling, the porch broken and sagging. It breaks my heart to see that house now, knowing it the way I do.

At the corner of Summit and Centennial, across the street, there's now a flat, concrete-block strip mall with a convenience store and pizza parlor, which thankfully Henry never had to see. And right by the corner on this side of the street is a bus stop, where you can catch the metroline to take you down and around the city.

Sometimes I'll ride the Number Two around town just to see how things have changed. It carries me down Centennial—now three lanes wide in each direction—into the heart of the old city, past the bank building where the Winkler Sausage Factory had been, then under the interstate and east, over the river and out toward the hospital and university. During the workday, everything bustles with noisy activity, the streets and parking lots filled with cars, the shops and offices animated with young people moving about like busy ants. Overhead, jet airplanes rumble across the sky, low and descending, on their way to the airport farther to the south. So much has changed, when you get away from Summit Avenue.

Now if you were to take the Number Two bus early in the morning and get off at Hawthorne, on the east side of the river, you could walk south into a maze of apartment buildings. With disingenuous names like "Oak Meadow

Manor" and "Hillsdale Estates," they stand like brick fortresses, two and sometimes three stories high. In the early morning a random patchwork of light shines from their long rows of identical windows as the hundreds of residents make their preparations for the day. And if, in the half-light of early morning, you were to approach a modest two-story, twenty-unit brick structure deceptively named "Paradise Gardens," you would be walking smack into the middle of this story.

Chapter Two

Exactly halfway down the inside corridor of the first floor of the "Paradise Gardens" was the door to Apartment 105. On this particular early morning, the door to #105 opened at about the same time it always did on workday mornings, and Carole Browning, Attorney-at-Law, dressed in a worn robe and floppy slippers, walked to the glass door entryway to retrieve the morning newspaper. Through the glass she could see the sky lightening; it promised to be another beautiful spring day. A slim woman in her late twenties, Carole yawned as she made her way back to the apartment with the paper, her blue eyes perplexed, still struggling to focus. Thank God for Morning Thunder tea, she thought. It's going to be a three-cup morning.

Back inside the apartment, Carole made her way to the cup of steaming tea sitting on the cluttered kitchen counter, stopping several times to stick her finger into the dirt of a potted plant, checking for proper wetness. Carole could grow anything, and from her husband Carlos's perspective, judging from the jungle of greenery overrunning the tiny apartment, was growing everything.

Gratefully taking a sip of the strong tea, she could hear the soft sound of Carlos's labored breathing in the bathroom, and the clink of his vice-grips as he finessed open the sink trap. Her eyes scanned the cramped living space. While everything was scrupulously clean—Carlos had what Carole referred to as an anal compulsion for cleanliness—the tiny apartment was crammed with so much stuff that it looked more like a storage unit than a place for human habitation. Where most people would have a dining table, Carole had a desk. Law books, legal briefs, and procedure guides, stacked high and ordered in a way only Carole understood, filled the desk and encroached like slowly flowing lava onto the surrounding floor space. In the misnamed living room, a small sofa and coffee table fought for space with Carlos's art equipment: a jerry-rigged board-and-brick bookshelf holding art supplies, an easel in the corner holding a half-finished cartoon, artist's sketch pads scattered haphazardly about.

Taking another sip of tea, Carole turned her attention to the newspaper, slipping off the green rubber band and eagerly extracting an inside section. Through the wall came the sound of loud arguing: John and Linda Stone, their neighbors to the immediate north, were having another hard time starting the day on friendly terms. But unlike Carlos, Carole had an uncanny knack for blocking out unwelcome sounds. "I guess I'm just concentrating," she'd say when Carlos asked her, as he often did, how she could stand the ruckus.

What Carole was concentrating on now was the cartoon that appeared every Wednesday in the "Happenings" section:

A moral dilemma.

Carole laughed out loud, pleased with the morning treat. She liked Carlos's cartoons, and often actively conspired with him on them. But what she most liked seeing was Carlos's work in print, and the scrawling C. Estrada below the drawing.

Carole carried the paper into the bathroom, where Carlos, his tall, lean body contorted like a pretzel, was just then successfully removing the S-shaped drain trap.

"Good one, Carlos," she said.

"Which one is it?" Carlos asked, a thin stream of water running onto his face as he looked up to her.

"The lawyers' convention," she replied. "Where'd you get that idea?"

"That A.B.A. conference you dragged me to in Milwaukee," Carlos said as he struggled out from under the sink.

"No kidding," Carole said.

With errant beads of water dripping off the side of his lean, clean-shaven face and down the back of his dark ponytail, Carlos tipped the S-trap and tapped it patiently until an earring fell into his brown palm.

"Here you go, honey," he said, handing Carole the earring.

"All right!" Carole exclaimed happily. "The opinion of others aside," she drawled in her Southern Belle imitation, "I hereby declare you to be a True Gentleman and my Own Personal Hero." Her Southern Belle imitation was one of her favorites.

From the other side of the wall came another chorus of the Stones' strident duet.

"Cabrona!" Carlos exclaimed in Spanish, raising his hands in a futile gesture of exasperation.

Carole's face softened with sympathy, and she gave him a kiss on the forehead before heading for the bedroom.

"All my life it's small apartments," Carlos complained to Carole's back, "with thin walls and loud neighbors who're bad cooks."

He followed her into the bedroom and watched as she shed her robe and, in slip and hose, began searching the packed closet for a dress.

"I die and go to hell, they'll put me in an apartment," he said.

"Poor baby," she said, finding the beige business suit she was looking for.

Carlos liked watching Carole dress. For one thing, he enjoyed the female rituals—the hair curling, the makeup, the odd layering of clothes—that after three years of marriage were still new to him. For another thing, he thought happily as he watched her step into the skirt and fluidly pull it up over the slip, Carole had it in all the right places. At their wedding reception a law school friend, tipsy on champagne, had revealed her secret nickname: "Callipygian Carole."

Buttoning her blouse and slipping her feet into her shoes, Carole moved past Carlos back to the bathroom, pulling curlers from her hair as she went.

"Want to meet for lunch?" she asked.

Carlos followed her to the bathroom doorway. "Can't today," he said. "I've got to fix the Hansens' toilet, the Rogers' linoleum, and Mrs. Espinoza's leaky faucet," he said, ticking off the jobs on his fingers.

In exchange for free rent, Carlos fixed things around the apartment complex. It was a good deal, allowing Carlos time for his cartooning and a little freelance advertising copy work, forestalling, for the time being, the necessity of getting a real job. And if Carole could grow anything, Carlos could fix anything. He'd learned the art of fixing—and he considered it an art, like his graphics work and cartooning—at the hands of his father, a building superintendent in New York City, and later as an electrician in   the

19

army. He proudly had what Carole called "hardware fingers," and it was his third love, after Carole and his cartoon creation, "The Halfway Inn."

As Carole prepared to leave for her work day, putting the finishing touches on her makeup and teasing the ends of her hair one last time, Carlos stood at the kitchen counter, finishing his second cup of coffee and making Carole a sandwich for her lunch. As he was slipping the sandwich into a plastic baggie, Carole emerged from the bathroom, searching for a last gulp of tea, her mind already on the day before her.

"So what's up for today?" Carlos asked, handing her the sandwich and an apple.

"Hmmm," she said, dropping the lunch into the looming darkness of her briefcase. "I've got to meet with a new client. Easement dispute, from what I gather." Her eyes widened and her lips tightened, sending the borders of her pink mouth tipping slightly downward. This meant "who knows," and was a good sign.

Just then their comparative quiet was jarred by the sharp, loud sound of a piece of electrical machinery coming to life, first whining, then throbbing rhythmically through the walls.

"Sheesh!" Carlos exclaimed, reacting to the sound.

"What is it?" Carole asked, still a little slow at piecing together Carlos's anxieties.

"Mrs. Bartlett's doing her laundry," Carlos answered ruefully. "Why don't you win some big case, and we can move up to a double wide trailer."

Over the sound of Mrs. Bartlett's machine entering its wash cycle, Carole leaned over to Carlos and gave him a long, loving kiss. "Our ship'll come in," she said. "You'll get 'The Halfway Inn' syndicated and I'll get my school loans paid off. We'll live in a castle."

They walked together to the front door and passed through into the inner corridor. Carole tilted her head up for a kiss. "Bye," she said as she moved down the corridor toward the morning.

"A castle on a mountaintop," Carlos called after her. "With a moat. And insulated walls."

She turned for an instant and smiled back as she walked. Carlos watched her light brown hair bouncing lightly off her shoulders. He remembered when her hair was shorter, when they had first gotten to know each other. He was finishing up his MFA degree and she was in her second year of law school, and they both had work-study jobs shelving books in the university library. They had an ongoing game they'd play with authors' names. "What would you name your kids if your last name was Cheever?" she'd ask. Her answer: "Under A. and Over A." "What would you name your son if your last name was Boyle?" he'd query. His answer: "Lance." And on and on, groan after delicious groan.

He'd had to ask her out. It seemed to him downright pathological not to, since they seemed to enjoy each other's company so much. He'd been surprised when she'd said yes, fighting his own racial demons; the perceived incongruity of the brown-skinned barrio kid going to school on an equity fellowship and the GI Bill, and the blue-eyed American dream girl with the soft creamy-white skin.

So they went to a movie, where Carlos declined to touch her, content with her close, warm presence and the faint jasmine smell of her perfume. Later, over coffee, they'd talked about backgrounds, about Carlos's large Puerto Rican family in New York City and the neighborhood he'd grown up in. When he asked her about her own background, he was surprised that she didn't know.

"I'm adopted," she'd said. "My adopted parents were English and Norwegian, but that's no help. I'm clearly not African-American, and I don't think I'm Hispanic. What do you think?"

Sitting across the table from him, her mouth open into a half-smile, she'd been light, almost flippant about it. But the way her small white teeth had tapped together pensively and the touch of hardness he'd seen in her powder blue eyes had hinted to Carlos that there was more at stake than idle good humor.

Around mid-morning, Carole sat behind her desk leaning forward, her chin resting comfortably in the palms of her hands, listening intently to the elderly lady sitting across from her. Sunlight from the windows behind her illuminated the lady's face, outlining the contours of her weathered skin and making her close-cropped white hair iridescent. Her name was Stella Phillips. Carole guessed her to be in her mid-to-late seventies, and from the dull gold band on her left ring finger and the fact that she was alone, that she was a widow. Stella had an easement problem, and like ninety-five percent of Carole's clients, was mad and frustrated.

"And then," Stella was saying, her dark eyes flashing, "not more than two weeks later I get this letter from his lawyer informing me that I was to take down my fence and move my rose bushes so that he can build a road...on my land!" Her mouth snapped shut, underlining the indignity of it all.

"Did you bring the letter?" Carole asked.

"You bet I did, honey," Stella answered firmly. She sifted through a file folder sitting on her lap, extracting an official-looking document typed under the letterhead of one of the larger law firms in the city. "A pox on their house," she muttered as she handed the letter to Carole.

As Carole sat back and scrutinized the letter, Stella continued to talk. "Well," she said, "I told my sister that anyone can get a lawyer to say damned near anything. No offense intended," she added.

Carole looked up from the letter and smiled. "None taken," she said. "Lawyers are mirror reflections of their clients."

A few seconds passed as Carole finished reading the letter. "It's the legal equivalent of a gorilla thumping its chest," Carole said, looking up to the old lady. "He's claiming there's an easement that gives him the right to twenty feet of your land for ingress and egress," she said.

Stella laughed lightly. "Honey," she said, "you're talking legal mumbo-jumbo. Talk plain to an old lady."

"You share a property line with this guy, right?" Carole asked.

"Right," Stella answered. "The old poop," she said under her breath.

"Okay," Carole continued. "He's saying that in the deed to your property there's a clause, what we call an easement, that guarantees him the right to use the edge of your land for coming and going."

"These things, these easements, they exist?" Stella asked nervously.

"Oh yeah," Carole said. "They're common."

"So the old bugger's got me," Stella said dejectedly, her lip turning up as if she smelt something bad.

"Maybe he has, maybe he hasn't," Carole responded.

Stella's right eyebrow cocked up, a glimmer of sweet hope holding back the tide of bitter defeat.

"First of all," Carole said, "there may or may not be an easement in your deed. And even if there is, easements can be abandoned, or they can sometimes be lost through what we call adverse possession."

Carole rose from her chair and walked around the desk to Stella. "Tell you what," she said. "Send me a copy of your deed and I'll do some digging."

Carole helped her to rise from her chair. "I'll do that," Stella said. "I'll take it down to the Kinko's and send you one of those faxes. I've never done that."

"That'll be fine," Carole said. She was starting to like this woman.

In the reception area, Carole held open the door as Stella left into the morning sun. "Do you have a ride?" Carole asked.

"I ride the bus," Stella answered.

"Well, take care," Carole said.

"You too, honey," Stella answered. She looked smaller and older in the bright sunlight as she turned away and started down the sidewalk toward the busy traffic on the avenue. Slightly hunched over, the circle of her wild white hair bright above her long brown trench coat, she seemed to Carole as old people so often do: overwhelmed by the energy around her, abdicated. Still, Carole thought, there was steely intellect in those eyes, and dogged humor.

Carole turned from the doorway and walked the few steps to Sandy, the receptionist, who was just then hanging up the phone. God help us, Carole thought, if we ever permanently lose our sense of humor.

Sandy handed Carole a pink message slip she'd just recorded. "From Riley, Robinson and Sweeney," she said. "You have a case with them?"

"Huh-uh," Carole said, moving her head slowly from side to side as she read the cryptic message. "Thanks," she said, then retreated to her office to make some tea and find out what this guy Riley wanted.

Her call to Riley, Robinson and Sweeney didn't reveal much. Riley was away at a deposition, and had asked his secretary to set up an appointment with Carole as soon as possible...something to do with a will that Riley was probating. Both of their schedules were booked for the day, so Carole agreed to an appointment at noon the next day, and for the next twenty-six hours it was business as usual.

After dinner and dishes and another couple of hours of legal work, Carole was finally able to crawl into bed with Carlos, who lay in his boxer shorts reading *The Hobbit*. "What's up with Bilbo and the gang?" Carole asked as she snuggled up next to him.

"Not so good, counselor," Carlos replied as he flipped the page. "They're lost in Mirkwood."

For a few seconds, Carole watched him intently read. "Oh, boy, my back just aches," she said hopefully.

"Yeah?" Carlos responded, flipping the page and continuing to read.

"I must have lifted something too heavy," Carole persisted, grimacing slightly as she stretched around to rub her lower back, groaning softly. Carlos didn't notice, concentrating, as he was, on the events of Middle Earth. "Hope I didn't pull anything," she offered a bit louder.

This time it worked, and Carlos left the plight of the dwarves and hobbit and turned to her. "Where is it?" he asked.

"Right back here," Carole said, gingerly touching the small of her back.

As hoped, Carlos put the book down and moved to her, lifting her nightgown and examining the small of her back with his fingertips. "Pretty tight down there," he said. "You want me to massage it a little?"

"Couldn't hurt," Carole said, rolling away from him onto her stomach so that he couldn't see the twinkle she was sure was in her eyes, confident now that she would spend the last minutes of the day in the best possible way.

23

The next day, at 12:15 p.m., she found herself sitting in the plush reception room of the law offices of Riley, Robinson and Sweeney, eating the sandwich Carlos had made for her and studiously making marginal notes in a brief she was preparing to file. Riley, Robinson and Sweeney was old and well-established, and the offices, occupying the entire twelfth floor of one of the newer steel and glass downtown office buildings, reflected the gracious extravagance of thirty years of billing by the quarter-hour.

At 12:30, Riley finally emerged from his office, escorting a plain-looking middle-aged woman to the door. His hand was on her shoulder, and he talked to her softly and encouragingly as he said his goodbyes. The woman's face was flushed and puffy; she'd been crying. A divorce case, Carole thought.

Riley turned to Carole and walked quickly to her. He was a short man in late middle age, gray at the temples, with a round, clean-shaven face and intense gray eyes. He was impeccably dressed: thirty years of billing by the quarter-hour hadn't done *him* any harm, either. Carole rose as he approached, a few errant bread crumbs from her sandwich spilling onto the Persian rug.

"Carole?" he asked, extending his hand to her.

"Yes," she said. "Carole Browning."

"Jim Riley," he said as they shook hands. "I'm glad we could get together so quickly."

He led her into his office, which seemed by Carole's first impression to be all leather and richly stained wood. The north wall was all window, so that from his twelfth-floor sanctuary Riley had a spectacular, unobstructed view of the city as it climbed upward to the houses and trees of Summit Avenue on the highest point on the hill.

He seated Carole in one of two identical leather armchairs sitting side by side and looking out and took the seat next to her. "Sorry I made you wait," he said.

"That's okay. A taste of my own medicine," Carole responded with a smile.

"That's right, you're an attorney too," Riley said. "Where'd you go to school?

"Northwestern," Carole replied.

"Good school," Riley said. "So you left the big city and came back home."

"That's right," Carole said, wondering with some unease how he knew that she was a local product.

"Well, I've got to tell you," he said, "you were one well-hidden devisee. It took my paralegal forever to pin you down."

The word "devisee" set off red flags for Carole. To be a devisee is to be the beneficiary of a will. But her adopted father was very much alive. Who could have possibly willed me something? she thought, except...possibly... She could feel the blood draining from her face, and her stomach turned. Very possibly, she thought with a mixture of hope and raw apprehension, a door that had been closed to her was being thrown open.

She sat forward in her seat and forced herself to speak evenly. "Is this about my birth family?" she asked, her eyes boring into Riley.

"It appears to be," Riley responded. "How much do you know about them?"

"Next to nothing," Carole said. Which was true. She'd been adopted when she was two, and Mom and Dad Browning had told her later what little they'd been told, which was that her unnamed parents had both died suddenly in an accident.

Riley walked to his desk and returned with a bulging file. "This is the last will and testament of a man named Henry Winkler, executed by me in 1974," Riley began. "Henry died in 1977, leaving his estate to his grandson William Jr. for his natural life, then to his great-granddaughter Carole."

Carole listened quietly, sitting small and childlike in the thickly padded chair, her hands limp in her lap. "That's you, Carole," Riley said softly. "You're Henry's great-granddaughter."

The will itself had been an interesting one for Riley to write. The property part had been easy: his house and personal property to William Jr., then to Carole. But what Henry had wanted done with his financial assets was unique. He had Riley establish a trust, to be used to pay for the expenses of the house through William Jr.'s natural life, in effect, ensuring the house a life of its own. Upon William Jr.'s death, the house, property, and trust were to be turned over to Carole.

Carole wanted to know what Henry had looked like, but Riley's twenty-five-year-old memory was understandably vague. He seemed to remember that the old man had been short and bald, round but not fat, tired-looking. If there were any other Winklers floating around, Riley was unaware of them.

Carole's drive back to her office was on remote control, her mind hostage to the complex dimensions of Riley's surprise. She called Carlos shortly after arriving back at her office, catching him just as he was finishing off a chili dog.

"Holy cow!" he exclaimed after listening to Carole's report, his mind racing. From their first date he'd known that Carole's status as an orphan was in some important way a discomfort to her. But in the few years   they'd

25

been together, she'd yet to talk about it, and Carlos, opting for caution, had never brought it up. In the happy unfolding of their lives, it had become a non-issue. But now, he thought excitedly, finally she had the key to the past she missed. Here was her chance to get to the bottom of it all, to explore the unknown terrain of these Winklers, her ancestors. And a house to boot, right here in the city! He was already imagining himself behind the wheel of the U-Haul, bidding an un-fond farewell to the Paradise Gardens.

He was so excited, in fact, that he entirely missed an important signal. He'd come to have a sense of Carole's emotions and their disguises: hurt masked as indifference; anxiety camouflaged as anger. But the voice that had delivered the extraordinary news had been cold and businesslike, monotone, as if she had been reading a stranger's obituary. It was her poker voice, and it signaled something entirely different.

When Carole got home late in the afternoon, Carlos was at his easel, at work on a cartoon. "I'm home," she sang out as she entered. "The happy devisee."

Carlos had absolutely no interest in the practice of the law and was blissfully ignorant of legal terms and their meanings. He moved to her and kissed her. "What's a devisee?" he asked.

Carole dropped her heavy briefcase and walked to the kitchen. "A devisee," she said in her most professorial tone, her index finger pointing upward, "is one who is the beneficiary of a will." She drew a glass of water and took a long drink. "Thus a devisor," she continued, "is one who leaves to another, in the form of a will or trust, that which he or she has ownership of." She refilled her glass and took another drink. "The devisee-devisor relationship is necessary because, as we all know, and as one Henry Winkler proved to be true, you can't take it with you."

She pulled a tarnished key from her coat pocket and dangled it by its paper ID tag, for Carlos to see. "Want to go check out a house?" she asked, raising her eyebrows and forcing a half-smile.

The sun was low in the cloudless western sky as Carlos guided his old Ford pickup up Centennial Drive. Carole sat next to him, her head buried in the will and court documents, oblivious to the noise and rush-hour commotion around her on the busy street.

"So if this Henry was your great-grandfather," Carlos said loudly, above the noise of the old pickup, "then who was your grandfather and your father?"

Carole looked over to him. "Don't know," she said with a hint of bewilderment. Her face disappeared back in to the mass of paperwork.

After a few moments of silent driving, Carlos tried again. "Isn't there a family tree or something in there?" he asked.

26

There was no response from Carole, who flipped a page and continued to read.

"You got a family tree there?" Carlos asked more loudly.

Finally Carole looked up, irritated. "All that's here, Carlos," she said curtly, "is Henry's will and probate documents."

The pickup reached the top of the hill, and Carole spotted the street sign. "There it is," she said, pointing.

Carlos made the left turn onto Summit Avenue and slowly headed west into the sun, following the route taken by Wilhelm, Sophie, and little Ellen over a hundred years earlier as Wilhelm sprung his great surprise.

"Hoo-lee cow!" Carlos exclaimed, drinking in the sight of the large, magnificently restored old homes with their wide lawns, lushly green from the spring rains. "Old Henry must've been rich."

Carole was feeling rather unworldly as the pickup passed slowly by what seemed to her, as it had at first glance to Sophie, to be a continuing row of mansions. "I don't think so," she responded. "There's a small trust fund worth around $50,000, but no pot of money."

The homes were all numbered in the 100s, so Carlos correctly assumed that the one they were looking for—number 228—would be on the next block. Carlos slowed as they passed by 208 and 218, then pulled to a stop in front of what had to be number 228.

Carole's mouth fell open in shock. Though Riley had told her that the house had been uninhabited for over twenty years, she was totally unprepared for what she saw. The poor old house was almost entirely devoid of paint, the weather-beaten wood dark and bare, like the walls, she thought, of houses in ghost towns. The long front porch seemed to sag precariously, ominously, and the porch railing was broken in several places. The lawn was thick with weeds and knee-high crabgrass.

It looked, Carole thought, like a cartoon haunted house, something Carlos would draw. Compared to the beautiful homes around it, it was like an ugly bruise.

"Beautiful!" Carlos offered softly, his eyes locked on the house, scanning it from weathered filigreed top to broken cut-stone bottom.

"Maybe to the Munsters," Carole snapped, "but not to me."

Carlos barely heard the put-down, mesmerized by the magnificent structure standing majestically before him. "Wow!" he said. "And it's yours...all yours."

"Not for long," Carole replied.

"Let's go in," Carlos said excitedly.

"No way," Carole declared flatly, shaking her head firmly from side to side.

"Come on," Carlos persisted. "It won't bite you."

After a bit of intense persuasion, he finally convinced her to take a quick look inside. Carole clutched Carlos's arm tightly as they walked up the cement path to the front porch, her eyes darting about nervously. Reaching the broken porch, the old house loomed over them.

"I don't like the feel of this, Carlos," Carole said hesitantly as they climbed the creaking steps to the front door. "It feels...I don't know...creepy."

"Well, hell," Carlos said cheerfully, "if you'd been treated this way for twenty-five years you'd be pissed, too."

As Carole fumbled in her jeans pocket for the key, Carlos examined the big door and heavy frame. "Look here," he said, running his hands lovingly over the weathered wood. "This is all solid oak, the door and frame both. And the craftsmanship is just superb."

He was in another world now, one measured by miters and dovetails, by joints and planes, and one that was as foreign to Carole as the practice of law was to him. "Of course, it needs some sanding and refinishing," he said studiously as Carole handed him the key.

The lock was hard to turn, but finally gave way to Carlos's gentle prodding. With a forceful push, the door rotated inward, screeching against its rusty hinges. Then, with Carole firmly attached to Carlos at the arm, they stepped across the portal into mysterious darkness.

Carlos's eyes drank in the interior, bathed in geometric patterns of shadow and bright light streaming in from the west windows: the winding staircase with its massive railing, the oak-framed passageway leading down the length of the house, the half-hidden furnishings visible through open doorways around him, everything covered with a thick coating of dust. On the walls around them, loosened wallpaper hung in limp sheets.

"Poor neglected baby," Carlos said sadly.

Carole, providing a second, independent set of eyes, looked around apprehensively. "One spider and I'm outta here," she said.

"Just look at this," Carlos said, moving to the staircase and reverently touching the thick, sculptured banister. "Walnut...and hardwood floors," he said mostly to himself.

He spotted a nearby hole in the wall and moved to it, exploring the hole with his finger. "Lath and plaster," he said. "They just don't make 'em like this anymore."

Carlos led her slowly toward the back of the house, peeking as they went into the rooms off the hallway. The furniture seemed to be a mixture of the old and the older. Half appeared to be antiques as old as the house itself, half potluck at the Salvation Army. In the parlor, a sculpted davenport and

28

cherry wood breakfront combined with a seventies-era television and a La-Z-Boy rocker. In the study, Wilhelm's huge roll-top desk stood proud against the north wall, his worn leather armchair and ottoman by the south wall, next to a long bookshelf crowded with dusty clutter.

The dining room stopped Carole in her tracks. The impressive Winkler dining room table and matching chairs were still there, but what she was most taken with were the two walnut cabinets built into the north and south walls. Even in the half-dark they were strikingly beautiful with their delicately carved drawers and glass doors crosshatched with thin strips of sculpted wood.

"Wow," she offered softly. "That belongs in a museum."

"This whole *place* is a museum," Carlos replied.

They entered the kitchen. Sophie's antique wood stove was gone, and the stove and refrigerator were all sixties-era.

"Let's see how old the plumbing is," Carlos said, moving to the sink and bending to the low cabinet door. As he opened it, a startled mouse came scurrying out.

At the sight of the mouse, Carole let out a sharp, involuntary cry. "That's it," she said, her eyes wide and her voice wavering. "Adios." She turned on her heel, intent on making a beeline for the front door.

Carlos grabbed her arm. "Come on," he said soothingly. "It's just a little mouse. Probably the only one in the house," he lied. He put his arms around her, giving her a moment to calm down. "There's nothing in here that can hurt you," he said softly into her ear.

The color was returning to Carole's face. She breathed in slowly, then exhaled. "You're right," she said firmly. "I'm a grownup. I can do this."

They walked back through the downstairs, then climbed the wide, curving staircase to the second floor. Carlos pushed open the door to Wilhelm and Sophie's front bedroom and, standing in exactly the spot where little Ellen had stood one hundred years earlier inadvertently witnessing the creation of her baby brother, took in the ancient four-poster bed and antique chests of drawers and dressing table. "Wow. That furniture's as old as the house, guaranteed. Really something, huh?" he said, turning to Carole.

"Yeah," Carole said.

They looked into the adjoining small side bedroom, brightly lit by the setting sun shining in through a west-facing window. A stack of comic books lay on an end table next to the bed, and the floor was littered with small brown pieces of wood.

"What are all those little pieces of wood?" Carole asked.

Carlos entered the room and knelt over the pieces, picking one up and examining it. "Lincoln Logs," he said.

29

"What?" Carole asked.

"Lincoln Logs," Carlos said again. "You build things with 'em. You know, houses and forts and stuff. You never played with Lincoln Logs?"

"A kid's toy," Carole marveled. "A *kid* lived here."

"Lots of kids lived here, I bet," Carlos answered.

"Yeah, sure," Carole said, "but in 1977?"

Carlos shrugged.

When they pushed open the door to the bathroom, Carlos's eyes became wide with excitement. "Oh man!" he exclaimed. "Look at this, honey!" he said, entering the room. "This is all original," he said, admiring the ancient, stained and chipped claw foot tub and the old water closet with its high wooden tank.

Having no historic or artistic interest in plumbing, Carole watched disinterestedly from the hallway. Her gaze traveled down to the end of the hallway, to an east-facing doorway that stood half-open. Summoning her nerve, she left the safety of Carlos and moved down the hallway toward the beckoning door.

In the bathroom, Carlos was marveling at the copper plumbing. "Unbelievable," he said, touching the old pipes reverently. "This whole house is plumbed with copper, I bet. You know what this would cost today?" When he got no response, he turned, realizing that he had been talking to himself. "Honey?" he asked the room.

He left the bathroom and stood for a moment in the empty hallway. "Carole?" he called out. Then he saw the open doorway, and walked to it. "You in here, honey?" he asked as he entered the room. It was a feminine bedroom, with white lace curtains and flowery wallpaper. Matched single beds contrasted with an old oak dresser and armoire.

Carole stood in the middle of the room, unaware of Carlos's presence, staring at an oversized and very old photograph hanging on the wall. When Carlos saw the painting, his breath inadvertently, forcefully sucked in. Hung in an ornate gilded frame, it was a photograph of a family: a father and mother in middle-age, a young man in his early twenties, and a somewhat older women. It was the young woman that was commanding Carole's, and now Carlos's, attention. She had blonde hair pulled forcefully back into a bun, and the most troubled eyes Carlos thought he'd ever seen. And except for the hair and the eyes, she was the spitting image of Carole.

After staring silently at the photograph for the longest time, Carole simply said "no way," turned on her heel and marched out of the room, down the stairs and out the front door, to sit sullenly in the pickup cab waiting for Carlos.

30

Carole chose to handle the shock of the photograph in the same way she always handled unnerving possibilities: by ignoring it. Back at the apartment, she threw herself into Stella Phillips's easement dispute. Dressed in nightgown and robe, she sat on the floor surrounded by law books, intently taking notes on a legal pad, occasionally taking sips from a cup of herbal tea.

Carlos, who'd changed into sweat pants and t-shirt, stood at his easel sketching, a half-empty bottle of beer within easy reach. Taken with the picture of Carole's one-hundred-year-old look-alike, he was re-creating the picture in charcoal. And doing a pretty good job, too, given that the model for the face was sitting ten feet away.

Through the wall came the unmistakable voice of Lawrence Welk. "What can we do to improve Mrs. Bartlett's taste in music?" Carlos asked.

Carole looked up from her writing. "Huh?" she said.

"Mrs. Bartlett is treating us to Lawrence Welk again," Carlos said facetiously.

"She's hard of hearing, honey," Carole said, burying her head back in the thick law book.

Over the past year, since the seventy-year-old widow had moved in next door, Carlos had come to be a reluctant expert on *The Lawrence Welk Show,* which Mrs. Bartlett conscientiously watched whenever the numerous re-run opportunities presented themselves. Having never seen their smiling faces, Carlos nevertheless felt himself to be intimately familiar with the gang: Myron Floren, the Lovely Lennon Sisters, Larry Hooper, the dancing pair of Bobby and Cissy, and with Mr. Welk himself.

"Hello, friends," Carlos said to no one in particular, enthusiastically mimicking the voice of the Polka King, "and welcome to another hour of champagne music."

For a while Carlos sketched in silence. When he was more or less done, he stepped back from the easel and appraised his work. He hadn't done justice to the eyes, he thought. He couldn't. "What do you think?" he asked, turning to Carole.

There was no response from Carole, only a momentary halt of the passage of her pen traveling rhythmically over the yellow sheet of paper.

"Honey?" he asked.

Finally she looked up from her work. "Nice job," she said, quickly returning to the sanctuary of her writing.

"So who do you think it is?" Carlos continued.

"How should I know?" Carole said testily, not looking up.

"Can't you tell from all that legal stuff?" he persisted.

Finally Carole had had it. She slapped down her pencil and slammed the law book closed. "Okay," she said, standing to confront him, her blue eyes

31

on fire. "Here's what I know, Carlos, and all I know," she said, her voice cold as ice. "There was a guy named Henry Winkler, an old man, who *claimed* to have two heirs, a grandson named William Jr., which implies I suppose that somewhere there was a William Sr., and a great-granddaughter named Carole, who, I'm told, is me. Only there's no real proof of that, because you can leave your property to whoever you want. And that's it, Carlos. That's the whole fucking enchilada." Her mouth snapped shut, and she plopped down on the sofa.

Carole rarely swore, and almost never used the f-word. Looking at her as she sat staring sadly ahead, her pink lips closed into a tight line, Carlos thought he saw in her unfocused eyes a hint of what he had tried to capture in his sketch, and it frightened him.

He went and sat next to her. "I thought you'd be happy...you know...to learn about your family," he said softly, rubbing her leg.

"But they're all dead," she said with a mixture of anger and dismay, still staring straight ahead. "I get them as an afterthought. And last but not least," she said, "when everyone else is done with it, I leave my broken down old house to dear little Carole."

She turned to Carlos, her eyes like blue steel. "And what I'm asking myself is so what?" she said flatly. "I've got a good life. I don't need this shit."

For several moments Carlos appraised the sad face staring back at him. "So what do you want to do with the house?" he asked.

Carole thought for a moment. "Tell you what," she said finally, her eyes softening. "I give it to you. Do what you want with it." Which was exactly what Carlos had hoped to hear, stated in exactly the wrong way.

Moments later she rose from the sofa, announced that she was going to bed, kissed Carlos lightly, and dragged herself out of sight into the bedroom. There would be no massage tonight.

Carlos sat alone on the couch, finishing the last of his beer. When the beer bottle was empty, he rose and followed Carole's path into the dark bedroom, clicking on the small lamp next to the bed. The soft light revealed her huddled under the covers on the very edge of the bed, her head facing the wall, away from him. She didn't move.

Carlos decided he wanted a shower. As he stripped in the dim light, his eyes fell on the small framed photograph of Carole and her adopted parents sitting on her cluttered dresser, behind the gold chain with the small piece of stone that was Carole's favorite necklace. It was serpentine, she'd told him, and had been hers for as long as she could remember.

Carlos picked up the photograph and inspected it carefully. They were at a carnival, and Carole stood between the adults. She was holding each by the hand, a yellow paper crown on her head. She was seven or   eight, all skinny legs and wavy hair falling into her face. Carlos noticed how different the expressions of the parents were. While the man smiled confidently into the camera, the woman stared ahead with a look of bewilderment, as if she were waiting for the cameraman to answer some troubling question. This was all she'd had, Carlos thought sadly.

In the shower, Carlos reviewed all that he knew of Carole's life with the Brownings. Mom and Dad Browning were kind and decent people and gave Carole all the love they would have given their own child. But when Carole was ten, Dad Browning went away on a business trip and never came home. He'd met another woman, one who didn't need tranquilizers and therapy sessions to make it through the day. After the divorce, he'd remarried and moved to the west coast. He was as loving to Carole as he could be from two thousand miles away, and when economic success in the burgeoning computer industry came, he willingly shared it with Carole and his ex-wife, so that neither physically wanted for anything.

Over time he slowly disappeared from both of their lives. And while the ten-year-old Carole seemed to have found a way to deal with the loss, Mom Browning never recovered from what was for her a catastrophe. Her new lover became vodka, so that by the time Carole was fifteen she was in charge of the house—cleaning, preparing all the meals, paying the bills. Shortly after Carole went away to college, Mom Browning had been killed in a car accident. Her blood alcohol level had been twice the legal limit.

Soaping himself down, Carlos's thoughts drifted back to his own large and boisterous family, and he remembered, inadvertently it seemed, something his grandmother had told him when he was a little boy. He remembered that he was sitting on her lap eating a pastry, and the plump, toothless old woman was hugging and pinching him lovingly. "In the center of everyone's heart there is a flower," she'd said. "Look for the flower, Carlos, and you will find happiness."

Carole, Carlos knew, had found her flower. But standing in the steaming shower, as the water cascaded over his head and down his arms and back, he appreciated for the first time what a lonely, daunting search it must have been.

Epistle

During the first years of the war, Henry Winkler was my only friend. Henry lived alone then, his son Will having joined the military at the first opportunity, and it became a comfort to me to look after him as much as he would allow. Not that Henry needed looking after. He was a robust and active man back then, in the prime of his life, really. True, he was beginning to go bald, and had begun the journey into roundness that many of us seem to take with time, but he was in excellent health, and his sharp blue eyes were filled with energy and curiosity.

During those years I came to know that house as well as my own. Henry kept it spotlessly clean and in perfect repair, and it responded with welcoming grace. On spring and summer days the sun would shine in through its many large windows, playing off the rich wood and gay wallpaper. In winter it would be a warm sanctuary, its windows tightly curtained against the cold, its rooms and hallways made small and intimate by the dim light of electric lamps.

In those days of so much sadness, at least the house was happy. It invited me to explore it, and I wandered through it at my ease, marveling at its beauty and mystery: the front parlor with its elaborate old furniture, like the setting from a Victorian novel; the small basement where Henry kept his tools, and from where he so often seemed to be emerging, smiling, wiping his hands clean; the upstairs bedrooms, lush with rich carpeting and dark wood, like a posh hotel.

Many nights I would cook dinner, which we'd eat sitting at one edge of Henry's huge old dining room table, listening to the war news on the radio. Then we'd do the dishes, and on fair evenings would retire to the front porch, where Henry would sit in his rocker smoking his pipe and drinking a bottle or two of the dark beer he loved. So often surrounded, as I was, by a half-century of Winklers, I'd often try to get Henry to talk about his family. This wasn't easy, for although Henry didn't mind looking backwards, he had cultivated the habit of concentrating his attention on the present, knowing, as I would come to learn, that it's the safest place to be.

Once, just once, he talked to me about his wife Clara. He talked only briefly, until the utter sadness of the memory, rushing from his heart and springing like a fountain from his eyes, overcame and silenced him. I went to him then and hugged him, and he hugged me back.

Sometimes, though, he would talk about his mother Sophie and father Wilhelm, and his sister Ellen, all gone to early graves. His memories of Sophie were of warmth and gaiety. Her strength, he felt, was the gift of gentle

34

acceptance. He remembered Wilhelm as a bundle of energy and activity, and from his loving tutelage Henry felt that he had learned to trust in himself and his instincts. His strength, Henry thought, was in his simplicity, in his ability to see straight through to the truth of things. Of his sister Ellen Henry had almost nothing to say, as if the weight of her memory left him tired. But the little that he did say made one thing clear: If his father's strength was in his studied aversion to self-delusion, Ellen's weakness, Henry had concluded (and as you may also soon enough) was in her susceptibility to it.

Chapter Three

On a late Sunday morning in early June of 1906, nineteen-year-old Ellen Winkler sat primly in a pew of St. Paul's Lutheran Church, surrounded by her family, listening intently to the sermon being delivered by Reverend Schneider. It was already hot, and the sanctuary was alive with the motion of hand-held wooden fans as the heavily dressed women tried to cool themselves.

Sophie, beads of sweat dripping down her neck, sat politely fanning herself, occasionally dabbing at her damp forehead with a linen hankie. Ten-year-old Henry fidgeted in his seat, tying and untying his shoes, then staring with childish wonder at the bright church interior with its high, vaulted ceiling and rows of tall, narrow stained-glass windows.

What awe Wilhelm had ever found in the architectural wonders of the church had dulled over the twenty-odd years of his reluctant association with it. Doubly dulled by the heat and Reverend Schneider's rhythmic monotone, he sat hunched forward, his chin in the palm of his hand, fighting a losing battle with sleep. His eyes would grow large, then close, then snap open again. He had to pee, and hoped, against experience, that today's tedious exercise in spiritual instruction would be blessedly short.

Of the four Winklers, only Ellen was paying any attention at all. Reverend Schneider, now in his sixties, was still going strong. He was a big and exceedingly ugly man with wild, bushy eyebrows, puffy jowls set in a constant disapproving frown, and a large red nose and ears, from which sprouted tufts of black hair. But this very ugliness, combined with the solemn authority with which he spoke of the hazards of the mortal world, commanded young Ellen's attention, if not quite her respect.

He was in fine form that morning, standing at his high pulpit in his black robe, advising his assembled flock with forceful authority. "Never forget that our God is a jealous God," he said sternly. "Oh yes! Never forget it, my friends. He tests us in many ways, and the Bible tells us that, indeed, 'strait is the gate and narrow is the way.'"

Wilhelm grunted, adjusting himself on the hard bench and loosening his tie and collar. He was trying mightily to stay awake, but the heat and the stultifying voice of Reverend Schneider were too much for him. Soon his eyes blinked and closed, his chin fell forward onto his chest, and the soft, distinct sound of a nasal snore—as if he were blowing his nose in reverse—became distinctly audible.

"Never doubt the interest of God in our daily lives and habits," Reverend Schneider continued on ominously. "And never doubt the cause of damnation."

Damnation, Ellen whispered to herself. She was testing the ability of the old man to read her thoughts. She liked doing this, proving to herself that she could do anything she wanted to inside the secret passageways of her mind.

The old man didn't seem to notice, carrying on without hesitation. "He watches us always," the Reverend continued, "and tests our mettle against the temptations of the flesh." He scanned his audience with approbation. "Tobacco," he spat out. "Liquor," he sneered.

Damn! Ellen thought forcefully. Damn you! she thought again, as if the old man in the pulpit might be hard of hearing. When she tired of mentally harassing the old preacher, she turned her attention to the handsome young man seated three rows ahead of her. His name was Thomas Hastings, and he was spending the summer as a guest of the Schneiders. He was tall and muscular, with an intensity in his eyes that drew Ellen to him like a magnet.

After the service, Wilhelm had run for the bathroom, then stood outside with a group of men admiring Herman Klatt's newfangled horseless carriage—a gleaming 1906 Oldsmobile. While the men oohed and aahed the noisy contraption, Ellen stood with Sophie as she made light conversation with Martha Williams, a plump, jolly lady of fifty, and Louise Klatt, a small, wiry lady close to Sophie's age. The three women were the most lighthearted female members of the congregation, and drew to each other naturally.

"My, that's a pretty dress," Mrs. Klatt said to Ellen.

"Thank you," Ellen replied politely. "Mama made it."

"A pretty girl in a pretty dress. I see young men on the horizon," Mrs. Williams said, her eyebrows rising mischievously.

"No," Ellen replied softly.

"No?" Mrs. Williams exclaimed. "Why, if I had your looks, honey, I'd still be courting!"

The two women laughed, and Sophie smiled along with the fun. Ellen looked away.

Mrs. Williams was right; Ellen had indeed grown into a very pretty young woman. Gangly in adolescence, her body had filled in nicely. She was slim like her mother, with clear, almost luminous skin and thick, naturally wavy hair the color of clover honey. Her facial features were those that men would normally call beautiful: large, sky-blue eyes, a small nose framed by high, smooth cheekbones, and a full pink mouth.

If Ellen wasn't courting, it wasn't for lack of potential suitors. Of those there had been plenty. But none of them had appealed to her. And while she couldn't have put a name to it, their failing was simply that they were just too ordinary. They were nice boys, but inconsequential, and they left Ellen cold. All but this Thomas Hastings, that is.

Mrs. Williams wasn't the only person confused by Ellen's apparent lack of interest in the opposite sex. Wilhelm was too. She was, after all, nineteen and out of school, and in his book, what girls that age did was get married. Back from church and in their bedroom, changing out of their Sunday clothes, Wilhelm vented his concern.

"What's she going to do?" he asked Sophie as he shed the stiff white shirt he'd sweated through during the service. "She's gotta do something. She can't hide in the attic forever. She's a pretty girl. That porch should be loaded with young men. Yours was," he added, flashing Sophie a sly grin.

Wilhelm spent the afternoon cleaning the horse stall in the small carriage house set back from the house, then rounded up Henry and headed for the long back yard for a game of catch. Wilhelm was an avid baseball fan, having in his youth played on his high school team and later in the city league. He frequently took Henry to city league games where they would sit high in the bleachers, Wilhelm explaining the idiosyncrasies of the game to the bright-eyed boy.

"Here's a high one, son," Wilhelm called to Henry, then tossed the ball high in the air toward the boy thirty feet away.

Young Henry staggered awkwardly forward, gauging where the ball would come down, then lifted his leather-gloved hand above his head—correctly, Wilhelm noted happily—and stiffly caught the hard white ball. He grinned happily to Wilhelm.

"Good catch, son," Wilhelm called out. "Fire it over here."

Henry reared back and sent the ball sailing toward his father, who had to hurry back and to the left to snare the wild throw. The boy has a good eye and a good arm, Wilhelm thought.

It puzzled Wilhelm how two siblings could be so different. Where Ellen was solitary and insular, Henry was gregarious, never wanting to be alone, and never wanting to sit still or be quiet. Where Ellen was moody and quick to anger, Henry was joyful, his face always smiling, his eyes always bright with delight. Wilhelm summed it up in his own workmanlike terms: Henry was a Kielbasa, he thought; Ellen was a Bratwurst.

It was the Winkler tradition to eat their Sunday supper in the late afternoon. And while most families had for their grandest meal of the week a beef or lamb roast, it was the Winkler's habit to have sausages, as a conscious celebration of the worldly endeavor that had led to their economic success and to their beautiful house on Summit Avenue. So after a quick shower, as Sophie set the table with steaming bowls of sausages, hot potato salad, and ears of sweet corn, Wilhelm went in search of Ellen.

He knew exactly where to find her, so instead of going the length of the upstairs hallway to her room, he opened the attic door and called up the steep staircase. "Time for supper, Ellie," he announced. There was no response, so he patiently called up again. "Time for supper!"

Ellen, sitting in an old, torn easy chair she had dragged over to the east-facing dormer windows of the attic, didn't respond, and after a moment her father's patient but insistent voice trailed up to her. "You won't make us wait, now, will you?" it challenged.

"I'll be right down," she called to her father, and was relieved to hear the attic door close.

Her afternoon had been immensely fruitful. For over a year now, since finishing high school, Ellen had secretly fretted over the same issues that were bothering her father. She was out of school, and she was expected to do something. And that afternoon, sitting alone in the quiet of her attic sanctuary watching the light and shadows slowly shift as the sun moved on its westerly path, she had choreographed a perfectly acceptable path for herself. She would become a nurse. It was a splendid plan. There was a nursing school at the new hospital just across the river, so that she wouldn't have to leave home for several more years, and when she did, it would be to marry someone important, a doctor, maybe. Someone who looked like Thomas Hastings. As she rose from her chair, reluctantly heeding her father's call to dinner, she resolved to visit the school the next day.

In the dining room, she was met by the friendly smiles of her family seated around the table. Wilhelm was sipping from a large glass of beer, the perfect accompaniment, he felt, to the feast of sausages that awaited them. "Sit down, missy," he said happily, "and let's get this show on the road."

The four held hands across the table as Wilhelm said grace. Unlike most families, the Winklers did not have a litany for a mealtime prayer. Wilhelm couldn't imagine that God would appreciate the mindlessness of such an approach, feeling that He would be much more interested in something personal and contemporary. Sunday was the day for his weekly update.

"Well, Lord," Wilhelm began, clearing his throat and getting down to business, "it's been a good week for the Winklers, and we thank You for Your help. Everything's fine at the sausage factory. We're making the 'little dogs' now, and they're a big seller." He paused for a moment, considering his mental checklist. "And, uh...well," he continued, "we've been trying to look after the unfortunate in a Christian manner, the way we know You'd like us to. We've been giving sausages to the Salvation Army. Knockwurst mostly, they seem to like those best. And Sophie's been spending time with Mrs. Goodrich, who as You know isn't doing all that well."

Young Henry peeked a look around the table at the faces of his closed-eyed family. Wilhelm's head bobbed from side to side as he continued his presentation. Sophie yawned. Ellen stole a glance toward him, and their eyes met. She wasn't paying attention either.

Wilhelm was finishing up. "Anyway, Lord, we thank You for keeping us in good health, and hope that You'll continue to watch over us. And, uh, about the only thing we'd ask, I guess, is that You might check up on old Schneider, because some of us think that he's losing his marbles. Amen."

"That was a mean thing to say about Reverend Schneider," Ellen snapped.

Wilhelm spooned hot potato salad onto his plate. He was in a good mood, and didn't mind having a little fun at the Reverend's expense. "I was only trying to get him some help, Ellie," he said, winking mischievously to Sophie. "Everyone knows the man needs help."

"You're the one who needs help, Papa," Ellen responded.

Wilhelm's beer mug stopped midway to his mouth. "Now what does *that* mean?" he asked.

Ellen's eyes darted defiantly between the three. "I heard what Reverend Schneider said today," she said. "About liquor and tobacco."

She didn't mean any of it, of course. She didn't know enough to mean any of it. She did it because it was fun to be contrary, and because she could. Wilhelm didn't know this, though, and so he tried to reason with her. "Why, Jesus himself drank wine, Ellie," he said. "It says so right in the Bible."

"What about tobacco?" Ellen retorted.

Wilhelm thought for a moment. "Well," he said, "I don't think they had it back then. That's a shame," he added, smiling around the table. "What the Reverend needs is to quit making rules for a game he doesn't play," Wilhelm pronounced, lifting a steaming knockwurst from the bowl. "And what you need, missy," he said, offering the bowl of sausages to her, "is one of these wonderful Winkler sausages."

Ellen pushed the offered plate away. She was being beaten badly by her father in this game, and had only one way to trump him. "I don't want a sausage!" she cried, lurching backward in her chair, tears beginning to stream down her face. "I hate your sausages!"

She pushed herself out of her chair and ran from the room. Sophie watched her go in silence, then settled her scathing gaze on Wilhelm, as if the whole thing had been his fault.

"What'd *I* do?" Wilhelm asked defensively.

The anger in Sophie's eyes slowly transformed into dull sadness. After a moment, she rose and wearily followed after the girl.

Ellen didn't visit the nursing school on Monday, or any time that week, or any time that month. By mid-July, the nursing scenario she'd so elaborately constructed for herself had collapsed into a formless memory: another fantasy easier in the dreaming than in the doing. In between her hours in the attic fretting over the bleak and empty horizon that was her future, Ellen justified her continuing existence in her parents' household by convincing herself that her mother needed help around the house. Sophie didn't need Ellen's help, but obliged her daughter's conceit, knowing that it comforted her. In truth, she was in no hurry to see Ellen leave, knowing as she did how unprepared for the world the girl was.

As the end of the month approached, Reverend Schneider announced that Thomas Hastings, the young man he was tutoring for the missions, was prepared to leave, and scheduled a Saturday picnic for early in August as a chance for the congregation to bid him farewell. Both Ellen and Sophie planned to attend.

When Thomas Hastings's imminent departure had been announced, Ellen had been rocked. During the prior few weeks, he'd gone out of his way to smile to her, on several occasions had stopped to speak to her, and on one occasion had touched her waist as he helped her through a doorway. He had become something of an obsession for her. He was the only young man she had ever met that Ellen could see herself with, and so she imagined herself with him all of the time. When she walked down the street, she imagined Thomas Hastings to be beside her, her arm in his. When she ate her meals, she saw him across the table, eating with her. And when she went to bed, she imagined him to be next to her, kissing her and touching her. And, if not for the mission that brought him to her, he was, she was certain, hers to have.

The day of the picnic broke clear and warm. A perfect day for a picnic, Ellen thought happily as she moved lightly down the stairs, joining her father and brother at the breakfast table. "Morning, Papa," Ellen said brightly.

"Morning, Ellie," Wilhelm replied cheerfully, looking up from the morning paper.

At that moment, Sophie emerged from the kitchen with a pot of coffee. Dressed in her robe, her uncombed hair falling loosely around her shoulders, she labored unhappily, her eyes dark, her face tired and pinched.

"I don't think Mama will be going to the picnic, Ellie," Wilhelm said.

"I can still go, can't I?" Ellen asked anxiously.

"Of course you can," Sophie answered. "The sun will do you good."

"You go back to bed, sweetheart," Wilhelm told his wife. "We'll take care of the dishes."

Sophie needed no insistence. Whatever bug she'd caught had kept her awake most of the night, and she was exhausted. "I think I will," she said gratefully, slowly rising from her chair and heading back to her bed.

And so in the late morning, Ellen found herself walking the mile or so from her house to the picnic area at one of the city parks nestled against the banks of the river. In one hand, she carried a small wicker basket of fried chicken Ellen had helped Sophie prepare the day before. She'd tied ribbons in her hair, and had chosen to wear what she thought was her prettiest dress. It was a summer dress that Sophie had made for her the year before—Alice blue in color, with buttons running down the front. Ellen liked the way the light fabric discreetly complemented the soft curves of her body, and the way it danced around her feet when she walked. And that morning she was walking quickly.

There were over a hundred people at the picnic, all of whom waited their turn to wish the young Mr. Hastings good luck and Godspeed on his journey to Africa. Ellen sat at a picnic table with the Klatts, picking at her chicken and waiting for Reverend Schneider, who was shepherding Thomas Hastings from table to table, to get around to them. She sat between the two Klatt girls: Audrey, who was seventeen and a senior in high school, and Gwen, who was fourteen. Audrey was everything Ellen was not. She was witty, vibrant and outgoing, always the life of the party and the center of attention. The two girls despised each other.

As Ellen watched the two men move slowly from one table to another, she fussed over how she would get Thomas Hastings's attention—how she would get herself into a position to get his singular attention.

By the time the two men approached her table, Ellen had chewed away three of her fingernails. Lunch was all but over, and Gwen had run off to be with her friends. To Ellen's chagrin, Audrey, who found the young man every bit as attractive as she did, was in fine form. When reintroduced, she stood, a picture of bright eyes and shining teeth and happy energy, and offered her hand to him. Ellen's stomach turned over.

"And you know Ellen Winkler," Reverend Schneider offered, turning finally to Ellen.

"I do," Thomas Hastings said, looking down to her.

His eyes were sharp and strong and commanding, and Ellen feared that he might be capable of looking inside of her, or reading her thoughts. She forced herself to stand and offer her hand.

"Hello again," she managed to say.

"Hello," Thomas Hastings said, taking her hand and squeezing it lightly.

The two men had already eaten, so Mrs. Klatt invited them to sit for a glass of lemonade. The old preacher declined. Over the last few years he'd

42

developed a bad case of gout, and wanted nothing more than to get back to his study where he could soak his aching feet in Epsom salts. Thomas Hastings placed himself between the two girls, and, sipping his glass of lemonade, quickly became engaged in small talk with the two of them.

Louise Klatt could plainly see the competition developing between the two girls for Hastings's attention. She watched the flirting cautiously. A sharp-witted woman of forty-five, she had learned how to keep her eyes and ears open and had taught herself to be distrustful of surface impressions. And she knew a thing or two about life in general and about men in particular. She knew how arrogance could mask itself as self-confidence, and how the hardness in a man's eyes, so often taken as a sign of strength, could as easily signal a predator waiting for a target. She'd seen it all before—not in her own husband, who if anything was too much the opposite—but in other men she'd happily only encountered in the third person.

Her instincts told her that Thomas Hastings was not all that he purported to be, that there was more to him than met the untrained eye, and that it was hidden for a reason. And so when the girls asked permission to take Mr. Hastings blackberry picking, her quick answer was no.

"But why not?" Audrey argued back, dismayed.

"I don't want you girls to get your pretty dresses dirty," Mrs. Klatt offered weakly.

"Father?" Audrey complained, turning quickly to her alternate source of authority.

"Oh, come on, dear," Herman Klatt said to his wife. "They'll barely be out of eyeshot."

Audrey looked to her mother expectantly. For a moment her resolution held, then wavered.

"Well, all right," she said finally to Audrey. "But your father will chaperone."

"Louise?" Mr. Klatt objected.

"You'll go with them," Mrs. Klatt snapped.

"No, I won't," Herman Klatt retorted. "I've had a big lunch and I don't feel like a walk." What he did feel like was a cigar, and was looking forward to the opportunity to sidle off to the wagons and cars with a couple of his friends for a smoke.

"You needn't worry, Mrs. Klatt," Thomas Hastings said. "I'll keep the girls safe."

His offer caught Louise Klatt off guard. He was, after all, the reason for the chaperone. But of course he knew that. And in the end, as Thomas Hastings correctly guessed, she didn't have the means to call him on it, and so gave her reluctant consent.

"Stay together," she offered weakly to their backs as Thomas Hastings and the two girls skipped down the meadow toward the white footbridge spanning a narrow spot in the river.

On the walk to the bridge, and once on the other side, Audrey kept herself between Ellen and the young man, her head as close to his as she dared, talking nonstop, her big, winning smile on constant display. As they walked along the tree-lined river bank and into a maze of wild blackberry bushes, Ellen tried once, then twice, then a third time to get a word in. But as soon as she would get Thomas Hastings's attention, Audrey would take it away again. And so while Audrey monopolized the man, Ellen, her pink mouth round and small and angry, stood to the side half-heartedly plucking ripe blackberries from the vine and dropping them into her wicker basket. She was losing badly to Audrey, and was confronted with the gnawing likelihood that she would fail that day. She was getting desperate.

"Do you like blackberries, Mr. Hastings?" Ellen heard Audrey ask in her flirting sing-song voice.

"I do," Thomas Hastings replied.

"Then try this one," Ellen said, forcing herself to move to face him, smiling up to him, a plump blackberry between her thumb and forefinger, an inch from his mouth.

She'd acted impulsively and in truth hadn't known what to expect, but he took the fruit into his mouth, allowing his lips to touch her fingers.

"Mmmm," he said. "What could be better?"

"One of mine," Audrey countered, lifting a ripe blackberry to his lips.

"Just as good," he told Audrey when he'd eaten the berry.

"Here's the best one," she heard herself say as she picked a plump, wet blackberry from her basket. Then, as he cocked his eye and turned to her, as he lowered his face to receive the ripe berry, she quickly leaned to him and pressed her lips clumsily against his. From the corner of her eye Ellen could see Audrey's face in reaction—the wide-eyed shock of it, her mouth fallen open into a hollow "O."

For a moment Thomas Hastings stood silent, as surprised by the kiss as had been Audrey. Then he smiled. "Well," he said, "that *is* the best."

If Audrey couldn't quite feel the heat growing between the two of them, she could clearly sense it. She was a seasoned flirt—it was her hobby, of sorts, and was always fun. But this, she sensed correctly, was quickly becoming something more than just fun. And it wasn't just the kiss. She'd done that herself, just as brazen, though not in public and never with someone she knew as casually as this Thomas Hastings. No, it wasn't the kiss. It was the man. Never had she seen a man so immediately attuned to it, so sure of both what it meant and what it promised.

She was out of her league and knew it, and happily stayed quiet and a step behind the two of them on their walk back to the picnic. She watched from behind as Thomas Hastings talked to Ellen, his mouth close to her ear, his left hand first on her shoulder, then on her waist. And she was happy, very happy, when they were back at the Klatt's picnic table and she could excuse herself to go find her sister. And when, a minute later, Ellen and Thomas Hastings excused themselves—Mr. Hastings was going to escort Ellen home—Louise Klatt was more than happy to see them go. She was sorry for Sophie, and hoped that it wasn't as bad as it seemed to be, but mostly she was just relieved that it wasn't Audrey.

A half-hour later, Ellen and Thomas Hastings were walking up the stone walkway to the front porch of the Winkler home. On the walk back, Ellen had told him two things: that her mother was sick in bed, and that she had a secret place to show him. And so after they'd climbed the front steps onto the long covered front porch and she'd silenced him with a finger to her lips, he let her lead him by the hand through the front door and into the coolness of the shadowed foyer, then up the winding stairway and down the hall to the doorway to Ellen's secret. When the door opened, Thomas Hastings saw that it was the entryway to the attic. He climbed the narrow staircase behind her, watching the lovely swaying motion of Ellen's hips against the thin cloth of her dress.

Louise Klatt's gut feeling had been right: there was much more to Thomas Hastings than met the untrained eye, and none of it was good. This wasn't Thomas Hastings's first time in an attic with a receptive girl. Or in a cellar or a barn or the back room of a tavern. He was familiar with all of them. But what was new to him, and what he was considering as they cleared the stairwell and Ellen took his hand and pulled him to the front bay window to show him the view south down the long hill to the city below, was the girl. He had guessed correctly that Ellen, like himself, was someone who trusted in nothing, and that all the admonitions and rules for behavior patiently spelled out for her protection had washed off Ellen like water off a duck's back.

But if the attitude was familiar, the girl herself was anything but. What his experience had prepared him to expect from her was some kind of naughty mischievous excitement, or perhaps just hot, carnal desire. But what he saw in Ellen Winkler was neither. Rather, she seemed to him to be just...happy, really happy, as if she'd just won a pot of money or been voted homecoming queen.

When he put his hands on her, she stood still with her arms at her sides and passively accepted his first kiss. He kissed her again—harder, this time—then pulled his face back from her. She was smiling back at him, her eyes bubbling with that damned happiness.

"Kiss me back," he said.

And so she did, allowing him to instruct her in how to kiss—how to open her mouth and tilt her head to the side and push back against him. When he cupped his hand around her breast, she made no sound or movement, and when he began to undress her she docilely complied, as if all he were doing was helping her prepare for her bath. At the time he wasn't giving it any thought, but later, on the train headed for New York City, he would remember how odd it was. It was as if she was outside of her own body, a spectator to her own lovemaking.

Her only reaction to him was a low moan when he pressed his hand between her legs, and, some moments later, a sharp, startled "Oh!" as he pushed his way into her.

A minute later he was done, and stood over her, buttoning his pants.

"I'll write to you," Ellen said.

"Sure," Thomas Hastings replied, "I'd like that." He'd expected that the topic would come up, and had in fact been ready to offer it up himself as an exit line.

"And when you return we'll marry," Ellen said.

Thomas Hastings's first impulse was to laugh. But when he looked down and had a good look at her and her ridiculous serene smile, he was struck by how simple she was, how stupidly ingenuous. And what he saw moved him to an emotion he almost never experienced. It was pity.

"Yes," he said finally. "When I return, we'll marry."

He knelt and kissed her, and then he was gone down the rough narrow stairway. Sophie, half-asleep in the warm comfort of her bed, vaguely heard the sound of his footsteps as he moved quickly down the hallway and the stairs, and the sound of the screen door slamming shut behind him as he moved away from the house and into the soft light of the late afternoon. She made a mental note to find out who it was who had left, then turned onto her side and fell back to sleep. When an hour later she would awake again and rise from her bed, around the time that Wilhelm and Henry would be getting home from the ballpark, she would have no memory of the sounds she had earlier heard.

In the attic, framed in a square of afternoon sunlight shining in through the west-facing windows, Ellen sat naked on the rough wooden floor. She was as happy as she'd ever been in her life, and her pale blue eyes danced with sparkling energy. Thomas Hastings had been right about her—that she was someone who trusted in nothing. But he was wrong about what that meant. For him, trusting in nothing meant believing in nothing. But for Ellen

46

it meant something very different—almost, in fact, the opposite. For Ellen trusting in nothing meant that she could believe in anything. And what she'd chosen to believe in, with all of her heart, was Thomas Hastings and the sexual encounter that had consummated their relationship. To her mind, she'd given herself to him, just as she had seen her mother give herself to her father. And now he was hers, and her life was settled.

Chapter Four

Carlos turned the yellow pickup off Centennial Drive and traveled slowly down Summit Avenue. Finishing his second donut, his keen eyes drank in the early morning sights of the quiet street. Here and there Carlos saw old people—a gray-haired lady already at work in her flower bed, a gaunt old man sitting on his front porch, meeting Carlos's eyes with his own as the pickup passed by—but mostly he saw evidence of youth: men and women in business clothes leaving for work, children waiting for a school bus.

He pulled to a stop in front of Number 228 and sat for a moment, admiring the fractured beauty of the hundred-year-old Victorian. The deal he'd brokered with Carole had been disingenuous, he knew. Still, he thought as his eyes swept up and around the scarred exterior of the house, if she was ever to come around to his intent it would be slowly, in stages. "Seduction" was the word that came to mind.

Over breakfast he'd scanned the classifieds for homes for sale around Summit Avenue. He'd found two; both were old and big, and both had asking prices just as big. He'd asserted that they should restore the old house and sell it. Take some of the money Henry had left her, plow it back into the house to make it nice and pretty, then sell it and use the money to buy a place more to their taste. She'd gone for the ruse like a mouse for cheese, Carlos thought happily and without a shred of guilt over the deception.

Carlos twisted his lean frame out of the pickup and stretched in the chilly morning sun. The back of the truck was loaded with the tools of his trade—ladders and electric saws, rope and extension cords, silvery metal toolboxes filled with sundry small hand tools—all the things he would need to recreate century-old splendor. It was going to be a big job, he thought. Many months of patient, part-time work.

As he stood facing the house, an old gray-haired lady passed by on the sidewalk in front of him, hobbling along with the help of a metal walker. Her walker, Carlos noticed, was like her partner in a curious dance: first the walker moved forward, then slowly she would move to it, her head bobbing down, then up. Ahead with the walker, then up with the body, rhythmically moving forward, foot by foot.

"Good morning," Carlos called to her.

"Good morning to you," she replied, her white teeth flashing below her mop of steel-gray hair. "Looks like you got your work cut out for you."

"It's gonna be a pleasure," Carlos called back.

"Well, you be careful," she said.

"Always," Carlos replied. He watched her as she shuffled past. To his untrained eye the woman appeared to be a generic old person, seventy or eighty years old, maybe. Second generation Summit Avenue, Carlos thought, maybe even third.

He decided to walk the length of the property line. The Winkler house, like all the houses of its vintage, was built on a large, long and thin lot, half an acre at least. He walked down the west side of the lot, under a huge old sugar maple badly in need of pruning, its scraggly branches spreading literally from the side of the Winkler house to the manicured walls of its western neighbor. The walk took him gradually downhill through knee-high Johnson grass to the alleyway at the end of the lot.

From this low position, a good ten feet lower than the street above, the old house looked to Carlos like a looming fortress: weathered, gray, and formidable. He could make out the traces of long-gone pathways and flower gardens. A handful of oak and elm trees graced the expanse of the disheveled lawn, and under a huge old willow he saw the rusted shells of iron lawn furniture. It was a great yard, Carlos thought, and made a mental note to add the limitless gardening possibilities to his list of selling points.

Turning right, he walked along the alley for a hundred feet or so, then right again and back up the eastern boundary toward the house. He reached the old garage set back from the house on the eastern side. It seemed to be as old as the house itself, its side door locked tight with an ancient round, rusted padlock. Carlos peered in to the interior through a small window next to the door, but could see nothing but vague outlines in the darkness. A job for another day, he thought.

Carlos returned to the pickup and began to unload tools from the back. "That old lady's right, Winkle," he said to the house. "You don't look so good, brother. But don't worry," he said with self-satisfied authority, "I'm gonna fix you up good as new."

Arms loaded with equipment, Carlos made his way up the narrow concrete path toward the front porch. "When I'm done with you, you'll be smiling again," he said confidently.

Inside the house, Carlos pressed a nearby light switch. He'd arranged to have the electricity turned back on, and was pleased to see the musty entryway dimly illuminated by dusty light bulbs hanging from the ceiling. He'd already formulated his battle plan. First he would clean the whole house from top to bottom—no easy task, he knew—then make the numerous large and small repairs he would discover in the process. First there would be the structural repairs: the broken plaster, the wiring and plumbing, the dry rot. Then the external walls and the roof. Then the inside walls and floors. Then, if things worked out the way he planned, some remodeling.

He decided to begin with the kitchen and move forward, and made his way, clumsily carrying an armful of cleaning equipment, down the   hallway toward the back of the house. He began by vacuuming around the windows, talking to the house, philosophizing. "You know," he said, I think houses are a lot like people. We gotta get old, but we don't have to get ugly. And I'll be honest with you, someone let you get real ugly." Then he turned to his right and bashed his shin—a direct hit right on the bone—on the steel of the half-open oven lid.

"Ayee!" he called out, dropping the hose handle and falling butt first onto the dirty kitchen floor. "Cabrona!" Carlos exclaimed, rubbing his throbbing shin, the hose of the noisy shop-vac sucking clean air. He reached over and turned off the shop-vac, then looked around the kitchen defiantly, seeking out his unseen antagonist. Slowly his anger subsided. "All right," he said finally, contritely. "I take it back."

He could have sworn that oven lid was closed because just a few minutes earlier he'd looked inside, and remembered having to coax the old lid closed. So he sat there on the floor, tenderly rubbing the growing, aching knot on his shin, grimly assessing the mute walls and cupboards around him. He had hoped that the house would be benign, indifferent to his incursion, but now he now knew that he was in for it. This was to be a battle of wills.

As Carlos limped painfully out to his truck for his thermos of coffee, across town in her office, Carole stood at her desk pouring freshly brewed cups of Earl Grey tea for herself and Stella Phillips. It had been a week since their first meeting, and Carole had done enough digging to know that Stella had more than just a fighting chance in what she now felt was a straightforward easement dispute.

"Thank you, honey," Stella said, accepting a cup of steaming tea.

As she returned to her seat behind the desk, Carole noticed that the old lady's hands shook ever so slightly as she lifted the delicate cup to her lips. "Now what about this good news-bad news business you mentioned on the phone?" she asked when she'd returned her cup to its saucer.

Carole took a quick sip of tea before responding. "The bad news is that the easement is for real," she said. "The good news, though," Carole continued, pointing her index finger skyward like a school teacher, "is that the easement is old, real old."

"Why's that good news?" Stella asked.

"Because easements can be abandoned," Carole explained, a faint gleam in her eye. It was the look she got when she was on the chase and closing. "It's use it or lose it."

"Why, he's never used it," Stella quipped.

"Exactly," Carole replied, a hint of a smile now complementing the sparkle in her eyes. "And if the court agrees with us, then it's goodbye easement."

Stella, staring into Carole's eyes, was silent for a moment. "It must be nice to have all that legal knowledge in your head," she said finally. "It makes you powerful."

The compliment made Carole feel awkward, as compliments always did. "Yes," she said after a moment. "I suppose in some small way it does."

"I don't think it's so small," Stella said. "When I was your age, women just didn't become lawyers. I'm glad it's different now."

Stella was right, of course, and long after Carole had escorted the old lady to the door and bid her a good day, the memory of the excitement she had experienced during her years at Northwestern, as she became more and more empowered with a knowledge of the law, stayed with her. She'd made at least two remarkably good decisions in her life, she thought happily; the second one had been marrying Carlos.

Carlos was on her mind that afternoon as she plowed through a stack of discovery documents. She'd intentionally distanced herself from the Winkler incident by telling herself, quite convincingly, that she had neither the time nor the emotional energy to deal with a surprise family tree. Screw the Winklers and their many skeletons, she'd told herself. The problem, she now knew, was that in the process of distancing herself from her unwanted relatives she'd distanced herself from Carlos. The whole episode had made her tired. And irritable. And lonely.

She'd make things right tonight, she thought happily. She'd whip up a big pot of gumbo—one of his favorite meals—and get him a six-pack of Sierra Nevada Pale Ale—his favorite beer—and look forward to an evening of serious massage therapy.

She finally stumbled into their apartment around six o'clock, her arms laden with bags of groceries. "Hi, honey," she called out happily.

Then she saw him, sitting morosely in his boxer shorts on the couch, his long black hair wet from the shower. With his heels on the coffee table, he had cold compresses on both shins, and was holding an ice pack to his left eye. In response to her cheery greeting, Carlos grimly removed the ice pack to reveal a whopping shiner.

Carole stopped in her tracks. "Holy cow!" she exclaimed. "What happened?"

"We got off to a bad start," Carlos said, dolefully looking up to her from his perch on the edge of the couch. "Me and Winkle."

Carole didn't follow. "Winkle?" she asked.

"Me and the house," Carlos said.

51

"Ah," Carole said, finally putting the pieces together.

She put down the bags of groceries and moved to him. Lifting a cold compress from one of his shins, she was confronted with a livid red welt. "Yikes," she said, her eyes big.

As she gently replaced the cold compress, she noticed the dark bruises on the fingers of his right hand. "Oh, my," she said softly. "What happened to your fingers?"

"Winkle slammed a window on me," Carlos answered.

"You mean Wink*ler*," Carole corrected, kissing the outraged fingers softly.

"Wink*ler*," Carlos repeated.

Usually she would call him on the half-dozen or so elements of his belief system that she found absurd—like believing that material creations like cars and houses had personalities—but this time she correctly guessed that he wasn't in the mood for needling, and let it pass. Instead, she uncapped two bottles of the beer and plopped down on the couch next to him.

"Ahh, you're a lifesaver," Carlos said, accepting a bottle and taking a long, grateful pull.

Carole kicked off her shoes and curled her feet under her. Despite her genuine concern for Carlos's pain, she could begin to see a possible silver lining to the black cumulonimbus cloud hanging over him. "So have you had it with Winkler?" she asked, trying not to sound too hopeful.

Carlos's eyes hardened with grim determination. "No way," he pronounced firmly. "First of all, he's got me all wrong. I'm his friend, man. He just doesn't know it yet. And anyway, I'm smarter than he is. I can outfox him."

Carole wanted to say that calling yourself smarter than a house was only slightly superior to calling yourself smarter than a rock, but again wisely let it pass.

"Well, you'll need your strength, then," she said with an almost-straight face, kissing him on the cheek. "You'll be happy to know that I've got a treat planned."

In the end, the evening didn't go quite the way Carole had planned. Carlos was delighted with dinner, so that by nine o'clock the gumbo had been wiped out, the last bottle of beer sat unfinished on the coffee table, and Carole lay in her robe on the couch, her head in Carlos's lap.

"I've been a real bitch the last few days, haven't I?" Carole said quietly, offering up her confession.

"Oh, no, honey," Carlos responded. "You've been fine. Really."

It was a lie, she knew. She'd been cold and indifferent to him, easily angered, snappish. She'd slept on her side of the bed all week. But it was the kind of lie you tell someone when you're in it for the long term, when having a bad week doesn't change anything. But now she wanted it over. She wanted her sense of humor back, and her husband.

"I love you, Carlos," she said.

"I love you," he said softly, bending to kiss her head.

The relief of having said it, and of having it said to her, and of knowing that it was meant on both accounts, released the vice of tension that had been holding her prisoner all week. She felt warm and protected, and soon fell fast asleep.

And that's how the evening ended. Carlos sat for a half an hour with her head in his lap, listening to her soft, steady breathing and curling locks of her long, light brown hair between his fingers. Finally, despite his aches and pains, he rose from the couch and carried her into the bedroom. She never awoke.

Carlos did indeed manage to outsmart the house. The next morning he stopped by a second-hand sports equipment store for some strategic purchases, so that when he finally pulled his pickup to a stop in front of the Winkler house, he was ready for action. Exiting the pickup cab, he faced the house, matching its acrimonious grimace with his own look of stern determination. He cleared his throat.

"You don't know it yet," he said, beginning the entreaty he had composed on the drive up, "but I am your friend. I am kind. I am gentle. I am the Gandhi of home repairers." His dark brown eyes scanned the cold, looming facade facing him, looking for a hint of a response. None came.

"But," he continued, "I understand that there is no reason for you to believe this. And so until I can convince you of the honor of my intentions, I will be forced to protect myself."

With that he extracted a cardboard box from the back of the pickup and began to clothe himself with various items of protective gear: a pair of football shoulder pads, karate pads for his elbows and shins, and leather gloves for his hands. Picking up a mop and pail, he headed grimly toward the front door to begin his day of battle.

To the old lady with the walker approaching on the sidewalk, he must have looked like a modern-day Don Quixote, trudging forward with his shoulder armor flapping and his mop handle lance pointing horizontally forward, in anticipation of the tilt.

"Good luck," she called to him as he passed in front of her.

Carlos turned to her and nodded. "Thank you. I'm gonna need it."

As silly as Carlos may have looked in his jerry-rigged armor, it worked. Standing on the front lawn and pulling off the sweat-soaked gear at the   end of his workday, Carlos found only one small cut on an unprotected portion of his wrist. As he had expected, the house had struck out at him with blind, unreasoned fury. Carlos had counted seven blows in all: three to the hands and fingers, one to the shoulder, two to the shins, and one literal low blow to the groin that bounced harmlessly off the cup he had thankfully remembered to put on. And all except one, Carlos thought smugly, had been to no avail.

"So you see," he said to the house from the safe distance of the pickup, "I'm still here, and I'm not going anywhere." He popped open a cold Coca-Cola, took a long, gulping pull, and belched. "And look at the nice things I've done for you," he continued. "Three rooms nice and clean, drapes to the cleaners, one window frame repaired." He took another pull on the Coca-Cola. "Now I don't expect you to trust me yet, but, hey, actions speak louder than words, right? So be open-minded, okay? Be reasonable. You'll see."

And sure enough, as the hot summer workdays passed, the blows became fewer and fewer, until one day in mid-summer they stopped altogether. The turning point, Carlos later concluded, came inadvertently. Tired of the repetitive grind of cleaning and minor repairs, he'd one day diverted his attention to the wood of the built-in dining room cabinets. Though beautifully crafted and carved, the rich walnut was dull and bone-dry, like a skull in the desert. "Hmmm," Carlos had said softly. "I know just what you need."

So he'd spent a portion of the day feeding the cabinets coat after coat of beeswax furniture restorer, which they sucked up greedily, and more importantly, as it turned out, gratefully. When the wood's tremendous thirst had finally been quenched, Carlos stood back from the cabinets, admiring their rich, sparkling beauty. "You, my good friend, are beautiful," he said.

Over the last few weeks he'd gotten pretty good at detecting booby-traps, so that on that day, scanning the dark, gleaming wood, Carlos noticed the half-opened bottom cabinet door, waiting, he surmised, for an errant shin. "You'll have to do better than that, pal," Carlos said as he moved to the cabinet and gently closed the door. "I'm a fast learner."

He left the room for his toolbox, and when he returned, to his surprise he again found the cabinet door half-opened. Now, though, he was more curious than wary. He stared at the door for a few moments, thinking, then smiled softly, finally figuring it out. Walking to the cabinet, he opened the door wide. As was true of most drawers and cabinets in the old house, the inside of this one was crammed with the flotsam of seventy-five years of Winkler habitation. But as he had done from the start, Carlos deferred from investigating. "You know," he said softly, running his fingers appreciatively across the slick wood of the cabinet, "I think this should be someone else's discovery. But thanks all the same."

All through the hot, sweating days of summer, Carlos worked on the house. Some jobs were trivial, some back-breaking, some grindingly monotonous. Some jobs turned out to be easier than he had thought they would be; there was, for instance, remarkably little dry rot around the foundations or the plumbing, and very little termite damage. On the other hand, some jobs, like the electrical rewiring, were formidable and time-consuming. But for Carlos, all were labors of love.

By the middle of September, as the heat finally began to break and north winds brought dark clouds and cool, light rain, the first stage of Carlos's work had been completed to his satisfaction. All of the rooms, including the small cut-stone basement, were spotlessly clean, and structurally the house was in perfect working order. Clear water, both hot and cold, ran from its taps, light shone brightly from all the ceiling lamps, and doors and windows opened and closed smoothly and soundlessly.

There was still much to do: the outside walls needed paint as badly as the inside hardwood had needed wax, the broken front porch would have to be rebuilt, and the inside walls needed refurbishing and re-papering. Nevertheless, the old house seemed fresh and pleasant to Carlos, eminently livable.

By late September everything was ready, and on a particular Wednesday morning, Carlos launched his plan. He elected not to prepare Carole's customary sack lunch, instead inviting her to lunch at their favorite burger place downtown. They met at noon, and as they ate their cheeseburgers and curly fries, Carole excitedly described the Client From Hell belonging to Hank Cooper, one of her associates.

"He's called 'Mad Dog,' and it's his bazillionth offense, and Hank gets assigned to him, he's got no choice, see," Carole said, her eyes sparkling with humor.

"They can make you represent someone?" Carlos asked, munching on a curly fry.

"Let's just say they can make you an offer you can't refuse, which is one of many good reasons why yours truly doesn't do criminal law," Carole said.

She took a bite of cheeseburger and hurriedly swallowed it, anxious to resume the story. "Anyway," she continued, "I'm leaving to come over here and he's sitting in the waiting room. She leaned over the table and whispered. "Carlos, he's got 'fuck you' tattooed on his forehead."

"You're kidding me," Carlos said, his mouth falling open.

"I kid you not," Carole said. "'Fuck you.' The guy's a walking Kodak moment."

They both laughed.

"So he takes his civil liberties seriously," Carlos said.

"Tell you what," Carole said playfully. "When Claudia comes out for a visit, we'll have him over."

Claudia was Carlos's youngest sister, whose taste in men, to the chagrin of her family, tended toward the exotic. "No way," Carlos protested, his mouth full of cheeseburger. "She might like him."

Since Carole had brought up the subject of dinner, Carlos took advantage of it. "Speaking of dinner, I'm planning something special for tonight," he said nonchalantly.

"So what's the occasion?" she asked.

Carlos's eyes danced with mischief. "Not what, honey, but where," he said.

And so at around six o'clock, Carole pulled her old Toyota to a stop behind Carlos's pickup on Summit Avenue and got out. The sky was overcast, threatening rain. Holding herself against the unusual September chill, Carole surveyed the Winkler house; her house, she thought ruefully. She hadn't balked when Carlos had suggested the dinner; he was excited to show her the state of the renovation—but now, squarely facing the ominous brute, she wavered. The old, uneasy feelings were returning. Who *were* these people, these dead people, she thought, who'd been so rudely thrust upon her?

As she moved cautiously toward the front door, her shoes click-click-clicking against the cement walkway, she forcefully asserted to herself that they, like the old, ugly mass of wood and brick in front of her, meant nothing to her. They were of no consequence, she told herself. But as she climbed the sagging porch staircase and approached the open front door, her stomach tightened and for a moment she felt sick and weak.

Peering in, she knocked on the front door. "Knock-knock," she called in, trying to be cheerful. There was no answer, so after a moment she stepped into the foyer. She was astonished by the change. Where before the house had seemed cluttered, cramped and dirty, now it was open and ordered, and impeccably clean. And where earlier it had been dark and ominous, now it was airy and bright with light, almost inviting.

Carlos popped into view at the far end of the hallway. He was wearing a cooking apron, and was holding a large wooden spoon. "Hi, honey," he called to her.

"Hi," she replied.

"Gotta watch my shrimp," he said with a smile. "Take a look around." Then he disappeared back into the kitchen.

Carole walked slowly up the length of the first floor, looking into the tidy rooms to her left. She felt as though she was taking a tour of some famous old house where the doorways are cordoned off with red velvet rope, where she wasn't supposed to touch anything. She was stunned by the charm that Carlos had reclaimed from under the neglect and debris. While the weathered walls had lost most of their wallpaper, and the carpets and old upholstery were sometimes worn and threadbare, she could clearly see the antique beauty of the design and furnishings, and could understand the comfort the old house must have offered to generations of its occupants: her relatives. Carlos, she thought appreciatively, had done a magnificent job.

Standing in the dining room, admiring the shining beauty of the massive walnut dining room table and cabinets, she heard, from the kitchen, the sound of a cork popping. A moment later Carlos emerged with two glasses of red wine. He walked to her and gave her a light kiss on the lips.

"So what do you think?" he asked, handing her a glass of wine and taking a sip from his own.

Carole thought for a moment. "Remarkable," she said finally. "Simply remarkable."

"You like it?" he asked, smiling hopefully.

Carlos should have known better than to think that this particular sales job would be that easy.

"Let's just say I'm impressed with your handiwork," she said judiciously. "Frankly, I had my doubts that even the great Estrada had the magic for *this* job."

"He hasn't tried to hurt you, has he?" Carlos asked with concern.

"Who?" Carole asked.

"Winkler," Carlos answered.

Carole got it. "Uh...no," she said.

"Good," Carlos said, relieved. "I think he's over it, but you can never be sure. Watch where you put your hands."

Carlos went back to the kitchen, fearful for his shrimp. While he was cooking, Carole wandered through the first floor rooms, her hands held together behind her back, as if she were in a china shop.

The dinner that Carlos prepared was magnificent: Puerto-Rican-style shrimp scampi over pasta, a Caesar salad complete with anchovies, which Carole carefully picked from her bowl and transferred to Carlos's, and fresh strawberries with melted chocolate for dipping. They ate by candlelight.

By 8:30, Carlos had removed the empty plates and bowls, and the two of them sat at the huge dining room table, finishing the last of the wine. Outside the sky was darkening, and the candles sent gentle shadows flickering against the unfinished dining room walls.

To Carlos, the stillness of the evening around them was intoxicating. "Listen, honey. What do you hear?" he asked.

For a moment she listened to the house. "Nothing," she said finally.

"Exactly," Carlos pronounced happily. "Nothing! No street noise, no arguing, no Lawrence Welk. And all the room," he said, gesturing to the empty space around them. "I feel like a cowboy on the open range."

Carole stifled a yawn. "Yeah, well, pardner," she said in her best western drawl, "we oughta be thinkin' about amblin' back to the bunkhouse, 'cause this filly's been rode hard today."

Now's the time, Carlos thought. It's now or never. "Come on," he said, rising to his feet and offering Carole his hand. "I want to show you something."

Holding her hand, he led her up the L-shaped stairway to the second floor, then guided her to the left, into Wilhelm and Sophie's old bedroom. When he flipped on the light, Carole was amazed by the elegance of the big, immaculate bedroom: the gleaming, antique cherry wood dressers and matching vanity and mirror, the two intricately carved old chairs with needlepoint seat covers, a lovely small writing secretary, a Tiffany floor lamp, and the ancient Winkler four-poster bed, covered with a beautiful old double-ring patterned quilt.

The beautiful quilt called to Carole, and she walked to the bed and gently handled its edge. She could see that it was all hand-stitched.

Now Carole was gullible to a point, but she was no fool. She quickly began to put the fishy pieces together. The sheets on the bed were clean and new and smelled distinctly of Bounce fabric softener; the candles and matchbook on the end table; the red wine. And finally, the black overnight bag next to the bed: her bag.

"What's in there?" she asked suspiciously, pointing to the black bag.

There was nothing left for Carlos to do but to push forward. "I just brought over a few things from the apartment," he said gaily, grinning foolishly.

"Oh, no," Carole said, her blue eyes hardening and her pink mouth snapping shut defiantly. "No, Carlos. No way."

"Aw, come on," Carlos complained.

"It's spooky in here, Carlos," Carole said. "This is somebody else's room...somebody else's bed."

"Hey, it's your room and your bed, remember?" he argued. "And there's good vibes in here, I can tell. Good people slept in this room."

"You're sure of that?" Carole said, raising a skeptical eyebrow.

"Sure I'm sure," Carlos answered winningly, sounding more and more, he knew, like a used car salesman. "Think of it as a night in an old, elegant bed-and-breakfast."

She wasn't giving in, but she wasn't being adamant, either, Carlos thought optimistically. "Look," he continued. "We've got everything we need here. Electricity. Plumbing. Hot water. Coffee and oranges for the morning. And tea…I brought tea."

Her face was softening. Carlos nibbled her neck. "Clean sheets on the bed," he said into her ear.

He tickled her, and she laughed.

"Me," he added.

He grabbed her around the waist and fell with her onto the bed. "Come on," he said softly. "Just one night." Then he kissed her on the lips, and she kissed him back, wrapping her arms around him.

Sometimes Carole made love to Carlos out of raw lust, sometimes out of playfulness, occasionally out of affectionate obligation, and sometimes, like that night, out of an urgent desire for safety; to attach herself to him and hide herself in him. Afterwards, Carlos fell quickly asleep in the quiet chamber. A gentle breeze stirred the curtains at the open windows, and the full moon in the clearing night sky bathed the room with soft, mysterious patterns of light.

Carole lay awake for a long time, unmoving, her eyes traveling worriedly around the strange room, looking, perhaps, for a ghost. Finally she turned away from Carlos, molded her body to his, pulled his limp arm protectively around her, and closed her eyes.

Usually Carlos awoke before Carole, but the next morning she awoke first, to the chill of the early morning and the sound of birds outside the open windows. Slipping out from under the warm sheets, she found Carlos's shirt and put it on. Tentatively she began to explore the room. She gently touched the wood of the dressers, and ran her fingers across the gilded frame of an old photograph on the wall. It was a wedding photograph: the thin young man in the photo appeared proud and strong, his eyes sharp and energetic; the young woman, almost as tall as her husband, had a soft smile, and the gentlest eyes Carole had ever seen.

She moved away from the photograph and walked soundlessly to the old vanity. Seating herself in front of the tall, oval mirror, she saw herself: her hair hanging at her shoulders in limp curls, her eyes still dull and puffy from sleep. Behind her on the bed, she could see Carlos sleeping soundly.

Cautiously, Carole opened the middle drawer of the vanity. Inside, right in the front, she found a pair of very old hair brushes, ornately crafted in silver and inlaid with mother of pearl. Feeling like a thief, she reached in and gently removed the brushes. Whose were these? she thought as she delicately examined them. The hair in the brushes was light brown, just like hers. She stole a look to the photograph on the wall; were these yours? she silently asked the woman. After a long moment, she turned back to the vanity and began to brush her hair.

Epistle

There's no reason, nowadays, why houses can't live forever. True, there will always be Acts of God—tornados and earthquakes and such—and true, fires still sometimes consume houses, but in the absence of these calamities, a house, with proper care, can live on and on.

Unlike people, who break easily and in ways that are too often irreparable, there is virtually nothing in a house that can't be put right if it malfunctions or wears out. In a house, plumbing can be replaced, wiring repaired and updated, structural elements revamped and reconstructed. I watched Henry Winkler, as self-appointed physician and plastic surgeon to the Winkler house, do all of these things, and more. And while over the long years time took its toll on Henry, while he lived that house remained young.

Also unlike people, who grow weak and frail with age, houses often seem to grow stronger with the passage of time. I once watched Henry repair a hole in the wall that had resulted from inadvertently leaving his grandson Willy alone in the living room with a hammer. Henry cleaned away the broken plaster and lath, revealing a piece of the thick oak framing of the house's immense skeleton. I watched as Henry tried to hammer a nail into the fifty-year-old wood; the force of the hammer blow bent the thick iron into a wobbly "S," as if it had hit a rock. Old hardwoods, like oak and maple, just get harder with age, Henry had explained as he searched through his toolbox for a hand drill. If only it were so for my old bones!

As commodities, houses are bought and sold at people's whims, leaving them to contend as best they can with the vagaries of whomever chooses to inhabit them. Like a marriage between strangers, these random couplings are sometimes serendipitous and sometimes ill-advised, becoming by chance joyful and loving, or passionless and barren, or even mean. And while I was at first reluctant to believe it, I now realize that houses, like people, respond in predictable ways to the people in them and the events that unfold around them.

Some more than others, of course. My own house, for instance, is for the most part indifferent, responding to the long cycles of love and acrimony, of hope and enmity in ways that are barely noticeable even to a trained eye. The Winkler house, on the other hand, has always been animated, wearing its heart, as it were, on its sleeve.

I have a story to tell you about how I began to come to this realization. One day during the war I was dusting in the back bedroom of the Winkler house—in the bedroom that had been Henry's sister Ellen's—when I heard a distinct thud from the closet. When I looked in, I found a small cardboard *box, old and cracked and tied together with string, lying in the middle of the closet floor. Thinking not much about it, I returned the box to its place on the high shelf and left, returning to my dusting. Some moments later I again heard the thud, and again found the box on the floor.*

When I took the box to Henry and told him what had happened, he smiled knowingly and nodded. He had had many similar experiences, he said. The house, Henry explained, had given me a gift. Gifts of discovery, he called them. Gifts from a friend.

Inside the box, Henry found dozens of old photographs his father had taken with his Brownie camera. He had thought them, like his wife and parents, to have been forever lost, and was overwhelmed with joy that they had so graciously been returned to him. I left him to be alone with his private memories, in wonder at the plainly animate force I had witnessed for the first, but not the last, time, and wondering, to be honest, how those photographs ever got to their hiding place in Ellen's closet.

Chapter Five

It was two-thirds of the way through the year, and 1917 was not turning out to be a happy one for Wilhelm Winkler. The United States had entered the war in Europe in April, and since then Wilhelm, as a first generation German-American, had been forced to endure a tempest of anti-German sentiment. Worse still, Congress had passed a conscription bill in May, and in June, his son Henry, now twenty-one, had been one of the nine-and-a half million young American men who had been obliged to register with the Selective Service. Wilhelm, who was adamantly and vocally opposed to U.S. involvement in the war, was faced with the real possibility that his son would have to fight in it.

On a late Saturday morning toward the end of September, Wilhelm sat in his bedroom reading the editorial page of the newspaper. Approaching his fifty-fourth birthday, he was as lean as ever, though his face had weathered and his hair had grayed and thinned, so that his pink head could be seen from several angles. He was dressed in his Sunday best, and sat chomping testily on an unlit cigar.

Ten feet away, Sophie, also in her best clothes, sat at her vanity combing her hair and admiring the silver hair brush set Wilhelm had given her for her birthday a few weeks earlier. Like Wilhelm, her hair was streaked with gray, and the skin of her cheeks and chin was beginning to loosen.

"Idiots!" Wilhelm growled loudly.

"Idiots?" Sophie asked as she began to wind her long hair into a loose bun. She could see his reflection in her mirror, his mouth folded into a sulking frown. It was an ugly look reflecting an ugly mood, and was to her both unfamiliar and unwelcome.

"Loyalty oaths. They're calling for loyalty oaths."

Sophie's hands froze for an instant. She, too, had felt the recent tension and hostility: the stares on the street, the hushed whispers from behind her back. Resolutely she continued to wind her hair.

"We're in a democracy, sweetheart," she said calmly. "People can say anything they like."

Sophie rose from her chair, quickly checking the details of her dress and hair in the vanity mirror. "Well," she said, turning to Wilhelm and forcing a smile, "our business prospers and our health flourishes." She moved to Wilhelm and straightened his tie. The tight collar and agitation had caused his skin to redden, so that, to Sophie's bemused eye, his head looked vaguely like a hairy tomato. "And we shall enjoy this day," she concluded, emphasizing the "shall": it was an order.

Wilhelm chuckled, following his wife's command to lighten up. "All true," he said, letting his anger go for the time being. "No matter what they say, they still enjoy eating Winkler sausages." He took the wet cigar from his mouth and placed his hands on his wife's waist, kissing her. He ran his hands appreciatively up her sides to her armpits. After almost thirty-five years, he still enjoyed the feel of her.

There was a quick knock on the half-opened door, and Henry popped his head into the doorway. "Mr. Brumbaugh's here," he said. Today was the day the Winklers had arranged for a family photograph, and Brumbaugh was their photographer.

Henry had grown into a handsome young man. He was short and dark-haired like his father, but bulkier, like the men on his mother's side. He had the clear complexion of Sophie and the crisp, almost chiseled facial features of Wilhelm. His blue eyes were a hybrid—quick and inquisitive like Wilhelm's, but soft like Sophie's.

"Ah, good," Wilhelm said. "Come along, son," he said to Henry, "let's try and roust your sister."

The two men left the bedroom and walked down the hallway, Wilhelm inspecting his cigar as he walked. He had planned to smoke it after the photograph session, but in his agitation he'd reduced the end to a wet, pulverized mush. A waste of a good cigar, he thought sadly.

Stopping in front of the door to the attic, Wilhelm knocked. "Ellie, honey, the photographer's here," he called out encouragingly. There was no response from within.

"Ellie, honey," he called out again, knocking harder on the door. Still there was no response.

Wilhelm tried the doorknob; it was locked. Frustrated now, he banged on the door and called out to Ellen angrily. "Ellen Winkler, open this God-damned door!"

"Shame on you, Papa," came Ellen's high voice trickling down from above, "taking the Lord's name in vain."

"And why are you locking yourself in the attic in broad daylight?" Wilhelm called out, dismayed.

"I'm working," came the distant reply from within.

"Ahhh!" Wilhelm exclaimed, giving up. He left the door and walked with Henry back toward the staircase. "In the old country they'd say 'sie hat ein vogel,'" he said, pointing his finger to his head and making small circles. Wilhelm loved and cared for his daughter, but she exasperated him be- yond belief. Thirty years old, she still lived at home. She had no vocation, and she had no husband: while several decent young men had shown inter- est, Ellen had coolly and consistently rebuffed their modest advances. She

63

was "spoken for," she claimed, though exactly who was the speaker remained her secret.

And then, out of the blue two years earlier, she'd come home one day from a church meeting to announce that she'd joined the cause of prohibition. Wilhelm vividly remembered how she'd looked that afternoon. It had been winter, and her face was flushed from the cold air outside. Her mouth was open into a small continuous smile, as if the ends had been lifted up and pinned to her cheeks. Her eyes had been wide and vacant and had appeared to Wilhelm to be slightly crossed. She'd looked, ironically, as if she'd been drunk.

The shock of it had quickly worn off. She was an impressionable girl, Wilhelm and Sophie both knew, and had fallen, they correctly concluded, under the influence of someone's strong personality. The someone, in this case, was the wife of Reverend Haselbush, St. Luke's new minister. A dour and pinched women forever given to wearing funeral black, she was the ringleader of the local temperance movement. On the strength of experience, they'd hoped that Ellen's interest in the cause would fade quickly, as had all of her previous interests. But in this case, time proved them wrong. Ellen's commitment to the cause had grown steadily, until neither Wilhelm nor Sophie could deny that it had become her life.

At the stairway they met Sophie, who had just emerged from the bedroom. "Talk to her, Mother," Wilhelm said, jerking his thumb back down the hallway.

Sophie needed no more of an explanation. She walked to the attic door and knocked briskly. "I need to talk to you, Ellie," she called out loudly, forcing her voice to penetrate the thick wood of the locked door. After several moments she heard soft footsteps on the attic stairs. A moment later the door lock clicked open, and the footsteps retreated quickly back up the attic stairway.

Sophie wearily opened the door and began the climb up the steep steps to the attic. Ellen had made the attic a shrine to her obsession. On one rough wall were large photographs of Frances Willard and Carrie Nation, surrounded by colorful banners of the Women's Christian Temperance Union. On and around the small desk Ellen had placed under one of the east-facing dormer windows haphazard stacks of brochures, books, and magazines dedicated to The Cause, and stacks of yellowing back issues of *The Crusader Monthly*, the official publication of the WCTU.

Ellen had returned to her desk. As she'd been instructed at breakfast, she'd done her hair and dressed for the photograph session. She'd chosen to wear what was still her favorite dress—the old Alice blue summer dress Sophie had made for her, and that she'd worn to the church picnic so many

64

years before. Above her left breast she wore the cameo brooch Wilhelm and Sophie had given her for her thirtieth birthday. She sat writing feverishly, holding the side of her head, and didn't look up as Sophie cleared the stairway and moved to her side.

"Another headache, dear?" Sophie asked sympathetically. Over the last few years Ellen had come to be plagued by occasional headaches that often debilitated and occasionally ravaged her.

"It seems to be my burden, Mother," Ellen answered. "But it won't keep me from my work."

Finally she looked up. "Look, Mother," she said, holding a page of writing out for Sophie to read. The page was entitled "Why Mere Temperance Is Not Enough." "It's my best work yet," Ellen said proudly.

Sophie looked dispassionately at the page of rough scribbling. She had seen a hundred of these by now, and the sight of them made her feel tired. She had tried in every way possible to shepherd her daughter away from her singular compulsion toward the everyday world of simple human pleasures. But she was out of ideas and out of energy. All she had left was love.

"That's nice, dear," she said softly.

"Oh, Mother!" Ellen said, her eyes shining with excitement. "These are exciting times. The amendment has passed!"

Sophie gently nudged Ellen out of her chair. "Let's go down for the photograph, darling," she said.

Ellen's eyes gleamed. "We'll remove this scourge once and for all," she said firmly. "We'll break this pestilence. Then…"

Ellen's entranced smile faltered, and her eyes clouded. In a moment she was crying, first softly, then violently, her shoulders heaving, her head in her hands.

"There, there, honey…there, there," Sophie said softly, rubbing the young woman's shoulders.

Sophie could feel Ellen's shoulders shiver under her fingers as Ellen sat weeping into her hands. Sie hat ein vogel, she thought. She was crazy— Wilhelm's simple explanation. But it wasn't that simple; Wilhelm just hadn't been there to see it. He'd been at work at the sausage factory, or at the ballpark with Henry, or in his study. Only Sophie had been there to see it…all of it, day after day: the string of letters to Thomas Hastings returned as undeliverable; the long, barren, empty days; the crushing solitude.

Sophie bent down and kissed Ellen on the arch of her neck. "There, there," she said, her heart aching for the girl.

Downstairs, Wilhelm and Henry entered the parlor to find Mr. Brumbaugh, the photographer, setting up his boxy camera on a tripod.

"Mr. Brumbaugh," Wilhelm said happily, extending his hand. "It's been several years, I think."

"Yes indeed," Brumbaugh answered, taking Wilhelm's firm grip. "The last time I saw young Henry here he was still in knickers."

Wilhelm patted Henry's shoulder affectionately. "We're very proud of our boy," Wilhelm said. "He's working with me down at the factory. He'll be taking over soon, once I'm good and sick of it."

"You're a lucky man," Brumbaugh said. "I was hoping I could say the same about my boy, but he up and joined the army."

Wilhelm and Henry exchanged a wary look as Brumbaugh shook his head sadly.

"I'm with you on the whole matter," Wilhelm finally said. "It's lunacy."

Henry listened as Wilhelm and Brumbaugh continued talking the politics of war. Like many young men of the time, he had been attracted to the pageantry and drama associated with the war effort: the parades, the impassioned speeches, the calls for patriotism and sacrifice. He had watched as several of his friends had enlisted, seduced by the promise of adventure and the guarantee of manhood, swept away by the pure energy of a society mobilizing for war. He, too, had been tempted. And while he respected his father's position, what had stopped him had nothing to do with ethics or politics or economics. She was five feet tall and weighed ninety-five pounds, and had auburn hair tinged with red, and sharp, sparkling green eyes. Her name was Clara.

When Ellen finally arrived, Brumbaugh got to work positioning the four family members around the large breakfront in the parlor. The daughter was a handsome young woman, he thought, and his camera would capture all of her beauty. What it would hide, if he used his talents well, would be the pale, almost sickly skin and the worry in her face, which he could usually override momentarily with a pun or a funny joke. But what he would not be able to hide, he knew, would be the eyes: dull and sad and far away, they seemed to him to be the eyes of a woman on her death bed.

Brumbaugh took five photographs altogether: one of the family together and then one of each of the four. Wilhelm and Sophie would hang the individual photographs in the various bedrooms, while the family photograph would be hung in the parlor. And while the first four would come to be lost, the photograph of the family would survive. It would eventually find a home for itself on the north wall of Ellen's back bedroom, where it would offer, to the odd assortment of visitors who would find their way into that room over the long years to follow, a fortuitous glimpse into the past—and, perhaps also, from a certain perspective, a glimpse into the future.

After lunch, Henry got the keys to the delivery wagon from Wilhelm and behind the wheel of the Model-T Ford, began the long, clattering journey down Centennial Drive to Klein's grocery store. They'd had the truck for four years now, and Henry loved driving it. He was a better driver than Wilhelm, who was awkward with the controls and uncomfortable with the high speeds, which Henry knew from his own calculations approached 50 miles per hour. "We're lucky we don't kill ourselves with these contraptions," Wilhelm would say. Still, the automobile represented progress, and Wilhelm was all for that.

Henry pulled to a stop in front of the small grocery. The Kleins were not as prosperous as the Winklers, and still lived in the second story above the shop. Like the Winklers, they were second- and third-generation Americans of German origin.

He entered the store and found Clara at the counter, packing boxes of food to be delivered, and when she saw him, she broke in to a wide smile.

"Hi," she said cheerfully.

Henry hurried to her. "Hi," he said, taking her small hand. He looked around quickly to make sure they were alone, then kissed her on the lips. It made his heart jump.

"You're early," she said.

"Then I'll help you pack," Henry said.

For the next half-hour Clara directed him through the aisles of the small store, consolidating into boxes and bags the sundry items from her lists. He loved the sound of her voice. It was soft and melodic, deep for a woman so small, like a cello.

Clara was two years younger than Henry. He had known her vaguely during his last two years of high school, but had never done more than to say hello to the tiny, reserved girl who always looked like she was twelve years old. When Henry started delivering sausages to the Klein's store a year earlier, he had been shocked by the change, almost not recognizing her. The skinny adolescent had matured into a beautiful young woman, and her sharp green eyes danced with amusement and delight, and with quick thought.

He'd taken her to a baseball game and then to a picnic. Then to dinner to meet his parents and his odd sister. Henry had been amazed at how fluidly the courtship had progressed, at how quickly and firmly, and how joyously, he had discarded his independence in exchange for the growing fruits of love. He could no longer imagine life without her, and like most young men stricken with the same affliction, saw no danger in this.

Saturday afternoons, when he would use the truck to help Clara with her deliveries, were the high point of his week. It was just about the only time when they could be alone, when they had time to relax and talk at their ease,

67

uninterrupted. After the deliveries, Henry would sit in the Kleins' parlor with Clara and Fred Klein, drinking cold beer and talking baseball.

On this day, though, as he and Clara rolled along the elm-lined streets in the warm afternoon sunshine, Henry was uncharacteristically uneasy. Shifting his eyes back and forth between the road and Clara's animated face, he was having trouble listening, preoccupied instead with the task ahead of him, the task that in its planning had seemed so easy and straightforward, but which now terrified him, making his hands sweat and his stomach churn.

From her seat next to him in the cab of the bouncing delivery van, Clara had been enjoying the beauty of the day as much as her conversation with Henry, so it wasn't until this point that the oddness of his responses finally made her ask him if he was all right.

"Sure I'm all right," Henry responded, his stomach churning ever more violently, his neck now beginning to sweat.

Clara continued to appraise him, unconvinced. "Are you sure?" she asked.

"I'm fine," Henry insisted. "But I have something to ask you."

"All right," Clara answered. "I'm all ears."

With great determination, Henry steadied himself as best he could and dove in. "Clara?" he asked.

"Yes, Henry," Clara said.

He cleared his throat. "Clara," he declared.

"Yes, Henry," she again answered quizzically.

He thought he was getting dizzy, but forced himself to continue. "Clara," he began for the third time. "We've...I mean you and I...uh, well, for a year now we've..."

He was sweating profusely now, and his words were bouncing around, caught in his throat, as if trapped in a maze. By then, of course, Clara was fully aware of the source of Henry's torment, and watched only for a moment before coming to his rescue.

"I will, Henry," she said gently and happily.

Henry's mouth fell open. "You...you will?" he asked, incredulous.

"Of course I will. Marry you, I mean," she said, smiling up to him.

A wave of sheer joy passed over Henry's face. "You will," he asserted happily, looking straight into her sharp green eyes.

"Uh huh," she said, nodding.

"She will!" Henry yelled to the street, laughing. "She will!"

The black delivery truck wove crazily down the narrow, shaded street, narrowly missing several parked cars as Henry Winkler, delirious with joy, tried to drive and to kiss and hold his new fiancée, all at the same time.

They saved their secret from the Winklers for a week. Henry planned to present Clara with a ring over Sunday dinner, and arranged with his parents to have her over. He assumed that he could pull off the surprise. After all, Clara coming over for Sunday dinner was nothing new. The day would be innocuous: he would go to church with his sister and parents as he always did, then later travel down the hill to the Kliens' to pick her up. Nothing fancy or special for dinner, just the familiar centerpiece of Winkler sausages.

Sunday arrived, and after the church service, as planned, Henry found himself behind the wheel of the Winkler delivery van driving his mother and father up Centennial Drive toward Summit Avenue. Ellen, as always for the past several months, had stayed behind, huddled together in the Sunday school classroom with the handful of pinched and dour women who composed St. Luke's temperance contingent. It was the high point of Ellen's week, and the low point of Wilhelm's day.

"What in God's name do you think they do in there all afternoon?" Wilhelm asked.

"They're plotting ways to make us all stop drinking, Father," Henry replied absent-mindedly; his thoughts were on other things.

"I *know* that, son," Wilhelm said. "But for the whole afternoon?"

"Well," Henry said after a moment of thought, "I'm sure they spend a great deal of time congratulating themselves on their wisdom and virtue."

Wilhelm's eyes twinkled with delight at the droll comment. Henry, he thought happily, was a chip off the old block.

Henry tried hard to care for his older sister, but in truth, he knew, he felt nothing for her; neither love nor enmity, neither fondness nor contempt. Ten years of age and an ocean of differences lay between them, and Henry had grown up both ignoring, and being ignored by, the reclusive, self-absorbed woman. Still, she was his sister, and the cold spot she forced on his heart discomfited and frustrated him.

Back home, Henry quickly changed clothes and headed back down the hill to fetch Clara. They arrived back around two, and for the next hour, the four congregated in the kitchen while Clara helped Sophie prepare dinner. By three, dinner was ready but Ellen had not yet gotten home, so with the dinner warm in the oven, the four settled into chairs in the parlor, drinking from tall glasses of lemonade and continuing with their comfortable conversation. By four, Ellen was still not home, and Henry, protesting that he was dying of hunger, insisted that they start without her.

Wilhelm was just starting on his third knockwurst and his second glass of beer when Ellen finally arrived. She breezed into the dining room, her face animated and her eyes all aglow, oblivious to her tardiness.

"I have wonderful news!" she said excitedly. "You'll never guess who's coming to our city."

"Take off your coat and sit down, missy," Wilhelm said. "And say hello to Clara."

Ellen noticed for the first time that Clara was at the table. "Hello, Clara," she said coldly.

"Hello, Ellen," Clara responded.

There was no love lost between the two of them. Ellen, for her part, hated having to be around the tiny woman. She was smart and opinionated and, Ellen had discovered to her chagrin, daunting in an argument. And so Ellen despised and feared her. For Clara's part, if she had a fault, and if it was a fault, it was that she was unable to suffer fools, which was exactly what Clara knew Ellen to be. She was wary of her, for fools, she knew, were capable of doing mischief to more than themselves.

Ellen removed her coat and took a seat at the table, helping herself to vegetables and bread. Ever since her dinner tantrum twelve years earlier, she consistently refused the plate of sausages.

"So tell us," Sophie said cheerfully, "what is your good news?"

"Oh, Mother," Ellen gushed, her eyes once again sparkling, "the most wonderful man will be coming here soon!"

"Mr. Wilson is coming to our city?" Clara asked innocently, winking to Henry.

Ellen stared dumbly at Clara; it took her a moment to realize that she was referring to the country's president.

"I'm referring," she said tersely, "to Mr. Earnest H. Cherrington."

"Ah," Clara replied, returning to her dinner.

"And who's he?" Wilhelm asked.

"Mr. Cherrington is General Secretary of the World League Against Alcoholism," Ellen said proudly. "The amendment has passed, Father. Now we must work to have it ratified by the states."

Wilhelm's stomach turned at the reference to the Eighteenth Amendment. First the war, and now this, he thought. The world was going to hell in a hand basket.

"Don't you think, as women, we'd be better off working for universal suffrage?" Clara asked politely.

"No I do not," Ellen snapped. "Remedying sinfulness must be our first purpose."

"Is it sinful to have a beer with your dinner, as we do here, or to be drunk with hard liquor?" Henry asked.

"One leads to the other," Ellen replied after a moment, proud of her quick thinking.

"Oh, God," Wilhelm moaned softly. He looked to his wife for support, but Sophie sat still, her head bowed to the contents of her plate.

"Then Christ himself was a sinner, since the Bible..."

"Stop it now," Sophie snapped softly, stopping Henry in mid-sentence. "There'll be no more of this talk," she said firmly, surveying the now silent table.

"But I must respond to that last..." Ellen began.

"You will not," Sophie commanded softly. "We're here for good company, not for arguing."

The brief contention had taken its toll on Ellen, and a jolt of pain passed through the side of her head, signaling the onset of a headache.

"You'll excuse me then," she managed to say before rising and hurriedly leaving the table.

And so Ellen missed the happy occasion where, over a dessert of cake and coffee, Henry produced the diamond engagement ring he had purchased months before.

Lying on her bed in her room above the dining room, Ellen could hear the muffled sound of the happy celebration below. She could vaguely hear the sound of raised voices, and of laughing and hand-clapping. It seemed to Ellen, holding her head against the pain and nausea of her headache, to go on forever.

Two days later the results of the draft were made known, and draft notices sent to the chosen. Among those chosen was Henry Winkler. After much serious and sometimes tearful discussion, Henry and Clara decided to move their wedding date forward to accommodate Henry's imminent departure. They planned the wedding for a Saturday in late October, and decided to challenge the weather and hold the ceremony in the Winklers' lush and broad back yard, under a young willow tree Clara was taken with. This time their luck was good, and the day dawned bright and unusually warm.

By noon the back yard was filled with over a hundred celebrants. Wilhelm, in a new suit, had taken on the role of master of ceremonies, dragging Henry from group to group, happily shaking hands and slapping backs. Sophie, in a bright new dress Clara had helped her select, bustled about making sure everyone's punch glass and hors d'oeuvre plate was filled. Clara, abiding by tradition, remained secluded upstairs with her mother.

When Reverend Haselbush arrived and it was time for the ceremony, Henry stood under the willow tree and watched as Clara's father led her across the grass to him. His heart filled with joy as the tiny, beautiful woman approached, and his eyes never left her until she was beside him, and her hand was in his.

71

Ellen watched the ceremony from the north window of the attic, safely hidden behind lace curtains. She couldn't hear the words the minister was saying, but she could easily read the happy couple's lips as first Henry, and then Clara, said "I do." Alone and small, she watched as they exchanged rings, and as they kissed. Her legs went weak and she moved awkwardly to a chair and sat, and after a moment she began to cry.

For their wedding present, Wilhelm and Sophie gave the couple a big double bed with an ornate oak headboard and a newfangled innerspring mattress. Wilhelm preferred his feather bed, but the new style was all the rage. They moved the bed into Henry's northwest bedroom, where the couple would stay until Henry left for the army. For a month the newlyweds went to bed early and slept late. During the day they would take long walks together under the chilly November clouds that enveloped the city, threatening snow.

Henry left three days after Thanksgiving. The railway station was crowded with people gathered to see off the young men. Clara was there, of course, as was Wilhelm and Sophie and the Kleins, along with several of their closest friends. Henry tried to be upbeat, smiling and joking, promising to send postcards and to stay out of the taverns, but the mood was unmovingly somber as the eastbound train pulled into the station. Henry stayed on the platform until the last possible minute, shaking hands and saying his goodbyes.

"Goodbye, my son," Sophie said as she hugged Henry, tears running down her face. "Come back to us."

"I promise," Henry said, kissing her cheek.

"Goodbye, son," Wilhelm said, hugging Henry tightly. "Never stop using your good sense."

"I'll remember that always," Henry said. He extended his hand to Wilhelm, and father and son shook hands.

"You have our love," Wilhelm said.

"And you mine," Henry answered.

Wilhelm and Sophie watched as Henry and Clara made their way to the carriage. They stood together by the carriage entrance, holding each other and talking softly. Finally, at the conductor's gentle insistence, Henry kissed Clara one last time, then turned and boarded the train.

As the train slowly began to move, Sophie moved instinctively to Clara and took her in her arms. Together they tried vainly for a glimpse of Henry through the passing row of carriage windows. Then the last car passed them by, and they watched the back of the train until it was out of sight around a bend.

The crowd quickly and quietly dispersed, and as the three Winklers turned to leave, Sophie's attention was drawn across the track to a small group of women waiting for the arrival of a westbound train. There she saw her daughter, waiting with the others in anxious anticipation of the arrival of the Great Man.

Chapter Six

Carlos's campaign to win Carole over to the idea of actually living in the house had been easier than he thought it would be. For one thing, it was eminently reasonable: they would have tons more space, Carlos would have more time for his cartooning, and Carole would be ten minutes closer to her office. So after several weeks of gentle persuasion, Carole agreed to the move, casually, as she might have agreed to the choice of toppings for a pizza. For her it was purely practical, or so she told herself.

On the day in late October when Carlos and Carole moved into their new home, the rain held off until late afternoon. Then the dark sky opened up in a torrent of wind and ice-cold rain, so that Carlos, who had misplaced his raincoat, was soaking wet and freezing. He had the U-Haul van backed in close to the porch so that the loading ramp stretched horizontally from the van to the porch like a narrow, rickety metal bridge. Shivering and miserable, he doggedly moved the last of the boxes and odd pieces of furniture across the treacherous strip of wet metal and into the inviting warmth of the house.

Carole, warm and dry under a poncho, stood on the porch with an open umbrella. As Carlos, breathing unevenly from the weight of a heavy box, began inching his way across the ramp, she moved out with the umbrella, clumsily attempting to offer him some shelter from the pelting rain. With the wind blowing in every direction, it was a mostly futile gesture, and while Carlos appreciated the effort, he secretly wished that she wouldn't even bother.

Carlos's foot slipped an inch on the wet metal, and the carton he was carrying tilted and wavered as he fought to steady himself.

"Don't drop that, Carlos," Carole yelped. "That's my teapots."

"Then you carry it, counselor," came the testy reply from behind the carton.

"Oh, no, this was your big idea, buster," Carole replied, teasing him. She began to mimic his Puerto Rican accent. "Oh ho-nee," she said facetiously, "theenk of all the room...theenk of the peace and quiet...theenk of the great sex in front of the fireplace."

Carlos's only response was labored breathing as he moved awkwardly over the ramp in six-inch steps, Carole moving backward as he moved forward, the umbrella off-target and tilted just enough to allow a thin stream of water to trickle down onto his head.

"Oh, no, you're on your own, pal," Carole said, her voice back to normal. "And if I see as much as one cockroach, you can forward my mail to the Holiday Inn."

At that moment Carlos stepped on her foot.

"Ow!" Carole yelped. "Watch the foot."

Carlos, who couldn't watch for anything, struggled to regain his balance. The carton danced erratically as Carlos bobbed from side to side, seeking equilibrium. In an instant he knew the attempt was futile—he was bent over almost double, with his rear end hanging out over the edge of the ramp. With a last heroic effort, he was able to set the carton down on the ramp before falling with a yell over the side.

Landing in a puddle in the abandoned flower bed in front of the porch, he lay on his back staring skyward, raindrops beating on his face, the icy-cold, dirty water quickly enveloping the entire back side of his body. After a moment Carole's head appeared above him, her damp hair stringing out like light brown fringe on the blue of her parka hood.

"Are you okay?" she asked. "Boy, that was a close one."

By eight o'clock the sundry boxes and pieces of furniture had all been unloaded and sat haphazardly cluttering the downstairs rooms. Upstairs in the bathroom, Carlos stood in his boxer shorts watching the old claw foot tub fill with water. It had been a long, hard and uncomfortable day, and the clear, steaming water looked to Carlos like heaven. He looked forward to a long, languid soak followed by the warmth and comfort of the bed.

When the tub was full, he dropped his shorts and slowly climbed in, stretching out his long limbs as best he could. The hot water, along with the perfect silence of the steamy room, worked on him like an anodyne, soothing and relaxing his aching muscles and clearing his mind. He ducked his head under the water for a moment, then lay still with his eyes closed, his long black hair floating around his head and shoulders like seaweed.

After what might have been either a few moments or several minutes—Carlos couldn't tell—he heard the sound of soft footsteps on the chipped bathroom tile, and opened his eyes to find Carole smiling down to him. She was wearing a bathrobe over nothing at all, and in each hand she held a glass of red wine.

"Room for one more?" she asked.

"Oh, yeah," Carlos said languidly.

He accepted a glass of wine, and when Carole had discarded her robe, moved his legs apart so that she could climb in opposite him.

"Man, this is good," Carlos said appreciatively, tasting the wine.

"It's special," Carole said, taking a sip from her glass. "Hank Cooper suggested it." Hank Cooper the wine snob.

It was Carole's housewarming present, which, unexpected as it was, gratified Carlos immensely. He watched Carole as she took up a washcloth and began to gently soap his legs. He was getting his good mood back.

"You're gonna like it here, honey," he said happily. "I know it."

Carole's response was less sanguine. "It'll be okay," she said, paying attention to her busy washcloth.

"The house doesn't scare you anymore, then?" Carlos asked hopefully.

Finally she looked up to him. "Not with you here," she answered.

"I won't always be here," Carlos said, taking a sip of wine.

"So what's to be afraid of? You yourself told me with great authority that there are no ghosts," Carole said with only a hint of sarcasm.

"Yes, I'm quite sure of that," Carlos answered earnestly, entirely missing the humor. "So just be nice to him, and watch where you put your fingers for a couple of weeks."

"Okay," Carole said, smiling softly.

Finally Carlos recognized the patronizing smirk. The juris doctor was humoring him. "Go ahead," he said dismissively, taking another sip of wine. "Be a skeptic."

Carlos watched her as she washed his legs, then moved up to his stomach. The soft curves of her lithe body and the smooth, gentle motion of her small hands were all lovely to him. Her hair, damp and twisted at the ends by the rain and wind, hung limp around her shoulders and over her face. Steam from the hot bath was condensing into little droplets on her forehead and upper lip, and on her breasts. He was becoming aroused.

"My my my," she said in her best Southern Belle imitation, "I do believe that some hard evidence is presenting itself." Her eyes sparkled with happy mischief.

Carlos laughed, put down his wine glass, then drew her to him and kissed her on the lips. Then he settled back in the water and let her make love to him.

Afterwards they sat in the tub drinking their wine, then dried and went straight to bed. Carole lay on her side, reading by the dim light of a table lamp. Carlos, pink and wrinkled and fully relaxed, fell immediately asleep.

Around midnight, Carlos rolled over in his sleep, and in a movement familiar to married couples, instinctively reached out to find his wife, as if to assure himself of her presence. And when his fingers, searching on their own for familiar flesh, found nothing but sheet, he fully awoke. The low light from Carole's reading lamp confirmed that he was alone. Forcing himself up, he pulled himself from under the warm covers, put on his robe and slip-

76

pers, and left the room in search of her. It wasn't that he feared for her safety; she just wasn't where she was supposed to be, and he wanted her in his radar.

Guided by the light emerging from the right-hand doorway at the end of the hall, he found her sitting in her robe on the edge of one of the small twin beds. She'd taken the photograph of the Winkler family from its place on the wall, and sat holding it in her lap, intently examining it. She looked to Carlos as he entered, then returned her concentrated gaze to the photograph.

"Does she look like me? I mean really?" Carole asked.

"Yes, she does," Carlos answered.

"But she looks so sad," Carole said softly.

"She looks scared," Carlos said. "Scared to death."

"She's beautiful," Carole said.

"Yes, she is," Carlos said.

Carole silently considered the portrait for several moments. "I want to know who she is," she said finally, resolutely, her eyes never leaving the portrait.

The answer she desired, and the answers to many other questions, would be theirs to discover. And while Carole would have to wait some weeks for her discoveries to begin, Carlos's began the very next day. When he'd unloaded the U-Haul, Carlos had put all of his tools—his sundry saws and drills and tool boxes—in a pile in the study, and so the next morning, after breakfast and after Carole had left for work, his first job was to relocate the tools into the small garage at the end of the driveway on the east side of the house.

After his first confrontation with the padlocked garage door, Carlos had more or less put the structure out of his mind. He had more important things to do, and in any case, as with the locked door to the attic, he chafed against the idea of either breaking down or breaking in. But that morning he needed in to the garage, so despite his reticence, he found his hacksaw, donned his old army field jacket and work gloves, and patiently went to work on the old padlock that was barring his way.

"Now I'm not hurting *you*, so don't get pissed, okay?" he argued to the closed door. "If you like, I'll get you a new padlock."

It was a long, tedious job, cutting through a quarter-inch of steel with a hacksaw, and by the time the lock was cut, Carlos's face and ears were red from the cold of the raw, sunless morning, and inside his leather work gloves his fingers were numb. Removing the lock, he was finally able to swing the door inward and enter the stale, gloomy interior of the old garage. The open door let in just enough light so that Carlos could find the light switch on the wall. It was old-fashioned, like the light switches in the house, and Carlos had his doubts that it would still be functional. But, giving it a twist, he was gratified to find the room instantly filled with the dusty light of two light bulbs hanging from the inverted "V" of the garage roof.

He was disappointed to find the center of the garage empty; he half hoped for something interesting, like an old car. Carlos moved to the double front doors, and lifting off the wooden brace that held the doors closed, swung the doors fully open to the morning light. Despite twenty-five years of dust and cobwebs, the old garage was surprisingly clean and in order. Work benches lined both of the side walls, and above them old tools hung in orderly patterns from their places on the walls. It was as if the garage had been cleaned right before it'd been locked up—which didn't surprise Carlos, who took it for granted that everyone kept their workplaces as clean as he did.

And then he saw it, parked at the far end of the garage, low and squat and covered with a stiff tarp that disguised its shape. Carlos smiled as he moved to it, hoping for something old and mechanical. He wasn't disappointed. Pulling aside the tarp, his eyes went wide and he broke into a long, appreciative whistle.

Around six o'clock, Carole pulled into the driveway, and was surprised to find dim light spilling out into the dark evening from the side window and the cracked open garage doors. Leaving her car, she walked to the garage and peered in. There she found Carlos stretched out on the floor, working on something that was low and red and that she couldn't quite make out. Pushing open the creaking door, she entered.

Carlos turned to the sound. "Hi, honey," he said, smiling up to her from his place on the cold cement, his eyes bright with a low, warm sparkle. She recognized the look immediately. She called it his hardware look—the look he got when something with moving parts had captured his interest.

"Okay, what is it?" she asked, moving to him to get a better look at what it was he was working on.

"It's a motorcycle," Carlos said, his eyes already back on his work.

"Ah...I see that," Carole said, getting a full view of the contraption for the first time. "Man, it looks old."

Carlos had a pan of soapy water next to him, and was cleaning the small, odd-looking engine with a toothbrush. "It *is* old," he responded. "This here's a 1927 Indian Scout," he offered, twisting his face around to look up to her. His face was streaked with oil and dirt.

"How d'you know that?" Carole asked.

"Found the owner's manual," Carlos replied, turning his camouflaged face back to his business.

78

Carlos had spent much of the day in the garage with his shop-vac and had stumbled on the owner's manual in a drawer. He'd also found the registration papers.

"Found out whose it was, too," he said, twisting again to face her, his eyes bright with energy.

For several weeks after that first discovery, life was uneventful at the Winkler house. Carole was working long hours at the office, and Carlos was busy replenishing his stock of cartoons, which had dwindled during the long months of home renovation. On the weekends they would work together on the house, refinishing the hardwood surfaces, removing stained and peeling wallpaper, and laying new tile in the kitchen and bathroom.

Carole had begun her search for the identity of her sad look-alike by enlisting Carlos in an attack on the drawers and cupboards of the various bureaus and cabinets, which were packed with the detritus of seventy-five years of everyday life. But the sheer volume of the massive paper trail proved to be daunting even to Carlos, who was by nature the nosier of the two. The vast majority of the information jammed into the various drawers and boxes—canceled checks and receipts and business correspondence—was of little value in reconstructing the flesh and bone of the long-dead strangers who had preceded them. And so after half a day of digging, as they sat cross-legged on the floor of the parlor surrounded by piles of paper from the drawers of the huge breakfront dominating the south wall, the futility of it caught up to Carole. Dropping the yellowed appointment book she'd been perusing, she rubbed her eyes wearily with the knuckles of her fingers, then directed a sour look toward Carlos.

"I give up," she said.

"Yeah," Carlos agreed. "I don't think we're gonna find much interesting this way," he said. "Junk, mostly, huh?"

Carole nodded her agreement, then sighed. She sat still for a moment, allowing her discouragement to fully settle in. But then her eyes hardened.

"I *gotta* find out who she is, Carlos," she said, her lips pressed together into a thin, determined line.

Carlos nodded. "I know," he said. "I guess we'll have to be patient, and wait for a little luck." And maybe a little help from their new friend, he thought secretly.

The first break came by way of luck. It happened one afternoon as Carlos was cleaning off the shelves of the bookcase in Henry's study, which he needed to store his art supplies and drawing equipment. All of the books were old—some, leather-bound and cracked, were very old—and the range

79

of titles, even to Carlos's untrained eye, were remarkably eclectic. There were books on history and religion and psychology. There were textbooks on physics and mathematics, and picture books of art and architecture. And novels by a variety of writers, some of whom Carlos remembered from his days of shelving books at Northwestern: Somerset Maugham and Earnest Hemingway and Joseph Conrad. And it was in a sagging cardboard box, under a stack of three large volumes by someone named Marcel Proust, that Carlos made the first critical discovery.

When Carole arrived home that evening, she was in an exceptionally good mood. It had been a good day. She'd settled a rather sticky case of premises liability in pretrial conference, much to the advantage of her client, had successfully gotten another client dismissed out of a contract violation action, and had taken on an interesting zoning case.

Entering the house and closing the door against the cold autumn evening, she dropped her bulging briefcase and hung her heavy wool coat on a peg by the door.

"Hey Carlos," she called out energetically, "guess what?"

"I'm in here," came Carlos's voice from the study.

Carole skipped into the study, where Carlos stood at his easel putting the finishing touches on a cartoon.

"The Dog walked," she said, her eyes dancing with humor.

"The what?" Carlos asked.

"Remember 'Mad Dog,' the guy with 'fuck you' tattooed on his forehead? He got off. Hank Cooper got him off. The Dog walked...get it?" Her eyes danced with humor.

"So maybe he's ready for adoption," Carlos offered. "Free to a good home. Adoption fee waived if we agree to have him neutered."

"Where would he sleep?" Carole wondered.

"On the floor next to the bed, of course," Carlos answered.

They were both feeling good and having fun. Carole for the first time noticed the cartoon on Carlos's easel:

"Good one," Carole said, chuckling. "What made you think of that?"

"That day on the lake in Wisconsin," Carlos replied. It'd been the last day of an ill-fated camping trip they'd taken shortly after they'd gotten married.

"Ah…right," Carole said, nodding in agreement. "That was bad news."

Her reference to bad news reminded Carlos of his good news. "Oh, hey, honey," he said, "look what I found."

He led her to the roll-top desk, where he had placed the worn and broken cardboard box he'd found.

"Wow," Carole said as she gently touched the ancient container, then gingerly opened it to reveal the mass of yellowing photographs. "Where'd you find this?" she asked.

"Under Marcel Proust," Carlos answered, gesturing toward the closet.

"*Remembrance of Things Past,*" Carole whispered softly, intent on the photographs. "How appropriate."

They moved the box out to the dining room table, where they sat sipping hot lemonade, examining the photographs. There were daguerreotypes, luminous and barely discernable, of still, unsmiling men and women. And wedding photographs of a happy young couple, the woman soft-eyed and quiet, the thin, wiry, mustached young man energetic and confident. They were the man and woman in the photograph upstairs.

81

Further on they found a photograph of the same man, this time in an apron, standing in front of an old building, the words "Winkler's Pure Pork Sausages" stenciled on the window. Later there were baby pictures, and later still family portraits of the couple and their two children. Like the stop action on a fast-moving motion picture, the children grew and the parents aged from one photograph to another, until Carole soon recognized the daughter who was to be her twin.

"Look, Carlos, there she is," Carole said.

Carole stared at the photograph for a long time, then turned it over, and found, written in pencil: "Wilhelm and Sophie, with Ellen and Henry, 1915."

"Here they are, Carlos," she said excitedly. The girl's name was Ellen," Carole pronounced, handing the photo to Carlos. "And the younger boy is Henry. He must be the Henry Winkler who left me the house."

"Ellen," Carlos repeated. "So if Henry was your great-grandfather, then Ellen was..."

"My great-aunt," Carole said. "And Wilhelm and Sophie were my great-great grandparents."

Carole gently returned the photograph to the album. "I feel like a burglar," she said, turning to Carlos.

"Hey, they're your relatives," Carlos said encouragingly. They didn't write their names on there for themselves. They did it for you."

It was the perfect thing to say, and Carole smiled over to Carlos gratefully.

Carlos left for the kitchen to prepare dinner. A half-hour later Carole was still at the table, her lips pursed, intently considering the faces in the old photographs.

The second break came on a Saturday two weeks later. Carlos and Carole awoke to the first light snow of winter. After breakfast and a shower, Carole went to work tending to the needs of the dozens of potted plants that now decorated the bedroom and the downstairs. She made her way from room to room, doting over the plants like a grandmother, carefully clipping off dead leaves, fertilizing and watering, and checking for insects and disease. Finally her labors brought her into the study, where Carlos stood at his easel, sketching out an idea for a cartoon.

"Whatcha drawing?" Carole asked as she probed the dirt of a coleus plant with her finger.

"Not sure," Carlos said, intent on the easel.

Carole duly noted that Carlos was in creative mode, the time of blank stares and one-syllable answers. She left him to his imagination, moving around him with her watering can and ending up at a philodendron sitting atop Wilhelm's roll-top desk. She'd become a big fan of the tall, ancient desk with its many small drawers and alcoves. She was beginning to think that it would look great downtown in her office.

"How old do you think this desk is?" she asked, looking up to Carlos's ponytail.

"Old," the ponytail replied.

She moved her hand lovingly over the golden wood, opening and closing the small drawers. But when she tried to open the large lower drawer, she found that it was locked. And, strangely, there was no key hole.

"How do you open this drawer?" she asked the ponytail.

There was no response from the ponytail.

"Honey?" she persisted.

Finally Carlos turned to her, looking as if she'd just jabbed him in the ear with a pin. "What?" he said tersely.

"Sorry," Carole said. "Never mind."

"No, go ahead," Carlos said. Carole noted that his eyes were actually focused on her—a sign that the self-induced spell holding him had at least temporarily been broken.

"Well," she said, "look at this drawer. It's locked, but there's no key hole."

"Yeah, that's weird, huh?" he answered. "I haven't figured that out yet."

With that he returned to his drawing.

"Humph," Carole grunted, considering the drawer. The wood was rough and dry to her touch—too dry, she thought—so she fetched a cloth and bottle of wood polish from the kitchen, and for the next hour, as Carlos drew intently, she applied coat after coat of the polish to the thirsty wood.

When she was done, she stepped back to admire the softly glowing wood. Her eyes traveled appreciatively over and down the heavy desk, then stopped abruptly. Goose bumps formed on her arms, and she breathed in sharply.

"Carlos," she said softly.

Carlos, who was in the process of deciding that he didn't much like the cartoon he had just finished, answered without looking. "Yeah, honey," he said.

"Carlos, look," she said in a monotone, her eyes glued to the desk.

Carlos turned to the desk and brightened. "Hey, that's nice, honey," he said, admiring the softly shining wood.

"Look," she said, pointing to the door.

The lower door that had been locked now stood cracked open an inch.

"Wow," Carlos said. "How'd you get it open?"

"I didn't," Carole answered nervously. "Maybe I sprung a latch somehow."

Carlos knelt and spent a few moments examining the door, running his fingers along the edges of the inside. "Yeah," he said finally, "I can feel the latch. But what triggers it I have no idea."

"I might've hit something without knowing it," Carole offered.

"Unlikely," Carlos said as he stood to face her. "I think it likes you."

"Who's 'it?'" Carole asked.

"The desk," Carlos said.

"Oh, right," Carole replied caustically. "The desk has a crush on me. Maybe it wants to go steady."

"It's giving you a present, maybe," Carlos persisted. "Go ahead, take a look inside."

And so Carole, sitting cross-legged in front of the open door, investigated the contents of the mysterious compartment. It didn't take her long to find the treasure: hidden under several inches of loose paper was a heavy, leather-bound volume. Gently, she opened the cover, the binding cracked and stiff and the pages yellowing. The title, written in German, read: "Die Heilige Bibel."

She called to Carlos, who ambled over and considered the writing. "Know what that says?" he asked.

"It's a bible," answered Carole, who had taken German in high school and college. She held it for a moment, then set it down gently in front of her. Then, looking to Carlos for support and taking a deep breath, she opened it, feeling once again very much like a thief.

On the inside cover she found her present. Across the top of the page, in faded ink, was written: "Der Herr ist mein Hirte."

Carole pointed to it. "The Lord is my Shepherd," she read aloud.

Under that, descending down the length of the page, were a series of names and dates, written in successively different hands.

"Wow, there they are," Carlos said.

The list began with a couple:

Heinrich Winkler 1831-1885
Luisa Winkler 1835-1867

Below and indented were three names:

Leona Winkler 1857-1859
Wilhelm Winkler 1864-1918
Sophia Winkler 1865-1918

Without realizing it, Carole's heart was beating faster. She pointed to Wilhelm and Sophie's names. "They're the parents in the photograph," she said excitedly.

"And look," Carlos said, pointing to the line above. "Wilhelm had a sister."

"Yes," Carole said sadly, considering the short life of the girl. "And look at the dates of death for Wilhelm and Sophie. They're the same year."

"Maybe they died together," Carlos said.

Carole shrugged her shoulders.

Below Wilhelm and Sophie were three more names:

Ellen Winkler 1887-
Henry Winkler 1896-
Clara Winkler 1898-

"There's Henry," Carlos said, pointing.

"And there's Ellen," Carole said.

"And no death dates," Carlos said, disappointed.

Finally, written below, was simply a list of names, added, it seemed, by some unknown person as a final gesture of completion:

William
Rachel
Willy
Carole

As Carole considered this last list of names, her index finger moved to her mouth, as if for protection. And when she reached the last entry, her own name, her mouth closed tight, and tears began to roll down her cheeks. Carlos reached for her and held her, and kissed her warm mouth.

The third break came as a result not of luck, or as a gift, but of several hours of dogged research. As much as she wanted to, Carole couldn't get away from her office on Monday or Tuesday, but on Wednesday she was able to leave early and head for the county courthouse. There, armed with the dates of Wilhelm and Sophie's deaths, she sat in the dusty archives room in front of a dimly-lit microfiche machine, a pencil between her teeth, making her way methodically through the record of death notices for 1918.

She was almost through the month of October, and was getting nervous and fidgety, before she finally hit pay dirt. There on the screen in front of her was the name Sophia Winkler, who had died on October 23, 1918.

"Oh, my God," she said softly to herself as she read the death notice. In her mind's eye she saw, perfectly clearly, Sophie's gentle, kind eyes, closed now for so many years.

She was almost out of days in the year when she found Wilhelm. The small, mustached, dark-haired man with the sharp, probing eyes had died on December 24, 1918.

When she got home shortly after five, Carlos was reclined on the couch in the parlor, sipping a beer and listening to the evening news on the public radio channel. A fire in the brick fireplace sent cheerful orange light flickering around the shadowed room.

"Hi honey," he called to her as she entered out of the cold.

"Hi," she said.

She took off her coat, walked to him and kissed him.

"You look pissed," he said. "Bad day?"

Carole caught her mood, and her eyes softened. "No," she said. "I found out how Sophie died."

She took the photocopies she'd made out of her briefcase and handed them to Carlos, who read the first one quickly.

"Sophie died of influenza?" he asked incredulously. "People die from the flu?"

"Oh, yeah," Carole responded. "In 1918 there was an epidemic. Thousands of people died."

Carlos read the second page quickly, then read it again. "I don't get this," he said finally. "There's no cause of death."

Carole sat down wearily next to Carlos. "No," she said, shaking her head. "There's nothing."

"Maybe he died of the flu, too," Carlos ventured.

Carole took a drink of beer from Carlos's bottle. She sat for a moment, vaguely considering the bottle's label. "Maybe he died from a broken heart," she said.

Epistle

One of the curious features of antique furniture is that they will often times contain secret compartments skillfully hidden in their design and taking the form of small, thin drawers disguised as ornamental borders or shelve partitions, or of false walls or bottoms accessible by means of a well-hidden latch.

I learned this inadvertently one day when I entered Henry's study to find him sitting at his father's great roll-top desk, reading a letter. A six-inch section of the carved border of the desk lay open on a hinge, revealing a thin, empty compartment. The existence of the secret drawer, now so clearly visible, amazed me, for I had dusted and straightened that desk a hundred times by then, and had never had even a hint of any irregularity in its smooth joints and surfaces. Which, of course, is as it was intended.

"Now isn't that clever," I said, startling Henry out of a deep reverie.

He looked up to me with sudden alarm, and his first reaction was to cover the document he was reading with his hand. I immediately realized that I had blundered into something private, and, embarrassed, suggested that I should leave. For just a moment he was silent, hurriedly performing in that instant the calculus that constantly defines the shifting boundaries of friendship.

"No, no," he said, stopping me as I turned for the doorway. "Come and look."

I walked to the desk and carefully examined the secret drawer.

"See how the carving is designed to hide the edges?" he said, opening and closing the curved cover for me. "And there's more. Father was very keen on these. Before I went in the army he took me around and showed them all to me, I'm not sure why."

Under his hand was an old, yellowed telegram, worn from many fold-ings and unfoldings, along with several pages of handwriting.

"When I got back from the war I found this inside," he said, handing me the telegram.

It was from the War Department, dated November 1918, and announced to Mr. and Mrs. Wilhelm Winkler that their son Henry was missing in action and presumed dead.

"My God," I said, "your parents thought that you had died?"

"Only my father," Henry said softly. "Mother had already died. And this," he said tersely, nodding to the pages of handwriting, "this indecipher-able scribbling, must have been father's last writing."

He gently and carefully folded the pages and returned them to their sanctuary. This, his calculus informed him, he would not share.

Though my hand was on his shoulder, for several moments he was lost to me, away in far-off memory. Then he forced himself to return. "Come," he said, smiling, "let me show you the others."

And so he took me around the house, showing me the handful of secret drawers and compartments in the desks, dressers, and cabinets that furnished the house.

I'm not sure why.

Chapter Seven

H ere is how Henry came to be missing in action and presumed dead. In October of 1918, Henry, who had been made a common infantryman, was participating in the allied campaign in the Meuse-Argonne in northern France, the last major battle of the war. For several days the trench warfare, as it always had, see-sawed back and forth. Some days the allies would gain territory, finding freshly dead Germans in the captured trenches; some days they would lose that much, leaving their own dead for the advancing Germans to discover.

During the brief lulls in the fighting, the soldiers would take what little pleasure they could: smoking, eating cold rations, playing cards, or just sleeping in the cold mud of the trench floors. On the event of one such lull, Henry found himself with three comrades under a makeshift lean-to made of scrap wood and railroad ties, huddled against a driving rain. Henry, who had come to loathe dirt, took the opportunity to attempt to clean himself. Stripping naked, he left his clothes with his sleeping comrades and walked out into the rain, where he proceeded to wash his filthy body as best he could with a scrap of lye soap.

He was standing in the open trench letting the cold, hard rain wash the dirty soap from his body and urinating against the muddy wall when the incoming shell hit. By chance, as most things are in war, the shell made a direct hit on the lean-to, obliterating the three sleeping men and sending shattered wood flying down the trench at tremendous force. Pieces of flying wood tore into Henry's legs, breaking them both, and a large fragment of railroad tie smashed into his head, cracking his skull. He fell over backward into the mud, knocked unconscious.

And this was how the Germans found him when they retook the trench some moments later. It was a wonder that they didn't simply kill him. Perhaps, naked as he was, and looking every bit the German he was, they mistook him for one of their own. Or perhaps, as is equally likely to be the case, they were simply tired of killing. In any event, they evacuated him to a field hospital in the rear.

When the allies recaptured the trench two days later, the mush of body parts in the destroyed lean-to were unidentifiable. No one was even sure how many bodies were there or which bodies were whom, so Henry, along his three unlucky comrades, were all listed as missing in action, presumed dead. Condolences were sent to the next of kin.

At roughly the same time that the remnants of Henry's infantry unit were picking through the remains of his comrades, Henry was finally waking

89

up. As soon as he began to moan and move, an orderly anxiously called over the surgeon. He was an old man with white hair and very bad teeth, and the large mole growing from the right side of his nose was the first thing Henry's eyes saw as they began to focus. The old man pulled back Henry's eyelids, looking for the lingering effect of a concussion.

"Wie heissen Sie?" the surgeon asked.

Henry, who had picked up quite a bit of German from his parents, knew what was being asked. "Henry Winkler," he said.

The surgeon and orderly looked to each other with surprise. This was no German accent.

"Sind Sie Deutsch?" the surgeon asked.

"Ich bin ein Americaner," Henry answered.

The old man stared down on him incredulously for a few moments, then began to laugh. "You are lucky, Americaner," he said in fractured English. "Fate has smiled. You will survive this war."

All in all, the Germans treated Henry very well. Between the German soldiers' halting English and Henry's own limited German, they were able to communicate quite well. The German soldiers—conscripts like himself, Henry learned—were anxious to learn about America. A few were from the area around Bremen from where Henry's grandfather and father had emigrated, and one actually knew some local Winckels.

When the armistice was signed a month later, Henry, his legs still in casts, said goodbye to his hospital friends and transferred to a POW holding camp in southern Belgium. A few days later he was repatriated to the allies and sent to a hospital in Paris. It was from there that Henry was finally able to make telegraph contact with Clara. The next day he received word back from her. Her telegraph read:

> Out of death and darkness come
> life and light. I love you. Clara

It was two weeks later when Clara's first letter arrived. On that afternoon Henry was bundled up against the January cold and sitting on the long front porch of the hospital, watching a cold rain fall on the open lawn around him and puffing on a pipe a German soldier had given him in the field hospital. When he was handed the letter, the sight of Clara's handwriting cheered him and warmed his heart, and he tore at the envelope greedily.

But, as Clara had known it had to be, it was a ruse—a sucker punch—and after the few moments it took him to read the first paragraph, the pipe he was smoking fell from Henry's hand, the bowl cracking in half when it hit the rough wood of the floor below his feet. Clara had refused to use the terse language of the telegraph to tell him what she was obliged to, so it was in this first of her many letters to him, in her familiar, flowing script, that Henry learned that in the span of the few short weeks that he'd been missing to them, both of his parents had died. His mother Sophie had died of the influenza epidemic that was still ravaging half the world. Of his father Wilhelm, Clara gave no cause.

And in that instant Henry's young life once again changed, as he experienced for the first time the loss of someone he truly loved; and next to Clara, Henry had loved no two people more. In the black days of his mourning only Clara's letters offered solace and hope, and lying on his cot Henry would read them over and over, as if they were scripture.

By the end of January Henry was back on the front porch. There he spent the wet winter days, wrapped in blankets and puffing on a pipe he had purchased from the hospital store. He dwelt bitterly on the absurdity of it all, of how he, who had been most imminently available for death, had lived, while they, tucked away safely in the mundane affairs of peacetime life, had died.

He longed for Clara, and for the familiar sights and smells of his small city, deep within the borders of America. And when he finally took his leave of Europe, he left bent with the weight of a new knowledge, fully understood but not yet fully accepted, that even outside of the madness of the Argonne Forest, even in the absence of the self-inflicted horrors of war, still, there was no sanctuary.

On the icy gray day when his troop ship finally docked in New York City, the soldiers were treated to a celebration. There was a band playing, and red-white-and blue banners, and a throng of happy relatives waving little American flags crowding the snow-covered dock. As the long line of khaki-clad young men disembarked in single file down the narrow gangplank, Henry scanned the mass of waving flags for a sight of Clara. As he slowly descended the rickety gangplank, he finally saw her, waving happily to him as she pushed her way forward. He remembered now how small she was, and how beautiful, and for the first time in well over a year his heart filled with joy, and he laughed out loud. Then they were together again, and he kissed her hard on the lips.

"Welcome back, my love," she said, her eyes dancing with delight.

"Yes," he said, his face beaming like a child on Christmas morning. "I've made it back, haven't I?" he asked with the happy astonishment of the lottery winner he knew he was.

He wrapped his arms around her small body, and for several moments held her tightly, burying his face in her hair, remembering the long, solitary months that he had ached for her. Clara's shoulders began to shake slightly,

91

and he knew that she was crying. Finally he let loose of her so that he could kiss her face. "I'll never leave you again. Never ever," he said.

They checked into a cheap hotel, and after their love making, lying together under thick blankets in the quiet of the darkened room, they talked.

"Tell me what happened," he said, running his hand over the length of Clara's smooth skin.

Clara struggled to find words that would gentle the unhappy story she was obliged to tell. "When the telegram from the war department came," she said hesitantly, "...oh, Henry, it was on the same day we buried your mother."

Henry's eyes closed.

"I was with him when it came," Clara continued, "and I can tell you that right then, in an instant, something deserted him. Something important for life. His, eyes..."

Henry turned to her. "What about his eyes?" he asked sharply.

"They...changed color," Clara answered softly. "They turned to gray."

Henry's heart sank. He had seen men's eyes change color—at the Somme, and in the Argonne Forest—and he knew full well what it meant.

Henry pulled himself from under the covers and sat on the side of the bed, facing away from her. "Tell me more," he said.

Clara spent a moment remembering. "For several days he wouldn't leave his room, and when he slept, he would cry out in his dreams. Then he would wander the house, or sit at his desk writing. Then he got sick, and took to his bed. On the afternoon of Christmas Eve, I brought him some broth...and he was gone," she said, her voice small and weak, as if Henry was listening from a long way off.

"Where were the doctors during all of this?" Henry asked bitterly. "And where was Ellen?"

"The doctors came and went, always without an answer," she said sadly. "And Ellen," she continued, her voice now tinged with her own brand of bitterness, "Ellen railed against alcohol."

Henry rose from the bed, walked gingerly to a dresser, and poured himself a glass of water. Rage rose up inside of him: rage at the war for taking him away, rage at the existence of the indiscriminant killer named influenza, and at the bankruptcy of doctors. His hand shook slightly as he took a drink.

"Not Father," Henry pleaded to the wall, shaking his head. He turned to face Clara. "I've seen men lose their will to live, Clara, but they were young men, and frail, and in an impossible situation. But Father? He was so strong."

Clara rose from the bed and took a step toward him. "Yes," she answered, "he was very strong. But then losing you, the last that he truly loved maybe, Henry, maybe that was his impossible situation."

"You thought I was dead, too, and you didn't just up and die," he spat out.

The savage comment hit Clara squarely, jolting her back, as if she'd been hit by an icy wind. "I never thought you were dead. Never!" she shouted back, her voice high and tight and breaking.

She quickly turned from him and walked to the window. Parting the thick drapes, she stood with her back to Henry, staring out at the cold, gray, snow-covered brick and steel world on the other side of the glass.

For a moment Henry watched her in silence, then sighed deeply and rubbed his eyes. Then his anger turned inward. Just for a second, in the time it had taken him in earlier days to squeeze a trigger and take a life, he had allowed himself to forget the location of his treasure.

He moved to her and wrapped his arms around her. "I'm so sorry," he said softly into her ear. "I never once doubted your love for me."

She turned to him. "I know that," she said gently, kissing him on the lips. She pulled him back into the bed and wrapped herself around him.

They stayed in the hotel for two days as Henry mustered out of the army, collecting his medals and back pay and discharge papers. On the afternoon of the third day, they checked out of the old hotel and made their way through the busy city to Grand Central Station. There they boarded a train for home.

When the train arrived early the next morning, Clara's parents—Fred and Minnie Klein—were there to greet them, along with Hank Dietrich and Irwin Meyer, two of Henry's army buddies, members of the group that had been offered up to war by the town. Henry stepped from the train into the crisp, early morning air, grinning happily, alternatively hugging and shaking hands and slapping backs.

Back at the Klein's apartment above their grocery, Henry and Clara were treated to a huge breakfast. It was good plain Midwestern food—eggs and ham and potatoes, and freshly brewed coffee—and Henry dove into it greedily. As he finished, Clara stifled a yawn. She was done in. Henry, who had developed the knack of sleeping anytime and anyplace, had slept like a log during the miles of Midwestern darkness. Clara, though, being used to quiet stillness and the constant comfort of a soft mattress, hadn't slept a wink.

"I've got to rest or I'll collapse," she said to the group, rising wearily from the table.

Henry followed her into the bedroom and watched as she crawled wearily out of her wrinkled traveling clothes and slipped into a sleeping gown. She slid between welcoming sheets, and Henry climbed onto the narrow bed and laid beside her. For a few moments they kissed lightly. Then she closed her eyes and lay still, and when Henry was sure she was asleep, he rose from the bed and left the darkened room.

Henry took a long, hot bath, then changed into the civilian clothes that Clara had fetched from the Winkler home. He was lighter than when he had left, and the clothes hung loosely around his chest and stomach; it would take a month of Minnie's cooking to get them to fit properly.

At the railway station, Henry had arranged to meet his two army buddies downtown, so at two o'clock he left the Klein's apartment and walked the six blocks to Otto's Tavern. The place was almost empty. Hank and Irwin, his two friends, waved to him from a table in the back.

"Sit down, my friend," Irwin sang out, pushing a vacant chair away from the table with his foot.

Henry sat and shook hands with his two friends, then took a long pull on the beer they had waiting for him. "So how long you two been back?" he asked.

"Since just before Christmas," Hank replied. "We got lucky. Got on the first convoy of troopships home."

Henry was never one to begrudge another man his luck. "Great!" he said, smiling broadly.

In truth, Hank and Irwin's luck had extended further back than their recent boat ride home. Before the war, both young men had, like Henry, worked for their fathers: Hank as a baker and Irwin as an auto mechanic. Once in the army, Hank had been made a cook, and Irwin had been put to work as a tank mechanic. And so, with the exception of an occasional mustard gas scare, both had passed through the war as spectators. Unfortunately for Henry, the army had had no need of sausage makers.

But Henry was also feeling lucky. He had escaped from the carnage in one piece in the most unlikely of ways, and had a beautiful young wife to come home to. He smiled happily, enjoying his beer, as his two friends filled him in on the latest news and gossip. Inevitably the conversation turned to the fate of the group that had gone.

"You're the last to be accounted for," Irwin said.

"How many made it back?" Henry asked.

"All but three," Hank answered.

Henry's eyes darkened. He had already had news of the deaths of two of the group. Stan Adams and Woody Kirk, friends from high school, had died together, only instants apart, during an assault on a machine gun nest in the Second Battle of the Somme.

"Who was the third?" Henry asked.

"Jim Owens," Irwin said solemnly. "Typhoid."

Henry sighed. Typhoid, he thought. Another scourge of war.

"So what will you do now?" Hank asked Henry.

"Not sure," Henry said, turning his beer schooner in a slow circle on the surface of the table's rough wood. "What about you two?" he asked, looking up brightly from the tabletop. "You both back to work?"

"Yup," Irwin said. "Dad's selling Buicks. They're a lot like tanks."

Everyone laughed.

"And how 'bout you?" Henry asked Hank.

"Back at the bakery. Four o'clock every morning," Hank said.

For a dozen years they would see themselves as best friends. But then Hank Dietrich would take his wife and children and quietly desert the small town for the chance of a better life out west. Like hundreds of his neighbors, the Great Depression would ruin Hank, even as it would almost ruin Henry. Irwin Meyer, like Henry, would survive the Depression, and the two would remain the best of friends long into the future.

The next day dawned clear and unusually warm, and after church, Henry and Clara decided to walk home.

"Are you sure your legs can handle it?" Clara asked, wrapping her head in a scarf.

"They'll complain a bit, but they'll handle it," Henry answered as he pulled on the heavy black woolen overcoat that had belonged to his father. It fit him perfectly. When he got his weight back to normal, he would find, to his great disappointment, that the coat would be too small.

They walked arm in arm under a bright blue sky along the red brick sidewalks of downtown, past closed shops and cafes and offices, the sun dazzling against the patches of roadside snowdrift. Henry puffed contentedly on his pipe, sending small streams of bluish-gray smoke into the still air behind them. They were in no hurry and walked slowly, enjoying the crisp, cold air and the stillness of the deserted streets.

Henry led the way, turning left at this street and right at that, so that before long it was clear to Clara where their detours were leading. When the two-story red brick sausage factory had come into full view, Henry stopped in his tracks, and for several moments silently surveyed the cold, still structure he'd come to know so intimately. Once filled to bursting with bustling activity, it now stood empty and lifeless, like the bodies of the dead men he had seen on the battlefields of France and Belgium. Here again, he was learning what it was like to outlive the things that he loved.

Henry sighed deeply, then turned to Clara. "Okay," he said, smiling wryly. "I've paid my respects."

"Is it too early to think about the future?" Clara asked.

"Not at all," Henry replied. "I've been thinking about it a lot lately."

"So tell me what's on your list," she said.

"Well..." Henry replied. Then he chuckled. "Well..."

"Go on," Clara persisted.

"I was thinking of the railroad."

"The railroad?" Clara responded, dismayed.

"Just a thought," Henry answered.

"You know you could work for Father in the store," Clara offered.

"Like I said, I was thinking of the railroad," Henry said, smiling. They laughed. There was nothing of the shop keeper in Henry Winkler.

"Well, time will tell, my darling," Clara said, patting his arm. "But I certainly hope it's not the railroad. My bed has been empty long enough."

As it turned out, the answer to their uncertainties was only a short walk away. As they climbed the narrow side stairway and entered the Klein's small apartment, they were met by Fred Klein and a man Henry didn't know. The two men rose from their chairs as Henry, unbuttoning his coat, entered the parlor. The middle-aged man was tall, at least six-foot-two. His face was thin and his eyes flat and weary, like his sister Ellen's when she was fighting a headache.

"Henry," Fred Klein began, "this is Mr. Owens...Jim Owens's father."

Henry walked to the man and shook his outstretched hand. "I'm so sorry about Jim," Henry said. "I got to know him in training. He was a fine man."

"Yes," Mr. Owens said. "Jim thought the same about you."

Henry stood silent for a moment, embarrassed by the compliment.

"I'll not take more than a moment of your time," Mr. Owens began, his voice earnest and businesslike. "I'm a printer by trade, Henry. It's an honorable profession, and I make a good living, if not a lavish one. Jim was to join me in my shop, but now...that cannot be."

Henry lowered his eyes for a moment, then brought them back to face the solemn man.

"I don't know what your plans for the future entail, but if you have an interest, I can offer you an apprenticeship in my shop," Mr. Owens said. "The pay will be adequate, I think, for a man and a wife, and the opportunities are promising. My business grows with the community."

Henry was floored by the offer, coming, as it did, out of the blue. "You've caught me off-guard," he stammered. "I've never...considered the possibility."

"Then think it over," Mr. Owens responded. "Come down to my shop tomorrow if you'd like. I'll show you around."

"I will," Henry said, stealing a look of happy astonishment to Clara. "Thank you."

Henry watched as the tall man donned his coat and hat and said his goodbyes. And what Henry saw in the man caused his heart to ache. It was love. Love with no place to go.

Henry spent a long afternoon at Mr. Owens's print shop on Monday, and on Tuesday, after lunch, walked back downtown with Clara to visit Cecil Eatman, the Winklers' long-time attorney.

Eatman greeted Henry and Clara warmly and ushered them into his large, cluttered office. In addition to being the Winklers' legal counsel, Cecil Eatman had been a good friend of the family. When his wife had been alive, the Eatmans had been part of a bridge group that included Wilhelm and Sophie. Like Wilhelm, and unlike the two women, Cecil had been a lousy bridge player.

With his prematurely graying hair, bushy eyebrows and wild, muttonchop sideburns, Cecil Eatman had always looked old to Henry. Now, standing behind his desk, thoughtfully packing a large, curved Meerschaum pipe, he looked to Henry positively ancient.

Seated with Clara in front of Eatman's huge cherry wood desk, Henry watched the man light his pipe, sending a cloud of blue smoke upward into the stream of soft light shining in through the tall windows to his back. Then he sat, facing the two across the expanse of polished wood.

"Prepare yourself for this, Henry," he said solemnly. "I wish I had some good news for you, but I don't. Since your father's death there has been nothing but mischief from Summit Avenue."

Henry and Clara shared a knowing look. They had expected trouble.

"Surely she can only do what father's will allows," Henry ventured.

"Ah, the will," Eatman said, sending a cloud of smoke toward the   ceiling. "Yes, this story begins with the will. Your father's will left everything in equal shares to you and Ellen. But Wilhelm knew your sister well, Henry, and named you as executor. You were to control the disposition of assets." He paused for a moment. "But then," he continued, "you were presumed dead."

Henry and Clara glanced to each other. Henry took her hand.

97

"Well," Eatman continued, "in a nutshell, she took control of everything. She transferred Wilhelm's bank account into her name, and, as you know, promptly sold the sausage factory. What she's done with the money God only knows."

Eatman paused again, remembering the gay enthusiasm Ellen had shown, so soon after the death of her father and the presumed loss of her brother, in taking control of the Winkler property. Over the course of his long career, he had seen this before, of course, but it never failed to sicken him. "I'm sorry, Henry," he finally said. "I was powerless to stop it."

Henry let out a long, deep breath. "Then it's gone," he said.

"Oh, no," Eatman said adamantly, sitting up straight and leaning forward. "What's left I don't know, but you're still entitled to half of the original value." His eyes narrowed, dark with anger. "Now you get that silly girl down here. Here's what I want you to tell her."

For the next several minutes Henry and Clara listened. When the old lawyer was finished, they looked to each other, then nodded to Eatman. They would remember every word.

That evening after dinner, they bundled themselves against the cold, borrowed the keys to Fred Klein's new Ford delivery truck, and began the long climb up Centennial Drive to Summit Avenue. Clara had filled in Henry as well as she could on what was known of Ellen. Not unexpectedly, she had jumped full-bore onto the Prohibition bandwagon, and #228 on Summit Avenue had become something of a headquarters for the local activity. When Clara had visited Ellen to pass on the news of Henry's miraculous reappearance, she had found the parlor walls covered with banners and solemn portraits of the founding mothers and fathers of the movement, the bureaus and tabletops littered with documents and brochures, and the house populated with a handful of dour-faced women.

Henry and Clara were talking of these things as Henry brought the truck to a stop in front of his home. "What did she do when you told her I was alive?" Henry asked wryly.

"Well," Clara said, "her mouth fell open, and she dropped her teacup." Clara thought for a moment. "She tried to smile, you know. She really did. Poor girl, spilled tea all over her pretty white dress."

They left the truck and stood for a moment surveying the house. It still looked wonderful, Henry thought; the care that Wilhelm had taken in its upkeep was still visible. The downstairs windows were all ablaze with light, and the faint sound of singing could be heard from within. It had begun to snow, and the cascading, heavy snowflakes curtaining his view gave the house a postcard-like quality. It was exactly the kind of view of the house that Henry had idealized in his mind during the long months that he had been away at war.

A light shone dimly from the curtained front second-story windows: from the grand room that had been his parents' bedroom. The vague outline of a woman passed quickly through the frame of light, and a moment later the light went out.

Henry's heart ached. "Let's get this over with," he said to Clara.

Inside, in the parlor, Ellen Winkler stood with a group of middle-aged men and women sipping punch and listening to a quartet of young women singing. She wore a dark woolen dress buttoned modestly to her neck, and had her long blonde hair pulled back severely into a bun.

Ellen stood listening to the women singing in their high, slightly off-key sopranos. From the look of her, with her eyes bright with energy and the edges of her mouth ratcheted up into a toothy, almost sardonic, grin, one would have thought she had been transported into the company of a host of angels from heaven. She silently mouthed the words she knew by heart:

For God and home and ev - 'ry land,
Our cause speeds on to - day;
For jus - tice, truth and right we stand
You'll find us here to stay...

Her blissful concentration was interrupted by a hand on her shoulder. Jarred from her reverie, she turned to the touch. Deborah Christianson, a heavy set woman in her late thirties, had entered from the foyer with the news that Ellen had two visitors waiting on the other side of the front door. "I think it's your brother, ma'am," she said solemnly. "Him and his wife."

"Oh, dear," Ellen said, the edges of her mouth snapping down into the more familiar pout.

"You want I should tell 'em to come back later?" Deborah asked.

Ellen thought for a moment. She knew she would have to confront him sooner or later, and as she thought about it, she would rather have it over with while the house was filled with her allies. "No," she said finally. "Let them in. Bring them to my study."

As she hurried to Wilhelm's study to prepare herself, she half-listened to the continuing chorus of young women:

For God and home and ev - 'ry land
Our cause is speed - ing swift - ly on...

99

Deborah ushered Henry and Clara past the crowded parlor and down the hallway to the study. As they entered, she moved away from the door to a spot just out of eyesight, so that she could listen.

Inside, Clara looked around the room that had been Wilhelm's sanctuary. His beautiful roll-top desk was stacked to overflowing with papers and leaflets, and a bottom door hung loose on a broken hinge. His wall-to-wall bookshelf stood empty, with crates of recently-packed books stark against the west wall. Ellen sat regally in Wilhelm's old leather chair, the right side of her face illuminated by the dim light of Wilhelm's reading lamp.

"Hello, sister," Henry said finally. "You look well."

"Yes, I am, thank you," Ellen said.

"And what do you think of me?" Henry asked lightly. "I look well, too, wouldn't you say? For a dead man."

"Yes, brother, you look well, too," Ellen said. Her eyes met his only for an instant, then darted away.

Ellen shifted uncomfortably in the big chair. Her eyes shot over to him as a cat's might to a nearby dog, assessing its safety. "I've been very busy, brother," she said weakly.

"Yes, I can see that," he responded.

Ellen's eyes sharpened with confidence. "We've won, you see," she said. "The amendment has been ratified. In less than a year's time, the nation will be free of the scourge of alcohol." Her smug smile was empty and joyless.

"Perfect," Henry said. "Since you've won, all these nice people can leave and my wife and I can finally return home."

Ellen's victory smile faltered. "That's not possible," she protested, her eyes nervously darting around the room. "As you can see we're quite full, and there is much more work to do. Much more work."

"This isn't a hotel, Ellen," Henry said. "It's the Winkler home. Yours and mine. As are all of Mother's and Father's assets." His words were hard now. "You're going to account for it," he said sternly. "You're going to account for the mischief that's been done in my absence."

Ellen's eyes blazed with anger, and she involuntarily rose from her seat. "Don't you call my life's work mischief," she said, her voice shaking. "My work is a true and noble cause. For God and home and every land!"

"Actually, it's Cecil Eatman's term," Henry said coolly.

The fire in Ellen's eyes vanished as quickly as it had surfaced. She took a step backward, as if Henry had struck her, and fell back into the chair. Cecil Eatman meant the law, and the uncompromising reality of the law was something that even Ellen, with all of her practiced ability, could not fantasize into something other than what it was.

For several moments she stared sullenly in the direction of her brother. "What will you have, then?" she asked meekly.

Henry told her what to do. Under the threat of a lawsuit, she was to bring all financial documents pertaining to the disposition of the Winkler estate to Cecil Eatman's office, where they would be independently appraised and evaluated. As charges of criminal negligence were a distinct possibility, Cecil Eatman's advice to Ellen was that she retain her own legal counsel.

As Henry and Clara left the darkened study and moved toward the foyer, Deborah entered and moved quickly to Ellen, who sat still in the chair with her head in her hands. As she bent close to the woman, Deborah could see that she was crying.

"He was supposed to be dead," Ellen sputtered into her hands. "He was supposed to be dead."

On a late afternoon early the next week, Ellen dutifully met Henry at Cecil Eatman's office. She sat warily in a high-backed chair, fidgeting uncomfortably and absent-mindedly biting a fingernail as the two men examined the bundle of documents she had brought along. After an hour of tedious examination, it was clear that precious little of the Winkler estate remained. Ellen had given most of it away: to the church, to the Women's Christian Temperance Union, to fellow-traveling politicians, to cheats and frauds and anyone else who could beguile their way into her pocketbook.

Cecil Eatman removed his spectacles and wearily looked up to the woman. "You've...given...so much away. How did you plan to live, girl?" he asked.

"Oh," Ellen said, her eyes wide and round. "I'm on the payroll at the Temperance Hall. I'm an officer." She nodded earnestly, as a child might when explaining the existence of Santa Claus.

Eatman closed his eyes and sighed. "Go home, Ellen," he said softly. He wasn't angry with her any more, just tired and frustrated.

Ellen nodded, then gathered up her coat and moved to the door.

"Oh, and Ellen," Eatman called to her. Her hand froze on the doorknob. "Don't give away one more penny. Understand?"

Again Ellen nodded dutifully, then she was gone.

Later that day, Henry met the lawyer at Otto's Tavern. For several minutes they sat in the dim light of the half-filled tavern, sipping their drinks in silence, surrounded by the muffled, animated sounds of people who had something to be happy about.

"She's still a little girl, really," Eatman said finally.

"I know," Henry said.

For several moments they were again silent. "I can turn her out of the house. Hell, I can send her to jail if you'd like," Eatman said, looking into Henry's eyes.

Henry rolled over the statement in his mind. It sounded so odd, so matter-of-fact, so absolutely true in the power of its application, yet so unthinkable as an option.

"I don't want to hurt her, Cecil," Henry answered, "and I most certainly don't want to send her to jail."

Cecil Eatman looked up to Henry and saw that he was smiling. "But where," Henry continued, "other than jail, can we count on her being taken care of?"

Eatman grinned wryly, then chuckled, accepting, as Henry had, the comedy of their impossible predicament. By the time their glasses were empty, they had decided. Henry would take what little cash Ellen had left, which he would save and use to help establish himself in his new trade. Ellen would have the house, although she could not sell it, and it would revert to Henry or his heirs on her death.

They left the warmth of the tavern into the shadowed overcast of the late afternoon. Turning up their collars against the winter chill, they shook hands and parted, Eatman to start the wearisome contractual paperwork, and Henry to tell Clara of his decision. She would accept it without a word, and they would turn their attention to the future. The next day Henry would start his apprenticeship.

Deborah Christianson was watching from the doorway when Ellen, returning home, turned from the sidewalk and progressed up the slippery walkway toward the porch. She walked with her head down and tilted to the side, as if she were walking into a stiff breeze.

"How'd it go, ma'am?" Deborah asked as Ellen passed through the doorway.

"Fine, Deborah," Ellen answered, offering an unconvincing smile. "Not to worry, love."

"They'll not take the house, will they, ma'am?" Deborah asked earnestly.

"Over my dead body," Ellen answered. Her hand moved to the side of her head, and her eyes closed momentarily.

"You've got another headache, ma'am," Deborah said, her voice soft with concern.

"Yes," Ellen said, "it seems to be my fate." Her eyes moved around the downstairs. The house was quiet and, except for the two of them, empty. "Where is everyone?" she asked.

"Down at the headquarters, ma'am. Stuffing envelopes," Deborah answered.

"Ah. Good," Ellen said as she took off her hat and coat, handing them absent-mindedly to Deborah. Her eyes winced from the pain growing in the side of her head. "I've got to sit down," she said.

"Would you like some tea, ma'am?" Deborah offered.

"That would be lovely," Ellen said, forcing a pained smile. "You're an angel."

As Ellen wearily took a seat in the welcome darkness of the parlor, she was thinking of what a godsend Deborah had been, appearing one day, out of the blue, at the Temperance Hall. Despite the hardship of the life she had tearfully described—a father who gambled, a husband lost to alcohol—she had remained sweet and kind, and dedicated to making the world a better place for others.

Deborah Christianson was thinking similar thoughts as she stood in the kitchen, boiling water for tea. Ellen Winkler was proving to be a godsend to her. As she turned to the cupboard, she barked her shin on the sharp edge of a half-open cabinet door.

"Ow!" she cried, then angrily kicked the thin door hard, sending it slamming into the face of the cabinet. Goddamned door, she thought as she bent to rub her aching shin. It was the second time that week her leg had liaisoned with that same cupboard door, and each time she had been sure that the damned thing had been closed.

Contrary to Ellen's high opinion, Deborah Christianson was no angel. Her name wasn't even Deborah Christianson. Her real name was Etta Mae Blumberg, and a very unflattering photograph of her was at that very moment on display in the police stations and post offices in and around New York City.

Until three months ago, New York City had been Etta Mae's home. And contrary to the story she had so tearfully and convincingly related to the Temperance workers, her father had not been a gambler. Rather, he was a hardworking and honest, if slow-witted, man who made a somewhat less than modest living loading and unloading merchant ships twelve hours a day. Etta Mae, it turned out, had grown up in a tenement only a stone's throw from the site of Henry's recent return from the European war.

By the time she was fifteen, Etta Mae—an observant girl—had come to several important conclusions about the hand she had been dealt in life. She realized, for one thing, that she was poor, and she knew from watching the world around her that poor people never got rich, at least not by doing honest work. For another thing, she was, she had to admit, exceedingly unattractive. While other girls' bodies blossomed, hers just grew, and her round face, with

103

its overly large mouth and small, porcine eyes, could not even qualify as plain. No, she was flat homely, and homely, she had learned, carried its own liabilities. She had almost no friends, and as even her own mother had said, she would probably never marry and should get used to the idea of being someone's maid. Now Etta Mae could get used to being homely, and she could get used to doing without men, but she could never, she concluded, get used to being poor.

Unlike her loutish father, Etta Mae was bright, and unusually perceptive. She came to understand that for women, homely translated into benign. Homely women, she learned, were assumed to be both stupid and virtuous, and were implicitly trusted. And so, during her teenage years, Etta Mae built on her strengths and slowly perfected the art of deception. When valuables disappeared from the homes of neighbors, Etta Mae was never suspect. And when police would come to investigate a burgled local business, they never for a moment suspected the dumpy, solitary young girl perched on the tenement steps, drinking a root beer. When she thought she had enough money, Etta Mae simply vanished.

As could be expected from an independent-minded woman with brains, drive, and absolutely no scruples, Etta Mae did very well in the complex and dangerous criminal world of turn-of-the-century New York City. A savvy businesswoman, she developed partnerships and profit-sharing arrangements with an assortment of petty crooks and strong men, and soon was busily engaged in thriving enterprise. Her business interests were eclectic, and included prostitution, drugs, and various clever bunko schemes.

Oddly enough, despite her unhappy childhood, Etta Mae grew up to be neither violent nor mean. She took no pleasure from the human misery that was almost always collateral to her endeavors, and genuinely regretted the few times she had been forced to use the stiletto she kept hidden in her corset or the Colt pistol she kept in her purse.

When the end came, it came suddenly and irrevocably. The recently-passed Clayton Antitrust Act did not apply to organized crime, and in the deep of a cold December night, Etta Mae and her colleagues became the target of a hostile takeover. Etta Mae escaped with her life, the clothes on her back, and just enough money for a train ticket to a two-bit Midwestern city she'd never heard of.

Now as a successful businesswoman, Etta Mae understood that good and bad fortune traveled in cycles. Though her bad fortune had never been this serious, she had recovered from setbacks before, and would, she was certain, recover from this. And so, shortly after leaving the train, stiff and tired from the long night's journey, when she stumbled upon the Temperance Hall, a glimmer of hope arose in her. Zealots, she knew, always welcomed fellow travelers. And when as Deborah Christianson she was introduced to the silly Winkler woman with the big house, her hopes rose still further. What Etta Mae's trained eyes saw in the gushing, starry-eyed, too-earnest woman was self-deception. And those who foolishly deceive themselves can, she knew from long experience, most easily be deceived by others. Ellen Winkler, she was now convinced, would be the source of her next good fortune.

Standing over the Winkler stove, carefully pouring boiling water into Sophie's blue china teapot, Etta Mae was considering her strategy. She had already profited modestly from her live-in relationship with Ellen, having stolen a substantial amount of money both from the Temperance Society and from Ellen herself. In addition, it was clear that most of the other girls' interest in prohibition were as feigned as her own. What they needed was leadership, of the type that Etta Mae was most able and willing to provide. The possibilities excited her.

There was only one weak link that she could think of. Ellen was fond of her, and Ellen trusted and confided in her, but she still was not indispensable to her. And Etta Mae knew that to exert real control over someone, you had to be in some important way indispensable.

Etta Mae had a plan for remedying this deficiency, which she was considering as she carried the tea service up the hallway to Ellen. It was, she knew, a dangerous plan, and if it failed, she would have to be on the next train out of town. Still, she thought, nothing ventured, nothing gained. She turned into the parlor and stopped for a moment. Like a rattlesnake appraising a mouse, her small, veiled eyes considered her quarry, who sat sprawled on the sofa in a very unladylike fashion, her eyes closed, her hand to the side of her head.

"Here's some nice tea for you, ma'am," Etta Mae said finally, setting the tea service down on the coffee table in front of the sofa.

Ellen's eyes opened. "Oh, thank you, Deborah," she said sitting up. "You're a dear."

Etta Mae poured tea into two of Sophie's delicate blue and white china teacups, then handed one to Ellen. "Here you are, ma'am," she said.

Ellen took the teacup and held it to her face, letting the rising steam warm her. She took a sip, then closed her eyes against the throbbing pain in her head. The headaches were getting more frequent and worse, and she was approaching her wit's end. She'd tried everything—aspirin and hot compresses and herbal elixirs—all to no avail.

"It's no better, ma'am?" Etta Mae said softly, taking Ellen's hand.

"No," Ellen snuffled. "I don't know how I can go on standing it."

When Etta Mae saw the desperation in the woman's eyes, she made her decision. "I...might have something that can help," she said, smiling gently with all the sisterly warmth she could muster. "Something you haven't tried yet."

Ellen's eyes brightened with hope. "What is it?" she asked.

"It's a special medicine they use in Europe," Etta Mae said. She hadn't considered the story she would tell, and was thinking on her feet. "A friend of mine in the east, she has the same malady as you, ma'am. Her husband's a ship captain, and he brings it back for her. I wrote her to send me some, just for you to try."

"What's it called?" Ellen asked.

Etta Mae was ready for this. "My friend calls it 'blessed relief.'"

Ellen hesitated. She didn't seem leery, Etta Mae thought, just indecisive, as if waiting for someone with authority to tell her what to do. "I'm sure it will help, ma'am," she said confidently.

Ellen winced, jolted by a wave of sharp pain. She let out a deep breath, then sat silently for a moment, her hand to her head, her eyes closed. Then her eyes opened, and she licked her lips. "Let's try it," she said.

Etta Mae helped her up from the sofa and led her out of the parlor. "We'll go to your room, ma'am," Etta Mae said. "The medicine will make you want to rest."

"Rest," Ellen said wistfully. "That would be wonderful."

Etta Mae, her arm around Ellen's narrow waist, walked her up the winding staircase to the second floor, then down the hallway to the attic door. "You go on up, ma'am," she said, opening the door for her. "I'll follow along directly."

As Ellen climbed slowly up to her third story sanctuary, Etta Mae hurried up the hallway to her front bedroom. While the other girls doubled up in the small bedrooms, Etta Mae had this one—the largest and best—all to herself. She'd discarded the old feather mattress for a new innerspring, which made the room perfect. She walked quickly to Sophie's dresser and extracted a small cardboard box from the bottom drawer. Checking the contents quickly, she hurried back down the hallway and onto the attic stairway, closing and locking the door behind her.

Ellen had converted the north end of the attic into a sleeping and working area, complete with an armoire and dresser for her clothes, a small writing desk and bookshelf, and a narrow single bed. Etta Mae found Ellen draped across the bed. It was very dark in the vaulted, heavily draped room, and to Etta Mae's surprise, unexpectedly warm.

"I'm here, ma'am," she said.

106

Ellen opened her eyes. "Oh," she said, sitting up. "You've got the medicine?"

"I do," Etta Mae said, smiling and nodding reassuringly. She sat on the bed next to her. "Now this isn't a pill, ma'am," she said. "It's an herb...very highly concentrated." Now for the plunge, she thought, taking a deep breath. "And you don't swallow it, ma'am. You light it, and breathe the vapors."

"It's not tobacco, is it?" Ellen said warily.

"Oh, no, ma'am," Etta Mae protested gently. "It's a flower. And you don't smoke it. Oh, no. You breathe the vapors."

Ellen nodded dumbly. So far, so good, Etta Mae thought. She opened the box and extracted a thin, delicate pipe. "Now we put the flower in here, and we light it, and you just breathe in," she said, smiling encouragingly. "It helps my friend. I'm sure it will help you."

What little sense Ellen had was warning her of the impropriety of all of this, but her desperate need for relief from the throbbing pain in her head won out. "Well," she said. "If it works for your friend, I'll try it."

"Good," Etta Mae said. She took a tiny metal tin from the box, and using a small, sharp knife cut off a wedge of gooey opium and placed it carefully in the bowl of the pipe. "Here," she said, passing the pipe to Ellen. "Now when I light it, you breathe in the vapors. They'll be harsh, like the taste of strong tea, but you pay it no mind."

Ellen took the pipe and held the stem to her pink lips. Etta Mae struck a match and held it to the bowl. "Now breathe in deeply," she said.

Ellen sucked on the pipe stem, then coughed as the acrid smoke attacked her lungs.

"It's okay," Etta Mae said quickly. "Try again."

The next draw was not so bad, and the one after that even milder. After five good draws on the pipe, Etta Mae could see the expected change in Ellen's eyes. Half-closed now, they had become vapid, like a deep, dark pool of water. Her mouth hung limply open, as if she were about to laugh.

"How's the headache, ma'am," Etta Mae asked hopefully.

"About gone," Ellen said. "It's a miracle."

"Yes, ma'am," Etta Mae said. "Here, then. One more draught."

She held the pipe to Ellen's mouth for a last deep draw. As Ellen slowly breathed out, the pipe slipped from her lips into Etta Mae's waiting hand.

Ellen, in the grasp of a delightful, playful opium dream, was quite out of touch with reality as Etta Mae helped her to stretch out on the narrow bed.

After a moment, Etta Mae moved away from the bed to the north-facing window. Opening the window wide, she reached into the pocket of her dress and brought out a crumpled pack of cigarettes. Lighting one and breathing in the sweet smoke, she turned her gaze back to Ellen. As she watched, Ellen moaned softly, then rolled onto her side and tucked her legs up under her, like a little girl.

Chapter Eight

Stella Phillips sat in a cushioned rattan chair in front of Carole's desk, sipping the Darjeeling tea Carole had offered her and listening impatiently as Carole explained the current state of their campaign for dealing with Stella's easement dispute. She was frustrated at how slow the process was. Here it was early spring—almost a year since she had first met with Carole—and they seemed to be no closer to a resolution than when they had started.

"This sure is taking a long time, honey," Stella finally said.

"Don't I know it," Carole answered, setting down her teacup and picking up a pencil from the surface of her desktop. "He's a tough old buzzard."

Carole's eyes turned steely as she got serious. "We're going to court," she said, tapping her pencil on the desktop. "We're going to claim adverse possession, which means you've used it and he hasn't."

"That matters?" Stella asked.

"Oh, you bet it does," Carole answered. "It's your property, and if for twenty years he acts like he doesn't need to use it, and you do, then a judge is free to tell him to go jump in a lake."

"The truth be known," Stella said, "I really don't use it that much."

"Baloney," Carole objected strenuously. "It's your flower garden." Carole had made a trip to Stella's to inspect the disputed property line, and had admired the long line of well-tended gladiolas and rose bushes. "So no more talk...with anyone, Stella," she said, looking the old lady hard in the eye, "about that strip of property being of no value to you. Got it?"

Stella stared back blankly at Carole, thinking, of all things, of the wonder of how such a pretty young face could become, in just an instant, so commanding. Then she smiled. "I get it.

Carole softened and smiled. "There you go," she said.

Stella's eyes twinkled. "Why, I don't know what came over me," she said earnestly, raising a wrinkled hand to cover her mouth. "That strip of land...why...I don't rightly know what I'd do without it...my flowers mean so much to me." She looked to Carole earnestly and innocently, her hand resting at her neckline, shaking slightly. "How's that?"

"Very good," Carole said, relaxing. "That's the attitude."

Picking up the teapot, Carole refilled their cups. "Was this your family home?" she asked.

"Oh, no," Stella said, reaching for her teacup. "My family first lived up on the hill, back in the early forties. No, Herb and I saved for eight years for the down payment on our place. Put in my roses a year later." She smiled up to Carole, then fell silent, a shadow of sadness falling across her face. "He's been gone for six years now, my Herb."

After a moment Stella brightened and smiled. She pointed to the framed picture of Carlos sitting on Carole's cluttered desktop. "That's your husband, I take it."

"That's him," Carole said, smiling back. "His name's Carlos."

Stella picked up the photograph and examined it. It was a recent favorite of Carole's, a snapshot of Carlos in his favorite Hawaiian shirt, a black smear on his face, surprised as he turned from his easel.

"Good lookin'," she finally said. "What's he do?"

"He's a cartoonist," Carole answered. "That's charcoal on his face."

Stella considered the photograph for a moment longer, then replaced it on the desktop. "He's good to you?" she asked.

"Very," Carole answered.

"Then sit back and enjoy it, honey," Stella said resolutely. "And don't ever get old."

When they were done, Carole walked Stella out into the mid-morning sunshine. It was crisp and chilly, the kind of early spring day when the young sun, low in the pale blue sky, was able to warm only around the edges. Carole stuck her hands into the pockets of her sweater as Stella buttoned her coat and arranged a loose knitted cap on her head, tucking the loose strands of her silver hair under the hatband.

"Where you off to now?" Carole asked.

"To the 'Y' for water aerobics," Stella said. "Thirty old women in spandex. Not a pretty sight." She grinned over to Carole, her eyes twinkling. "But I'm the best looking of the lot," she said.

As Carole stood outside the doorway of her office building watching Stella walk slowly toward the bus stop, Carlos sat on the roof of the house. All winter Carlos had had a nagging worry about the roof. Though he had patched it as best he could before the rain and snow came, it was old, and old roofs, he knew, were prone to be disingenuous. If he had been able to enter the attic, he could have checked the rafters for signs of a leak, but he was still unwilling to brutalize what he presumed to be the attic door, and all of the attic windows were curtained and locked tight.

And so, relying on a promise from the six o'clock news of an extended period of dry weather, he had allotted the week ahead of him for roofing. While physically hard and tedious work, roofing was mentally easy, requiring little more than an eye for a straight line. Carlos was actually looking forward to it, being certain that his straying mind would be certain to uncover fruitful grist for "The Halfway Inn." Far below him, the old lady with the walker was doing her familiar three-step down the sidewalk. One, two, three. The walker forward, then up with one foot, then up with the other. One, two, three.

Planting his feet firmly on either side of the roof's peak, he began to scrape away at the old shingles with an ancient hoe he'd found in the garage. They came away easily, revealing the wooden lath to which they had been nailed. "Wow," he said, surprised. He'd thought there'd be a layer of wood under the shingles, but before him was nothing but lath and air.

Bracing himself on his lower legs, Carlos peered down between the lath into the attic. Except for two long lines of rough attic flooring made visible by the weak sunlight, Carlos couldn't see a thing. "All right!" he said happily. Now he realized he could finally get in the attic without having to damage the locked door.

After a trip down and up the ladder, an apology to the house, and ten minutes of work with a hand saw, he had a clean, three-foot square hole into the attic. Below him, daylight now revealed a small square of clear flooring. He was smiling now, excited. He climbed into the hole, then lowered himself, grunting occasionally, until he was hanging by his hands from the attic roof, his feet dangling several feet above the attic floor below. "Okay...here goes," he told himself, then let go.

The drop wasn't as bad as he had feared, and while when he hit he fell backward onto his rear end, he was unhurt. Getting up and dusting himself off, he peered around into the shadowed corners of the steeply pitched walls, breathing in the musty-scented old air. While he couldn't make out the exact nature of the darkened objects around him, there was enough light from the hole in the roof to allow him to make his way around the length of the attic, pulling back the heavy, dust-laden curtains at each of the many windows. Only then, turning away from the dirty glass of the front bay window, did he consider the contents of the attic. He stood still for several moments, then raised a hand to scratch his head. "Wow," he said finally.

The twenty-foot dumpster that Carlos had rented to accommodate old shingles occupied the driveway in front of the garage, so that when Carole arrived home in the late afternoon, she had to park on the street. Leaving the car and pulling her sweater tight against the chill, she walked slowly up the walkway toward the wide front porch, her heels click-clicking methodically against the cement. She was beat from the long, pestering day, and was looking forward to a hot bath in a quiet, dark room.

Carlos had heard her arrive, and stood at the open front bay window of the attic. High above her, he watched as she approached the house, admiring the way her loose skirt flowed against the outline of her slim legs.

111

Carlos's cat whistle stopped Carole in her tracks. She looked around, her eyes seeking him out. Again the cat whistle. Carole's eyes darted around vainly for the source of the sound. "Where are you?" she finally asked, exasperated.

"Look up," Carlos's voice suggested.

Carole lifted her gaze up to the second story, then higher still to the attic, where she found Carlos hanging out of the front window. "Come on up. You gotta see this," he called down to her.

Carole entered the house, dropped her briefcase in the foyer, and moved slowly up the stairway to the second floor. Halfway down the hallway, the attic door, unyielding for so long, now stood open. Carlos was there to meet her.

"How'd you get in?" Carole asked when she reached him.

"Through the roof," he told her.

Carlos's eyes were dancing and his mouth was open in a wide, toothy smile. He was excited, wound tight by whatever he'd discovered. "Come on," he said, turning from her and beginning to climb back up the stairs. "You won't believe this."

Carole hesitated for a moment, then slowly followed behind him. As she passed through the doorway, she appraised the huge deadbolt lock that had defied all of Carlos's attempts at picking, then began to climb the steep, rough wood staircase. She was halfway up the stairs before she began at all to realize that she didn't want to be doing this. She wanted her bath and a big glass of wine, and the musty, dust-filled air of the attic was unwelcome and oppressive. Carlos's enthusiasm, most often infectious, was at that moment singularly unappreciated.

When Carole's head had cleared the attic floor, she looked around the cluttered, dusty expanse of attic, then stopped cold on the stairway, her mouth half-open. "Oh, jees," she complained involuntarily. The house had caught her in a weak moment, and had once again disarmed her. For what she saw was unmistakably someone's bedroom.

"Cool, huh?" Carlos asked, his eyes dancing with mischief. "Another mystery."

Carole's feet reluctantly began to move again, and she climbed the remaining steps and moved slowly to Carlos, her eyes flitting nervously from item to item as she catalogued the long-untouched contents of someone's rooftop sanctuary: the small bed, neatly made; the writing desk stacked with curled and yellowed papers and pamphlets; the tall armoire with its mirrored door; a light summer dress hanging limply from a wooden coat rack. Absentmindedly, she pulled her sweater tight around her. She'd had enough of mysteries.

"The desk is locked up tight," Carlos said, bending over to pull futilely on the low cupboard door. "But if you're wondering who lived up here, I think I can tell you," Carlos offered, picking up a dust-covered pamphlet from a pile on the desk.

"I wasn't," Carole decided.

Carlos handed her the pamphlet. Hand written, it was entitled "Fighting the Good Fight: The Next Chapter," by Ellen Winkler.

"God, not her again," Carole moaned.

"Yup, your twin relative, back at it again," Carlos said happily. "Don't ya love it?"

"No, Carlos," she said coldly, "you love it. Me, I'm just stuck with it."

Carlos, caught up in his excitement, missed the weariness in Carole's response. "Look here," he said, moving to the writing desk. "There's dozens of 'em."

Carlos began to flip through the pile of yellowed pamphlets. "Looney-toons, man!" he mumbled to himself.

Looney-toons. She was doing okay until looney-toons, pacing herself to deal with the fatigue and the unpleasantness of the stuffy, rough-walled attic with its unwanted surprise. But looney-toons was too much. On her good days Carole was at least marginally open and interested in her long-dead and previously unknown relatives, willing to learn about their lives and their relationship to her, but on her bad days, like this one, she wanted to disown them, to forget about them, to ostracize them for their unwitting role in her deception, and for the loneliness of her youth.

"And check out this dress," she heard Carlos saying.

Carole watched as he moved to the coat rack and lifted the fragile cloth from its hook. Walking to her, he held it open for her to see. It was the color called "Alice blue," and buttoned primly up the front, a small cameo pinned to it above the heart.

"So where've you seen this before?" he asked, his eyes bright with playful energy.

She knew immediately, of course. It was the dress her sad look-alike was wearing in the photograph in the back bedroom. Carole's stomach turned. The steeply angled, rough-wood walls seemed to close in on her, making her feel claustrophobic.

"I bet it fits," Carlos was saying. "Ten bucks says it fits." He was teasing her, having fun—the kind of harmless good humor they both enjoyed, and that was a common part of their friendship.

"Come on," he said, grinning out at her. "Try it on. I dare you."

It took just a second for Carole's distress to overwhelm her, to turn her eyes steely cold and snap her mouth shut.

113

"Fuck you, Carlos," she spat back at him, then turned on her heel and moved quickly down the stairway without looking back.

Once before dinner Carlos tried to apologize for whatever it was that he'd done wrong, but Carole had no use for it. "Just drop it, okay?" she'd said, interrupting him. So Carlos had shut up and geared himself for the wait. As darkness overtook the house, they ate their dinner quickly and in silence, their faces down, the thin sound of knives and forks on plates conspicuous in the eerie stillness.

After the dishes were done, Carlos retreated to the study to work on his cartoons. Carole, who normally would have joined him, opted instead for the davenport in the parlor, where she sat alone, an unread deposition in her lap, the orchestra of conflicting thoughts and emotions slowly suffocating her. She wanted to be at her office, or in her old apartment—anywhere other than where she was.

When she couldn't stand the walls around her any longer, she grabbed her coat and left the house, walking the length of Summit Avenue and back, then walking it again. When she returned to the house the second time, she saw that the light in the study was out—Carlos had gone to bed. She stood for a moment wearily appraising the old house, still now, and dark except for the porch and foyer lights Carlos had left on. Having nowhere else to go, she slowly climbed the porch steps and entered the house, and put herself to bed next to her sleeping husband.

The next morning, after a fitful sleep, Carole rose early, showered and dressed, and left the house as soon as she could, eager to throw herself into her work. Her morning was fine—packed to the brim with phone and email messages and client visits and memos to respond to—but in the early afternoon, after her last client of the day had left, she found herself alone with her thoughts, which took her single-mindedly back to the house on Summit Avenue. And as much as she tried to leave—time and again forcing her mind back to the reality in front of her—inexorably, like a compass needle, it would return north to the house, and to the attic with its bed and table and pretty Alice blue dress, and the long, sad, unknown tale that only the rough walls of the attic could tell.

There was no way to rid herself of them, she knew: Wilhelm and Sophie and Henry and crazy Ellen, and the others, like her mother and father, still unaccounted for. They were as dogged in their claim on her as the spectre of death, as unrelenting as life itself. For better or worse, she was stuck with them.

Entering the house, she met Carlos in the foyer. For a moment she stood still, watching him, her eyes soft and questioning. Then without a word she moved to him, her open arms asking him to hold her. It was over.

114

After a good, long hug, Carlos pulled his head back from her. "Don't worry about all that crap in the attic," he said. "I can pack it..."

Carole put her finger to his mouth, stopping him. "I want to try it on," she said, her jaw set and determined.

Carlos didn't try to talk her out of it. He knew the look by heart, the one that informed him that she had made up her mind. "Betcha' it doesn't fit," he offered as they climbed the narrow stairway into the attic.

"Betcha' it does," Carole said back.

When the attic light came on, Carole's stomach jumped at the sight of the limp cloth hanging formlessly from the coat rack. She moved slowly, resolutely to the dress, hesitated momentarily, then reached out and took it from the coat rack. It seemed light and gossamer to her; almost weightless, as if it had been washed a hundred times. For a few moments she held it out in front of her, appraising its fabric and color, its cut and design. She admired the stitching, all hand-done, she knew.

She shook it gently, trying to remove decades of dust. Slipping out of her clothes, she took a deep breath, then raised the dress over her head and allowed it to slide down over her. As it passed over her head, she smelled it; it was dry and musty, and faintly woody, like dead leaves. Like dead leaves crumbled in her hand.

She moved to the armoire and swung open the mirrored door to best catch the weak light from the overhead bulb. When she came into full view, the sight shocked her, sending goose bumps arching like electricity up her arms and legs. The dress fell modestly to several inches above her ankles, then rose to fit snugly around her hips and waist, then smoothly up to cover her chest and shoulders. The Cameo brooch hung on Carole as it had on Ellen: above the heart. It was, as Carole had bet, a perfect fit.

Finally Carole considered the face, and her stomach turned again as the past she had so studiously and adamantly sought to avoid stared back at her, unblinking. This was no circumstantial evidence. This was hard evidence of sperm and egg, as indisputable to her as DNA. She shuddered imperceptibly, as if struck by a chill wind.

Carlos approached her from the rear, and she was relieved to see his lean, brown face in the mirror beside her own. She felt the comfort of his hands on her waist. It was a feel she had come to love, of strong, adoring hands separated from her naked skin by a thin, fluid veneer of soft cloth.

Carlos moved closer to her, overlapping his hands around her stomach. "I think it's a pretty dress," he said.

"It's a beautiful dress," Carole answered. "All hand-stitched. Someone who loved her made it for her special."

Carlos, who was being very careful with his mouth, thought for a moment before speaking. "Who loved her, do you think?" Carlos asked finally.

Carole thought for a moment. "Her mother and father," she said finally. "A man, maybe."

"I bet there were more than a few men who wanted to," Carlos said. "It doesn't look like she was into that, though."

"Into what?" Carole asked.

"Love," Carlos answered.

Carole thought for a moment, then nodded sadly.

"And that, my beautiful darling, is how you're different from her," he added.

And there, in those few words, was the plain truth of it. Carole smiled softly, then turned her head to kiss him. And when she turned back, it was her own face in the mirror, and her own body. Yes, she thought, this is Carole, not her. And like a fever breaking, whatever fear she had of her long-dead look-alike fled from her like smoke in the wind, leaving only a mildly aching, free-floating sorrow. What crime had this Ellen committed, Carole thought, other than, perhaps, the commonplace kinds that people so often practice against themselves? And what crimes had the Winkers committed, other than stumbling through their own lives, passing on their genes, generously and lovingly, to generations they would never know?

Carole took off the dress and hung it carefully back on the coat rack. Picking up her clothes, she left the attic for her bedroom, where she removed her pantyhose and the serpentine necklace she'd chosen to wear that morning. She turned the small piece of rock over in her hand, examining it. It wasn't a valuable stone, she knew, just pretty in a simple sort of way. And old, like Ellen's cameo. She'd always assumed that it'd been a gift from the Brownings, because she couldn't remember ever not having it. But then she wondered, for the first time, if it might have been an even earlier gift.

Gently depositing the necklace onto the top of her dresser, she changed into a sweat suit and got to work helping Carlos fix dinner. Later that evening she took a long soak in the tub, then climbed into the bed next to Carlos, who sat propped against a pillow reading from the last book of the Tolkien trilogy.

"How are the hobbits doing?" she asked cheerfully.

"Not good," Carlos said, shaking his head. "Frodo's been captured by Orcs."

"Oh, I bet he'll be just fine," she said.

Carlos put down the book. He had sensed the change in her, the softening release. But he wanted to be sure. "And how 'bout you?" he asked, turning to her. "Are you just fine?"

116

"I am," Carole said assuredly, the white tips of her teeth showing now as her smile turned sly. "Except," she said, rubbing her shoulder lightly, "I've got this sore muscle in my shoulder…"

Carlos finished the roofing that week, and after a couple of days unsuccessfully trying to get the old Indian motorcycle to run, set to work wallpapering the upstairs bedrooms and hallway. Like most home repair jobs, it wasn't hard once you'd mastered a few basic techniques, and was either blindingly tedious or blessedly cathartic, depending on the home repairer's disposition. For Carlos it was almost always the latter.

He had insisted that Carole pick the wallpaper, and had been surprised, and at first somewhat disappointed, at how closely it resembled the torn and faded remnants of the original. But as he carefully hung line after line of the paper in the front master bedroom, he came to change his mind. The pattern was soft and delicate, almost playful. It was modest in its beauty, like Carole.

He had made his patient way through both of the front bedrooms and out into the long hallway when the good news came. Like all artists seeking to sell their work, Carlos had learned that only bad news comes by mail. And so as he knew it had to, the good news came by phone. The call came around one o'clock on a Friday, just as Carlos was putting the finishing touches on the monstrous hot pastrami sandwich he had prepared for himself. As the phone rang he jealously eyed the sandwich, then hurried to the phone in the study, hoping that the call would be short.

"Hello," he said into the receiver.

"Is this Mr. Estrada?" a female voice queried. Carlos correctly placed the accent as pure New York City.

"It is," he responded.

"Oh, good," the voice said.

Carlos listened, his mind on his sandwich, ready to hang up at the first hint of a marketing ploy. But this was no telemarketer, and after ten minutes, his face flushed and happy, he finally hung up. He immediately called Carole's office, only to be told that she was with a client. Fifteen minutes later, as he was just finishing his sandwich, she called back.

"Guess what, honey," he said happily into the phone. "I just got a call from New York. They're interested in syndicating 'The Halfway Inn.'"

"Oh, honey," came Carole's excited voice over the receiver. "That's just great. Just so great. I told you, didn't I? Didn't I?"

The "they" turned out to be a publishing company in New York City— one of the half-dozen or so that Carlos had been doggedly courting—that packaged "Life and Leisure" pages for newspapers around the country. The

117

page contained tongue-in-cheek essays, light op-ed pieces, relationship advice, and one-box cartoons of the type Carlos drew. As the woman had explained to Carlos, one of their cartoons had stopped being funny, and they thought that "The Halfway Inn" might be a perfect replacement.

Carole left the office as soon as she could and stopped on her way home for a bottle of good wine. As she entered the house, she looked around excitedly for Carlos. Searching the rooms on the ground floor, she found him on his knees in the study, sorting through a pile of photo reductions of his cartoons. For a moment she stood in the doorway watching him, filled to the brim with happiness for him, and for the long-awaited success that now seemed imminent. Then he looked around and saw her.

"Hi," he said. "Whatcha got there?"

Carole assessed the wine bottle dangling from her right hand. "A victory celebration," she said.

Carlos rose from his knees and walked to her. "They haven't bought anything yet," he said, kissing her lightly on the lips.

"Oh, but they will," Carole responded, her eyes twinkling.

To tell the truth, Carlos was a bit reluctant to celebrate. He'd come close before, and knew that unlike Carole, whose professional success depended solely on brains and hard work, his commercial success depended on some stranger's haphazard and capricious reaction to his work. Did she get a good night's sleep? Was he happy in his marriage? Was the Prozac working?

But Carole was not to be denied. She was cognizant of the many celebrations Carlos had orchestrated for her: law school graduation, passing two state bar exams, the winning of the occasional big case. But Carlos's insular and solitary work life offered few possibilities for real celebration. And so after their dinner, they sat on the front porch, bundled against the chill, and toasted Carlos' success. When the bottle was half-empty, they abandoned the porch for the bathtub to continue the celebration.

Carlos spent most of the weekend wallpapering. It was good therapy, giddy as he was over his upcoming trip, and kept his hands busy and his mind engaged. He worked steadily for two days, moving methodically down the length of the hallway and into the back bedrooms, listening to the animated chatter of an oldies radio station, and to tunes from groups he knew only as history: The Beach Boys, The Temptations, The Supremes.

When she was done with her weekend chores, Carole chipped in to help, and he taught her how to cut the paper to match the pattern, how to spread a thin layer of wallpaper paste evenly across the wall, and how to smooth the wallpaper to prevent bubbles from developing. "Be patient," he would say.

"There's no hurry. You're only going to lay this piece of paper once, so try to make it perfect."

By late Sunday the entire second floor, with the exception of the west wall of the hallway, shone with the pristine glow of beautiful new wallpaper. Carlos spent the early days of the next week preparing for his trip: updating the portfolio of his published work and outlining for himself the many directions he was prepared to go with "The Halfway Inn."

Then, on Thursday morning, Carole drove him to the airport. He was booked on a continuing flight from Chicago to LaGuardia, and as they sat near his departure gate waiting for his plane to arrive, Carole studied him as he silently sipped coffee from a paper cup. "What are you worried about?" she asked nonchalantly, squeezing his hand. "They already love it. All that's left is reading the fine print."

"Right. Like Chicago," Carlos retorted. He was thinking of the time the winter before when he'd driven west through a snowstorm to meet with a newspaper editor, only to be confronted with a disinterested secretary with no record of the appointment. Worse still, on his way out of town, he'd been rear-ended by an out of control SUV, splitting open his lip as it bounced off the steering wheel. Injury added to insult.

To burn some time, they walked the length of the terminal, then stopped in a newsstand so that Carlos could buy a magazine. "Where's the *Hustler?*" he asked, intently examining the crowded, colorful shelves of magazines.

Carole cocked a cynical eye toward Carlos. "Out of reach of little boys," she answered.

After Carlos bought a sports magazine they hung around the newsstand perusing the lines of paperback books. "What would you name your daughter if your last name was White?" he asked. His answer: "Lily."

Carole chuckled, then quickly scanned a line of books. "Okay," she said, "here's one. What would you name your kid if your last name was Schwartz?" Her answer: "Bermuda."

Twenty minutes later she was waving to him as he walked down the jetport. From the distance between them, he seemed thinner than before, and older. "Bye, honey," she called to him. "Stay out of the barrios."

Carlos laughed and waved back, then he was gone around the corner and into the plane. Carole stood by the window and watched as the little jet backed out and turned. As it slowly taxied away, she looked vainly for Carlos's face in one of the windows. Five minutes later she watched it roar by on the runway, its nose lifting gently, leading the plane smoothly into the air, speeding east.

Carole left the airport and spent a hectic day at the office, then went home with more work, scrambling to meet filing deadlines for a contract she was working on. Around eight Carlos called from his parents' house. Both of his parents and two of his brothers insisted on talking with her, so the call went on for more than an hour.

Later, she took a long, leisurely bath, lingering in the hot water until her fingers and toes were pink and wrinkled. Then she made herself a cup of herbal tea and climbed into the big four-poster bed. Alone in the big bed, she felt awkward, overwhelmed by its size. It was an hour later in New York City. Carole wondered whether Carlos was asleep yet. Her eyes darting nervously around the room, Carole knew she wasn't ready for sleep. She reached across the bed to Carlos's nightstand and picked up the book he was reading. It was the third volume of the Tolkien trilogy, which Carlos had been slowly working his way through. She took Carlos's pillow and stuck it behind her head for support, and as she read, she slowly became aware of the faint smell of him coming from the pillow. Maybe it was the smell of his hair after he washed it, or his aftershave, or maybe just him. For Carole it was a delicious, quieting smell, and so, warm under the covers and surrounded as she was by Carlos's subtle presence, she read until her eyes wouldn't stay open.

The next day was one of those rare days without appointments, which meant that Carole could trade in her business suit for slacks and a sweater and spend the day holed up in her office with her teapots and computer, doing research. She worked hard until mid-morning, the time when she could reasonably expect that Carlos might call with news of his meeting. After that she became increasingly distracted, spending more and more time staring at the phone and the clock, and less and less time focused on her computer monitor. By noon there had still been no call, and Carole, now thoroughly peeved by the waiting, left the computer and began pacing.

Finally, around 12:45, the call came. With her receptionist out to lunch, Carole took the call. "Law offices," she said hopefully.

"Oh, thank God," a male voice said. "I'm over here at Centennial and Summit, and there's a woman down in the crosswalk. We need a lawyer here fast."

Carole was smiling from the beginning. It was Carlos's unmistakable voice, and the line had become a favorite of his ever since he learned that lawyers refer to the pedestrian crosswalk as "the pay zone." She was smiling for another reason, too. He wouldn't be joking around, she knew, if the news was bad.

"Good news, I take it," she said confidently.

"Yup," came Carlos's reply. "Two hundred newspapers, three days a week plus Sundays."

"You did it, you big lug," she said softly. "Congratulations."

120

She made him carefully describe the deal, which, based on the research she'd done, was standard. The pay was a bit low, she thought, but would increase substantially if the spot was renewed after six months.

"Couldn't be much better," she said finally.

"Yeah, I know," Carlos responded. "I'm pinching myself."

When they finally hung up, Carole knew she wouldn't get any more work done that day. Every once in a very long while, Carole knew, a day comes along that is as good as it can possibly get, and this was one of them. Carole was so happy for Carlos, and so excited for the future, that she wanted to run and jump and yell. And so she shut down her computer and deserted the office for the day.

She spent some time padding the corridors of one of the gigantic malls located near her office, stopping for an Orange Julius and looking for a present for Carlos. Then, not knowing what else to do, she went to a movie, where she stuffed herself on buttered popcorn.

When she finally got home, the sun had just fully set in the western sky. Still filled with happy energy, she decided to go for a walk. Pulling on her favorite sweat shirt—thick, hooded, and showing its age, with "NORTHWESTERN" printed across the front in faded purple block letters—she left the house into the early evening.

With her hands stuck deep into the pockets of her sweatshirt against the evening chill, Carole walked the half-mile length of Summit Avenue, then crossed the street and walked back on the other side. She walked slowly, examining the muted outlines of the tall houses she passed. Inside the lighted windows she occasionally glimpsed snippets of the lives inside: TV sets soundlessly popping from scene to scene, a boy playing a computer game, a girl practicing on a clarinet.

As she came even with her own house from across the street, she stopped to assess it. Dimly illuminated in the yellow glow of a nearby streetlight, the house seemed smaller to Carole than it did in the light of day. Pale light shone from the two front parlor windows and from the entryway. But above the long porch, the house was all in darkness, and the filigreed second-story windows and steep dormered roofline seemed to blend with and disappear into the background of the darkening sky. It seemed to Carole like a giant cat, curled up and half asleep. A light wind sent the budding branches of the two old trees in the front yard gently swaying, creating, in the dim light, the illusion of movement. The house, Carole thought with surprise, seemed to be breathing.

Six months earlier she would have dismissed such a thought as ridiculous, the kind of thing Carlos would dream up. But at that moment she found the possibility tantalizing in a playful sort of way, like a guilty pleasure   she wouldn't dare share with anyone. She wondered how the house had looked in earlier times, in the seventies when the man named Henry had last lived there, or earlier, when Ellen had been alive, or still earlier even. She thought of Christmases and Thanksgivings, of the possibility of toys littering the front porch and bicycles lying on their sides in the front lawn.

She stood watching for a few moments longer, her lips pursed, as if she were offering the house a distant kiss, then quickly crossed the street and returned to her front door. She wanted a hot bath and a warm bed, and maybe some quality time with Carlos's Tolkien characters. She was in the mood for magic. The real magic, though, wouldn't occur until very late the next day.

Carole awoke early the next morning, and after brewing a pot of strong tea, sat at her computer in the small southwest bedroom. Of the three spare bedrooms she'd chosen this one—the one where they'd found the Lincoln Logs—for her office. It was a cozy little room with good light from its south- and west-facing windows and, like the master bedroom adjacent to it, with a commanding view of Summit Avenue. Like most people who work with their brains, Carole's work was often lonely, and the occasional interruption of human activity on the shaded street below kept her company.

Dressed in a sweat suit, her uncombed hair curling haphazardly around her face like pale brown confetti, she sat sipping tea and munching on an English muffin, composing a letter. It was the type of letter lawyers refer to as a "nastigram," whereupon the attorney advises the recipient of the letter of their legal obligations to her client and the dire consequences of disregarding this obligation. In this case the client was Stella Phillips, and the recipient was her next-door neighbor, the object of Stella's ongoing easement dispute. She pecked away at the keyboard, spelling out the potential dire consequences of his transgression, which included arrest, civil prosecution for property damage, and having both of his legs broken. "You, sir," she typed, "are one of the reasons that there are so many lawyers employed in society—smart, hard-working men and women like myself who could otherwise be making a positive contribution to humankind: educating...healing the sick...laying asphalt." She was on a roll. "You, sir," she continued, "are living proof that the good die young. You should be kicked squarely on your septuagenarian keister, put in stocks for public ridicule and tickled unmercifully."

Carole took a sip of tea and read what she had written. Someday, she thought, nearer to the end of her career, she'd actually send a letter like that. Highlighting the paragraph, she deleted it, ended the letter with a stern warning and a polite "Yours sincerely," and printed it out.

After dropping the letter into the mailbox, Carole returned to the house for a long, hot shower. Emerging from the steamy bathroom and wrapped in

Carlos's old terrycloth bathrobe, she stood in the hallway, rubbing her hair dry with a towel and admiring the gleaming new wallpaper adorning the walls of the long hallway. She loved the way it opened the hallway up and made all of the rooms seem bigger. As she rubbed, her eyes traveled down one side of the hallway and back up the other, to where the new wallpaper ended. About fifteen feet of hallway remained to be papered, the bare stretch of stained and patched plaster ugly in its emptiness. Carlos will finish up on Monday, she thought as she headed for the bedroom.

Because she was fresh and energetic and feeling good, as she dressed she allowed herself to consider a heresy of sorts. Why wait for Carlos to do it, she thought as she pulled on an old pair of faded blue jeans. I can paper that hallway. I can finish it myself and surprise him. Show him that I'm more than just the dummy on the other end of the string. Carlos had carefully shown her how to do it, and she'd listened, as earnestly attentive as a first year law student. So instead of putting on the pink cotton sweater she'd lain out, she donned Carlos's favorite bowling shirt and went to work.

Her thinking was both right and wrong. She was right in believing that she could do it. It wasn't that hard. She would cut the paper to match the pattern, leaving an excess on the top and bottom, then apply the paste thinly and evenly, the way Carlos had shown her, then, holding the paper up and in front of her, smooth it into place, then trim the ends with an exacto knife.

As it turned out, she was right that she could do it, but was wrong about how long it would take. She thought it would take her a couple of hours, leaving her time in the afternoon to go downtown and buy Carlos a home-coming present. Instead, lunch was long-missed and the sun was low in the western sky when Carole finally approached the end of her job. As her eyes scanned the length of the wall, comparing her work to Carlos's, she rubbed her aching arms. "Okay," she said aloud, "that looks pretty darn good. I hope you're satisfied with this paper. It's the closest to the original I could find."

Then she caught herself and realized that, intent as she was on her work, she'd been talking to the house for the past couple of hours, telling it how pretty it looked and the plans she and Carlos had for remodeling the kitchen and painting the outside and rejuvenating the flower gardens. "Ahh!" she yelled. "I'm talking to a house. Why am I talking to you?" she asked. "It's that crazy Puerto Rican. It's rubbing off!"

She quickly finished laying the last column of wallpaper and cleaned up the mess she'd made. Then, pulling on a stray bottle of Sierra Nevada Pale Ale she'd found in the back of the refrigerator, she headed for the telephone in the study. Plopping down into the big leather chair, she picked up the phone and quickly dialed the New York City number. She was ready for some human conversation.

Her reward came around 11:45 that night. She'd lain in bed reading from the Tolkien trilogy until her eyes wouldn't stay open, then switched off the reading lamp and, her head cradled in Carlos's pillow, fallen almost immediately into a sound sleep. Soon she began to dream, a funny little dream that had her back in law school wandering the corridors of Mayer Hall, looking for Carlos. Softly at first, she would hear a distinct wooden "thump," as if a loose shutter was somewhere banging against a window frame. As she searched for Carlos, the thumping became louder and more frequent, so that in her dream she would stop and look around for the source of the noise. And when she realized that the noise was not part of her dream, she woke up.

Warm under two of Sophie's quilts, Carole lay still for several minutes, listening to the soft banging sound coming every few seconds from somewhere in the house. When she was convinced that she wouldn't go back to sleep until she found the source of the noise, she flipped on the reading lamp and reluctantly crawled out of bed, donned slippers and robe, and headed out into the darkened hallway.

At first she wasn't afraid, just disgruntled at having been rudely woken out of a perfectly good sleep and, maybe, a bit on-guard. She could tell that the source of the sound was not downstairs, but was rather somewhere in front of her. Switching on the hall light, she walked slowly down the hallway, past the new wallpaper, listening intently. When she was halfway down the hall, she realized that the sound was coming from above, from the attic. Thump...thump, thump came the persistent sound.

Shoot, she thought. It was the one place in the house where she didn't want to go alone in the middle of the night. She stood at the attic door, holding herself, debating her options. She could go back to bed and hope that the sound would go away, or maybe go downstairs and sleep as best she could on the davenport in the parlor. The problem was that the first option was unlikely, and the second would involve admitting that she was afraid to go up there. And this she was doggedly determined not to do. And so, after several moments of indecision, she set her jaw and opened the attic door.

With the attic door open, the thumping was immediately louder, and the sound sent the small hairs on the back of her neck rising. Reminding herself that she didn't believe in ghosts, she forced herself forward and upward, out of the protective light of the hallway and into the looming darkness of the attic. As she climbed the steep stairway, she could smell the old rough-cut wood and dust surrounding her.

Clearing the stairway, soft moonlight shining in through open windows illuminated the shadows of the interior, so that Carole easily found the light switch. And with the light safely on, the hairs on the back of Carole's neck settled back down.

124

Looking quickly around, Carole soon spotted the source of the thumping. Powered apparently by a breeze coming through the open windows, the bottom door of Ellen Winkler's desk was banging against a wooden chair. Yes, Carole thought happily, relaxing. This was the sense of it. Carlos had opened the windows to air out the attic, and the night wind was blowing the open door erratically against the chair. Yes, she told herself. She could feel the breeze on her back as she stood there.

She bent over the desk and gently closed the open cupboard door, which firmly snapped into place. Then she walked to the west windows and pulled them shut. There, she thought, well-pleased, as she smacked dust from her hands, assessing the now-still attic. A natural solution to a natural problem. She felt proud of herself, having overcome an irrational fear, all by herself in the middle of the night. As she reached for the light switch, though, she heard it again: thump. And as she turned, surprised and unnerved, to the sight of the open door again banging against the chair, she remembered that the desk's door had been locked tight, that Carlos had tried unsuccessfully to open it.

And that was when Carole came unglued. Her stomach rolled and her knees went weak, and as she slipped to her knees she let out a soft, guttural moan, very much like the sound she imagined a ghost would make. Her heart racing, she stared wide-eyed at the cupboard door, her lips moving soundlessly, as though they were trying to form words. In the midnight chill of the attic, Carole knelt like a supplicant before the cupboard door, which had ceased its thumping and now stood wide open and still. She looked wildly around into the shadows of the attic, her eyes like saucers. But after a few moments, when doom failed to materialize, she slowly began to pull herself together, and when her heartbeat had returned to some semblance of normal, she confronted the desk.

"Don't hurt me, okay?" she asked. "Hey, I'm family, right?"

Then she caught herself, and groaned. "Oh, jees," she said softly. "I'm talking to a piece of furniture." She wearily blew a stray wisp of hair away from her face, then stared at the cupboard door for a few moments longer, summoning her courage.

"Okay," she said finally, as if she were a card player calling a bluff, "so what's in there? You got something bad in there to show me? Something good?"

With her jaw set, she scooted herself the few feet to the open cupboard door and began, carefully and tentatively, to search through its crowded contents. She found a dozen or so letters, old and yellowed, tied together with string. They were from Miss Ellen Winkler, addressed to a Mr. Thomas Hastings, care of a missionary station in the Belgian Congo. The letters were unopened, and had been returned as undeliverable. She found a garland of dried flowers that might have been worn by a woman in her hair, as Carole had done at her wedding. The delicate petals were bone dry and paper thin and fell apart in Carole's hand.

She found a cigar box containing a pipe and matches, a small pen knife, and a brightly covered tin resembling a snuff container. For several moments she examined the pipe with its delicately carved pattern of Chinese characters, then replaced it in the box and set it aside.

Finally, in the very back of the cupboard, she found an old diary, its black leather cover cracking, its lined pages yellowed. Gently opening its cover, she found that it was Ellen's diary, for the year 1932. For the next hour Carole sat on the rough wood floor of the attic, reading from Ellen's diary by the dim light of the bare electric bulb above her. She was as careful with the old book as she would have been with a new-born baby, holding the book lightly and turning the fragile pages gently and carefully. At first the entries were long, often stretching to several paragraphs. But toward the end the entries were incoherent and incomplete, and the strong handwriting Ellen had exhibited earlier disintegrated into an erratic, wavering, and often indecipherable scrawl.

The entries for January of 1933 were entered on scraps of paper, which Carole found folded behind the last page of the book. As best Carole could make out, these were the last four entries:

January 2
I saw the lights again. Could it be?

January 7
The anguish! Oh, that I could start anew.

January
Thomas, my beautiful Thomas.

January
I know now what the lights mean.
I've found my windows to heaven.
Thank God, for my trial has become

Around two o'clock in the morning Carole closed the book, carefully replaced all of the items into the cupboard and gently closed the door. Then she slowly rose, flipped off the attic light, and started down the attic steps.

When her chest was even with the attic floor, she stopped, turned her head, and took a last look around into the shadows of the darkened room.

"Thank you," she said softly, to no one in particular.

Epistle

When I was a young woman attending the university, I took, as part of my major, a course in Romantic poetry. It was tough going, wading through the long and elegant pages of Coleridge and Blake and Wordsworth. But every once in a while a line would hit me that made me sit up and pay good attention, and made me wonder. One of these that I remember, and have thought about often the last few years, is from a poem by Wordsworth:

"Bliss was it in that dawn to be alive,
But to be young was very Heaven!"

At the time I was just newly married, and heaven was the way I would have characterized the state of my own life. But what did "young" have to do with it? It hadn't occurred to me that the young might be happier than the old.

One day I was over at the Winkler house helping Henry with his gardening. We were on our knees in the front yard pulling weeds when I decided to ask him what he thought of the passage. Henry, who thought about everything, it seemed, was often clever at deciphering meanings. When I'd quoted the lines to him, he nodded quickly and turned back to his work.

"It means what it says," he said matter-of-factly. "Everything's better when you're young."

"Why?" I asked.

"Well, first of all," he said, "you have to be old, or at least older, to know one way or the other, right?"

"That's true," I admitted.

"And when you're old, you know it," he continued. "But you'll have to take my word for it for about thirty more years."

"So what will be different then?" I asked.

"Your body, for one thing," he said. "Look at the differences between you and me. You're young and strong. I'm middle-aged and tired."

"You're not tired," I said.

"Oh, yes I am," he said, turning to me and arching an eyebrow. "And my body complains. Your body doesn't complain."

"But you're happy, aren't you?" I asked hopefully. I'd always assumed he was, because he was so accepting.

For a long moment he was silent, as though, possibly, he knew something he didn't want to share, or knew something he couldn't find the words to say. "I'm content," he said finally. "And sometimes more than content. Like right now, because I know your world is filled with joy."

I leaned to him and kissed him on the forehead, and held his head to my cheek for a moment. Then we went back to work in the garden. Some moments later he stopped and again turned to me.

"And even if I was as happy as you, there'd still be another difference," he said. "You young people, you think it's going to last forever."

He was right. I did. For a long time. And that, maybe, is the difference between bliss and heaven.

Chapter Nine

On early weekday mornings, when the alarm would jar them from sleep, Clara and Henry would take turns leaving the warmth and comfort of the bed to quickly brew up a pot of coffee, the half-asleep reluctant volunteer returning to the bed some minutes later with two steaming mugs. They would prop their pillows against the headboard and sit in the semi-darkness, their bodies touching and their covers pulled high around their chests, sipping their coffee and allowing wakefulness to slowly and gently triumph over sleep. Then they would rise, bathe and dress, and share a quick breakfast before leaving for work.

Clara continued to work for her parents, who paid her a dollar a day for keeping the shelves of their small store stocked and the books balanced. And so, on workday mornings, the two would leave their small apartment and walk south two blocks together before splitting in opposite directions: Clara west to the old neighborhood and Henry east to the downtown area, a stone's throw from the old Winkler sausage factory, where James Owens Sr. had his bustling print shop. Almost always, after their paths had split, they would stop and wave and blow kisses to each other, and often, when Henry had finally turned his back to her, Clara would stand watching him as he made his way down the wide sidewalk, the cap on his head bobbing with each step and his metal lunch box glinting in the morning sun. She would notice how his pace quickened once they separated, making sure that he would be early to work.

While Mr. Owens hadn't known it at the time, he couldn't have picked a more able and energetic apprentice than Henry Winkler. The work, requiring both patience and gentle precision, was an ideal match for Henry, who had his mother's agile hands and sharp eye for detail, and his father's inclination towards perfection. Most important, though, Henry very quickly found in the work a transfixing beauty that focused both his energy and creativity, and that brought him unexpected joy. And so, as Henry quickly passed from apprentice to journeyman, Mr. Owens knew that in Henry Winkler he had more than just a craftsman; he had an artist.

It took longer than anyone thought for the inevitable to happen, and it wasn't until early spring of 1922 that Clara found herself to be pregnant. After visiting Doc Smith one late afternoon, who confirmed what she had suspected for several weeks, she skipped the half mile back to their apartment to share the news with Henry.

She entered the apartment to find Henry exactly where she knew he would be, sitting at their small dinner table, his shoes off and his feet propped on a chair, puffing contentedly on his pipe, reading the newspaper, and drinking the single bottle of bootleg beer he allowed himself every day after work.

"Hi," he said, looking up to her as she entered. "How's Doc Smith?"

"Fine," she said, unbuttoning her coat. "His hands are starting to shake," she added, referring to the mild case of Parkinsonism that had recently begun to show itself.

"So what's he think?" Henry asked, bending forward to tap ash from his pipe into the soup can he used for an ashtray.

Clara dropped her coat onto a chair and walked to the dinner table. "He thinks I'm pregnant," Clara said matter-of-factly, focusing on Henry's eyes for a reaction. They were soft, and to her surprise, playful.

"Well, hell," Henry responded, his mouth flirting with a grin, "I could've told you that."

Now she smiled, and reached out to take his hands. "And why would that be?" she asked, her eyes twinkling.

"Well," he answered, "it's the only explanation why someone with such pink cheeks could be throwing up every morning."

"Are you happy about it?" she asked.

Henry stood and wrapped his arms around her, and kissed the top of her head. "I'm as happy as a man can be," he said into her ear. They stood like that, in each other's arms, for a long time.

It was spring, and the days that followed unfolded warm with sun and fresh in the morning from light evening rains. Henry, now a journeyman, was making good money, so that in addition to planning for the birth of their baby, they took the opportunity to move to a bigger apartment. They found what they were looking for a few blocks to the north, on a lovely tree-lined avenue that had been on the route Henry had driven so many years earlier as he chauffeured Clara on her Saturday grocery deliveries. It was just what they needed: two bedrooms on the ground floor with a large kitchen and a cheery, front-facing parlor that looked out onto a green lawn and a long line of neatly ordered rose bushes.

As spring passed into summer, Henry took pleasure in watching the slow, almost imperceptible changes in his wife. Like a flower slowly opening, Clara's stomach and breasts began to grow, her face became more round, and her hair, Henry thought, shone with a new luster.

Clara and Henry had gotten into the habit of taking long walks on the weekend. They would be gone most of the day, walking leisurely along the shaded lanes and meandering through the several small parks dotting the city with their green squares. Sometimes they would work their way through the cobbled streets of the downtown, window shopping. And just as Wilhelm and Sophie had done thirty years earlier, they would talk of the day when they could afford a house of their own. Never, though, did they speak of the house on Summit Avenue, or of the bargain Henry had forced on his sister. Instead, when they talked of their home it was always in the abstract, the style undecided, the location vague, the floor plan malleable and ephemeral.

As summer drew to a close and Clara's middle continued to grow, the weekend walks became shorter and shorter, until it was all Clara could do to slowly and awkwardly negotiate the sidewalk and six concrete steps leading from the front door of the apartment house to the street. So rather than forfeiting the pleasure of their weekend outdoor excursions, Henry went down to Irwin Meyer's Buick dealership and got a good deal on a 1914 Ford Model-T. Irwin's father, retiring early, had sold the dealership to his son a year earlier. The car, Irwin said, had been won in a poker game, and sold to Irwin for quick cash. Irwin, good friend that he was, sold the car to Henry for substantially less than he paid for it, and threw in a full tank of gas and two spare tires.

After that, as August faded into September and the oppressive heat of the summer began to break, Sunday afternoons would find Henry gently guiding the pyriform Clara down the walkway from their apartment building and into the passenger seat of the Model-T. Then they would head off for an afternoon of exploring, the Model-T clackety-clacking down the narrow country roads like a noisy sewing machine.

On a cool and breezy Sunday afternoon in mid-September, they decided to travel north, to follow the river into rolling farmland. Turning onto Centennial Drive, they made their way slowly up the long grade. As they reached the top, Clara's eyes stole up to Henry's to see if he would hazard a look down the length of Summit Avenue. When his eyes never veered from the road in front of him, Clara's gaze fell to her swollen stomach.

"Any more thoughts on a name?" she asked, smiling over to him.

Henry looked over to her. "Nope," he said honestly. "I haven't."

Clara watched him drive for a moment. "If it's a boy," she said seriously, "how about Henry?"

Henry thought for a moment. "Nah," he said dismissively. "He needs his own name. If it's a boy and he ends up liking me all right, he can name his own son after me."

And that was when Clara knew that if it was a boy, it would be named William.

As consumed as they were with the unborn child growing inside Clara's middle, Henry and Clara barely noticed as late summer slipped quietly away. Soon, the face of autumn was full upon them: the days shortened and wet with rain, the leaves quickly gone from the trees. Before he knew it, Henry

132

was shoveling coal into the big boiler in the basement to heat the building against the then unrelenting cold. And before he knew it, it was Thanksgiving, and their child's birth, estimated by Doc Smith to be in mid-December, was only a handful of days away.

Three days later, on a Friday afternoon, Clara's water broke. Clara's call came to Henry at work, just as he was finishing the type setting for a store advertisement. He called Minnie, Clara's mother, and told her to meet them at the hospital. Ten minutes later Henry was home, and he was helping Clara into the front seat of the Model-T. And ten minutes after that, at the hospital, he and Minnie stood watching as a nurse led Clara through a set of swinging double doors. The doors had small porthole windows in them, and Henry stood peering through one of them until Clara was out of sight down an inner hallway.

"What do we do now?" he asked, turning to Minnie.

"We wait," Minnie replied, moving to a row of padded chairs lining a wall of the waiting room and plopping down in the chair nearest the window. "So relax and sit down."

Henry tried sitting, but after a few minutes found himself up and pacing, moving every so often to the porthole windows to peer in. Mostly he saw empty hallway, but occasionally a nurse or orderly would move in and out of the hallway from one room to another, and after several minutes Henry saw Doc Smith entering one of the delivery rooms. Henry and Minnie were the only people in the big room, and the only sound to be heard was the click of the wall clock as the minute hand jerked clockwise from minute to minute.

Though it seemed like an eternity to Henry, the birthing came quite fast, and after something just short of three hours, Henry watched through the porthole as Doc Smith left the delivery room and moved down the hallway toward him. He seemed to Henry to be grim and preoccupied, and his white smock was red with blood.

"He's coming," Henry said to Minnie, who put down her magazine and rose to join him.

For the first time Henry considered the possibility that something might be wrong, and as Doc Smith pushed through the swinging doors, his stomach tightened.

"You have a baby boy," the doctor said to Henry. "Healthy and perfect." The news made him smile. "And Clara?" Henry asked hopefully.

For just a moment Doc Smith hesitated, then forced his hard eyes on Henry's face. "Clara's bleeding," he said.

The smile deserted Henry's face, and he looked first to Minnie, then back to the doctor. "That's expected, isn't it?" he asked.

"Yes," Doc Smith replied. "And it's expected that it'll stop. Clara's not stopping."

In that moment the world turned on Henry, and his happy optimism abandoned him. He was small and vulnerable and impotent, and as he confronted the doctor, his mouth opened into a hint of a smile, a fool's smile.

"But she'll be all right," he pleaded.

"I hope so, Henry," Doc Smith replied. "We'll be doing all we can."

And with that the doctor turned and left them, disappearing back inside the forbidden hallway behind the double doors. Henry and Minnie helped each other back to the row of seats. For a moment they sat in silence, Henry staring at the double doors, Minnie resting her head in her hand.

"She's going to be okay, isn't she?" Henry asked finally.

Minnie raised her head from her hand and opened her eyes. Her face was tired and pinched, her lips closed and small. "I don't know," she answered.

Then they broke, the two of them, and sat holding each other. For an hour they sat there waiting, until once again Doc Smith emerged from behind the swinging doors. Henry watched anxiously as he walked to them, intent on his face, hoping to decode something of what he was about to tell them. When he reached them, he held out a hand for each of them to take. "I think she's going to be all right," he said, his eyes soft.

They didn't let Henry see her until the next morning when, as he had been advised, precisely at seven o'clock, a nurse escorted him down the hallway of the maternity ward to Clara's room. He found her sitting up in bed, bone-pale but cheerful, holding the day-old baby as he suckled at her breast. He stood for a moment in the doorway watching her, for the hundredth time in the last twelve hours thanking a God he had no longer thought he believed in. Then he moved to her and kissed her, and took his son William into his arms.

Later that day Doc Smith joined them, and after examining Clara and the baby, sat with them for a long while, talking about bleeding disorders and the grave danger Clara had been in. And after they'd talked it all through, Clara and Henry made their decision: William, who would be called Will by everyone, would be their only child.

In an ongoing effort at self-improvement, Etta Mae Blumberg, a.k.a. Deborah Christianson, read the morning newspaper from cover to cover, building slowly but surely on the rudimentary reading skills she had obtained by way of the New York City public school system. After breakfast, and after instructing the three live-in girls on their morning activities, she would retire to her bedroom with the newspaper and a pot of freshly brewed coffee, where she would sit in the good light of the big front bay window, reading and smoking cigarettes, and occasionally consulting a dictionary. It was in this way, as she perused the weekly birth notices, that she discovered that Ellen's brother and his wife had had a child.

"Well, I'll be damned," she muttered to herself.

Stubbing out her cigarette, she carried the newspaper down the long upstairs hallway, then through the attic door and up the narrow, rough-wood steps to the attic. As she thought she would, she found Ellen sitting at her desk, writing.

"Guess what, ma'am," Etta Mae said as her feet reached the attic floor.

"Not now, Deborah," Ellen said, not looking up. "I'm very busy."

"Oh, you'll want to hear about this, ma'am," Etta Mae persisted.

Ellen reluctantly looked up from her writing. "What, then?" she snapped.

"You're an aunt, ma'am," Etta Mae said, moving a loose chair next to Ellen and sitting.

"What?" Ellen asked.

"You're an aunt," Etta Mae repeated. "Your brother and his wife just had a baby. Sticking the folded newspaper in front of Ellen's face, she pointed out the entry. "It's a boy, and they've named him William. See?"

Ellen stared blankly at the newsprint.

"Aren't you happy for them, ma'am?" Etta Mae asked with just a hint of reproach. She was toying with the woman, knowing full well that Ellen would instinctively resent any small grain of success or happiness visited upon her brother and his wife.

"I suppose I should be," Ellen finally responded. "But I do fear for the child, you know."

"Of course you do, ma'am," Etta Mae offered soothingly.

Ellen, still young by most standards, was beginning to show signs of premature aging. Crows' feet had begun to furrow out from the corners of her eyes and mouth, and the skin on her face and hands was beginning to noticeably lose its tone. Her straw blonde hair, once thick and wavy, was now streaked with gray, and hung limp and dull around her shoulders. At 36, Ellen looked like a well-preserved 60. Remarkably, though, her body remained essentially the same. Most likely due to the opium, which dramatically reduced her appetite, Ellen could still wear the dresses her mother had made for her when she was a teenager.

Etta Mae noticed that she was wearing one of the old dresses. It was Alice blue and buttoned up the front all the way to the neck. A cameo brooch was pinned to the dress above the heart. It was a summer dress, Etta Mae

135

noted, way too light this time of year for any place other than this dusty, overheated attic.

Ellen had turned back to her writing, and Etta Mae watched her for a moment, admiring the effort. Ellen wrote slowly and clumsily, mouthing the words as she labored to connect them to the written page. The result, Etta Mae knew, would be as bad as always. Facile, she thought, contentedly remembering the wonderful new word she had recently learned. But, my, she thought, what dogged determination the woman had.

"That's a pretty dress you have on," Etta Mae said.

Ellen once again looked up from her work. "Thank you," she said, smiling.

It was a pretty smile, Etta Mae thought. The kind of smile that would be common if the woman had been normal. With a laugh to go with it. But then neither of them were normal, she thought.

"My mother made it for me when I was a young girl," Ellen offered. "It was to be my wedding dress."

"You don't say, ma'am," Etta Mae offered encouragingly. She'd heard this story several times before.

"Yes, indeed," Ellen said. "I was engaged to be married in the summer of 1906. My fiancé was from Cleveland."

"Is that so, ma'am?" Etta Mae responded.

"Yes," Ellen nodded. She lingered for a moment, her lips pursed, dreamily half-smiling in her memories. "His name was Thomas," she said finally. "He was very handsome. Yes, tall and handsome." Then the half-smile faded. "He's gone missing, you know," she said sadly.

"Gone missing, ma'am?" Etta Mae asked.

"Yes," Ellen answered, her lips beginning to tremble. "In Africa."

As Ellen began to cry, her hands lay still in her lap.

"I'm so sorry, ma'am," Etta Mae said softly, covering Ellen's small white hands with one of her own. "You bear such terrible burdens," she said. "No wonder you have the headaches."

"I'll bring you your lunch in an hour or so," she said, her voice subdued. "Then we'll have your afternoon therapy."

Ellen, wiping her eyes, nodded to the wall.

Etta Mae made her way down the steep attic steps and returned to her bedroom. She was as happy in the Winkler house as she had ever been. She'd winnowed down the house's other boarders to two young women with ambitions more in line with her own.

In addition to the daily comforts of life in the splendid Winkler home, Etta Mae was finding that life in a small Midwestern city, as opposed to New York City, offered its own pleasures. Against her own expectations, the

136

slowed pace of her life, and the general peace and quiet of Summit Avenue, were surprisingly enjoyable. In the spring and fall months, and in the early mornings during summer, she would take long walks along the elm-lined streets of the neighborhood. She became an avid bird watcher, and would often take a picnic lunch to one of the city parks where she would stroll for hours, bird manual in one hand and binoculars in the other, her eyes looking up expectantly into the tangle of tree branches above.

Temperance had proven to be highly lucrative for Etta Mae. In the early days of her association with Ellen and the other temperance workers operating out of the old St. Paul's Lutheran Church, Etta Mae had been astonished by how easy it was to get strangers to give you their money. All that was needed was the right pitch, in this case, "for God and Home and every land," and the right look, in this case, piety.

Still, skimming the cream off the modest pot of donations made to the St. Paul's group translated into pretty small potatoes for Etta Mae, so as soon as Ellen was safely on her way toward opium addiction, Etta Mae had, with Ellen indisposed in the attic most of the day, free reign over the household, and had begun her own Temperance enterprise. Summoning her proven entrepreneurial skills and calling herself the president of the Frances E. Willard Society, Etta Mae and her two housemates began a fundraising campaign of monumental proportions. Soliciting funds through the mail, Etta Mae's flyers would always begin with a concocted story of some woman whose life had been savaged by alcohol: a ruined father, an abusive husband, children forced into prostitution. The ad would then ask for donations to help the multitude of victims get back on their feet, followed by a long list of fabricated names of endorsers, most with "Dr." or "Rev." before their names. In contrast to most mendicant organizations, Etta Mae's strategy was to never ask the same person for money more than once. Her reasoning was that familiarity would breed interest, and she didn't want anyone to get too interested in the Frances E. Willard Society...as in wanting to join, or worse yet, getting suspicious. "Remember girls," she would tell her two young charges, "one bite of the apple and all they get is the sweet taste. Two bites and they might find the worm."

Before long, the money was rolling in nicely, and after a year Etta Mae had to rent a larger post office box to handle the increased volume. It was hard work, having to cast her net, as it were, in ever different directions, but Etta Mae thoroughly enjoyed both the challenges and the rewards. Like most good capitalists of the day, Etta Mae had become enamored with the stock market, and studied it on a day-to-day basis. When she'd convinced herself that she understood the fundamentals of the market and could reasonably distinguish potential winners from losers, she began to invest her sizable profits. Sometimes, sitting in Wilhelm's overstuffed easy chair and sipping from a glass of bootleg Canadian whiskey, she would almost have to pinch herself. Making money had never been so safe and so enjoyable, and all from the comfort of a lovely Victorian home on a quiet street in the middle of nowhere.

She was, in fact, counting those very blessings as she carried Ellen's lunch tray up the narrow attic stairs. The tray contained a bowl of steaming potato soup left over from the last night's dinner, along with two liberally buttered pieces of the coarse white bread Etta Mae preferred. The soup bowl clattered lightly against the plate as Etta Mae maneuvered the staircase. As she gained the attic floor, she found Ellen sitting at her desk staring at the wall in front of her, as if she was searching for some meaning from the grain of the rough wood paneling enclosing the attic eave around her.

"Ma'am?" Etta Mae asked softly as she approached with the tray. "Ma'am?"

As Etta Mae set the tray down in front of her, Ellen's trance was broken. She looked first down to the tray of food in front of her, then up to the coarse features of her good friend and confidante.

"The soup's delicious, ma'am," Etta Mae offered. Which was true. Sally, the younger of Etta Mae's housemates, was an excellent cook.

Ellen's eyes traveled back down to the tray in front of her, then once again back to Etta Mae. "It looks very good," she said.

"Try a bite, ma'am," Etta Mae said encouragingly.

Ellen hesitated for a moment, as if summoning the energy to lift the spoon. "In a moment, Deborah," she said finally. "I'd like to finish the letter first."

In front of Ellen lay a partially composed letter, with Ellen's spidery handwriting filling two-thirds of the page. Etta Mae could clearly see to whom the letter was addressed. "And who are you writing to?" she asked.

"My fiancé," Ellen answered. "Surely he's been found by now, and will want to hear from me." She looked up to Etta Mae hopefully, her mouth slightly open, the edges of her pink lips turned almost imperceptibly upward. Then the mouth closed and the lips grew small and began to quiver. "Don't you agree?" she pleaded.

Etta Mae saw that the woman's eyes were pooling with tears. "Of course I do," she said gently, smoothing Ellen's hair with her short, thick fingers. "Now don't cry, ma'am," she continued softly. "One day our prayers will be answered, and all of your devotion and sacrifice will be rewarded." Not bad, she thought to herself, happy with her spontaneous choice of nouns.

Ellen took Etta Mae's hand from its resting place on her neck and gently kissed it. "You're so good to me, Deborah," she said in a whisper. "You've given me so much.

"Now finish your letter there, and I'll have it in the afternoon post. Then eat your lunch," she said encouragingly, "and we'll have your afternoon therapy."

As she descended the attic stairway some minutes later, Ellen's letter in hand, Etta Mae could hear Ellen's soup spoon clinking against its bowl. Good, she thought. The woman needs to keep up her energy. It wouldn't do for her to become malnourished.

Returning to her bedroom, she plopped herself down in her easy chair, kicked off her slippers, lit a Chesterfield, then tore open Ellen's letter and read through it quickly. The same drivel, she told herself disdainfully. "I love you I miss you I'm waiting for you I'm saving myself for you." Blah blah blah. She drew heavily on her cigarette, blowing out the smoke slowly and luxuriantly.

Etta Mae was, by that time, thoroughly versed in the Thomas Hastings matter. Early on, while Ellen dozed blissfully in an opium haze, Etta Mae had found and read the stack of returned letters dating back to 1906. The letters themselves were generally uninteresting, canned reruns of the "I love you I miss you I'm waiting for you" theme. But a number of vague references to Hastings himself, and to the nature of his relationship with the Winkler woman, had piqued her curiosity. What did she mean by "the blessing we shared"? Etta Mae wondered. And what was Hastings's "duty" that took him away? And where had he come from?

Etta Mae knew instinctively that Ellen was in some fundamental and critical way deceiving herself regarding Mr. Thomas Hastings. And deception, especially self-deception, intrigued her. And so she had resolved to get to the truth of the matter. She began her inquiries at the logical place, which was St. Paul's Lutheran Church, where for three years she and Ellen had faithfully gone every week to Sunday morning services. Lately, though, Ellen hadn't had the energy to go, so Etta Mae had been going alone. At first, none of the longtime members of the church had any memory of the boy named Thomas Hastings. Finally, though, in a conversation over punch and cookies with the Klatt widow, her luck changed.

"And how is Ellen doing, Deborah?" Mrs. Klatt asked.

Etta Mae shook her head sadly. "She tries so hard, but she's so frail. I keep trying to get her to see the doctor…" Etta Mae let the sentence trail off as the two women nodded their heads sadly.

Etta Mae paused for a moment to allow Mrs. Klatt to nibble on the edge of a cookie. "Ellen spoke to me recently of a man named Thomas Hastings. Was he a member of the church?" she asked innocently.

Mrs. Klatt thought for a moment, trying vainly to place the name. "I don't seem to recall..." she began to answer. Then she began to remember. "Oh," she said. "Wait a minute now."

After working for several moments to kick the cobwebs out of her brain, Mrs. Klatt could vaguely recall the young missionary boy that the church had agreed to sponsor years earlier. She remembered that he had been from Cleveland and had spent a couple of weeks at the church before leaving for New York City and Africa. She remembered that he had been very handsome, and that for some reason he had never arrived in Africa. The church had had to find another missionary to sponsor.

A call to the Lutheran churches in Cleveland was all it took to continue the story. On the fourth call she found the connection, and soon the mystery of Thomas Hastings was unveiled. Thomas Hastings had been the second son of Rev. George Hastings, now deceased. He had been a fractious and worrisome boy, in and out of mostly minor trouble with the law, and had agreed to a missionary assignment as an alternative to the county jail. On the eve of his departure for Africa he had cashed in his boat ticket and disappeared. Six months later he was sent home to Cleveland in a box. The funeral had been closed casket, the rumor being, someone remembered, that he was missing the back of his head.

After finishing Ellen's latest letter, Etta Mae sat quietly, languidly drawing on her cigarette and thinking about what a bad boy Thomas Hastings must have been. Stubbing out her cigarette and rising slowly from the depth of her easy chair, Etta Mae moved to Sophie's walnut vanity. From a side drawer she extracted her opium kit. She would prepare three doses for Ellen's afternoon therapy. If Ellen wanted more, as she had the day before, Etta Mae would tell her she was almost out. Ellen's habit, even at the heavily discounted prices Etta Mae paid, was getting expensive.

Henry Winkler awoke when the early sun had risen far enough to overtake the sill of the open bedroom window and dispatch a thin ray of bright sunlight over the floor, onto the bed, and right into his eyes. It was almost eight o'clock on an already warm August Sunday morning.

Henry rolled onto his back and stretched under the light linen sheet, then crawled out of bed and, scratching his head absentmindedly, went looking for Clara and the baby. He found them where he knew they would be, on the davenport in their tiny parlor, and both asleep. The boy, now nine months old, lay on his back at one end of the davenport, loosely wrapped in a   blanket and propped on all sides by pillows. Clara lay at the other end of the davenport, her head on the armrest and her feet curled underneath her, her long auburn hair falling loosely around her shoulders and onto the gentle rising and falling of her chest.

Henry took a few minutes to brew a pot of coffee, then sat quietly opposite the two, sipping his coffee and watching them sleep. After a few minutes, Clara's eyelids fluttered, then opened, and her hand moved to her face and scratched her nose. "Hello," she said to Henry after a moment.

They sat together on the couch for half an hour, talking softly, laughing now and then, their hands gently touching. When Will finally stirred and began to complain, they reluctantly rose from their languid comfort to begin the day.

As they did every Sunday morning, they would bathe and dress, then drive across town to attend church with Minnie and Fred Klein. While Clara's faith was for her own reasons strong and unwavering, Henry's was, given the simple and undeniable reality of his war experience, shaky at best. Where was God at the Somme? he would ask himself. Where was God at the Ardennes Forest? Still, the tone of the services at the small church they attended was one of Christian love and charity, so that Henry never begrudged a moment he spent there. After church the tradition was to gather with Clara's parents for dinner, often, in honor of Henry's father, consisting of sausages and bootleg beer.

As they consumed their sausage and sauerkraut, the conversation around the dinner table was small and happy, the four of them simply pleased to hear the sound of each other's voices. There was, though, something important Henry needed to share, and he waited until the apple pie was served to bring it up.

"Mr. Owens told me Friday that he's going to sell his business," he said offhandedly, pushing his fork through a triangle of pie.

This new piece of information, as Henry knew it would, stopped everyone's fork in mid-movement. Mr. Owens was Henry's employer, and Henry was Mr. Owens's only employee.

"What?" Clara asked impatiently. "Why didn't you tell me this earlier?"

Henry, his mouth full of pie, could only raise his hands in equivocation.

"When, Henry?" Minnie asked.

"And why?" Fred piped in. "He's too young to retire."

Henry finally got down the piece of pie. "He doesn't want to retire, but he needs to move," he said. "It's Mrs. Owens. She's got arthritis, and the docs tell her a drier climate would do her good. So they're off to Arizona."

"Where's Arizona?" Fred asked.

141

"Next to California," Henry answered. "Hot and dry."

"So what will you do, Henry?" Minnie asked.

As Henry lifted another piece of pie to his mouth, his eyes moved to Clara, who stared intently back, her small, sly smile exposing a glimpse of white tooth.

"Let me guess. We're going to buy it," she said.

And buy it they did. It took all of their small savings and a hefty loan from the bank, but by mid-November, Mr. Owens and his wife were on their way to a city named Phoenix, and Henry and Clara were established in the small apartment above the print shop. It had been the Owens' first home thirty years earlier, and for the last twenty years had been used for storage. Now the cycle was beginning again.

Henry had by that time mastered all of the arts and crafts of his trade, and the business prospered. While Henry printed, Clara, with Will on her hip, managed. She handled all of the paperwork: the billing, the advertising, the taxes. They were working like dogs, and were as happy as they'd ever been. They'd make love when the work was done and the baby was asleep, and sometimes when the work wasn't done. Christmas came, and then another, and then another. In the quotidian joy of health and success and the closeness of each other, time and care had no meaning.

The magic would last one more year, through the spring and summer of 1926 and on into the autumn, when Clara once again found herself walking home from Doc Smith's office with news. She'd planned to walk first to her parents' grocery where she'd dropped off Will, but chose instead to go directly home. The November morning was gray and icy cold, with a strong north wind blowing a confetti of snow onto her coat and hat. She'd underestimated the cold when she'd left the shop that morning and had dressed too lightly, but now, weighted with the troubling news she bore, inside the cotton and wool that clothed her she was sweating heavily, the perspiration soaking her hair and the back of her blouse. For a moment she was overcome with nausea and thought she was going to be sick. Holding on to a lamppost, she rested for a moment, letting the nausea pass, then turned north for home, pushing doggedly into the wind.

When she finally entered the print shop and pushed the door closed behind her, Henry looked up from his work, smiling to her from across the room as he always did. Wearily pulling her hat from her soaking hair, she looked back to him, her eyes dull and tired, her face blank.

"I'm pregnant," she said.

A half-hour later she was climbing out of the tub of lukewarm water she'd drawn for herself to arrest the sweating, and Henry was drying her with a big cotton towel. While she lay in the water, they talked of Doc

Smith's explanation of how this could have happened: of the ruthless unreliability of the rhythm method they had employed since Will's birth. They could even guess, they thought, the exact day that it had happened, on the Saturday afternoon in early September when Will was asleep and they'd just put fresh sheets on their bed.

Their discussion of the options later that day took less than a minute. There was staying the course and there was abortion, and when Henry mentioned the possibility of the latter, Clara's eyes become hard and small.

"No," she said flatly. "Not that."

"But Clara," Henry persisted. "You could die."

Clara raised her hand in front of her, stopping his voice the way she might have stopped traffic in the street. "It's a blessing," she said. "Just like Will was. And I won't die."

Her jaw was set, and like blinds being drawn, her eyes clouded over, shutting him out. And with that the long wait began.

There was Will to take care of and work to be done, so that at first, on the surface, at least, Clara and Henry's life returned to normal. There were games with Will and Sundays with the Kleins and lovemaking in their big bed—and laughter, too, as the pernicious gamble they faced, scheduled by Doc Smith for June of the next year, was put out of mind.

But as the new year came and the tight grip of winter gave way to spring, the reality of the deadly risk that was soon to be reckoned with could no longer be ignored. An outsider to their home would have noticed it: the unnatural quiet of the two of them, passing around each other, touching instead of speaking, as if they were both waiting for the phone to ring.

It was decided that Minnie would move in with them during the last weeks of the pregnancy, when her help would be most needed. And so on a Saturday afternoon in late May, Henry carried up from the store room the light cot Minnie would sleep on and set it up in the second bedroom she would share with Will. The room was small and cluttered with Will's clothes and toys, but it would have to do, so on the next Monday, after breakfast and after Henry had descended the narrow stairway to his shop to begin his workday, Clara took up the task of preparing the room for Minnie's imminent arrival. Henry had flatly told her to stay out of the room and to leave that kind of work to him, but Clara, on that Monday morning, was feeling unusually strong and energetic and decided to surprise him with a finished job by lunchtime.

And so as Will played in the parlor, she slowly attacked the bedroom, making up the cot with freshly washed sheets, clearing a space in the closet and the chest of drawers for Minnie's clothes, and collecting the scattering of toys that littered the floor around Will's bed. She was almost done, and was

143

feeling pleased with herself for having successfully negotiated a project that Henry had considered too daunting for her, when she misstepped.

She was carrying one last armful of Will's toys to a wooden box at the end of the bed when a toy car slipped from her hand and landed in front of her. And as her foot made contact with the metal of the toy her knee buckled and she fell, straight forward, her belly and head hitting hard against the wood floor.

For a moment she lay there, stunned by the fall and aware only of the throbbing of her head. But in the moments that followed, as her head cleared, she felt the steady searing pain coming from her stomach. It was as strong a pain as childbirth itself, as strong a pain as Clara had ever felt.

A moment later Henry heard her screaming, and dropping the printing plate he was working on, dashed up the stairs to her. Passing quickly through the kitchen and the parlor, he ran to the high and terrible sound of her voice, to the bedroom doorway where Will stood, looking in at the growing pool of red that encircled his mother.

When Clara saw Henry, she stopped screaming and held out her arms to him plaintively, her eyes begging him for help. A sound, involuntary and low, escaped from Henry as he rushed to her, kneeling in her blood and wrapping his arms around her.

"I'm sorry," Clara said, her voice already weak.

Henry pulled up the length of her dress to find the source of the bleeding. It was streaming from her freely, from deep inside of her, like water from an overflowing sink. And the old forgotten terror was once again upon him, the rage and terror that he had come to know so well in the trenches of World War I, whenever death visited.

Leaving her, he ran to the telephone and screamed to the operator for an ambulance. When he returned a minute later, Clara's face was white: as white as alabaster, as white as the newly-washed sheets on Minnie's cot. He knelt again and took her into his arms. One last time she looked to him, her face now calm, her eyes blinking, as if she were being seduced into a deep sleep.

"Goodbye, my love," she said to him in a whisper.

And in that moment Henry's heart broke. He held her tight to him, unaware of his own sobbing, or, some minutes later, of the sound of the ambulance screeching to a stop outside the shop. He sat in her blood, rocking her, his face buried in her neck.

For the three days before Clara's funeral and for six days afterward, Henry Winkler gave himself up to black and utter grief. Deep in her own mourning, Minnie opted to stay with him, forcing herself to be useful taking

144

care of Will and offering Henry the saving grace of her constant gentle presence. In those first dark days, Henry seemed to her to be diminished by the tragedy not just spiritually, but in some actual physical sense as though, once vital and unmistakable, he would now be easy to miss in a crowded room or on a busy sidewalk.

At night she slept on the cot in Will's room, awakening often in the early hours to the soft sound of Henry's bare feet on the wooden floor as he wandered the apartment like a ghost. Around three or four in the morning, the telltale sounds of his movements would cease. Exhaustion would overtake him, and for a short time, in the early hours before daylight, he would sleep.

Two weeks after Clara's funeral, Henry Winkler got up, bathed and shaved, and went downstairs to work. He had, after all, a son to raise. Luckily, he was skilled enough that even without enthusiasm he was able to deliver satisfactory work.

A few days later, Minnie went home to her husband, and Henry was left to cope alone with the trials of everyday life. The effort exhausted him, as though all day long he was walking into a stiff wind. At the end of the day, with Will finally asleep, he would collapse into an armchair, pack his pipe with tobacco, and begin work on several fingers of bootleg bourbon obtained weekly from Otto's basement. When the pipe was empty and everything was good and fuzzy, he'd grope his way to bed.

After spring had passed into summer and summer into early autumn, it was at a Sunday dinner with the Kleins that something small and remarkable happened. Henry Winkler laughed. The three adults were lined up in the kitchen doing the dinner dishes, with Minnie washing, Fred rinsing, and Henry drying. As they talked softly among themselves, Will scampered into the room, naked from the waist down and wearing Henry's brown Homburg hat, which engulfed the little boy's head down to his small pink mouth. "Daddy," he said, "I'm ready to go for a walk."

All three adults laughed involuntarily, then looked around to each other and laughed some more. A few seconds later, as they quieted down, Minnie's eyes sought out Henry's. Her eyes were soft and light and loving, telling him that it was okay to laugh at something funny, and telling him that she hoped that he thought it was okay, too. Henry looked away from her for a moment, then, forcing himself, looked back to her again. Then he stepped to her and hugged her. "Will," he said to the boy, moving to him and removing the hat, "don't you think you should put on some pants? You might get a sunburn."

That evening, after Will had been put to bed, he poured the contents of his whiskey bottle down the drain, opened a bottle of cold bootleg beer, lit his pipe, and for the first time in six months, turned on the radio.

Pleasure returned to his life in small, almost imperceptible increments, and sometimes in unexpected ways. In the early fall of 1928, he paid a visit to Irwin Meyer with the intent of trading in his Model-T Ford for a newer model. He found Irwin, now the owner of the largest Buick dealership for 100 miles, sitting in his wood-lined office with his feet on his desk, reading the sports page of the morning paper. The years since the war had been good to Irwin. His belt size had increased by about a half-inch per year, so that his crisp white shirt ballooned out noticeably over the top of his wool pants and his ample rear end neatly filled the wooden desk chair.

"Hey," Irwin said, looking up as Henry entered. "How's it going?"

"It's going okay," Henry answered.

This was the best response Irvin had heard in six months, so he took it at face value. He searched hard into Henry's eyes for confirmation, and was happy to see a glimpse of life there, maybe even the beginnings of humor. "Good," he said finally, tossing the newspaper to the side and raising himself out of his chair. "So you're tired of crankin' the Ford," he said, referring to the laborious, frustrating, and sometimes dangerous business of starting the Model-T.

"How'd you guess?" Henry responded.

"Having cranked my share, I can testify that it's almost never a happy experience," Irwin answered. He grinned over to Henry. "Want some coffee?" he asked.

"Sure," Henry said.

They left Irwin's office and headed out across the courtyard toward the showroom where Irwin kept fresh coffee and doughnuts for the customers. "I think I've got just the car for you," Irwin said, stopping in the middle of the courtyard to light a cigarette. "A '26 Buick, fender bender, less than ten thousand miles, picked it up from the insurance company for a song." They were walking again. "Nice car," Irwin continued. "Electric start, of course."

Henry's eyes strayed across the courtyard toward the showroom, and that's when he saw it, leaning up against the wall, red and gold, shining in the mid-morning sun. Henry stopped in his tracks. "Whose motorcycle?" he asked Irwin, pointing to the machine.

"Mine," Irwin replied. "It's an Indian Scout. Almost brand new. Won it in a poker game." Irwin's luck in poker seemed to grow with his waistline. They walked to it.

"It's gorgeous," Henry said, running his hand lightly over the smooth, polished surface of the gas tank. It was, in fact and without a doubt, the most beautiful piece of machinery Henry had ever laid his eyes on.

"Didn't know you liked these contraptions," Irwin said.

"Well I always thought they'd be fun," Henry responded, "but I've never seen one that was so...beautiful."

Now Irwin, in truth, had been looking forward to having a lot of fun with the Indian, but he was too good a friend to pass up any opportunity he had to help Henry. "You want it?" he asked off-handedly.

"You don't?" Henry asked back.

"Nah," Irwin lied. "You want it, it's yours."

"How much?" Henry asked, ready for the let-down.

"I'll sell it to you for what the guy owed me. Fifty bucks," Irwin lied again.

And so Henry Winkler, who was destined to fall in love with only one woman in his life, began a love affair with a motorcycle. He would keep it all of his life, long past the days when he was comfortable riding it and even into old age. The first thing he did was to order the optional back seat from the Indian dealership in Cleveland, so that very quickly he and Will were out together on the roadways, visiting nearby towns and exploring the countryside.

At first Will was terrified of the machine, which seemed to him to roar and shiver like a wild animal. But after several short trips around town sitting on his father's lap, he settled down to riding comfortably on the new seat, his small hands locked onto his father's belt. They rode together that year until the cold rains came in early November.

At six, it was still not perfectly clear to Henry what his son would grow up to look like. He was slim, like Wilhelm, with Henry's dark hair and dark brown eyes. The features of his face, and his hands, were delicate, like his mother's. His small pink mouth and rows of straight white teeth were those of his Grandmother Sophie and of his sister Ellen.

What he would grow up to *be* like was, of course, even more of an unknown, and was a question Henry had no interest in addressing. He presumed, as most parents do, that his boy would grow up to be a good man. But if Wilhelm and Sophie had been alive, they would have caught certain subtle mannerisms and behaviors that Henry missed. They would have noticed how the little boy's eyes clouded when he was angry, and how pleased with himself he could be. They would have been reminded of Ellen as a little girl, and they would have begun to worry.

The stock market crash of October 1929 laid on Etta Mae Blumberg, like millions of benighted investors, one hell of a sucker punch. In two months she saw her hard-earned and, she had thought, shrewdly invested stock portfolio fall in value from just shy of $50,000 to less than $5,000. She was, quite simply put, all but wiped out. The catastrophic loss shook her to her bones. Her experience, more so perhaps than most people, was to foresee danger and threat in physical form: a flood or a fire, a thief or a con artist. But the stock market and the banking system? These were bedrock institutions run by intelligent and magnanimous men. The kind of men they named bridges after.

As a result, in the months following the crash as the American economy slipped quickly into the grips of the Great Depression, Etta Mae was, for the first time in her life, rudderless. Day after day she wandered aimlessly through the house, or sat in front of the big bay window in her bedroom smoking her Chesterfields, overwhelmed with feelings of hopelessness and betrayal and hating herself for feeling the way she did. What was wrong with her? she thought. She had recovered from adversity before, so why not now?

The answer, she knew, for her as for so many Americans ruined by the crash, was no further away than the upright mirror centering Sophie's dressing table. She was approaching fifty years of age, her hair was almost completely gray, and she was getting tired. She just didn't want to have to work that hard again.

As she had expected, donations to the Frances E. Willard Society had fallen to a trickle, so that she had been forced to send away the two girls with whom she had shared the Winkler home and, to a modest degree, the plunder from their enterprise. One of the girls went willingly, understanding that the con was about over and allowing Etta Mae to buy her a one-way train ticket to a town where she had family who would take her in. The second girl had gone less willingly and had made the mistake of threatening to go to the authorities. For this she got a beating she had to have thought only a man could deliver, and the feel of Etta Mae's Smith and Wesson revolver in her ear was all it took to have her hurrying on her way.

Even with the two girls gone, weekly revenues were barely enough to keep Etta Mae in modest comfort and Ellen in opium, and Etta Mae knew that even this small amount would further whither. No, something definitely needed to be done, and Etta Mae was trying mightily to identify what this might be as she climbed the narrow stairway into the attic to deliver Ellen's dinner of soup and bread, and the small black balls of smoking opium that would be her dessert.

"Good evening, ma'am," she said cheerfully as she cleared the attic floor.

148

Ellen, encircled by the soft light of a reading lamp, sat at her writing table laboring over an entry she was making in her diary. Etta Mae approached her with the tray of food. "I said, good evening, ma'am," she repeated.

Finally Ellen looked up from her writing. "Good evening, Deborah," she said, smiling up weakly from the circle of light.

Etta Mae set the tray down on the edge of the desk. "Your dinner, ma'am," she said. "Home-made vegetable. Your favorite." This was a lie. Etta Mae's culinary skills were almost nonexistent, so that virtually everything they now ate, including the soup before Ellen, came from a can.

"Did you bring my medication?" Ellen asked hopefully.

"Oh, yes, ma'am. Yes indeed," Etta Mae said.

"I'll have that first," Ellen stated matter-of-factly, as if she were consulting a menu at a restaurant.

"I think you should eat first, ma'am," Etta Mae offered flatly. It was a command, not a suggestion. Etta Mae didn't want Ellen to become sick from malnourishment, and over the last several months, as Ellen moved steadily toward a singular interest in opium, she had had to withhold the drug until Ellen had dutifully eaten her meals.

For a quick second, Ellen's eyes smoldered, challenging Etta Mae the way they had challenged her father when she was a girl. Then, as before, they clouded and dimmed. "I suppose you're right," she said flatly, putting down her pen and picking up the soup spoon.

Etta Mae watched as she ate. Her long fingers, once smooth and delicate, now looked twisted and bony, and shook slightly as she moved the spoon back and forth between the soup bowl and her lips. After several of these round-trips, watery red splotches dotted the dressing gown she had loosely pulled around her.

"Have some bread, ma'am," Etta Mae ordered.

Ellen looked up to Etta Mae, then obediently picked up a thick piece of buttered bread and took a bite. Silently watching Ellen chew, Etta Mae wondered what kind of nonsense the silly woman was writing in her diary. She had read all of the entries, of course, and had correctly concluded that the woman was losing her marbles. The writing was mostly gibberish, with repeated references to her darling Thomas.

"What are you writing in your diary, ma'am?" she asked after a few moments.

Ellen looked up from her soup, a line of tomatoey broth dribbling down the side of her chin. "I've seen a set of bright stars," she said. "Every night they pass low over the house. I think they're searching for me."

"Oh, how very interesting, ma'am," Etta Mae said. She wished the woman would eat faster, so that she could get back to the vexing business of figuring out how to save herself from her current mess. She didn't need to stick around the attic anymore while Ellen got high; Ellen had been self-sufficient in preparing her own pipes for a long time.

From the long distance down the hallway and two flights of stairs, Etta Mae heard a knock on the front door. It was a forceful knock: a man's knock. Visitors came less than rarely to the Winkler home those days. Probably a salesman, Etta Mae thought. He'll go away.

But the knocking continued, even more forcefully.

"What's that sound?" Ellen asked.

"Someone's at the door, ma'am," Etta Mae answered.

Ellen stared ahead blankly for a second, allowing the statement to register. "Well," she said finally, "I suppose you should answer it."

Which is what Etta Mae had already concluded she was going to have to do. She was sure this would be quick. Almost always the dimensions of her scowl were enough to discourage even the most enthusiastic peddler. But when she flipped on the porch light and cracked open the front door to take a look, she received a shock that startled the scowl right off of her face. For standing on the porch, his collar up against the cold and stomping snow from his feet, was the very man who had to be, from her memory, Ellen's estranged brother. Henry, she thought she remembered his name was. With him was a young boy she assumed to be his son.

"Yes?" she asked, offering no hint either of friendliness or recognition.

"I'm Henry Winkler," the man said. "I need to see my sister."

Etta Mae's sharp mind raced, performing a hurried mental calculus. She knew she could make him go away. She could say that Ellen was ill, or that Ellen had instructed her never to let him in the house, or that Ellen had gone to church. But he'd come back, and maybe, if he was suspicious, he might come back with the police. No, she concluded, better to get it over with, whatever "it" was.

"I'll see if she's disposed for guests," Etta Mae said finally, pleased with the fancy word she'd used correctly. She closed and locked the front door, then hurried back up the stairs. So it's Henry Winkler, she thought. She had been correct in recognizing his face from thirteen years earlier when he had so forcefully confronted his sister. The same face, but with different eyes. Thirteen years ago his eyes had been sharp, and piercing with energy. But on the porch they had been small and dull, and surrounded by black circles. He was bone tired, she thought. Like everyone else. Maybe the Depression had already defeated him, she thought hopefully.

Henry and Will stood on the porch in the January cold for almost a half hour as Etta Mae washed Ellen's face and combed her hair as best she could and placed her in Wilhelm's big leather chair in the study. Finally, when she

150

had finished with all of the damage control she could do, she ushered the two chilled visitors into the house and down the corridor to the study.

Henry, who had neither spoken to Ellen nor been in the house for twelve years, was unprepared for what met him as he walked down through the middle of his boyhood home. Though nothing seemed to be broken, the house was dank and filthy, and stank of rotting garbage and rat turds and cigarette smoke. The sight and smell of it made his stomach turn and his heart ache.

As he entered the study, his first sight of Ellen made him stop dead in his tracks and almost took his breath away.

"Hello, sister," he said softly as he walked to her.

"Hello, brother," the old woman sitting in the chair replied.

She was all skin and bones, Henry saw, her fingers thin and bony, her ashen cheeks loose and concave, her breasts withered and sunken. Her thinning hair, he saw, was almost entirely gray and stuck out wildly from her head, as if she had been riding on the back of his Indian motorcycle. My God, my God, he thought, finding a sadness and pain for her that he would have thought impossible. He did a quick mental calculation: Ellen was forty-six years old.

"This is my son Will, Ellen," he said softly. "Will, this is your Aunt Ellen, my sister," he said to the boy.

"Hello," Will said to Ellen.

Ellen stared silently at the ten-year-old boy, her hands, resting limply in her lap, shaking imperceptibly. After several seconds her gaze turned back to Henry. "Put your faith in God," she said, remembering what Deborah had told her to say if he asked her for money. Then she smiled up to him awkwardly, as if the faith she demanded of him had already provided a soothing dose of grace.

Drowning in the utter sadness of it and the memories of better days, Henry knew he could not stay a moment longer. "Well," he said to Ellen, "I think Will and I will be going." He moved to her and bent over, so that from two feet away he was looking straight into her eyes. When it was clear that there was nothing there to see, he moved away.

"Goodbye, sister," he said sadly.

"Goodbye," Ellen replied.

Etta Mae held the door open for them as they exited. As Henry stepped through the doorway, down onto the porch and into the clean, cold air, he turned to the woman.

"You'll be seeing me again soon," he said flatly. Then he turned, took his son's hand, and made his way down the porch steps and into the falling snow.

As he walked down Summit Avenue toward the bus stop on Centennial, he couldn't get the disturbing sight of his sister out of his mind. Either drugs of some kind, he thought, or just plain dementia. True, the first seemed unlikely, but he had heard plenty of stories of seemingly normal people, right there in his own town, who turned out to be morphine or heroin addicts. And Ellen, he knew, was anything but normal. In any event, she was clearly not competent. He would visit Cecil Eatman on Monday, though he had no idea how he would pay the man.

Money, in fact, had been the reason why Henry had swallowed his pride and returned, hat in hand, to his old house. The growing Depression had not spared him, and slowly but surely his business had dried up. He was by then on a clear path to bankruptcy, and the bank had sent the first of what he knew would be a relentless stream of foreclosure notices. He had gone to Ellen in the hope of a loan.

At the corner of Summit and Centennial, a light dusting of snow collecting on his coat collar, he stood with his hands in his pockets watching as Will made a snowball, then wound up like a baseball pitcher and let the snowball fly toward a naked elm tree twenty feet away. How would he feed the boy? he wondered. And where would they live? Ellen had been his last, desperate hope. There was no one to save him, and he was damned if he knew how to save himself.

Etta Mae, in contrast, was busy about the business of saving herself. As soon as the front door had closed and locked on the man and boy, Etta Mae had known that this phase of her life was over. That she had no good plan was immaterial. The man would come back, most likely with the police and a court order of some kind. At best she would be expelled, and much worse than that was probable. No, if she had to leave, it was best for her to pick the hour. So after shepherding Ellen back up the stairs to the attic, she sequestered herself in her bedroom where, with her Chesterfields and the last of a bottle of bootleg French brandy, she hitched together the elements of a plan.

The next morning, being a Sunday, she went to church, and after the service spent an hour or so explaining to a handful of Ellen's old acquaintances how it was that the poor lady's health still kept her taken to bed. She was feeling better, though, Etta Mae reported, and was looking forward to receiving visitors in a week or so.

The rest of the day she tended haphazardly to Ellen and walked aimlessly through the big, silent house, getting a last good look at all of the rooms that had supplied her with such exquisite comfort. Twice during the long afternoon she had had to fight back a welling despair. Why was she not allowed to stay? she would ask. Why was she being denied such a small and

152

reasonable justice? She had established her place here, she argued to herself petulantly. She had risen from the gutters of New York City and earned her position here. She deserved to be able to stay here in the modest beauty of the big house on the quiet, tree-lined street.

The second time this happened, the strength of her self-pity astonished and repulsed her. It was all nonsense, she knew. Like the suicides, the wasted effort of the weak-willed. To wrench herself back into reality, she found a straight pin and plunged it deep into the back of her hand, embracing through clenched jaws the searing, mind-clearing pain. When it was done, she went to her bedroom and packed a small suitcase with a minimal assortment of traveling essentials. She then took a small wad of bills—the last of her savings—from its hiding place in the bottom drawer of Sophie's dressing table and packed it neatly into her bodice, where it lay snug against the hard surface of her stiletto.

Then, finally, she took the last of her opium stash, cooked it down and rolled it into a dozen small balls, and carried it, along with one last bowl of Campbell's soup, up to Ellen. Climbing the narrow attic steps for the last time, she wondered idly what would become of the woman. She'd be institutionalized probably, she thought. The brother would see to that.

She found Ellen asleep on her narrow cot, her mouth half-open, the thin gray tangles of her hair falling around her face like a spider's web. As quietly as she could, she put down the soup and added the collection of opium balls to Ellen's cache. True to her longtime nature, Etta Mae begrudged the Winkler woman nothing and had no desire to cause her unneeded pain. She could stay in her attic, the warm glow of opium coursing through her veins and orchestrating her dreams, until her brother came to break the sweet spell.

When it was good and dark outside, Etta Mae left. The snow, which had fallen lightly all day, had finally stopped and the sky was clear and filled with bright stars when Etta Mae, suitcase in hand, made her way through the front door and down the porch steps. On the last step, though, the heel of her shoe caught on a quarter-inch of bare nail that had come loose and worked its way out of the wood. She tripped forward, emitting a small cry of astonishment before falling in a heap on the snow-covered sidewalk. After a moment she picked herself up, rubbed the aching shoulder she had fallen on, and dusted the snow from her coat and legs. Curious, she took a step back to the porch and stooped to examine the porch step. It was as smooth as glass.

Etta Mae stared at the guilty porch step for a few moments, then began to laugh lightly. "Fair enough," she said to the house. "And good riddance to you, too."

With that she turned, picked up her suitcase, and walked away. She knew better than to look back. An hour later she was at the train station, her

153

modest stock of traveling money augmented with the contents of the morning offering stolen from St. Paul's Lutheran Church. An hour after that she was on a train heading east, back to New York City, where she would attempt to again find a place for herself in its busy and complex underworld economy. Halfway back, as the earliest rays of morning sunshine met the east-moving train, Etta Mae discovered that she'd forgotten her pistol. It lay wrapped in a rag in a drawer of the big roll-top desk, where she'd put it after cleaning it some days before. Damn, she thought as she fumbled for her cigarettes, I'm getting old.

Etta Mae Blumberg's remaining time on the earth would be brief, lasting less than one year into FDR's second term. That her death would come violently would not surprise her. And given that death had to come, it would come exactly as she would have wished it. Quickly, with no time for second-guessing.

When Ellen awoke, it was dark outside, the shadowy attic interior made visible only by the soft moonlight issuing in from the long row of west-facing dormer windows. She stared into the shadows around her for several moments until she finally realized that she was awake, then slowly swung herself off the cot and walked the five steps to her writing table. Switching on the light, she walked back to the bed and poured a glass of water from the clay pitcher on her end table.

"For God and home and everyland, our cause speeds on today..." she sang softly as she poured water into a glass. Lifting the glass, she drank greedily. She was thirsty, and the cool water soothed her dry lips.

"Deborah," she called down the attic stairway. "I would like some help to the bathroom." She had to use the toilet, and lately the steep stairway had been causing her problems. "Deborah?" she called again. When there was no answer, she walked to the edge of the steps and peered down into the black stairway. "Deborah?" she called out again.

A moment of panic seized her, which she attempted to bring under control by hurrying to her desk and sitting. She must be asleep, Ellen thought. Yes, she must be asleep. Slowly, sitting at her desk in the small circle of weak light, Ellen gained the resolve to attempt the stairway herself. As she rose from her chair, she looked around for her dressing gown and saw, inadvertently, through the east-facing window before her, two pricks of white light, high and far away and brighter than any of the stars in the cloudless night sky. She gasped, then stood motionless, watching intently as the pricks of light slowly grew.

"They've come back," she said out loud. "They've come back for me!"

The sight of the approaching lights filled Ellen's withered heart with soothing joy. The lights, like a lost lover, had returned to claim and save her. She felt giddy, almost dizzy. As the lights slowly grew she hurriedly fumbled with the window latch, throwing open the high dormer windows to the icy-cold winter air. The blast of cold air shot like electricity through her skin and out through the tips of her hair, invigorating her with an energy and purpose she hadn't felt in years.

Climbing clumsily first onto her chair and then onto her desk, she leaned her body out through the open attic windows. "I'm here," she screamed into the night as the white lights approached. "I'm down here," she screamed, waving her arms frantically.

The lights were approaching steadily, but they weren't descending. They would pass over and lose sight of her in just a few seconds. Desperate and panicked, Ellen climbed awkwardly onto the window sill, throwing a thin white leg over the sill and onto the steep slope of the rooftop. The lights were high above her now. As they passed by, Ellen rolled herself out onto the roof. The snow-covered roof was as slick as ice, and as Ellen slid down the side of it, she screamed up to the twin lights. "Wait!" she cried one last time, then pitched head-first over the edge of the roof, landing a moment later on the walkway by the side door. She lay with her arms outstretched, lifeless, her broken neck curled under her shoulder, like the broken neck of a bird.

Above and now to the southwest, the pilot of the Ford Tri-motor pulled back on the power and banked the airplane to the left, aligning its powerful twin landing lights with the twinkling lines of the airport runway lights shining clearly and steadily four miles to the south.

Chapter Ten

Carlos's sweet deal with the newspaper syndicator changed his daily life both for the good and for the bad. On the one hand, it validated the long years of his strained belief in "The Halfway Inn" and promised to bring in what was, for Carlos and Carole, a substantial amount of money. On the other hand, he was now under the gun to produce four quality cartoons each week, which ate into the time he could devote to the continuing renovation of the house and, more importantly, was beginning to put a strain on his creativity.

This last issue was foremost on his mind as he sat in Henry's big leather armchair in the study, idly tossing a Sharpie pen into the air and catching it, staring at the blank easel in front of him. Lacking a steady paying customer, his pace of composition had always been able to be comfortably slow, so that if the spirit didn't deliver a good idea, he'd simply do something else and wait until the next day to try again. But as Carlos sat there, a warm, late-afternoon May breeze stirring the curtains of the open study windows, the absence of the spirit, evidenced by the half-dozen sheets of drawing paper littering the floor, was beginning to take its toll.

He'd had it for the day, he knew. Tomorrow he'd go for a walk downtown and people watch, which almost always resulted in inspiration. Besides, he thought, consulting his wristwatch, it was almost four o'clock. Putting down the Sharpie, he hurried to the kitchen, quickly made a peanut butter and jelly sandwich, grabbed a Coke from the refrigerator, and returned to the study. Plopping back down in the leather chair, he reached for the TV clicker.

As it happened, "The Halfway Inn" was at that very moment on Carole's mind as she drove up the busy slope of Centennial Drive. She'd had a three o'clock court date that had ended early, and driving back to her office she'd seen the funniest thing. Stuck in traffic, she looked up to a billboard ad for "The Kit Kat Lounge," a retro-1940s bar and restaurant, announcing a new cocktail hour every night from four till six. And this got the wheels in Carole's brain turning until she had an idea for a dynamite cartoon. So instead of going back to the office, she decided to go home and share her idea with Carlos. As she drove up Centennial Drive, her eyes hidden behind sunglasses and her hair blowing in the wind of her open window, she was smiling to herself, imagining the cartoon.

Turning left off Centennial onto Summit Avenue, she cruised slowly down the two blocks to number 228, then pulled into the driveway and parked behind Carlos's truck. Grabbing her briefcase and leaving the car, she headed toward the front porch, stopping to assess the progress of the row of daffodils she'd planted a month earlier. They needed a good watering, she concluded. Maybe she could get Carlos to put in a sprinkler system, she thought hopefully as she climbed the porch steps.

And then she heard it: the faint sound of singing. Women's voices singing. She couldn't tell if the sound was coming from her house or from one of her neighbor's. But when she opened the front door and entered the foyer the sound—the sweet, melodic sound of a chorus of women's voices—became louder. It *was* coming from inside, and appeared to be coming from the study. As she moved down the hallway to the study, she was trying to place the voices. She'd heard them before, she was sure. But whose? And where had she heard them? As she moved even with the door to the study, the TV set came into view, and there they were, and Carole remembered. The Lovely Lennon Sisters. In extravagant but discreet evening dresses, their hair perfectly styled, their teeth white as snow. In four-part harmony.

In the two seconds it took her to understand what was happening, her eyes moved away from the TV set, and through the narrow crack between the half-open door and its frame she caught a glimpse of Carlos plopped in the big leather chair, munching on a sandwich, his eyes glued to the TV. It's *The Lawrence Welk Show,* she thought suddenly. He's watching *The Lawrence Welk Show.* It was all she could do to not laugh out loud.

She watched him for a couple more seconds, then silently retraced her steps to the front door. "Honey, I'm home," she called out loudly. Quickly the sound of the music died, and Carlos emerged from the study just as Carole reached the doorway.

"Hey, honey," he said, bending slightly to kiss her.

"Hi," she responded, smiling mischievously. "I thought I heard the sound of music."

"Yeah," Carlos answered. "It was…it was on the TV. You know, background noise." He was thinking fast.

"It sounded kind of familiar," Carole persisted, toying with him. "But I can't quite place it. What was that TV show Mrs. Bartlett used to watch every afternoon?"

Carlos looked blankly to her as his mind extrapolated the obvious from Carole's strange line of questioning and sly grin. "You caught me, didn't you?" he finally asked, his face reddening slightly.

"I sure did," she said back, smiling broadly up to him.

"It's not bad," he said hopefully. "You know, interesting. Music of a different era."

"Uh-huh," she responded. "A real history lesson." She watched him squirm for a few seconds more, then let him off the hook. "Let's check it out," she said, putting down her briefcase and entering the study.

Carole pulled off her pantyhose, then plopped onto the ottoman, pulling up her skirt to allow the warm breeze to gently wash over her legs. Then, with Carlos behind her in the armchair, they watched the remainder of *The Lawrence Welk Show*. It was a rerun from the early seventies, so that most of the men had stylishly long hair and gaudy plaid suits, and the women had shoulder-length wavy hair and sequined gowns. They caught the last three acts of the show, which included a solo number by Myron Floren on the accordion, a dance number featuring Bobby Burgess and Cissy King, and finally Lawrence Welk himself dancing with an old lady from the audience as the champagne band played a polka.

Later that evening, after dinner and about the time the sun had just begun to sink below the western horizon, they went for a walk. They walked west down Summit Avenue, slowly walking past the homes of their neighbors and assessing the state of their own home relative to those around them.

"Not as pretty on the outside yet," Carlos said as they reached the end of the first block, "but give me another six months." He was referring to the last, and in many ways the most formidable, of his unfinished refurbishing tasks, which was to prep and paint the outside of the house. Carlos hated to paint, considering it mindless, uncreative drudgery.

"It's gonna take more than six months for me to match these flower gardens," Carole said. "More like six years." Virtually all of the neighbors had expansive and impeccably maintained flower gardens, which Carole admired and coveted.

"They have lawn services," Carlos said.

"Who needs a lawn service when you have a husband?" Carole said with a sly smile, sneaking a look up to Carlos.

"I think I feel a disc about to slip," Carlos responded. It was his standard response to the thought of yard work. Yard work was the only household chore that Carlos hated more than painting.

As they continued to walk down the avenue, Carlos treated himself to several seconds of quick mental arithmetic. If he was not exactly excited by the prospect of a future marred by the specter of occasional yard work, he was very excited by Carole's offhand reference to a time frame. Six years, he thought. She said six years. In the back of his mind lay the uncomfortable memory of the deal they had made: to fix up the house and sell it. But with or without a world-class flower garden? Maybe her comment had been idle speculation, not meant as an amendment to the contract. He decided to take a leap.

"If you're serious about a flower garden, I'll put in a sprinkler system for you," he said, trying to sound off-handed.

"Sure I'm serious. Who needs flowerpots when you've got all this dirt?" she responded playfully.

"Okay," Carlos said, putting his arms on Carole's shoulders and kissing the top of her head. "I'll start on it right after I finish the floors." Damn right, he thought happily, and more than a bit triumphantly. Carlos, ever the realist, was perfectly happy taking the bad with the good.

As soon as he had gotten back from New York City, Carlos had taken up the task of refinishing the hardwood floors that covered the two stories of the house wall-to-wall. As was typical of the time, they were made of tongue-and-groove oak and, to Carlos's practiced mind, seamlessly fit and beautifully laid. But after one hundred-plus years of abuse, they were dry and pitted and stained, and badly in need of a sanding. And so Carlos had had his father, the apartment super, send out the old floor sander that belonged to the building, and for the past couple of weeks he'd devoted a few hours a day to the job. Now, hardwood floor sanding is not a task for the novice home repairer. Carlos's father was an expert and had taught him enough so that Carlos knew that if he worked slowly and very carefully, he could do a job he could be proud of.

Knowing that Carole would want her sprinkler system soon, Carlos speeded up the floor sanding, so that by the Sunday of the following week he had finished the entire house with the exception of the front parlor. As the hours passed, Carlos slowly worked his way with the growling, rumbling floor sander down the width of the room, moving ever closer to the gigantic cherry wood breakfront that stood like a fortress against the north wall of the room.

As Carlos sanded, Carole sat at her desk upstairs in the small front-facing bedroom, admiring wood. It had started with the freshly refinished wood flowing under her feet, which she had personally stained and sealed after Carlos had sanded it smooth, and moved slowly to the door and door frames, then on to the wooden windows and sills with their ingenious hidden counterweights for opening and closing. Getting actively involved in the remodeling of the house had awakened in Carole a long-dormant appreciation for craftsmanship, of how patience and skill were capable of transforming common objects, like raw pieces of wood, into things of beauty and function.

She had intended to get some work done on a limited liability corporation she was constructing for one of her clients, but for some reason hadn't been able to keep her attention focused on the computer monitor in front of her. So she'd abruptly shut down the computer, put her feet on the desktop, and willingly given herself up to the comfort of her complacencies. In fact, without quite recognizing it herself, Carole had come to develop a comfort level for the entire house that was quite unprecedented. Beginning with the joyless home of her youth and progressing through a series of college dorm rooms and apartments, Carole had always thought of a home as nothing more than a mailing address and a shelter, functionally necessary for life but nothing more. A year earlier it would have never occurred to her to sit quietly and sip her morning tea, as she now did most mornings, in the arch of the big bay window in their bedroom, listening languidly to the muffled movements of the awakening neighborhood. She was, in fact, and without understanding it well enough to acknowledge it, coming to enjoy the simple comforts of the old house as much as, if not more than, Carlos.

Her thoughts left the wood as her gaze traveled past the open front window, focusing on the gently swaying green-leafed branches of the old dogwood adorning the west side of their front lawn. As she watched a robin land on a branch in front of her, she was struck by how absolutely unlikely the chances were that she could be sitting where she was: in the quiet and tranquility of a gracious old house on a secluded, park-like avenue on a hill in the middle of the city. And if her hindsight had been sharper, she would have connected what she was feeling, in kind if not in intensity, to how she had felt after the first time she and Carlos had made love. Then, lying quietly in the embrace of the strong, happy man who handled her so gently, Carole had felt, above all else, lucky.

Her unfocused thoughts were interrupted by Carlos's voice calling up from below. "Hey honey," he called up. "I need your help."

What Carlos needed help with was the huge breakfront in the parlor. He had sanded right up to its edge and now needed to move it out of the way, which involved lifting each edge while Carole slid a blanket under its legs. Then, with the floor protected, he could pull the massive piece of furniture, one side at a time, away from the wall and on to the sanded portion of the floor.

And so it went, but as he finished pushing the breakfront clear of the flooring, something caught his eye. It was an old, fat, yellowed envelope, lying on the floor where the breakfront used to be. "Humph," Carlos grunted as he bent to pick it up. After examining the envelope, he called out to Carole, who was already on her way back upstairs. "Hey," he said, "take a look at this."

He handed the envelope to Carole, who spent several moments studying the envelope and its contents. "Jees," she said finally, looking up to Carlos. "It's a cemetery plot. In 1918 Wilhelm Winkler purchased a cemetery plot."

Carlos thought for a moment. "Well, sure," he said. "We never even thought of it, but they gotta be buried here someplace."

Carole hurried to the study to retrieve the old family bible and the death notices she had photocopied. Returning to the parlor, she plopped the material onto the ledge of the breakfront and studied it for several minutes. "Look here," she said finally. "Sophie, his wife, dies on October 23, 1918, and two days later he buys this cemetery plot." She looked again to the papers. "And then he died two months later." She looked up to Carlos, stunned by the tragic sense of it and bewildered that there was nothing more to say.

"Where's the cemetery?" Carlos asked.

Carole again consulted the purchase agreement, glad to have a task to perform. "Doesn't say," she said finally. "Just a post office box."

Carlos glanced over her shoulder to catch the name of the cemetery on the contract. "Chapel Hill Cemetery," he said. "Let's find out where it is."

They walked quickly to the dining room, where from a cabinet drawer Carlos extracted a large city map. Carole watched as he spread it out on the long dining room table, then searched slowly for the small patch of green that would identify the site.

"Here it is," he said finally, pointing to a patch of green directly to the west of the old town. "Wanna go take a look?"

Carole thought for a minute, then shook her head from side to side, first slowly, then more vehemently, her pale blue eyes floating wide and vacant in a sea of white. It would be a while before Carole would be ready for that particular journey.

The next weekend, on Saturday, Carole and Carlos hosted their first party in their new home. They spent a long Friday evening and all morning on Saturday cleaning and polishing everything in sight, and in the early afternoon, as Carole hurried to the A&P for a variety of forgotten items, Carlos mowed the grass and set up the croquet set and badminton net. It turned out to be a gorgeous day, cooler and less humid than usual for early June, so that when the guests started trickling in around five o'clock, everyone migrated quickly to the back yard.

The thirty or so guests were a mixture of Carole and Carlos's respective work acquaintances and their spouses, which meant lawyers on the one hand and artists on the other. To the untutored eye it would have seemed an odd mix—long hair and Birkenstocks contrasting with smooth, short $50 salon cuts and Eddie Bauer polo shirts. But the two groups mixed effortlessly, so that by six the backyard was filled with a swirl of brightly colored summer shirts and dresses and the low buzz of many conversations.

In the shade on the east side of the house, next to several coolers over-flowing with iced beer and soft drinks, Carlos stood before his Weber kettle mopping barbecue sauce on a grill full of chicken pieces and sipping from a cold bottle of Sierra Nevada Pale Ale. It was hot standing next to the kettle full of hot coals, and beads of sweat were forming on his forehead and on the back of his neck. He wiped his forehead with the edge of his "Grill Ser-geant" cooking apron, then flipped the chicken pieces and slopped on more barbecue sauce.

After a few minutes, a tall, statuesque woman wandered over to refill her wine glass. She was an artist friend of Carlos's who taught part-time at the university. "Hey, Carlos," she said as she pulled the cork on a half-filled bottle of red wine.

"Hey, Fiona," Carlos responded as he fiddled with his chicken.

"Big congrats on the syndication," Fiona said as she filled her glass. "That is so super."

Fiona was as Irish as her name implied. She had long, unkempt straw-berry blonde hair, green eyes, and pale, almost iridescent skin. She also, to Carlos's mind, always appeared to be a bit cross-eyed, and always seemed to smell of pot, even when she hadn't been smoking it.

"Thanks," Carlos said, smiling. "I'm still pinching myself."

"You need help there, you let me know," Fiona said.

"With the chicken?" Carlos asked.

"With the pinching," Fiona responded with a sly smile.

Carlos, who had begun to remove his chicken pieces onto a platter, could only chuckle and shake his head. It was more or less a standing joke between them, with both parties fully aware that Carlos was more than not available.

"You seen Carole?" Carlos asked as he began to scrape the grill clean with a long-handled wire brush.

"She's inside showing off your house," Fiona answered.

"You checked it out?" Carlos asked.

"You bet," Fiona said. "First thing I did. I couldn't believe it when I drove up. I said to myself, man, I've got the wrong address." She took a sip of her wine, then paused to light a cigarette. "Everybody's oohing and aah-ing," she continued, blowing out a thin stream of smoke. "They're all, like, it's a mansion, you know, with these high ceilings and all this polished wood everywhere. Carole must be doing okay, that's all I can say."

"She inherited it," Carlos offered.

"Yeah?" Fiona asked. "Like from her parents?"

"Like from her great-grandfather. It's a long story," he said as he began to lay out hamburger patties for the second round of grilling.

162

From a distance, Carlos saw Hank Cooper, the wine snob and office colleague of Carole's, approaching. "See that guy," Carlos said to Fiona, "he's single."

"No kidding," Fiona responded. "What's to recommend him?"

"He likes really good wine," Carlos answered. "And jazz."

"Hmmm," Fiona mused, narrowing her eyes to scrutinize the approaching man from the top of his wavy blond head to the bottom of his penny-loafered feet. "I like wine. I like jazz."

"Hi, Hank," Carlos offered as Hank reached the barbecue.

"Hi, Carlos," Hank said, reaching for an open bottle of pinot noir. "Now she's got you barbecuing. Is there anything you don't do?"

"Windows," Carlos responded. "I don't do windows." Which wasn't true. Carlos had washed all of the downstairs windows just a week earlier. "Hank Cooper...Fiona O'Donnell," he added, gesturing toward Fiona with his spatula.

"Hi, there," Fiona said, smiling invitingly and offering her hand, demurely, her wrist slightly downturned.

"I take it you're a lawyer," Fiona continued. "What kind of law do you do?"

"Criminal law," Hank responded, letting his eyes travel discreetly over Fiona's ample curves.

"Hmmm," Fiona said, smiling. "Well I'm innocent on all counts."

"Really?" Hank responded. "You don't look innocent."

By ten o'clock, Carole and Carlos had said their goodbyes to the last of the partygoers and stood side by side in the kitchen doing the dishes, with Carole washing and Carlos rinsing and drying. Evening had brought with it a chill, turning Carlos's thoughts to the warm quilt awaiting him upstairs and, naturally, to the prospect of the warm body that would be next to him. Carole was happy and animated and just a little bit tipsy, talking a mile a minute about one of the local attorneys and his young trophy wife.

"And so," she chatted on, gesturing with her dishrag, "it turns out, you know, to be one of those stories that goes from one person to another and gets changed a little bit each time, so, like, it goes from she's taking a cruise by herself because he gets seasick to she's taking a cruise by herself because she's sick of him to they're sick of each other."

"So what was it?" Carlos asked.

"None of the above," Carole said. "Margaret Coleman straightened it all out." Margaret was another one of Carole's office colleagues. "It turns out that *she* was sick and couldn't go on the cruise, so to make up for it she makes him buy her a new Beemer."

163

"You don't say," Carlos remarked. He was half-grinning now, like he was watching a funny movie.

"I don't say," Carole repeated, smiling happily. "And you know what else? Margaret's husband Bob—the guy who dumped a plate of potato salad onto his lap? Well, he's a realtor, and he told me that our little cottage here is worth a lot of moolah. Mucho dinero," she added, looking over to Carlos and cocking an eyebrow. "Viel Geld," she added in German.

"I coulda told you that," Carlos responded.

"Yeah, well, he said to keep him in mind if we ever want to sell," Carole said.

Carlos's stomach turned at the sound of the awful word. "So what'd you tell him?" he asked, trying to sound nonchalant.

"I told him we're not done fixing it up," she responded, handing him a bowl to rinse.

A hint of distress overtook Carlos's face. On a scale of hoped-for responses, hers was two out of ten.

"But then what could we get in exchange?" Carole continued. "Some place in tract house city with no trees? I don't think I'm ready for that."

Now that was more like it, Carlos thought, his face relaxing and brightening. A nine out of ten. "Yeah," he said. "Fiona thinks we're living in a mansion."

"Our own little Tara," Carole said in her best Southern Belle imitation. "I noticed, by the way," she added in her normal voice, "that Fiona and Hank left at the same time."

"Yeah," Carlos responded. "Probably too early to know whether *their* evening will be a success."

Carole's eyebrows arched. "Maybe too early for us, too," she said, flashing a quick smile in Carlos's direction.

Carlos hooked his dish towel around her neck, pulled her to him and kissed her. "You mean you haven't had too much wine?" he asked.

"What do you care?" Carole responded, her eyes twinkling.

Carlos laughed. "I prefer sex with the soundtrack," he said, grabbing her and tickling her until she screamed.

Their evening, it turned out, was in fact not quite over, and ended with sleep several hours later, at roughly the same time as Hank and Fiona's.

The following Monday was a busy day for Carole. She spent the entire morning at the courthouse, and then after an hour in the law library, where she hurriedly downed her ham sandwich while she scanned a handful of appellate court decisions, she returned to her office for a round of telephone calls. After an hour or so of calling, Sandy, the receptionist, tapped lightly on her door, then opened it and stuck her head in.

"It's Carlos," Sandy said.

"Tell him I'll call him back in five minutes," Carole replied, her hand over the end of the phone.

"Uh...I think you'd better take it, Carole," Sandy said nervously. "It's...uh... pretty important."

Shooting Sandy a quizzical look, Carole quickly switched over to the second line. "Hi, Carlos," she said. "What's up?"

Immediately Carole sat up straight in her chair, her eyes like big blue and white saucers. "What!" she exclaimed.

"I've been arrested," Carlos's voice repeated.

"What happened?" Carole asked, her stomach turning over at the news.

"I got into a fight," Carlos answered.

"You mean like a fistfight?" Carole asked.

"Like a fistfight," Carlos affirmed.

"Oh, jees," Carole heard herself say. "You okay?

"I'm fine," Carlos said.

"Where are you?" Carole asked.

"I'm in jail," Carlos replied. "This is my one phone call."

Carole's initial fright was turning into frustration. "Well I figured that, Carlos," she said sharply. "Which one?"

When she found out where he was being held, she reached for her purse. "Okay," she said, "stay put. I'll be there in fifteen minutes."

Fifteen minutes later, she was halfway to the station house, stuck in traffic behind a fender bender. As she inched along, she fretted over Carlos and, replaying in her mind the conversation they'd had, thought of what a dumb thing it'd been to tell him to stay put. Maybe someday they'd be able to get a laugh out of that, she thought hopefully.

Twenty minutes later, when she finally pulled into the station house parking lot, Carlos was outside sitting on the curb. As she brought her car to a stop, Carlos got up and walked to her. Carole could see that his shirt was torn and stained with red, and as he climbed into the passenger seat, she saw that his lip was cut.

"Oh, baby," she said softly, reaching out with her finger to softly touch his lip. He was calm on the outside, almost lethargic, but his jaw was set grimly and his eyes were small and hard. He was, Carole knew, still in a rage.

"How'd you get out?" she asked.

Carlos shrugged his shoulders. "Right after I called, a couple of witnesses came in to testify that I didn't start it, that I was just defending myself," Carlos said. "So they let me go."

"So what happened?" Carole asked.

"Son of a bitch called me a spick," Carlos said. "A fucking spick, actually. I got in his face about it and we were off to the races."

He was spitting out the words, his voice low and tight and angry. "I got him good, though," he said, twisting in his seat to face her. "I hope I broke his fucking nose."

As Carole drove Carlos across town to pick up his truck, she learned the whole sorry story: Carlos had driven down to the hardware supply store where he'd angered a couple of local hillbillies by parking his truck in a space they'd apparently been aiming for. Carlos had heard the horn blast and caught a glimpse of the middle finger as the car passed by, but hadn't thought anything of it until he'd entered the store. They'd been waiting for him in the entryway—two of them, a big guy and a little guy—and it'd been the big guy who'd wanted to fight.

"What started it?" Carole asked.

For just a second Carlos's rage cooled. His face relaxed a bit and his mouth opened into a hint of a smile. "I called him a pendejo," he said.

Carole dropped Carlos off at his pickup, then headed for home. Every once in a while, maybe once a year, Carlos had a personal confrontation with racial hatred. While these thankfully isolated events were almost never violent, Carlos always reacted to them in the same way, first with intense anger, and later with a deep sense of sorrow that bordered on depression. It weighed on him as if it were the curse of humanity, as if it were the tool of the devil, and the way the devil would win.

As Carole had feared, when Carlos got home, he was past the anger and deep into a profound sadness. Entering the house, he walked straight to the study and fell into the big leather chair, his eyes dull and distant, his body still and limp, as if the day had exhausted him. Carole watched him for a few moments, then hurried to the kitchen, took two leftover bottles of beer from the refrigerator, and returned with them to the study.

"Come on," she said softly. "Let's go sit on the front porch and put a lip lock on these babies."

So they moved to a couple of lawn chairs on the front porch, where they sat sipping their beers and watching the odd car or pedestrian pass by. The stony silence, so foreign to their times together, was spooky to Carole. She stole a look over to Carlos, who sat staring straight ahead, as if he were concentrating on some aspect of the house across the street.

"You know what this porch needs?" she asked finally. "A swing."

166

Carlos turned to her. "Yeah," he said blankly. "A swing would be nice."
Carole's hopes for a quick recovery sank. This was a bad one.

Carlos sat silently for several moments, then finally spoke. "His face was so...ugly," Carlos said softly, after a moment. "So...twisted and contorted...inhuman, really." He turned to Carole. "Like he had rabies."

"He does," Carole said.

Carlos thought for a moment. "Yeah," he said sadly.

All through the bottle of beer, and then later through dinner, the sadness continued. "Wanna play some Trivial Pursuit?" Carole asked as they did the dishes.

"No, thanks," Carlos answered.

"Wanna watch the *Blues Brothers?*" she asked. The *Blues Brothers* was their favorite old video.

"Nah," Carlos said.

"You're refusing to be consoled, you know," she said, running her wet hand down his back and grabbing a handful of rear end.

Finally he chuckled. "I'm sorry," he said. "I can't get that face out of my mind."

"So look at my face, then," Carole said, stage smiling and batting her eyelids.

Now Carlos was smiling back. "You're right," he said. "I have to share the earth with people like that, but I don't have to share my house."

"Exactly," Carole said. "So let's do something fun."

"Okay," Carlos said, nodding to her. "You name it. Anything you want."

Carole thought for a moment, tapping her teeth lightly, then turned to him and kissed him softly on the lips. "Okay, brown boy," she said softly into his ear. "Let's you and me go upstairs and make us a beige baby."

By Wednesday Carlos had completely forgotten the ugly racist incident and had returned to his normal self, which meant that he was looking for a job to do. So after a morning of cartooning, he polished off a huge pastrami sandwich, then headed the nose of the pickup down Centennial to the equipment rental, where he checked out a Ditch Witch trencher. If the yard was relatively free of roots and rocks, as he hoped, he figured he could dig the trenches for the sprinkler system in a day, then spend portions of the rest of the week laying and gluing PVC pipe.

As it turned out, the yard was in fact free of rocks, but, as he should have surmised from the half dozen or so hundred-year-old trees dotting the property, was anything but free of roots. By the end of the day, he knew he was in for it. He had only completed trenching the relatively small   front yard, and his lines of trenches were marred in a half-dozen places by knots of roots as thick as his legs.

Dirty and sore, he was determined to at least expel the roots from his trenches, and went in search of an axe he thought he remembered seeing in the garage, leaning up against the wall next to the Indian motorcycle. Walking to the garage he made a deal with himself. He'd count the number of swings of the axe it took to clear a path through the roots. If it was under a hundred, he'd reward himself with one bottle of beer. If it was over a hundred, he'd reward himself with two.

Inside the garage he found the old axe just where he thought it was. It was in good shape, but the blade was dull and badly pitted. "Puto," he grunted softly to himself, disappointed. He needed a file to sharpen the axe blade, and he didn't have one. He'd have to hope that Henry Winkler had had one, and that he could find it. His tasks were multiplying and the cold beer was moving further and further off into the future.

And so he went looking. But as he shuffled randomly through the old wooden drawers of Henry Winkler's workbench, he discovered, half hidden by an ancient pipe wrench, the oddest thing. It first appeared to Carlos to be a piece of dirty blue string, but after he had extracted and untangled it, it turned out to be a graduation tassel, like the ones he still had from high school and college. It had a little metal shield attached to it just above the fringe, and Carlos could make out the letters "CHS" and the number "1940." "Humph," he grunted, fingering the delicate blue fringe. Carole will be interested in this, he thought. So he stuck it in his pocket and went back to his search for a file.

When Carole got home two hours later, she found Carlos sitting on the front porch eating peanuts and sipping from a bottle of beer. He had swung the axe eighty-three times, and had to settle for just one beer. "Nice job," she said as she climbed the porch steps, admiring the neat, straight rows of trenches patterned across the front yard. Putting down her briefcase, she plopped down in the chair next to Carlos and kicked off her shoes. Leaning over, she accepted a quick kiss from Carlos, then borrowed his beer bottle and took a swig.

"Aye, there, counselor," Carlos warned. "That's my only beer."

"Easy job, then?" Carole asked. She was aware of Carlos's reward structure.

"Oh, no," Carlos laughed. "Hard job. I'm only, maybe, half done with the trencher."

Carole gave him a quizzical look.

"Roots," he explained. "Big ones. Big as your leg, but not nearly so pretty."

168

Carole smiled, enjoying the compliment. "Then treat yourself to another," she said. "I'll finish this one."

Carlos thought for a moment, doing a quick mental calculus of how the additional half beer could be justified within the complex framework of his self-control mechanism. "Talked me into it," he said after a moment, smiling. Tossing a handful of peanuts into his mouth, he got up and headed for the refrigerator.

When he returned a minute later, he had, along with the second bottle of beer, the dirty graduation tassel he'd found in the garage. Sitting back down, he handed the tassel to Carole. "Look what I found," he said.

Carole took the tassel and examined it. "Hmmm," she said. "CHS, that must be Central High." She looked up to Carlos. "Our rivals." Carole had gone to one of the other high schools in town.

"Look at the year," Carlos offered. "Nineteen-forty."

"Yeah," Carole answered. Lifting the dirty tassel by its long loop of string she blew gently on the fringe, making it dance in front of her.

"Who do you think it belonged to?" Carlos asked.

Carole blew again on the fringe of the tassel, then turned to Carlos. "Don't know," she said, "but I betcha I can find out."

Two days later, on Friday, she did. When an eleven o'clock settlement conference was abruptly cancelled, she had a perfect excuse to leave early for lunch and scoot over to the west side of town to Central High School which, she noticed as she parked her car in the visitor's parking lot, was gearing up for its June graduation. The lovely, ornate red brick buildings with white crosshatched windows had been preserved, so that if it weren't for glimpses of ripped jeans and multicolored hair among the crowds of teenaged boys and girls, Carole could have easily believed she was back in 1940.

After asking directions from a beefy kid in a letterman's jacket, she made her way through the courtyard and on to the school library. Ten minutes later, after explaining her situation to an enthusiastic librarian, she was seated in a back room perusing the yellowed pages of the school album for the 1939-1940 academic year. Compared to her own high school albums, this one was thin and plain, coming, as it had, from a time when photographs were expensive and incomes were low. Forgetting for a moment the urgency of her mission, Carole leafed slowly through the first pages, caught up in the history before her and captivated by the pictures, all in oval boundaries, as was the style then, of men and women long gone, and of young men and women long transitioned into adulthood and on into old age. The pictures moved from the faculty to the sports teams and clubs, and then to the senior class. Flipping to the "Ws," Carole quickly located the object of her search.

His name, as she knew from the Winkler family bible, was William Winkler. For several long moments she sat still, appraising his face. Like his father and grandfather, his hair was dark. But unlike them, whose faces were lean and angular, his facial features were small and soft, like a doll. He was, she thought, an astonishingly good-looking boy, more pretty than handsome.

As Carole considered the photograph, she found herself drawn back to the eyes. In the rough black and white of the old photograph they seemed to be light-colored, blue or maybe gray. There was something about them that Carole found puzzling—vaguely troubling—but she couldn't quite put her finger on what it was. She reached into her purse for her wallet and took out one of the several snapshots of Carlos she kept in the ID compartment. After looking back and forth between the two pictures, comparing Carlos to the Winkler boy and searching for the key to the difference, it finally came to her. Carlos's eyes, like most people's, looked out from the picture *at* you, as if acknowledging the camera. William's eyes, on the other hand, seemed to look inward, back at himself. Carole had seen those eyes before, in the portrait in the back bedroom: in Ellen's eyes. But those eyes were sad and distressed, revealing an inner torment of some kind. If the boy were hurt or frightened, Carole thought, he certainly didn't look it. In fact, he looked to be quite the opposite. He seemed to Carole to be smugly content, smirking into the camera, as if he were privy to a private joke.

Carole rose from her chair. Her first thought was to find a photocopying machine and make a copy of William's photograph to take home with her. But as she considered the photograph one more time, she abruptly changed her mind. Closing the album and gathering up her purse, she headed directly toward the librarian's desk to return the album and thank him for his help. She had known people who went through life with that exact same look, and she knew, from experience, that William Winkler was one guy she would never like.

A week later, Carole, dressed in cutoff sweat pants and a light tank top, stood in the kitchen sipping from a cup of tea and sorting through the various sections of the fat Sunday edition of the Chicago newspaper she'd had Carlos pick up on his way back from the donut shop. It was a lovely summer morning, and though it promised to be hot and humid as the day wore on, at that point in mid-morning it was deliciously warm, with a light breeze transporting the scent of lilac from their neighbor's yard in through the open windows. From the driveway to her right she could faintly hear the occasional sound of metal clinking on metal as Carlos worked on the old Indian motorcycle.

What Carole was looking for was the section of the paper that contained Carlos's inaugural cartoon. It was two months since his victorious return from New York City, and this was the date of his first syndicated release of "The Halfway Inn." After a couple of moments of searching she found the section, and then, a moment later, the cartoon. She laughed out loud when she saw it: it was the one she had had the idea for while stuck in traffic:

Cockatiel Hour at the Kit-Kat Lounge.

Chuckling to herself and eyes twinkling, she carefully folded the page containing the cartoon and placed it on a tray, then moved to the refrigerator and extracted a split of champagne she had hid on the bottom shelf behind a bag of salad. When she had popped the cork and arranged the tray with the bottle and two glasses, she carried the tray out through the side door to the driveway. Carlos sat cross-legged at the side of the motorcycle, his long straight hair falling around his shoulders, intent on some meticulous adjustment he was making to some small component of the engine.

"Hey, big boy," Carole said to Carlos's back, "got time for a break?"

Carlos twisted his head around to the sound of her. "What's the occasion?" he asked, spotting the champagne. As Carole had hoped and correctly guessed, he'd forgotten the importance of the date.

Carole was excited, and was feeling very, very good. She set the tray down, then sat next to Carlos on the cement. "It's the actual beginning, Carlos," she said as she handed him the paper, her small white teeth gleaming out from her wide grin. "The first one!"

"Hey, you're right," he said, considering the cartoon. "Think we should frame it?"

"Absolutely," Carole answered as she filled the two glasses, handing one to Carlos. "Here's to 'The Halfway Inn,'" Carole said, raising her glass.

"To 'The Halfway Inn,'" Carlos repeated, his eyes softly gleaming.

They clinked their glasses and sipped from them.

"I think we should call our house The Halfway Inn," Carlos said after a moment.

"What?" Carole asked, surprised.

"Sure," Carlos responded, taking a sip of champagne. "Hang a sign from the front porch. We're crazy enough."

"If you include the prior occupants," Carole said. Then she remembered. "Jees," she said. "I can't believe it. I forgot to tell you."

How it had so totally slipped her mind she had no idea, but she'd forgotten to tell him of what she'd found in the attic desk while he was gone. So as she explained, she pulled him away from his motorcycle and up the two staircases to have him see for himself. After he'd considered the last entries in Ellen's diary, he closed the book and gently laid it on top of the desk.

"What do you think?" Carole asked.

"Pretty bizarre," he responded.

Carole nodded, her mouth now tight and small, her eyes sad. "And guess what?" she offered. "She smoked a pipe."

"Yeah?" Carlos asked.

"Uh huh," Carole nodded. "Look."

Carole got the cigar box from the side drawer and handed it to Carlos, who spent several moments perusing through the contents. "Uh...honey..." he said, moving the delicate pipe with its intricate carvings around in his fingers, "...this is no ordinary pipe."

Carole's eyes narrowed and her head twisted quizzically to the side.

"It's an opium pipe," he continued, and these little brown balls, if I'm not mistaken, are dried up opium balls."

"Opium?" Carole asked incredulously. She took the pipe from him and examined it closely, then warily sniffed the bowl. "How is it you're so sure?" she asked, turning to Carlos and arching an eyebrow skeptically.

Carlos thought for a minute. "I dunno," he said honestly. "I guess somewhere I'd heard about how they do it, you know, with the little balls of opium. Besides," he added, "just looking at it, it doesn't look like something a university professor would be puffing on."

Carole weakly placed the pipe back in the cigar box. She had decided to try to be generous to her sad-eyed look alike who had inhabited the attic space where they stood. But sad-eyed had become weird, and weird had just become, as Carlos had said, bizarre. And now this opium business.

"How can someone write all this strident temperance stuff and then load themselves up on opium?" Carole asked Carlos as they passed down the steep steps to the second floor hallway.

To Carlos, a more practiced student of human nature than Carole, the question was rhetorical. "People can rationalize anything," he said simply. "Too bad," he added as he closed the attic door behind them, summarizing in those two words, better than he could have ever imagined, the verdict on Ellen's 46 years on the earth.

Two hours later, Carole was sitting on the front porch, sipping from a bottle of fruit juice and thinking about Ellen. She wanted to be able to talk to someone who had known her well to find out what had gone wrong in her life. She felt sorry for her, not strongly, to be sure, but genuinely, as she might for someone she had casually known. But she was also feeling defensive. If there were crazy monkeys in every family tree, she thought, why should she let this one cause her too much grief? True, they looked remarkably alike. But so what? There was a time, Carole thought, when the house had been Ellen's, and she'd made of it what she did. But her time was over, forever over.

A warm breeze blew through the open porch, sending the ends of her hair dancing gently against her shoulders and cooling the thin line of perspiration that had formed on her forehead. She took another drink of fruit juice, then made a decision. It was time, she concluded, for Ellen to come down from the elevated position she had granted her. Time for her to take her rightful place among the long list of Carole's predecessors, equal but no more important.

And so Carole spent the rest of the hot afternoon dismantling the attic bedroom that had been Ellen's sanctuary and prison cell so many long years earlier. She boxed up all of Ellen's personal items and clothing, sealed them tightly with masking tape, and, along with the portrait from the back bedroom, exiled them to storage shelves in the basement. The single exception was Ellen's sky blue dress with the cameo brooch. This, for some reason she refused to articulate to herself, she left hanging in the armoire.

As she climbed the basement stairs after depositing the last of Ellen's artifacts, she heard the sharp cough of a gasoline engine, then, a moment later another sharp cough, followed by the raw roar of a seventy-five-year-old motorcycle engine coming grudgingly to life. She hurried through the kitchen and out the side door to find Carlos straddling the roaring contraption, manipulating the hand throttle with one hand and making small adjustments to the motor with the other. When he spotted Carole he grinned. It was the

173

cocky smile of success Carole saw whenever Carlos successfully accomplished a difficult task.

"Hey honey," he called to her over the rough sputter of the trembling Indian. "Let's go for a ride."

The next Tuesday Carole left her office around a quarter to twelve and walked the half mile to the Italian restaurant where she had made plans to meet for a working lunch with Stella Phillips, the old lady with the easement dispute. When she got there, Stella was already seated and sipping from a glass of iced tea.

"Hello," Carole said as she slipped onto the bench opposite Stella.

"And hello to you," Stella replied cheerfully. For a moment she studied Carole's face. "You've been in the sun. You're brown as a berry."

"And you've gotten a perm," Carole replied, referring to the crown of tight gray curls adorning Stella's head.

"Just yesterday," Stella said matter-of-factly. "I suppose it's foolish," she said after a moment. "Old ladies getting perms. And putting on lipstick. As if anyone cares."

"Hey, it's fun," Carole said supportively. "Why not?"

A waiter came and took their orders, and Carole spent the time until their food arrived filling Stella in on the latest developments in her easement dispute. In response to the letter Carole had sent to Stella's next-door neighbor, he had hired an attorney who, after a lengthy and unproductive telephone conversation with Carole, had threatened to file a motion for summary judgment. In effect, Carole explained, he would be asking the court to dismiss Stella's claim as meritless. Carole was sure it was a bluff, and had urged him to please go ahead and do this, as he didn't have a snowball's chance of winning and would waste a substantial amount of the nasty man's money.

"I told him," Carole said, "that that would make my client very happy."

"Oh, and it would," Stella replied.

Their meals arrived, and for a few moments, the two women ate in silence. After a couple of bites of her meatball sandwich, Carole changed the topic of conversation. "What are you going to do after lunch?" she asked.

"I'm going mall walking," Stella responded. "A bunch of us from the Senior Center go there twice a week and do four laps. Got my walking shoes on and everything," she said proudly, sticking her feet out into the aisle for Carole to see.

"That's great," Carole said. "If I'm in anywhere near as good a shape as you when I'm your age, I'll be happy."

"I've been lucky, I'll admit," Stella replied. "I've fared the best in *my* family, that's for sure."

"You've got a sister, right?" Carole asked.

"Uh huh," Stella answered, making a fist and knocking on the wooden tabletop, "but not in very good shape."

Carole nodded, thinking, not for the first time, how strange it was to have been an only child. "Me," she said after a moment, "I've got no brothers or sisters."

"That's too bad," Stella said. "They make life interesting."

"Ain't that the truth," Carole said. "My husband Carlos, he's got a ton of relatives, brothers and sisters and aunts and uncles, and they're all good for a funny story. Sometimes more than just funny."

"Uh huh," Stella responded. "Sometimes flat-out strange."

Carole's eyes clouded as her mind drifted off to her own thoughts. Then, a moment later, they refocused on the table.

"Where'd you go off to, honey?" Stella asked.

"I was thinking of my great-aunt," Carole said, pursing her lips thoughtfully. "It appears that she was an opium addict."

Stella's jaw dropped open. "You don't say," she said, offering a toothy smile. "Now isn't that interesting. It's funny what you can find out about your relatives if you're game enough to ask."

Epistle

I can count the number of people I've loved over the years—truly loved, you understand, not just cared for—on both of my hands. In fact, I have one digit left over. The first time I actually got down and thought about it was many years ago when Henry Winkler, who is one of the nine, was still alive. I remember talking to him about it. It was towards the end of his life when he walked poorly and only with the aid of a cane, and it was after a dinner we had shared at his dining room table. When I quoted him the number he asked me who, and I told him.

I remember that he asked me to bring him a pen and paper from his study, and right there in front of me he composed his own list. His list was twelve, and it warms my heart, even now, to remember the sight of my own name midway down the list. I kissed him on the cheek and squeezed his hand.

"Not many, though, huh?" I said.

"What, twelve?" he asked.

"No," I responded. "Nine."

He looked over to me sideways for a moment before responding, his eyelids partially closed, the way he did when he thought I was being silly. "You think you've been ungenerous with your love?" he asked.

"I don't know," I answered. "It just seems like a small tally for a lady well into middle age, and one that won't likely be added to."

He nodded sadly, considering, I'm certain, what I hadn't said, which was that for both of us the list of the living was shrinking. Henry at that point had outlived all but three on his list, and I had outlived all but four. "Well, you never know," he said. "I found you later in life."

Since that day I haven't added a single name to that list, though I hold on to the small hope that I might. For the possibilities for love, it seems to me, can come most any time and often in surprising ways. And some is earned and some is not; some returned and some squandered. Love, that singular grace, is complex and convoluted, its logic often cryptic and sometimes seemingly absurd.

Hate, on the other hand, is wickedly straightforward.

Chapter Eleven

Will Winkler guided the Ford five-window coupe up Centennial Drive, steering with two fingers of his right hand while his left hand hung out the open window. It was three o'clock on a hot mid-western July afternoon, and Will was returning from his summer job at Irwin Meyer's Buick dealership, where for fifty cents an hour he did odd jobs for the mechanics in the auto shop. And though 1941 was turning out to be a decent year for the car business, that particular day had been slow and Irwin had sent him home early. Downshifting the Ford into second gear, he turned off Centennial onto Summit Avenue and cruised slowly down the street toward home, softly singing the words to a silly Andrews Sisters song he liked:

"'...I like oysters, lobsters too. I like the tasty Butterfish, foo...'"

He entered the second block of Summit Avenue and was beginning to slow for his driveway when he saw the two girls on the other side of the street. So instead of pulling into the driveway, Will glided the Ford to a stop in front of the house, switched off the ignition, and sat behind the wheel watching the two girls. They were, he knew, his new neighbors, moving into the Morris house that had been vacant for most of the summer. The front lawn was littered with boxes fresh from a delivery van, and the girls were picking up the smaller ones and carrying them into the house.

He was too far away to make out much about them. One had light brown hair, straight and cut at the shoulder. The other was taller and had dark hair, short and in a pageboy. Will watched as the dark haired girl carried a box into the house, then came back out, climbed into an old DeSoto that was parked in the driveway, backed out into the street and drove away. This left the girl with the lighter hair alone on the front lawn, struggling to lift and balance a box that was too big for her. Will left the Ford, crossed the street and walked quickly to her.

"Hi," he called out as he approached.

The girl looked up to the sound. Her face was thin, and she had brown eyes that matched almost identically the color of her hair. Will's trained calculus told him that she was pretty. Really pretty. "Let me help you with that," Will said, moving to her side and taking an edge of the box.

"Thanks," the girl said. "Let's just put it on the porch."

As they walked the box across the lawn and up the porch steps, Will scrutinized the girl more closely. She had a small nose covered with very light freckles, thin, pale pink lips the color of the inside of a seashell, and small teeth that were slightly crooked on the bottom. Beads of sweat pooled

177

on her forehead, and she labored slightly for breath as she struggled with her side of the box.

They set the box down on the porch, then stood to face each other. "Whew," she said, wiping the sweat from her forehead with the back of her hand and smiling wryly over to Will, as if the whole situation were mildly humorous.

"I'm Will Winkler," Will said. "I live across the street there." He pointed across the street to the Winkler home, which stood shining brightly in the new gray and white paint that had been carefully applied by Henry that spring.

"I'm Irene Adams," the girl said, extending her hand for Will to shake.

Fifteen minutes later Will had pulled the Ford into the driveway by the side of his house and was just entering through the side door. He was in a hurry. "Pop?" he called out into the cool, still interior as he moved quickly through the dining room toward the front of the house.

"Up here, son," he heard his father call down from somewhere on the second floor.

He found Henry on his knees in the bathroom, carefully breaking away the tile flooring with a hammer and chisel. Looking down to his father, Will could see the mottled skin showing through the bald spot growing on the back of Henry's head. He saw his father as he saw any other middle-aged man, which was to say rounded and balding and mildly irrelevant.

"Hi, Pop," Will said casually, stepping by Henry to get to the mirror hanging above the lavatory.

"Is it five already?" Henry asked, looking up and over to Will, his face smeared with a thin white paste of tile grout and sweat.

"Nah," Will said, checking the stubble on his face to see if he needed a shave. "Irwin let me off early."

"Want to give me a hand here?" Henry asked lightly, already knowing the answer he would get.

"Can't," Will replied. "Promised the new girl across the street I'd show her around town."

"Oh, well," Henry said, resuming his chipping. "First things first."

Will, turning from the mirror and moving around Henry and out the bathroom door, let the mild sarcasm slide harmlessly aside. "Be back in a bit," he said.

"In time for dinner?" Henry asked, but Will was well out of the room, and chose to ignore it.

In his room Will slapped on some aftershave, then headed out down the stairway and back towards the dining room and kitchen. Stopping at the door to Henry's study, Will stole a quick glance back down the hallway, then entered the study and moved to the big roll top desk where Henry kept everything important. Opening a side drawer, he found the cigar box tucked in the back as it always was. The box, Will had discovered some months earlier, was where Henry kept his money. Helping himself to a $5 bill from the box, Will carefully replaced the box, then headed out the side door to the Ford. The Cokes, he thought happily, would be on Henry.

In the bathroom upstairs Henry heard the sound of the Ford as it backed out the driveway. Gradually the sound dimmed, then disappeared as the Ford pulled away down the street. The car had been Will's high school graduation present, and as Henry chipped away at the tile before him, he wondered whether it had been a good idea. The car was providing Will with the means for constant escape, so that father and son rarely saw each other, much less spent time together. Still, Henry thought as he patiently chipped away at the tile, maybe the pulling away was a good thing. Will was eighteen going on nineteen and would be establishing his own life soon. And the disappointment of separation from the boy was not new. In truth, it had started soon after he and Will had moved back into the home on Summit Avenue in the wake of Ellen's death.

Will had grown up to be smart in school and reasonably well-behaved. As a young boy in grammar school, he'd been energetic and gregarious. But as Will entered his teenage years, his interest in friends and activities waned steadily, as did his desire for the company of his father. By eighth grade he'd dropped out of the Boy Scouts and quit baseball, and through his four years in high school he didn't seem to Henry to do much except study just enough for modest success, listen to the radio, and hang out with a succession of girlfriends.

He was, Henry had concluded, a good, if somewhat strange, kid, and for each of Will's personality quirks Henry had a well-rehearsed apology. That he had few male friends Henry blamed on the circumstances of his upbringing, and on a father who was himself more than a bit of a loner; except for his old friend Irwin Meyer and Minnie and Fred Klein, Henry had virtually no social contact and desired none. The fact that Will was girl crazy Henry attributed to having been raised without a mother. And the fact that he and Will hardly ever talked he attributed to there just not being a need: if there had been a need, they would have. The possibility that he knew his son not at all, he didn't even consider.

"Showing the new girl around" consisted of a quick tour of the downtown, a drive by Central High School where Irene would be entering her senior year at the end of the summer, and a stop by Schubert's Pharmacy for a soda.

179

"All the kids from Central hang out here," he said. "Plus a couple of old timers like me," he told her when they were seated with their drinks.

"When did you graduate?" Irene asked.

"Last year," Will replied. "I'm in college now."

"No kidding?" Irene asked, arching a thin eyebrow. The small farming town Irene had moved from rarely sent high school students on to college, and Will was the first college student she'd ever met.

"No kidding," Will assured her matter-of-factly. "Right here in town. I've got a deal with my dad. I stay in school, Pop pays the bills. So what brings you to town?"

"Mmmm," she said, pursing her lips as she chose her words. "Mom died, and Dad...I think he didn't want the memories, so we packed up and moved here."

"My mom's dead, too," he said lightly, sipping his Coke.

Irene, whose mother had been her best friend, was caught off-guard by the casualness of Will's response. "Don't you miss her?" she asked softly, her head tilted to the side and her lips small and thin.

"I didn't know her," he said flatly. "She died when I was six." Which was almost the truth. Will's memories of his mother were few and fleeting, and were flatly unresponsive to the photographs of her that Henry kept next to his bed and on the oak desk in his study.

An hour later, after he'd squeezed Irene's hand and said goodbye to her at her doorstep, he'd decided that he wanted her for his girlfriend. She was pretty and lithe and smart but not too smart. She was a virgin, he was certain.

And he was right about that. Irene had had boyfriends, to be sure. Plenty of them. But the customs of the small farming town she'd come from had in their own way sheltered her, setting boundaries on behavior and curbs on expectations. And her older sister, boundary breaker that she often was, had nevertheless taught her how to set limits on what went on in the back seats of the Dodges and DeSotos that had frequented her driveway. But that was the country.

As the last weeks of her summer vacation passed, Irene spent her days waiting hopefully for school to start. Her sister—three years older—had gotten a job waitressing at one of the restaurants downtown and had moved into an apartment closer to work, so that Irene rarely saw her. And her father, who had always been distant and reserved, became even more so as he struggled unsuccessfully to regain a sense of purpose after the death of his wife. Sadness and solitude overwhelmed the old house as Irene fell into the role of cook and caretaker for her father.

The start of school offered blessed, if transitory, relief. It was as if, Irene thought, she was transported daily between two worlds. Leaving her house in the morning for school, she would find herself in a world of fresh air, sunshine and happy energy. But returning from school in the afternoon, she would enter the house into a world of stillness and shadow, of empty corridors and curtained windows and the tired squeaking sound of her father's chair. She would have run away if it had been an option, and if she could have rid herself of the responsibility she had to care for her father.

But instead of running away, she ran across the street to the Winklers', and by the end of October was firmly established as Will's steady girlfriend. She liked him, she thought, because he was handsome and fun, and because he was happy. He was a sophomore attending the small university across the river, and on most school days was available to pick her up after school and, after a soda at the pharmacy, drive her home. On Saturdays they'd go out, usually to a movie but sometimes to a club where they'd dance to local bands playing Benny Goodman and Glenn Miller hits. Several times a week, after she'd fixed her father his dinner, she would join Will and his father Henry for theirs, helping Henry with the cooking and cleaning up and then sitting with them in the parlor listening to the radio.

As the weeks passed and autumn deepened, Henry, for his part, found himself becoming more and more drawn to Irene. She was polite and down-to-earth and surprisingly witty, and of all the girls Will had brought to the house over the years, was by far the most intelligent and thoughtful. She had an odd habit, whenever she was uncertain of something, of tilting her head until it was almost horizontal, so that a wave of her shoulder-length hair would hang like fringe from the side of her head, as if contorting her body would somehow squeeze out the truth. "Are you sure it's okay?" she would ask when he insisted on buying her something he thought she needed, her head tilted east and west, her eyes soft and doubting. The sight of her like that would make him chuckle, and he would go to her, use his big hands to pull her upright, and kiss her on the forehead.

At the Winkler house, Irene was almost always happy. The two men kept her in constant conversation, and Irene responded with a nonstop program of funny stories and pantomimes. Her favorite was a caricature of Mrs. Russell, her gym teacher. Holding a wooden ruler and standing with her feet planted firmly apart, she would pretend to blow a whistle, scowl dramatically, and bark out in a deep voice, "who wants to get their fanny whacked?" She would scowl out again for a few seconds, then break out laughing.

By November, Henry had come to consider Irene something of a fixture, and couldn't have been more pleased with his son's luck. Will, on the other hand, was not so confident of his good fortune. Sure, she was pretty, and fun to be with. And when they were parked alone in the Ford she was no cold fish. But whenever he tried to move his hand inside her dress and up her leg,

181

she'd stop him. "No, Will," her warm breath would say into his ear. "That's for love. For marriage."

So instead of dropping her for one of the less pretty but more experienced girls at the university, he began a campaign to convince her that he was serious about her, hinting at marriage and a life together after school, and buying her little presents with notes that ended with "All My Love Forever" and "Love Always." Toward the end of November, one like this had arrived with the corsage Will had sent her for the Central High School homecoming dance, with a line of poetry so beautiful she'd had to believe that maybe he really was in love with her, truly in love.

Around six on the evening of the dance, Will left the warmth of his house for the short walk to Irene's. A steel-gray bank of clouds lay low in the sky, obscuring the setting sun and threatening the first snow of the season. As he moved quickly across the street and westward down the block, a gust of wind blew open his coat to reveal his crisply-creased black pants, white dinner jacket, and tie. Feeling very much like Cary Grant, he turned up the walkway to Irene's front porch, climbed the porch steps and knocked crisply on the front door. A moment later he heard footsteps, and after another moment, Irene's father opened the door and allowed him to enter.

Mr. Adams was dressed in faded work pants and a wrinkled undershirt, and smelled of tobacco. "She'll be down in a minute," he said. It was all he ever said. An instant later he had disappeared into the dark interior of the house, leaving Will to stand alone in the silence of the dimly lit foyer.

Upstairs, Irene was in her bedroom with her sister Stella. Unlike her younger sister, Stella had some experience with the logistics of formal dances—the makeup and stockings and high-heeled shoes—and had come up earlier in the afternoon to help Irene prepare for her first. Stella was just finishing helping Irene with a pair of long, sheer silk stockings, new and fresh from the box. "Watch what you bump into, kid," she advised. "You look at 'em wrong and they'll run."

"I'll be careful," Irene promised.

Ten minutes later she was in the foyer with Will. She allowed him to kiss her on the cheek and pin the red rose corsage onto the shoulder of the party dress Henry had bought for her. A moment later she was in her coat and out in the fresh air. As they retraced Will's earlier path from his house to hers, he held her close to him, close enough to smell the faint sweet jasmine of her cologne. A few flakes of snow were falling as Irene and Will made their way across the street to the Winkler home. The plan was to have a special dinner Henry was preparing for them, then drive to the homecoming dance.

"Look at you!" Henry exclaimed as Irene and Will entered the steamy

182

kitchen. "You're as beautiful a girl as I've ever seen." It was the truth, too. She had curled her hair, and the elegant dress, silk stockings, and lithe curves of her body combined for nothing short of a magical transformation from bobby-socked teenager to sensuous young woman.

She pirouetted happily for him, then walked to him and planted a kiss on his cheek. "I just love the dress," she said, beaming. "Thank you so much."

"My pleasure," Henry replied. "And you," he said to Will, "are one lucky guy."

"Oh, I know it," Will said, putting his arm around Irene and pulling her to him. In fact, the issue of luck had been very much on his mind from his first sight of Irene that evening.

The homecoming dance was all light and magic for Irene. Multicolored spotlights sent colors cascading in all directions, and the band kept the tone lively and happy for the auditorium full of dancers. When they weren't dancing, she and Will sat with a couple Irene had gotten to know in school, eating cake and drinking punch, with Will telling jokes about the various teachers patrolling the perimeter as chaperons. As the dance neared its end, the band concluded with a series of slow songs. Irene, encircled by Will's arm as he guided her through the last waltz, felt closer to Will than she ever had before. As the last dance ended, Will kissed her on the top of the head. Her eyes lifted to meet his, and at that moment she was sure she saw love in them, kind and soft and pure.

After the dance, Irene and Will passed on an invitation to go with a group to an all-night diner. Irene sat close to Will in the Ford coupe, her head on his shoulder, as he guided the car up Centennial Drive. By the time they turned onto Summit Avenue, the Ford's heater had filled the coupe's interior with delicious warmth, and as they cruised slowly by the darkened houses, Will put his arm around her and began to unbutton her coat. When they got to the Winkler home, Will pulled into the driveway, cut the motor and let the Ford glide to a stop in front of the garage. Snow was falling steadily, and as Will moved to remove Irene's coat, large flakes of snow began gathering in clumps on the windshield.

"I'll get cold," Irene protested good-naturedly as her bare arms left the sanctuary of her heavy coat.

"No you won't," Will answered. Quickly shedding his own coat, he reached to the back seat and brought up a bed quilt he'd borrowed from the stack in the front bedroom closet.

"You think of everything," Irene giggled as he hurriedly unfolded the quilt.

Will smiled his best Cary Grant smile over to her, and as the blanket enveloped them Irene moved happily into his arms. For several minutes they

183

pressed together under the blanket, kissing. Will's kisses moved from her mouth to her eyes, then to her neck. He'd been aroused earlier in the evening at his first sight of her, and had stayed aroused throughout the dance, watching her, and watching other guys as their eyes moved up and down her. And now, finally, she was his. His hand moved to her breast, and he heard her moan softly as he caressed it. "Oh, God," he said into her ear. "I love you so much. So much." His voice was a soft staccato, almost panting.

As he pressed his lips hard against hers, she felt his hand move down to her knees and quickly up the inside of her dress. "No, Will," she said, pushing his hand back down her leg. "Not that."

"Oh, God," Will moaned. Again his hand slid up the inside of her dress, and again Irene stopped him.

"No, Will," she said again. "Please."

The windows of the Ford coupe were fully steamed up, and though it was bitterly cold outside, inside the coupe Will felt hot, and could feel beads of sweat pooling on his forehead. "Goddamn it," he said, "I told you I love you. You can't ask for more than that. Look what you're doing to me." His voice was high and angry, as if he'd caught her trying to cheat him out of something.

Irene, in the gloom of the Ford coupe's shadowed interior, was able to make out the wildness in his eyes. Then he was on her, his mouth hard on hers, his hand moving back up her leg, ripping at her stockings. She tried one last time to stop him, but as he moved his body to counter her struggling hand, his elbow caught her with full force square on her jaw and her face exploded in pain.

Moments later, when her mind cleared, Will had wedged himself on top of her and between her legs, and was awkwardly pulling at her underwear.

Later she would think of how she could have screamed and kicked and scratched, and years later she would chastise herself for not having done so. But at that moment, not knowing how someone who had just moments earlier said that he loved her could practice such violence on her, and, worse still, not being clear—not being crystal clear—about who was to blame, she froze. For the next few minutes she was severed from herself, as if she were outside her body. She was outraged, of course, but she didn't know enough to call it that. For her, at the time, it was simply another bitter disappoint- ment that life wasn't what it should be. What she would later remember would be the pain: the steady throbbing of her jaw, the screaming pain from the arm that was wedged tortuously behind her against the coupe's door, the sharp momentary pain between her legs when Will finally succeeded in forcing himself into her.

Then she was in the open air, following Will across the street to her house. Heavy snowflakes driven by a light southerly wind melted on her face and stuck to her hair. Her feet moved tentatively through the deepening snow, her black dress shoes carving a stumbling path toward her door. Behind her right shoe the remains of a shattered silk stocking bobbed along erratically as she walked. The long patch of torn silk slid effortlessly along the snow like a gossamer veil, the trail of its path so slight, so insignificant on the surface of the snow, that only Irene would have noticed its passing.

At the doorstep, Irene fumbled in her purse for her key, then somehow managed to unlock the front door. As she started to enter, Will's hand stopped her. Wearily, and with great effort, she turned her head and raised her eyes to his face.

"Thank you," he said.

For a full week, Irene stayed away from the Winklers. When she looked into the mirror she saw a different face. The open mouth and upturned lips were now shrunken and pinched, and her normally bright and energetic eyes looked small and defensive, as if she were alone in a strange and dangerous place. Luckily, she'd had her sister to talk to. Two days after the dance, she'd cornered her while she was helping fix lunch for their father, and had dumped the whole story on her.

"That son of a bitch," her sister had said, moving to Irene and taking the shaken, crying girl into her arms. "You could turn him in, you know," she'd said after several moments. "You're underage, kid."

"He says he loves me," Irene had said haltingly, and in a voice so small her sister could barely hear her. "He calls and tells me how wonderful I am and how much he loves me."

At this Irene's sister, who knew a lot more about men than Irene, came unglued. "Bullshit," she'd said. "He's a lying son of a bitch, and he'll hurt you again if you give him a chance."

Irene wasn't sure what she was supposed to do. She'd heard women talk of girls being "spoiled"; maybe now she was spoiled and nobody would want her. Maybe not even Will.

"Baloney!" her sister had responded. "Look, kid. This isn't the end of the world. Believe me. Any decent guy isn't going to care about that. Besides, you can always tell them the truth, that you were raped."

But Irene didn't want to have been raped. She wanted to be in love. And so, to her sister's chagrin, she returned to the Winkler house, determined in her own hesitant way to try to rediscover the warmth and security that had been the house's earlier blessing. Not surprisingly, Will chose to treat the whole thing casually, as if it had been a conspiracy—a sly, amorous secret they shared. And also not surprisingly, he wanted to do it again as soon as possible.

This was, in fact, the worry that consumed her, that kept her lips twitching from side to side. For if she was going to stay with Will, stay in the Winkler house and hope to recapture the joy of it all, she was going to have to find a way to endure it. But the very thought of Will on top of her and inside her made her physically ill. And so as November passed into December and steady snow came to cover the ground and blanket the roofs of the houses on Summit Avenue, Irene avoided being alone with Will, feigning obligations or illness.

Then, on December 7, the war came. Irene, who had been given the news by her sister early in the afternoon, hurried over to the Winkler house to find Henry puffing on his pipe in front of the radio in the parlor. He motioned for her to sit next to him on the davenport. After listening silently to the news broadcast for several minutes, she turned to him. "We'll be going to war, won't we?" she said.

"Oh, no doubt," Henry replied, tapping ashes from his pipe into an ashtray. "We've been heading toward it for a while. Now there's no turning back."

"You were in the Great War, weren't you?" she asked.

Henry nodded, relighting his pipe. "Yes, I was," he said. He knew what Irene really wanted to know—what it was like and how bad it was really and what would it mean for the people involved—but he knew better than to frighten her with the truth. "It's going to be hard, Irene," he finally said, as gently as he could. "Very hard. And it's going to be long."

He opened his arm for her and she scooted close to him, so that he could put his arm around her. His hand seemed to her to be big and worn, and seemed to cradle her shoulder like a giant paw. He smelled of pipe tobacco and Aqua Velva aftershave, and Irene buried her head in the side of his chest as he gently stroked her arm. "What will happen to Will?" she asked softly.

"I don't know, honey," Henry answered. "We'll have to just wait and see."

It wasn't long before Will was concerned with the same question. As the days passed and the nation readied for war, he knew that all bets were off for guys his age, that this war, like the ones before, would be fought by the youngest of the nation's men. Large numbers of young men were already joining the various branches of the services, and the peacetime draft was hurriedly being expanded.

"I'm not going if I don't have to," Will informed Henry and Irene at a Friday dinner shortly after war had been declared. "I look at it this way," he said as he cut a thick slice of pork roast into small pieces. "I'm in college, right?" He lifted a forkful of meat to his mouth, then chewed thoughtfully. "I figure the country's going to need us to keep things going smoothly here at home."

Henry stopped eating and sat with his hands resting on either side of his plate, a knife in one hand and a fork in the other, his gaze directed downwards at the food on his plate. "So a year of college and all of a sudden you're indispensable," he said finally, lifting his eyes to Will.

"A year and a half, Pop," Will replied. "And yeah, indispensable, in a relative sense."

When Henry spoke again, his voice was like ice. "And so," he said, "who's not indispensable, in a relative sense? Who gets to be the cannon fodder for this one?"

Will, intent on his argument, failed to catch the pathos in his father's voice, or to consider for even a second the bare essentials of Henry's own wartime experience.

"I don't know," Will offered off-handedly. "Unemployed workers, to start with. Then, you know, the factory workers...laborers."

"How about sausage makers?" Henry asked. His voice was low and his eyes bore down on Will like magnets.

Finally the light came on for Will. "Aw, come on, Pop," he said after a moment, twisting uncomfortably in his seat. "You know what I mean."

"That's the problem," Henry said. "I know exactly what you mean."

"So what do you want?" Will asked petulantly. "You want me to go? You want me to lead the charge?"

As quickly as it had come, the fire left Henry's eyes. For several moments his eyes, now soft and cloudy, seemed to gaze past Will down the hallway toward the parlor. Then he smiled sadly and shook his head. "I don't want anyone to go," he said sadly. "But they will."

Irene understood that if she was to remain with Will she was not going to be able to continue to deny him access to her body. So when she had found a way to endure his kisses, she reluctantly, and as seldom as she could manage, began allowing him to have sex with her. The liaisons weren't as bad as she had feared. There was really no pain involved, Will was generally finished in short order, and a hot bath helped to erase at least the tactile memories. She assumed, for her own self-preservation, that the experience would become enjoyable as love returned, and, further, that love would return.

By the end of the year, as Christmas came and went and 1942 made its somber debut, Irene had a new secret to share with Will, a secret that made it even more important than ever that love would return, for both of them. And if Irene's dogged clinging to the absurd hope of love was understandable if not defensible, so was Will's reaction.

"I've joined up," Will announced to his father midway through January. It was early evening, and Will had found Henry in the study, sitting in his father's big leather chair puffing on his pipe, reading.

"What?" Henry had asked, removing the pipe from his mouth and cocking his head sideways, the way Irene would have.

"I've joined up," Will replied, smiling happily. "The Air Corps. I leave on Saturday."

For several moments Henry sat in stunned silence, a thin line of blue smoke curling up from the bowl of his pipe, as he tried to digest both the words and their clear implications. "Why?" he asked finally.

"I thought you'd be happy, Pop," Will said. "This way some sausage maker can stay home."

The words struck Henry as if he'd been slapped in the face. "I never said I wanted you to join up, Will," Henry said softly. "I never even thought it."

"No matter," Will said with too much smile. "What's done is done."

"Does Irene know?" Henry asked.

"Nope," Will replied. He looked to his watch. "Gotta go. Gotta meet some guys down at the bowling alley. I'll tell her tomorrow."

And then he was gone from the room. As he headed down the hallway, Henry could hear him singing softly: "...I like oysters, lobsters too. I like the tasty Butterfish, foo..."

The next Saturday broke cold and overcast. It had been snowing lightly since the afternoon of the day before, and as Henry pulled into the train station parking lot he could hear the crunch of snow beneath the wheels of the Ford coupe. Once parked, the three of them—he, Will, and Irene—slid from their seats and walked toward the dim yellow light issuing from the terminal's cross-hatched windows.

Inside the building, the three stamped snow from their shoes and opened their coats to the warmth offered by a coal stove. There were perhaps twenty people inside the structure waiting for the arrival of the eastbound train. Among the group were a half dozen other young men who would be leaving with Will for the services.

"Hey, Bobby!" Will called to one of them.

Leaving the other two, Henry watched as Will walked to the young man, shook his hand, slapped him on the back, and began an animated conversation. "What branch you goin' in?" Henry heard him ask. "Navy, huh? I'm for the Air Corps."

188

As Will continued to talk, Henry's gaze turned to Irene, who stood next to him with a look that couldn't help but remind him of Clara's on the day he had begun his long journey to war. Irene hadn't handled the news well, and on the few instances that Henry had seen her the previous week, she'd had a hard time holding back the tears. And standing there in the terminal, she looked to Henry to be absolutely forlorn, as if instead of being separated from a boyfriend she was being set loose in a life raft in the middle of the ocean.

"He'll be all rright," Henry said to her, rubbing his hand affectionately up and down her back. "He'll get a desk job someplace."

Irene's look was unmistakable. But what about me? it said. Will I be all right?

Finally Will returned to the two of them. "Bobby Sinclair," he said by way of explanation. "He's headed for the Navy."

It was clear to Henry that something was very wrong between Will and Irene. Why wasn't he holding her, the way the other young men were holding their girlfriends, and the way he had held Clara? Why wasn't he having to pry them apart?

In an effort to give them some time alone, Henry excused himself to go find the drinking fountain. When he returned several moments later, he found them in earnest conversation. He stopped several feet from them, wanting to give them time to finish. Irene's back was to him, and he watched the back of her head bob as she talked. She had a hold of the lapels of Will's coat, as if to pull him to her. Will, Henry thought, seemed to be trying to calm her down. By lip reading, Henry could make out some of Will's words. "I'll be back" he made out, and "I promise" said three times in a row.

After a moment, the long wail of a railroad whistle announced the arrival of a train. As Henry rejoined the two of them, he saw that Irene's cheeks, still pink from the cold, were now covered with tears. He pulled a handkerchief from his pocket and gave it to her.

"Well, I guess this is it," Will said as the train pulled to a stop. He was grinning broadly, as if he were about to go for a carnival ride instead of leaving for a war.

They walked out to the tracks, and as soon as the handful of arriving passengers had disembarked, Will quickly hopped aboard. There would be no handshake or goodbye kiss.

"So long, Pop," he said from the safety of the boarding platform.

"Goodbye, Will," Henry said. "Take care of yourself."

"So long," he said, turning to Irene. "See you soon."

Irene's eyes were dry now as she looked sadly over to him. "No you won't," she said flatly.

"Gotta go," he said to no one in particular, then turned quickly and entered the coach. Irene and Henry stood on the platform and watched through the long row of windows as Will moved quickly up through the car, then disappeared through the door into the car ahead. Then the engine's whistle blew, and a moment later the train cars banged into motion.

When Henry turned to Irene, he could see that something was very wrong with her. "You okay, honey?" he asked, taking her arm. "You look like you're going to faint."

"I…I need to get to the restroom," Irene said weakly. She was breathing hard, like someone who had just run up a flight of steep steps.

"Come on," he said, putting his other arm around her and turning her toward the double doors of the terminal. After several steps, though, Irene, breathing even harder, broke free of Henry and stumbled to the side of the building. Falling to her knees, she threw up violently onto the freshly fallen snow.

For just a moment before hurrying to her, Henry stood watching her back heave. And in that moment it all came to him. Why is someone with such pink cheeks sick in the morning? he remembered. Turning his head back toward the departing train, the lights of the last coach could barely be seen, dim and failing against the falling snow. Idiot! he thought. What an idiot I've been. Because now it was clear to him why Will had been so happy. He wasn't going to war. He was escaping.

As Henry had suspected, after a hurried basic training, Will, having declined the Air Corps' invitation to become a pilot, was given a desk job. He was assigned to a fighter training squadron in Texas. There he stayed, updating training logs for the waves of pilot trainees passing through, until the spring of 1944 when he was shipped out to England to help prepare for what would be the D-day invasion. There, he was quite unexpectedly assigned to the Office of Strategic Services, the U.S. military's counter-intelligence unit that would later become the CIA, where he spent the remainder of the war updating road maps by day and frequenting London's pubs and nightclubs by night. Also as Henry had suspected, Will broke his promise, repeated three times, to return to Irene at his first opportunity, and it wasn't until after VJ day, in October of 1945, that Will returned to town.

Over the years that Will was away, his contact with Henry had been cryptic and utilitarian: where he was stationed, what rank he was, where to send the extra money he would plead he needed for one reason or another. His last message—a telegram from New York City—gave the date and time that he would be arriving back home by train.

190

And so on that day, Henry drove down to the train station to meet his returning son. It was a beautiful late October morning, and the leaves on the elms and oaks lining the station parking lot, like those throughout town, were just beginning to turn. Shortly after Will had left, Henry had given the Ford coupe to Irene, which she had promptly traded and gotten another. In its place, he purchased a 1942 Buick sedan from Irwin Meyer. Parking the Buick, Henry poured himself a cup of coffee from the thermos he'd brought, lit his pipe, and sat back to wait for the train.

As he waited, his thoughts turned back and forth between Will and Irene. He wondered what Will would look like after almost four years, and what kind of man he'd become, and whether Will had developed any qualities that would help erase the deep shame that Henry felt for him. His correspondence with Will had been equally cryptic, so that Will was unaware of most of what had happened in his absence. Of Irene, he was sure, Will knew absolutely nothing. And there was, it turned out, very much to know.

He was wondering how Will would react to these many changes when the westbound train announced itself with a long wail of its whistle. Leaving the car, Henry walked to the terminal and stood on the platform as the train came to a long, creaking stop. For the first years of the war, the trains had primarily taken the young men away, but for the last few years they had mostly been bringing them home, sometimes with all their pieces, sometimes not, and all too often in gray government-issue coffins. Will, one of the first to leave, would be one of the last to return, and with all parts working splendidly.

After a handful of people had disembarked, Will finally emerged, hopping lightly down the steps to the platform. He was dressed in his Army Air Corps uniform with sergeant's stripes, the white stub of a cigarette dangling from his mouth. Taking the cigarette from between his lips, he stood canvassing the small crowd of people gathered on the platform. Behind him, a short blonde-haired woman, struggling with two big bags, stumbled down the train steps and onto the platform. She had a small, very red mouth, and appeared to Henry to be either pregnant or very fat.

When Will finally spotted Henry in the crowd, he smiled and waved, then walked quickly to him. "Hi, Pop," he said, smiling even more broadly and extending his hand.

"Hello, son," Henry offered back, taking Will's hand and shaking it. He thought about adding a "welcome home," but decided against it. Will was all the family Henry would ever have, and the only living memorial to Clara, and Henry would always love him, or at least love the little boy who had held tightly to his waist from the back seat of the Indian motorcycle. But whether his return was welcome was still, Henry knew, to be decided.

191

"Great to be home," Will said, dropping the end of his cigarette and stepping on it. Henry was amazed. The young man, his bright eyes twinkling in the morning sun, was as full of himself as the day he'd left.

Will's eyes swept the parking lot and the buildings beyond. "Doesn't look like much has changed," he said finally.

"Yes and no," Henry responded, catching his son's eyes. "There are some things you'll be wanting to know." Just for a moment, Henry noticed, the bright confidence in Will's eyes faltered.

"Will," Henry heard a very British voice say. "Don't just stand there. Introduce me to your father."

Henry turned to the sound to find the blonde-haired woman standing right next to him. She was short, coming only to Henry's shoulders, and her face was round like a cantaloupe, with small blue eyes and a face full of makeup that was the worse for wear after the all-night train ride. Henry looked at her and then back to Will.

"Uh, Pop," Will said, trying to smile. "This is my wife Mary."

"Hi, Dad," Mary said. She smiled broadly up to Henry. "I'm the war bride," she said, opening her arms and stepping close to Henry, forcing a hug on the startled man.

It took Henry less than five seconds to circumnavigate an entire spectrum of emotions, beginning with shock, moving quickly to apprehension, and finally settling into anger. It was the same tired, impotent anger that Henry had come to know well in the first years of Will's absence, and the sense of it, returning instantly and in full force, made Henry sick to his stomach.

She was a plump girl, Mary, and very much "preggers," as she called it. "Six months in the oven," she told Henry happily as they walked to the car with Henry and Will dragging Mary's two large suitcases and Will's green canvas duffel bag. When they reached the car and Mary had piled into the back of the Buick, father and son were alone packing the suitcases into the trunk.

"So when did you get married?" Henry asked off-handedly, his voice as calm as he could make it.

Will turned to Henry, his eyes angry and defiant, as if the whole issue was none of Henry's business. Quickly, though, he melted under the scrutiny of his father's uncompromising stare.

"I had to marry her, Pop," he complained. "Her father's a general. They were going to court-martial me."

"So this will be two," Henry said calmly as he lowered the trunk and snapped it shut.

192

Will looked over to his father like a little boy who'd just been caught in a lie: mad at being caught, but in no way contrite. "Look, I'm really sorry about that, okay?" he offered after a moment.

"You think that's enough?" Henry asked, his voice hard. "You think you get to get off with just saying you're sorry, like you spilled a drink on someone's pants?"

For a moment the two confronted each other, their jaws set. Then came the sound of knuckles rapping on glass, and Mary's high voice calling out to them. "Will you two please hurry up? It's bloody awful cold in here," she complained.

"So what will you be doing next, now that the war's over?" Henry asked Will as they left the parking lot and headed for Centennial Drive.

"Probably headed for D.C., Pop," Will said, fishing a Lucky Strike out of the pack and lighting it. He drew deeply on the cigarette, then let the smoke out slowly. "Do what I did in the O.S.S.," he continued. "Five guys from my shop in London have already been offered jobs. I'm just waiting for the phone call."

Mary leaned forward, took a drag from Will's cigarette, and handed it back to him. "Will wants to be a spy, Dad," she said, exhaling the smoke into Henry's face. "He likes looking into bedroom windows." Mary caught Will's eye and they shared a laugh.

It took Mary and Will the course of that day to make themselves at home in the Winkler house. Mary oohed and aahed over the big front master bedroom and wanted it for theirs, but Henry adamantly refused, so they had to settle for two single beds in the back bedroom that had been Ellen's. After they'd unpacked their suitcases, they showered and slept for a few hours, made themselves a late lunch and headed out in the Buick to, as Will called it, "reconnoiter." They came home late, happy and smelling of gin.

The next day, around noon, the three of them were sitting around the big dining room table eating sandwiches and potato salad for lunch, and the topic of conversation was communists.

"If we knew what we were doing, we'd drop one of those A-bombs on Moscow," Will said as he spooned together one last bite of potato salad. "Mark my words, Pop. There's more mischief in those commies than there ever was in the krauts and japs. Not that I think much of krauts and japs," he added with a wink to Mary.

"You forgetting we're all 'krauts'?" Henry offered.

"You are?" Mary asked incredulously.

"A hundred percent," Henry answered, smiling. "Vink-el," he added, giving his name the correct German pronunciation.

"I mean Germany's krauts, Pop," Will responded. "And in five years *they'll* be commies if we're not careful."

"They've got commies right there in Ruslip, Dad," Mary added solemnly.

"Do they now?" Henry asked facetiously. "Right there in Ruslip, you say?"

Will caught the anger in Henry's voice even if Mary, who nodded back earnestly, did not. "I'm ready for a piece of pie," he said, hoping to change both the topic and the mood.

"Good idea," Mary responded happily. "I'm eating for two, you know." She got up and moved toward the kitchen. "How about you, Dad?" she asked Henry.

Henry shook his head no, and Mary, humming a tune from the hit parade, retreated to the kitchen. The two men silently avoided each other's eyes. Henry, his jaws tight with a dozen sources of anger, idly stirred a half-filled cup of cold coffee while Will fidgeted awkwardly in his chair. After several moments they heard a muffled thump and a cry of pain from the kitchen.

"Something in there doesn't like her," Will said with a smile, hoping to lighten the mood.

"I don't like her either," Henry said flatly, his eyes, now cold and hard as steel, locked on to Will. "I like the mother of your first child better."

Now it was Will's turn to be mad. "What do you want from me, Pop?" he said angrily in a low voice. "I can't have two wives."

"You shouldn't have either," Henry responded. "And what I want from you I don't think you have." As Henry vented his anger, his voice grew, so that he felt as though he were shouting at the cowed boy across the table from him. "I want you to care about your daughter, a beautiful little girl named Rachel, and I want you to care about Irene and the immense damage you've done to her. But most of all I want you to be a man. So if you want to stay in this house, after you eat your...pie...you're gonna get your ass over there and do your best imitation."

It wasn't a request, Will knew, it was an order. And sitting there passively in the grip of his father's iron authority, it was an order he knew he'd have to obey.

"You understand me?" Henry demanded.

Will swallowed hard, then nodded yes. Finally he was able to pull his eyes away from his father's face. His gaze drifted to the side, where he found Mary frozen in the kitchen doorway, a plate of pie in each hand, her eyes wide and her mouth half-open in stunned silence.

194

As Will and Mary poked at their slices of pie, Henry retreated to his study. The color had returned somewhat to Mary's face, and she sat across from Will trying to get the eye contact Will was determined not to make. When she finally spoke, her voice was small and hurt, like a little girl who'd just had her fingers slapped. "You didn't tell me you were married before," she said.

For several seconds Will's eyes went everywhere in the room except straight ahead. Finally he found her. "That's because I wasn't," he said.

"But you...you..." Mary's small voice trailed off to nothing.

"She says it's mine and Pop believes her," Will said flatly, answering her unfinished question.

"Is it...yours?" Mary managed to ask.

Will's eyes snuck a quick glance to the closed study door, then snapped back to Mary. "Listen," he said, his voice low and angry, his index finger pointing at Mary's face. "What happened before we were married is none of your business, and if you want to be married to me, you're gonna have to learn to keep your nose out of places it doesn't belong."

For just a second the tension held, then broke as Mary, tears beginning to run down her plump cheeks, dropped her gaze to the half-eaten piece of apple pie on the plate in front of her. After a moment she picked up her fork, cut a piece of pie, and with slightly trembling fingers lifted the piece of pie to her mouth.

When Henry emerged from his study several minutes later, he carried a white business-sized envelope, sealed and plump with its contents. Walking to Will, Henry dropped the envelope onto the table in front of him. "You need to take this over to Irene," Henry said sternly. The anger had left him, replaced with sad determination.

Will looked quickly to his father, then, glancing away, nodded.

"Now, Will," Henry said, as if demanding immediate payment for a debt long owed.

Five minutes later Will left the house and began his slow walk across and down the street. It was an inhospitable day—cold, overcast and blustery—and Will, the strong wind blowing his hair and battering his shirt sleeves, looked small and vulnerable, like a boat in a storm. As he approached the Adams' house, he could see what appeared to be a woman on her knees in the grass at the front corner of her house, digging in a flower bed. When Will was even with her, he stopped.

From the sidewalk, Will watched as she dug. She was bundled in an old jacket and wore canvas gardening gloves, and her brown hair was pulled back into a ponytail.

"Hello, Irene," he said finally.

195

Irene turned to the sound, so that for the first time Will saw her face. She was clearly Irene, but the face, flushed at that moment from cold and exertion, was not the face that Will had turned from at the train station years earlier. It was a woman's face: thinner than before, the eyes and mouth more pronounced, the attitude more reserved. She was, Will had to acknowledge, absolutely beautiful.

Irene put down her trowel and awkwardly pushed herself to her feet. "That stinker," she said calmly, bending to brush the dirt from her knees and removing her gloves. "He made you come over, didn't he?"

Will, who had been expecting trouble, was relieved by the composure she was showing. He thought she'd be angry at the sight of him, but all she seemed to be was disappointed. "Yeah," he said, "he did. He wants me to give you this." Will held out the envelope he was carrying, and after a second Irene took it.

"You know what this is?" she asked, her head involuntarily tilting to the side, the way Will remembered it would do when she asked a question.

Will shook his head no.

"My tuition money," she said. "Henry's putting me through college. I'm a junior. I'd be a senior, but I missed a year when Rachel was born. Dad kicked me out, of course, so I lived with Henry for a year, until Dad moved away." For a moment she drifted off in thought, her eyes going far away and her mouth closing into a halfsmile. When she came back a moment later, it seemed to Will that she was waking from a sweet dream. Then her eyes narrowed and her lips pursed, as if she were trying to find the answer to a question. "I think he wants you to see Rachel," she said after a moment. "Come on."

She led Will to a parlor window on the front side of the house and directed him to look inside. Cupping his eyes against the outside glare, Will peered into the dimly lit parlor and saw the little girl, dressed in a white cotton shirt and brown corduroy jumpsuit, sitting on the floor and scribbling a crayon drawing onto a piece of butcher paper. She had a round face and big dark eyes, and straight dark hair cut at her shoulders.

Watching the little girl from behind the glass of the window provided Will with the distance he needed to keep himself safely separated from the little human being he had been a part of creating. She was inside and he was outside, which was the way he wanted it and the way, he now realized, Irene wanted it. He was immediately relieved: there was no danger here, he concluded. Irene would not be demanding accountability. And so Will relaxed, and began to casually examine the little girl for Winkler characteristics, much the way he might have, out of casual curiosity, considered changes in the new line of Buicks.

"How old is she?" Will asked.

"She was three in August," Irene answered.

Will mentally calculated the nine-month gestation period: Rachel had been right on time. "She's got Pop's face," he said, turning to Irene.

"Yes, she does," Irene said. "She was lucky there." She made the statement earnestly, without smiling, so that even Will knew what she really meant.

"Look," Will said, "I'm really sorry..."

Like a traffic cop, Irene raised her hand to stop him. "Don't...I don't...don't talk to me about that...don't you even dare to bring it up," she said, her anger growing slowly with each word. For just a second the immense pain of what she'd endured flickered out through her eyes and through the twisting of her lips, then disappeared as she forced herself back under control. "I have a good life now," she said, her voice small but steady, "and a lovely daughter, and you're never ever going to be even a tiny part of it. So don't worry."

Behind him Will heard the screen door bang shut. He turned his head to see a man limping slowly across the porch from the front door to the porch steps. The presence of the man caught him off guard. He hadn't considered the possibility that there would be a man in Irene's life, and was doubly shocked because he knew him. His name was Jeff Mullins and he had been a year ahead of Will at Central High School. He'd been all-state in wrestling, Will remembered. Will watched as the man struggled down the porch steps, balancing carefully on his bad leg from step to step and using the porch rail for support.

"You remember Jeff Mullins," Irene said.

Will nodded yes. "Sure," he said.

"The war ended early for him," Irene said matter-of-factly. "He lost his leg at Guadalcanal."

The man completed the descent of the stairs and began the slow walk across the grass to Irene and Will. He had lost weight, Will thought, though his chest and arms were still big with muscle, the way they had been in high school.

"What's he doing here?" Will asked.

Irene almost laughed. Will had failed to notice the gold band on her left hand. "He's my husband," she answered.

For some reason the answer didn't seem to register with Will, as if somehow the answer she'd given defied the laws of physics.

"I know," she said in response to Will's vacant stare. "I didn't think anyone would want me either."

Then the limping man was very near, and Will could remember the chiseled features of his face and the boldness of his gray eyes.

"Jeff, you remember Will Winkler?" Irene said.

"Hi, Jeff," Will said, offering his hand earnestly, as if the two of them had some reason to be friends.

The powerful blow, which Jeff delivered so fast that Will never saw it coming, caught Will smack on his left eye, snapping his head backwards and sending him twisting into a heap on the ground. When he came to several minutes later, the eye had closed and the whole right side of his face felt like someone was beating on it with a hammer. He pulled himself up to his knees, then vomited his lunch onto the yellowing grass of the lawn. Struggling to his feet, weak-kneed and wobbling, he looked around with his good eye and saw that he was alone in the yard.

It took a week for Will's eye to begin to open, and another week for the enormous black shiner to fade to a shadow, an ugly stain that would remain with him for the rest of his life. Then, just about the time the last remnants of the black eye were disappearing, the call he had been waiting for came.

"It's happened, Pop," he said happily, stepping into Henry's study. "They've got a job for me."

"Doing what?" Henry asked, looking up from the book he was reading.

"Just paperwork for now," Will said, "but everyone's pretty sure they'll be forming a new agency. And yours truly will be getting in right at the bottom."

"So you and Mary will be leaving soon," Henry offered hopefully.

"Me first, then Mary later," Will said. It was meant to be a statement, not a request.

"Wait a minute..." Henry began, putting down his book and taking his pipe from his mouth.

"Pop," Will pleaded before Henry's objection could gain momentum, "I don't have a house, I don't have an apartment, I'll be staying in a hotel...give me a month, okay?"

Henry sat back in his leather chair, his heart sinking and his stomach twisting. "Okay," he said finally. "But no longer. She needs to be with you when the baby's born. You got that straight?"

"Got it," Will replied. But just as fast as Henry had agreed to his request, Will's eyes departed to new business in some far-off place.

Three days later, in mid-November, Henry was once again at the train station putting Will on an eastbound train, this time to Washington, D.C. As Henry stood on the platform, puffing on his pipe and sipping from a cup of hot coffee, his memories of Will's earlier departure came back into full view,

198

puzzling him with eerie similarities. As before, it was snowing. And as before, Henry realized, Will was leaving behind a pregnant girl. He stood watching from a distance as Will and Mary talked, Mary fighting back tears and Will talking earnestly to her, as if assuring her of something. As before, he could make out by lip reading bits of what Will was saying. "Don't worry" he made out, and "I'll send for you." But then, as Henry continued to watch the two of them, the shock of what he made out next sent the hairs of his neck standing and caused his pipe to drop from his mouth, bouncing on the wooden platform and scattering black ash, like pepper, over the white layer of new snow. The words were the same, but the time was different. It was January of 1942, and the girl was slim and afraid and very, very young. "I promise," Will said earnestly. Then again, and still again. "I promise."

When Mary's baby finally arrived, it was early February of 1946, a week early of its due date. For the last two months Mary had been a trial to live with, angry at being billeted with her father-in-law and hearing next to nothing from Will, and vexed by the ubiquitous discomforts of pregnancy. In the last weeks of the pregnancy, the doctor had recommended bed rest for her, which came as a great relief to Henry, as it meant that he had only to interact with her three short times a day when he brought her her meals. Henry had purchased a second radio for her room, so that Mary had no reason to leave her bed except to go to the bathroom or to sit by the window, smoking cigarettes and looking out onto the bare trees in the long sloping back yard. From his study below, Henry could sometimes hear her as she struggled to open the window to let out the smoke, and on one occasion heard her muffled cry when the window fell abruptly, pinching her fingers in the sill.

But with the birth of her child imminent, Mary added another emotion to her portfolio—panic. Immediately after her water broke, Henry heard her moving slowly down the upstairs hallway screeching out to him. "Help!" she called out. "Dad, help!"

When he got to her, she was standing halfway down the stairs holding tight to the banister, tears running freely down her pudgy pink cheeks, her eyes wild. "I can feel the contractions," she managed to sneak in between moans. "I don't think I can make it to the hospital." A wave of pain from an early contraction caused her to cry out and plop herself down on the steps. "Call an ambulance!" she pleaded to Henry through gasps of pain. "Call an ambulance!"

Instead, Henry called Irene. She found Henry and Mary still on the stairway, Mary babbling incoherently and Henry standing uselessly beside her. As she moved past Henry to bend down to the hysterical woman, Henry shrugged his shoulders.

"What's her name?" Irene asked.

"Mary," Henry answered.

"Get up, Mary," Irene said to her. "We have to go to the hospital."

"I can't," Mary said in a low moan, her eyes wide and blank, as if she were going into shock.

"You have to get up," Irene said with more authority, grabbing Mary by the shoulders and pulling.

For a moment Mary tried to rise, but a spasm of pain sent her falling backward onto the stairs.

"I'm going to die!" she called out wildly.

It was then that Irene slapped her. Not angrily, and only hard enough to make sure that she was getting her full attention. And it worked. Immediately the noise and movement stopped, and Mary sat frozen, her eyes fixed on Irene's face six inches in front of her.

"You're not going to die," Irene said sternly. "You're going to have a baby. It's going to hurt like hell, but you're not going to die." She instructed Henry to bring her a washcloth, which she rolled up and placed between Mary's teeth. "When it hurts, bite down on this as hard as you can," she said.

Together, Henry and Irene helped Mary down the remaining steps, into a coat, and out to the car. At the hospital, they stood on either side of her for six hours as Mary screamed and swore and cried until, mercifully, the baby was born. It was a little boy whose name would be William Winkler Jr. but who everyone would call Willy.

With Mary and the baby both asleep, Henry and Irene sat in the hospital cafeteria drinking coffee and waiting for Jeff to come pick her up.

"Thanks," Henry said. "That was beyond me."

"You're welcome," Irene said, her eyes showing mild amusement. "You're a good hand holder, though. I remember that."

Henry looked across the small table to Irene, then stretched his hands out to her. She took them, one in each of her small hands, and squeezed the rough fingers gently.

Chapter Twelve

The summer months seemed to run away from Carlos and Carole. June passed into July, and July into August, so that before they knew it, the stores were having back-to-school specials and Labor Day was approaching. It had been a summer of routines. Carlos's routine involved working on the house in the cool hours of morning, then retreating to his easel in the coolness of the study in the afternoon. That it was cool in the study in the typically hot and humid Midwestern summer was due to the first of Carlos's summer home jobs, which had been to install a central heating and air conditioning unit.

Carlos's second summer home job, which had been to prep and paint the outside of the house, had gone splendidly. Faithful to the color scheme he'd inherited from Henry Winkler, Carlos painted the house a light, almost platinum shade of gray, with white paint on the window frames and porch railings and carpenters' lace adorning the roof gables. When Carlos was finally done and the paint brushes and rollers were cleaned for the last time, the old house stood beaming in the big summer sun with a gleam that sent Carole scurrying for her camera.

Carole's routine involved her steady devotion to her law practice during the day, followed by work in her burgeoning flower gardens in the early evening and on the weekends. Carole, whose love affair with flowers had always been constrained to flower pots, reveled joyously in the sheer abundance of the raw material of her passion, which was dirt. Like a general preparing a battle plan, she'd mapped out every square foot of dirt in the large yard, from the back fence to the front sidewalk, and had begun planting trees, bushes, and flowers.

It was, in fact, while Carole was weeding around the gladiolus she'd planted along the side of the house that the final mystery of the Winkler house became evident. It was a Saturday morning in mid-August, and as she made her way slowly down the long line of orange and yellow gladiolus, she encountered first one, then another, basement window. Carlos happened to be working in the basement, doing laundry and sorting through boxes of junk, so that at each window Carole could look into the lighted basement and see Carlos at work inside. She'd rap on the glass of the thin rectangle, then make a face when Carlos looked up and over. But when she got to the last window at the back end of the house, it was black—apparently painted over from the inside.

Carole's first thought was that it was odd that she hadn't noticed the painted window earlier, either from the outside or from the inside on one of the countless trips she'd made to the basement. Her second thought was to consider exactly how many basement windows there were. From somewhere in her memory the number three asserted itself, but when she leaned back on her heels to assess the long side of stone foundation, she counted four. "Humph," she said to herself, rising to her feet and slapping dirt from her hands and the knees of her pants.

When, moments later, she came hopping down the basement stairs, she found Carlos transferring a load of wash from the washer to the dryer. A quick scan of the basement windows confirmed it: there were three windows on each side, the last one just a few feet from the far end of the basement, which was lined from wall-to-wall and floor-to-ceiling with wooden walk-in cabinets; the handiwork, presumably, of Mr. Henry Winkler.

"Hey, Carlos," Carole called over to him. "Did you know there's more windows on the outside than on the inside?"

Carlos started the dryer, then moved to her. "Uh-huh," he said.

"How come you didn't say anything?" Carole asked.

"Didn't want to scare you," he answered.

"Why would it scare me?" she asked.

"'Cause it means there's a secret room," Carlos responded. "And who knows what's in a secret room?"

Carole's gaze moved down to the cabinets at the far end of the room. "You mean, like, behind those shelves?" she asked.

"Yup," Carlos said, nodding. "Gotta be."

Carole considered the distant line of cabinets, her eyes narrowing and her lips curling up slightly, as they might if she were confronting an invading spider. "So there's a door someplace," she offered.

"I guess," Carlos responded. "I looked for it…looked hard for it. But no luck."

For a moment more, Carole stood considering the cabinets. "So, like, the door's hidden," she said.

"And hidden extremely well," Carlos said. "Someone really knew what they were doing."

Carole's imagination began to race. "Why a secret door?" she asked. "Why hide a room in your own house, when nobody but you comes down to the basement anyway?" She turned to Carlos, her blue eyes wide with the beginnings of serious alarm. "Maybe there's no door at all, Carlos," she said earnestly. "Maybe there's just a wall, with something behind it."

"Like a body, maybe," Carlos offered on cue.

"Yes, like a body," Carole answered. "And stop grinning at me. This isn't funny."

Carlos stopped grinning and put his hands on her shoulders. "Look," he said, "I don't know for sure what's in back of those cabinets, but whatever it is, it's not a body."

"How do you know that?" Carole demanded.

"Honey, I know this house," Carlos responded seriously. "If there was something really bad anywhere here, I would've picked up the vibes by now."

Carole, her pink lips pulled together into a pout, considered the assertion for several moments before rejecting it. "Let's break the glass," she said.

"Let's not break the glass," Carlos countered. "That would definitely piss off the house."

"Oh, we wouldn't want to piss off the house," Carole said with a hint of sarcasm. But only a hint, for Carole herself had come to appreciate, if grudgingly and certainly without full conviction, the mysteries of the old house.

And so they let the matter lie. But while Carlos, convinced that the house would reveal its secret when it was good and ready, put the matter out of his mind, Carole could not. Whenever she was in the house and not intent on a task, her thoughts would return to the basement cabinets and the blackened windows, and what might be behind them. Luckily for Carole, she didn't have long to wait to find out.

The next Saturday, after a morning of housekeeping, Carlos sat in the den eating a hot dog and watching a baseball game. They had a party to go to at five, and the ball game would nicely fill in the time in between. Carole, who was bored by the game, had wandered off to find something else to do. He was just finishing off the hot dog when he heard the scream. Instantly he was on his feet, the ball game forgotten.

"Carole?" he called out as he hurried down the hallway. Entering the kitchen, he called out her name again, then, seeing the open doorway to the basement, quickly moved to the narrow cement stairway and on down the stairs. And there she was, standing as if frozen in front of an open cabinet door at the far end of the basement.

"You okay?" Carlos asked, relieved that she appeared to be unhurt.

She moved to him quickly, seeking the safety of his arms. She motioned with her index finger for him to look past her, and when he did he let out a low whistle. "Holy cow," he said. "You found it."

Though shadowed by the dimness of the basement lights, Carlos could see, through the open door of the cabinet, that the back wall had opened at an angle. Clearly it wasn't a wall at all, but a secret door that led to the mystery room with the painted windows.

"How'd you find it?" Carlos asked.

Carole, still petrified, stood staring into the black interior on the other side of the secret door. "Don't know," she said finally. "I was looking for my tea pots," she said softly and a bit plaintively. "I must've hit something."

Carlos took two steps to the cabinet and peered inside, inspecting, as best he could, the construction of the secret door. "Very nice," he said appreciatively after a moment. "Very, very nice. We couldn't of found this in twenty years," he said to Carole. Turning his attention back to the secret door, he appraised it again for several moments. "Thank you, my friend," he murmured softly, patting the smooth wood of the cabinet wall.

As Carlos moved to a nearby shelf, Carole stood as if she were frozen, her arms crossed, holding herself. "What are you gonna do?" she asked.

Finding his flashlight, Carlos walked back to her. "Gonna take a look inside," he said. Passing by her, he entered the cabinet, letting the light lead the way into the mystery room.

"Watch out for spiders," Carole offered as Carlos's body disappeared into the dark.

A moment later, Carlos found the light switch, and the room filled with light. "Holy cow," Carole heard him say. Then, a moment later, "You gotta see this."

As carefully as she could, Carole stepped into the wooden cabinet and passed her head into the secret room, her eyes darting around on the lookout for spiders, her heart pounding in her chest. "What?" she asked when she'd gotten a good look at the interior of the room. "Are those what I think they are?"

"They sure are," Carlos answered.

"No way," Carole said, her eyes big.

Not surprisingly, the room was full of dust and, as Carole had predicted, spider webs. The surprise was what the room contained. At one end, under the painted over window, sat a huge steel machine the size of a car engine, which Carole had to believe was a printing press. Next to the machine were rows of shelving and work tables containing an array of bottles and cans and brushes. The remainder of the long room held perhaps a dozen clotheslines strung shoulder-high from wall to wall, upon which were pinned hundreds of little rectangular pieces of paper. Like little dusty flags, they hung limp in the stillness of the room.

At the end of one of the work tables was an old portable phonograph and a stack of phonograph albums, both covered with a thick coating of dust. "Hey," Carlos said, spotting the phonograph. "Check this out."

He moved to the phonograph and gently lifted the lid. On the turntable was an album ready to play. A moment later the secret room was filled with the sound of Ella Fitzgerald singing "How High the Moon." Closing the lid and turning away from the work bench, Carlos found Carole inspecting one of the little rectangular flags.

"What denomination are they?" he asked.

"Tens," Carole replied.

Two hours later, when the shock of it was over and the reality of Henry Winkler as a counterfeiter had been at least partially digested, Carlos, fresh from the shower, stood at the bathroom sink shaving. A moment later, Carole entered the bathroom, pulling curlers from her hair. She was wearing a slinky, sleeveless crepe summer dress that flowed so perfectly over the gentle curves of her body that even Carlos, who was familiar with all of Carole's curves and singularly uninterested in fashion, had to take a long second look.

"Wow," he said. "Pretty dress."

"Thank you," Carole responded, pleased to acknowledge the compliment.

"A pretty lady in a pretty dress," Carlos added, bending over to give her a kiss.

"You don't think I look fat?" she asked. She'd put on a couple of pounds in the last month or so, and was seeking Carlos's assurance that it wasn't showing up any place in particular.

"No way," Carlos responded. Which wasn't quite the truth. Her face did seem a little fuller to Carlos, and her torso seemed just a tiny bit curvier. "You've never looked better," he added, which was, to his mind, the complete truth. Carole's days in the garden had turned her skin a beautiful shade of light, light brown and tinged the ends of her hair with gold. And as for the curves, well, Carlos liked those too.

Turning back to the mirror, Carlos resumed scraping shaving cream from his face. "So what do you want to do with the money?" he asked.

"I guess we'll have to go to the cops," Carole responded as she teased out the ends of her hair with a brush.

"How come?" Carlos asked. "*We're* not counterfeiters. I mean, I understand that we can't spend it."

"It's evidence, Carlos," Carole argued back. "And yes, you can't spend it, or you'll be doing cartoons from Club Fed."

"But it's been, like, twenty-five years at least, right?" Carlos said. "Isn't there some kind of time limit?"

Carole considered this point for several moments. "This is true," she said finally. "The statute of limitations. Hmmm. I'll quiz Hank Cooper tonight at the party."

When they arrived at Margaret Coleman's home an hour later, the house was already filled with people. It was basically the same lawyer crowd that had been at Carole and Carlos's party earlier, along with a handful of people Carole either didn't know or didn't like. Slowly they made their twisting way through the groups of people, Carole stopping here and there to say hello and to exchange compliments on dresses and jewelry and occasionally to introduce Carlos to someone he hadn't met.

When they reached the drinks at the far end of the dining room, Carlos separated himself from Carole, poured her a glass of white wine, and was just able to deliver it to her before she was dragged away by Margaret Coleman to see their bathroom remodel. Temporarily left alone, Carlos returned to the drinks table and began to rummage through the ice chest in search of a decent beer. The offerings were disappointing, and after a thorough search, he settled on a bottle of mineral water. Spotting Fiona O'Donnell standing alone nearby, he walked to her.

"Hi, Fiona," Carlos said. "You here with Hank Cooper?

"Who else?" Fiona asked.

"So I take it you and Hank have hit it off," Carlos said.

"Oh, my," Fiona responded good-naturedly. "It's that obvious? The well-laid look?"

Carlos laughed. "Where's Hank?" he asked.

"Off getting something to drink," Fiona replied. "Ah, there he is," she added a moment later, spotting Hank moving toward them with two glasses of red wine.

When Carole finally emerged from the remodeled bathroom, she went looking for Carlos. They'd tossed around the idea of turning the little room next to their bedroom—the one Carole was using as her home office—into a master bath, and she wanted Carlos to see some of the nice touches Margaret had done to hers. Weaving her way around the odd clusters of partygoers toward the front of the house, she spotted Hank Cooper standing alone, sipping his wine and casually inspecting an abstract oil painting.

"Hi, Hank," she said as she reached him. "You seen Carlos?"

"He's out on the porch keeping Fiona company while she smokes a cigarette," Hank said. "What do you think of this painting?" he asked Carole, gesturing to the wall.

Carole, who knew nothing of paintings, did know when to keep her mouth shut. "At a minimum, it beats a blank wall," she said.

Hank smiled. "Fiona knows the artist," he said. "She claims he paints naked."

Carole again considered the painting. "Well," she said after a   moment, "in that case I hope it's not a self-portrait."

Hank laughed.

"Hank," Carole continued, remembering what she had intended to ask him, "let me give you a hypothetical. Suppose you had a client who found evidence of a crime in their house, but it was left by, say, previous owners..."

"Burn the money and destroy the plates," Hank offered off-handedly, taking a sip of his wine.

Carole, stunned, allowed her mouth to fall open.

"I already talked to Carlos about it," Hank added. "Mind if I see the money before you burn it? I've never seen counterfeit money."

And so the next day, Hank and Fiona came over for lunch, after which Carlos gave them a tour of the secret room and a look at the counterfeit money. Carlos had gathered it all from the clotheslines and consolidated it into ten neat rubber-banded stacks of twenty bills each—a cool $2,000 of fake money.

"Wow," Fiona said, carefully comparing one of the counterfeit bills to a real one from Hank's wallet. "Whoever did this was a real pro. I can't tell a bit of difference. Who did it?" she asked, looking up from the bill.

"Apparently my great-grandfather," Carole said. "The guy who left us the house."

"Cool, huh?" Fiona said, looking over to Hank.

"Very cool," Hank agreed.

Carlos snuck a look to Carole, who was standing holding herself, her mouth small, like a miffed schoolmarm. "You think this is cool?" she asked incredulously. "I think it's embarrassing."

Hank, who was standing next to Carole, raised his arm to pat her on the back. "God, Carole," he said. "You're such a Girl Scout. You should do some criminal law. Give you a whole new perspective."

After they'd finished admiring Henry Winkler's handiwork, they took the bills upstairs and Carlos burned them in the parlor fireplace. As Carlos was about to toss the last bill onto the flickering pile of ash, he turned to Carole. "How about saving just one?" he asked.

Carole, still holding herself, shook her head no.

"Aw, come on," Carlos urged.

Carole took two quick steps to him, plucked the bill from his fingers, and threw it into the fire. "There," she said in response to the chorus of disappointed "ahhs" from the others, "it's done."

Later, that night, very late when it was pitch dark, Carole and Carlos found themselves in Carlos's idling pickup parked on a country road at the near end of a bridge leading over the wide river that divided their city.

"Make sure no one's coming, Carlos," Carole hissed into the dark.

"Relax, honey," Carlos said from his seat behind the wheel. "The worst they can get us for is littering."

A car passed by from the other direction, and Carole hid her face as the car's headlights passed quickly over her. Then the road was empty.

"Okay...now, Carlos," Carole whispered.

Carlos, chuckling to himself, put the pickup into gear and pulled slowly onto the bridge, stopping midway across.

"Cut the lights," Carole hissed, looking nervously back and forth along the length of the bridge.

"No one's coming, so just relax, okay?" Carlos said flatly.

Getting no response, he pulled on the emergency brake, opened the door and got out, and pulled from under the seat the two heavy metal plates that Carole had wrapped in newspaper. Walking to the edge of the bridge, he removed them from their camouflage and tossed them quickly over the side.

From the cabin of the pickup Carole heard the distinctive "plush" of metal hitting water and managed to relax just a bit. "Okay, Carlos," she whispered through the open window, "let's beat it."

While far from complete, Carole's flower gardens were, by late summer, firmly established and vibrant with color. She had planted flowers along all four sides of the house, so that passers-by were treated to lines of meticulously maintained gladioli and snapdragons and hibiscus along the sides of the house and a long thicket of red and pink and yellow roses in the front below the porch. In addition, she'd planted a border of pansies and peonies and baby's breath along both sides of the cement walkway leading up from the sidewalk to the porch steps.

And so it was on a Saturday morning in late August, after her shower and tea and a breakfast of bacon and eggs that Carlos had prepared, that Carole took her garden shears and a wicker basket and slowly made a circuit around her flower beds, snipping a gladiolus here and a rose there until she had a beautiful bouquet of colors and textures layered in her basket like an artist's palette. Then, summoning Carlos, they climbed into the pickup and headed down Centennial, then west to Chapel Hill Cemetery. Carlos had called the cemetery the day before and had been given rough directions to the Winkler plot, so that as they passed under the iron gates at the entrance to the cemetery he knew vaguely where to park, and after that, where to walk.

As Carlos drove slowly down the narrow lane through the middle of the cemetery, Carole surveyed the expanse of carved stone around her. Her first sense was of disarray, of a sea of monument colors and sizes and designs mixed randomly, like the pieces of a patchwork quilt.

"There's no paths or anything," she complained aloud.

208

"What?" Carlos asked.

"I thought there'd be paths…you know, pathways," Carole explained. "It's a mess out there."

It took Carlos, who *was* experienced with cemeteries, a second to make sense of Carole's comment. "You never been in a cemetery before?" he asked.

"Uh-uh," Carole said. "Mom Browning was cremated."

The lane ended at a small parking area. Carlos parked and they got out, Carole with her bouquet of flowers, and, with Carlos holding Carole's hand, they began to walk due south, as Carlos had been instructed. "They're all little family plots…all different, see?" he explained as they walked.

Chapel Hill was typical of Midwestern cemeteries. The family plot would have a large memorial, four-to-six feet tall, of pink or gray stone, marking the graves of the oldest mother and father. These were the immigrants who had traveled the long distance across the sea to the broad and fertile farmlands of middle America. To the sides and in back would be smaller headstones marking the graves of their first generation sons and daughters, and sometimes the second.

Carole followed Carlos slowly through the maze of sculpted granite, stopping now and then to look at a name or date. The names reflected the mix of immigrants who had settled the city. Carole saw "Buchner" and "Meltzer" and "Vogel," as well as "Creswick" and "Parker" and "Leary." German, and English, and Irish. On their southerly path they passed by the graves of Irwin Meyer and his wife, who were buried beside Irwin's mother and father and sister, and passed within ten feet of the small headstone with a sculpted lamb marking the graves of Minnie and Fred Klein, Clara's mother and father.

"Here it is," Carole heard Carlos say.

He had gotten ahead of her and was standing in front of a modest three-foot-high marble monument in the design of a church steeple, which in the bright summer morning light appeared to be the color of pink pearl. Carole walked the twenty feet to him, then considered the inscription. Immediately below the small stone gable centering the monument were two sculpted praying hands, and below that, in small script, the words "Weider Zusammen."

Carole's hand pointed to the script. "Together again," she said softly.

Beneath the script, on either end of the stone, were the following inscriptions:

Loving Husband and Father	Dearest Wife and Mother
Wilhelm Winkler	Sofia Winkler
Nov. 14, 1864 - Dec. 24, 1918	Sept. 7, 1867 - Oct. 23, 1918

For several long moments, Carole and Carlos stood in silence before the graves. Carlos felt Carole squeeze his hand tight, then loosen it, then squeeze it again. Finally, she let go of Carlos's hand and stooped to place her bouquet of flowers at the foot of the monument. Then she stood upright, reached out, and tentatively touched the rough stone, the way she might touch something beautiful but foreign to her. Her face was intent but expressionless, as if she were making her way through a complicated legal problem.

Carole moved away from the graves of Sophie and Wilhelm, turning her attention to the small gravestones immediately to the right and slightly back from the main monument. To the right she found:

Rest in Peace, Sister
Ellen Winkler
February 22, 1887 - January 26, 1933

And behind the main monument:

Beloved Wife	Beloved Husband
Clara Winkler	Henry Winkler
August 4, 1898 - May 27, 1927	March 19, 1896 - April 3, 1977

Carole stood, her hands held together, considering the small gravestones. Intent as she was on the names, she failed entirely to take note of the small bouquet of wilted flowers lying at the foot of Henry's stone.

The huge cemetery was almost empty. To their right a hundred feet away, an old man sat on his knees cleaning leaves and twigs from a grave. To their left, way in the distance, an old lady could be seen tending to her own past. Under the climbing summer sun, the quiet of the cemetery was broken only by the occasional squeaking of a handful of robins parading in the newly cut grass.

Carole stood in front of the small graves, her sense of deep helplessness turning, for some reason, to outrage. She pulled away from Carlos and took several steps away from him and the gravestones. And then the anger broke, and she stood with her back to all of them, sobbing uncontrollably into her hands, her shoulders heaving. She cried as she hadn't cried in twenty years, since the time she was ten and her adopted father drove away from her home for the last time. Once again she found herself alone and confused, the unmoving gravestones the only testament to her abandonment. When the heaving of her shoulders finally stopped, Carlos moved to her, and when he touched her, she turned to him and hugged him, her face flushed and wet.

"I'm sorry," she said finally, letting go of him and wiping her eyes with the back of her hands.

"Don't be sorry," Carlos said gently. "I'm glad that there's someone to cry over them."

When they got home, Carole turned on the air conditioner, washed her face, then plopped down on the couch in the parlor, exhausted. She could hear the vague sound of music coming from the study: Carlos was listening to the old albums he'd brought up from the secret room. The way she had fallen apart at the cemetery had shocked her and even frightened her, and as she laid there, grateful for the soft breeze of cool air streaming in around her from the air conditioning vent, she tried to make sense of why it had happened. What was so utterly sad? That they had died? Yes, certainly. Carole, having almost no intimate exposure to death, feared it the way she feared a pitch-dark room. But there was more, she thought. There had to be more. She tried to sort through it, but as exhausted as she was, her mind soon stumbled and she fell quickly to sleep.

She must have been thinking of it in her sleep, because when she awoke an hour later, rolling her legs off the couch and sitting up, the answer quickly occurred to her. The house was almost perfectly still, the only sound the low hum of the air conditioning unit from outside the house. Carole got up, stretched, and walked into the kitchen. Pouring herself a tall glass of lemonade, she took a long drink, then went looking for Carlos. She found him in the garage, tinkering with the Indian motorcycle.

"Hi," he said, looking up to the sound of her approaching footsteps. "Have a good nap?"

"A great nap," she said, moving to him and kissing him softly on the lips. "And I want to thank you."

Carlos's quizzical eyes asked why.

"For guiding me to the answer I needed," she said softly. "I needed to know...I mean, I *really* needed to know...why I fell apart out there..."

"Aw, hell, honey..." Carlos began to offer.

"No, no," she said, stopping him. "Let me explain. I really needed to know what caused it. What was so damn awful sad. And I didn't know. And I couldn't get on top of it." She looked up to him and smiled. "Then I remembered what you said. You said 'I'm glad there's someone to cry over them.' Not 'for' them, but 'over' them. Remember?"

Carlos nodded, not remembering exactly what he'd said, but taking Carole's word for it.

"So when I woke up from my nap," Carole continued, "that was on my mind, and I saw the truth of it." She was talking earnestly now, but peacefully, drawing comfort from her thoughts. "I wasn't crying 'for' them. I was crying 'over' them. I was crying for me. The simple truth is that I *miss* them. I want to talk to them, to each of them. And I never will." And though her eyes were, one last time, pooling with tears, she smiled happily up to Carlos, then kissed him again. "So thank you," she said. "You're a very wise man."

Carlos, who didn't remember meaning anything by whatever he'd said, did the only right thing. "Glad to help," he said.

On Monday morning two days later, Carole got up at 5:00 a.m., had a quick shower, and sat down at her computer with two pieces of peanut butter and jelly toast and a pot of strong English Breakfast tea. Her plan was to spend a couple of early hours doing the routine transactional work she had planned for that day in order to free up the bulk of the morning for something else. And so, while Carlos slept in the adjacent room, Carole worked.

The "something else" she had to do had asserted itself the day before. All morning long, Carole had been bugged by her memory of the Winkler grave site. It wasn't the grave site itself; Carole was through that. Rather, it was the persistent feeling that something was vaguely not right, and Carole couldn't put her finger on what it was. And so, like trying to remember a name that hides right on the edge of memory, the elusive puzzle piece pecked away at her. Finally, as she was watering her houseplants, it came to her.

Hurrying into the dining room, she found Carlos sitting at the dining room table reading the Sunday newspaper and eating a sloppy joe sandwich. "There's somebody missing," she said, moving to the top drawer of the cabinet lining the south wall.

"Huh?" Carlos responded.

"There's somebody missing at the cemetery," she repeated, rummaging quickly through the drawer for their copy of the will that had given the house to her. "William Winkler Jr.," she said, looking up to Carlos. "His name was William Winkler Jr., Henry's grandchild. So where is he?"

"He's dead," Carlos mumbled, his mouth full of sloppy joe.

"I know that," Carole responded impatiently. "But what happened to him, and why isn't he buried with his family?"

212

This was the mystery that Carole was determined to unravel that Monday morning. She wasn't sure how she was going to do it, but she knew how she was going to start, so at 9:30, having finished her busywork, she called Jim Riley, the lawyer who had probated Henry's will, and was lucky enough to find him in and available.

After Carole told him what she was looking for, Riley pulled the Winkler file, and after some digging, was able to find a copy of William Jr.'s death certificate. "Hmmm," Riley said, consulting the death certificate. "He didn't live here when he died. The death certificate's from up north."

"You know what he was doing up there?" Carole asked.

"Uh-uh," Riley responded. "I know that shortly after Henry died, William Jr. ended up in state custody, and that's where I left the loop."

"State custody?" Carole asked.

"Yeah," Riley answered. He paused for a moment, thinking. "I outta know why," he said finally, "but if I ever did, I can't remember now." He consulted the death certificate again. "There's an address on this," he offered. "Why don't I fax this over to you? And if I think of anything else, I'll let you know."

When Carole arrived at her office an hour later, the fax was waiting. Riley had faxed over two sheets. The first was the death certificate, while the second was a blank piece of paper onto which Riley had scrawled the following: "William Jr. was arrested." Dropping her briefcase and plopping down into her chair, Carole took a deep breath, then turned her attention to the death certificate. The name was right: William Winkler Jr., aged 54. The cause of death: electrocution, accidental. The document also contained William Jr.'s last address. But what she was most hoping for—a telephone number—was absent.

"Scheiss," she said under her breath. Turning away from the fax, she directed her gaze out through the office window and past the parking to the busy street beyond. What next? she thought. After several moments of futile mental search for an easy answer, she reluctantly rose from her chair, grabbed the fax and her purse, and headed for the door. "Be back before lunch," she said to the receptionist on her way out.

The city library contained telephone books for most of the cities in the state, and Carole was able to find the right one fairly quickly. But then, sitting at a long, ancient wooden table with the yellow book before her, she was at a loss on what to do next. The telephone book was much thicker that she had hoped; William Jr. had died in a city almost as large as her own. She popped a piece of gum into her mouth and sat chewing, snapping the gum absent-mindedly as her mind tried to identify some strategy other than going through the pages line-by-line. If the address she had was for a private residence, she knew she was screwed. But what if it wasn't? Then what would it be for? A hotel? A nursing home, maybe? A retirement home? Maybe even, she thought, he'd been in jail.

She made a short list of these possibilities, then opened up the book to the yellow pages and started alphabetically. An hour later, she'd gone through all the way to "R," and had just finished striking out with the half page of listings for Retirement Homes. Having thought of nothing after "R," Carole sat dumbly at the table, the telephone book open before her. She was tired and dispirited, and mad at herself. Dummy, she told herself. Thinking you're going to find the needle in this haystack. She was about ready to close the book and head back to her office for her sandwich when her eyes were drawn to a pretty picture on the opposite page. It was a sketch of a long tree-lined driveway leading up to a Tudor-style home. It was an ad for Heritage House, which was a residential care facility. In large print was the telephone number, and below that, in smaller print, was the address. "Holy moly," Carole whispered when her eyes fell to the address.

Back at her office, Carole picked up her phone and quickly dialed the number. The phone rang and rang, and just when Carole was about to hang up, someone answered.

"Heritage House," said a voice that Carole could immediately identify as both old and female.

"Hello," Carole said into the phone. "My name is Carole Browning, and I'm calling about a relative of mine who was one of your residents. His name was William Winkler Jr."

"William Winkler Jr.," the voice said. Then repeated it, then repeated it again. For a long moment the line was silent. "Oh," she said finally. "You must mean Willy."

"He would've been about fifty-five or so," Carole said.

"That would've been him," the voice said. "He died, honey. A couple of years ago."

"I know," Carole said.

"He was a dear man," the voice offered. "Gentle as a lamb. Everybody here loved him."

"I understand his death was an accident," Carole said, probing.

"Yes," the old lady said. "So sad what happened to him, the TV falling into the bath and all. But he's with the Lord now, right where he deserves to be, with all the other angels."

"I wonder if you might know where he's buried," Carole said, getting down to the point. This, she had decided on the drive back to her office from the city library, was to be her mission. She was going to find William Jr. and bring him home.

"He's not buried anywhere," the old lady responded. "The state don't pay for no burials anymore."

"So what happened to him?" Carole asked, sitting straight up in her seat.

"He got cremated, honey," the old lady said.

"Oh," Carole said dully, her heart sinking. She imagined poor Willy's ashes being spread over some farmer's corn field, or dumped out a back window, or worse. "So what did they do with the ashes?" she asked, her voice flat.

"Well they didn't do nothin' with them, honey," the   old lady replied. "They're sittin' right here in a jar in the cupboard with the others."

The next Monday, after an early morning appointment with her doctor, Carole hurried to her office to meet with Stella Phillips. When she got there—thirty minutes late—the old lady was sitting patiently in the   lobby, her feet together and her hands in her lap.

"So sorry," Carole said as she ushered Stella into her office. "My doctor's appointment went over, so now I'll be behind all day."

"Oh, that's all right," Stella said dismissively, plopping herself into the armchair by Carole's desk. "I've got the time."

"Would you like a cup of tea?" Carole asked.

"You bet," Stella replied, smiling up to Carole.

Carole moved to a credenza, switched on her electric tea kettle and selected a Porky Pig teapot from her collection. "What kind of tea would you like?" she asked.

Stella twisted her head around to speak. "That kind we had last time was wonderful," she said. "Earl Green I think you called it."

"Earl Grey," Carole said, smiling. "I've got plenty."

As Carole prepared the tea, Stella watched from her chair. There's something different about the girl this morning, she thought. More energy and animation, and a nonstop smile. Finally she got it: Carole was, quite simply, very, very happy. And Stella suspected why.

As they sat sipping their tea, Carole outlined the latest development in Stella's case. They had a trial date set for two weeks from then, and Carole was just about ready to go. Plus, the old man on the other side had fired his lawyer and decided to represent himself.

"That good or bad?" Stella asked.

Carole took a sip of tea, then answered. "Good for us, bad for him," she said. "Representing yourself in court is almost always a bad idea. It's like trying to play poker if you've never seen a deck of cards. We're going to ask the court for what's called 'Quiet Title,' which is where the judge decides whether after all these years of nonuse there's any reason to burden you or your heirs with this silly easement."

"No heirs, I'm afraid," Stella said.

"No kids?" Carole asked.

Stella shook her head. "Herb and I tried, but no luck," she said. "We thought about adopting."

"I was adopted," Carole said.

"Now were you?" Stella asked, surprised.

Carole nodded matter-of-factly.

"Well, Herb and I would've loved to have a girl like you," Stella said.

Carole blushed, embarrassed by the compliment. "You didn't know me when I was thirteen," she said.

Stella laughed. "So how about you?" she asked. "Kids?"

"Not...quite yet," she said, her eyes glowing.

"I *thought* that was it," Stella said, breaking into a wide, toothy smile. "Why, you look like you want to run out and dance in the street. When's it due?"

"About seven months," Carole said.

"Congratulations, honey," Stella said.

Carole smiled back from her seat behind the desk, then popped up and walked quickly to Stella, bending so that the two women could share a big, long hug. She was as happy as she'd ever been.

Two hours later Carole pulled to a stop in front of her house. Exiting the car, she reached the sidewalk just as the old lady from across the street was approaching on one of her laps around the block. "Hello," Carole called to her.

"Hello to you," the old lady answered.

Carole waved happily to her, then skipped up the walkway to the front porch. As she passed into the foyer, she could hear music wafting softly from Carlos's study: he was listening to the old records again. She found him in a tank top and a pair of cutoff sweatpants, at his easel working on a cartoon.

"Hey," he said, surprised by her unexpected showing. "Come home for lunch?"

Carole thought for a moment. "Yeah," she said finally.

The music was Sinatra:

"It's not the pale moon that excites me
That thrills and delights me, oh no,
It's just the nearness of you..."

216

Carlos moved to Carole and kissed her, then put his arm around her and took her hand, coaxing her to dance. "You ever dance to Sinatra?" he asked.

"Never," Carole said.

"We called this 'makeout music,' " he said.

"You mean you made out with someone other than me?" Carole asked, pouting.

"Only once," Carlos responded, leading her through a slow spin, then back into his arms. "And I didn't inhale."

Carole laughed, relaxing in Carlos's arms and allowing him to direct her languidly around the room, the silky smooth voice of Sinatra caressing her ears.

"Uh...Carlos," Carole said after a moment, "you notice any-thing...uh...different about me?"

"What d'you mean?" Carlos asked.

"You know," Carole continued, teasing. "My shape. Am I, maybe, a lit-tle rounder?"

Carlos slid his hand down over Carole's bottom. "Don't think so," he said.

Carole laughed, pulling his hand away. "Not there," she said.

Carlos reached for a breast and Carole stopped his hand, laughing again. "Not there either," she said.

Then Carlos stopped dancing and eyed her curiously. After a moment, she took his hand and placed it on her stomach. Her mouth was half open in a tentative smile, the tips of her white teeth bright in the late morning light.

Carlos looked to his hand, then up to her face. "No kidding?" he asked, his voice soft and almost breathless.

"No kidding," Carole said.

In an instant Carlos's face was transformed, his eyes wide and shining, his mouth fallen open in pure, dumb joy. "Oh, man!" he said. "Man-o-man! Man-o-man!"

Epistle

For many, many years, there's not been a day gone by that I haven't thought of Henry Winkler. Certain familiar things have always brought back the memory of him: the sight of a motorcycle, the smell of Aqua Velva aftershave or of pipe tobacco, the rough feel of a woolen sweater. Sometimes, though, the oddest things would bring him into my mind's eye. When I was young, for example, the sight of a couple together would often make me think of him. It was the contrast, I'm sure...the plural versus the singular. When I first met Henry, he was already a widower, and while he lived to be an old man, he never remarried.

One day, after I'd gotten to know him well and my admiration for him and appreciation of him had begun to ripen into love, I'd asked him why. He was a hero to me, you see, and it astonished me that all of his strength and beauty—all of the good that he had to offer—would go wasting in the wake of the solitary life he'd chosen for himself.

He'd looked to me oddly for a moment, discomfited by the question, I think. Then his eyes had clouded over, his thoughts turning inward. When his eyes focused back on me some moments later, he was relaxed and open, at peace with the question. "I had my time with the brass ring," he'd said. "So will you."

I'd nodded my head as if I'd understood, but in truth I had not. And while at the time it went unexplained, I think I now know, these long years later, why remarrying would have been impossible for Henry. I think that he literally would not have known how to touch another woman. That's what having the brass ring can do to you.

In any event he was right about me. Soon after that conversation I fell in love myself, married, and had for fifty-one years as good a marriage as I could have ever hoped for. And then I became a widow, and, like so many women my age, have come to be alone. And when I see a couple arm-in-arm in the park, or talking over a meal in a restaurant, I'll admit that sometimes, despite my best intentions, I now think of myself.

I hate being alone. I hate the estrangement of it—the absence of talking to or touching or smelling other human beings—and the forced quiescence, and the damnable, incessant, galling silence. And I'll allow that sometimes, in the dark of the night, I despair of it.

But mostly I just carry on, grateful for church services on Sunday and pinochle games with my sister twice a week, and for the chance opportunities I sometimes get to make new acquaintances. But when I'm honest with myself, I'll admit that what I really want, what I ache for, are my old friends, *long gone. They were like the walls and roof of my house, protecting me from the elements and freshening my heart. They were my life.*

I wish I could have talked to Henry about these things. I wish I could talk to him now.

Chapter Thirteen

All through the spring of 1946, Mary waited impatiently for Will to send for her. Every week or so she would send a letter to a post office box address in Virginia that Will had supplied her with, filling him in on the news about Willy, complaining about the boring and lonely life she was leading. For his part, once a month or so Will would call with a new excuse for why the situation wasn't quite right for her to join him: proper housing wasn't available, proper housing was too expensive, he was due to be sent overseas on some secret assignment, and so on.

The existence of a newborn baby, of course, destroyed timely routine for both Mary and Henry. In the absence of Will, Mary presumed that Henry would take his place as a contributor to the routine tasks of caring for an infant, both day and night. Soon Henry was awakening automatically at 1:00 a.m., just as he had done twenty-five years earlier with Clara and Will, in anticipation of the imminent summons from across the hallway. First he would hear the muffled crying of the baby, then, a moment later, the sound of soft tapping on his bedroom door, followed by Mary's mournful voice. "It's Willy again, Dad," she would say.

The division of labor soon became clear. They would flip a coin, and the loser would head for the bathroom to change Willy's diaper while the winner would head downstairs to the kitchen to prepare a pot of hot chocolate. With the baby changed and back in Mary's bedroom, they would sit sipping hot chocolate—Mary on her bed and Henry in an armchair against the far wall—while Mary nursed the baby. Mostly they would sit and yawn, the only noise being the delicate and wet sound of Willy sucking first on one breast and then on the other. But sometimes Mary would want to talk, tentatively at first, hoping that Henry would be willing to listen. And when Henry showed a willingness to at least pay attention, she began to open up.

She would talk often of idle, trivial things of which Henry had no interest: the changing fashions, the prices of things, movies and movie stars. But as the nights passed, Henry encouraged her to talk of England, a place he had never been. She happily obliged him, taking him on mental tours of London and Bath and the seaside, and the gentle green hills of Gloucestershire, which had been her girlhood home before the war. She had been a disappointment to her parents, Henry learned, having done poorly in school and sometimes being guilty of what she referred to as "behaving badly." When she finished school in 1944, her mother and Brigadier father sent her off to London to work in the war industry and hopefully find a husband. She accomplished both, the former at a plant in Ruslip producing malted milk, the latter by way of a dance club in Soho where she had met Will.

"Swept me off me feet, he did," she explained one night as she switched Willy from one breast to the other. Then she laughed. "O'course, I always was a bit of a round-heel," she added wryly. When she saw that Henry wasn't familiar with the term, she explained. "A round-heel. Always falling over backward."

If the nightly sojourns together didn't make friends of them, they at least served to soften the initial repulsion Henry had felt for the girl. She was coarse and loud and to Henry's experience, remarkably crude for a woman, but far from being the monster he first thought her to be, she was, Henry discovered, benign in every respect. She was neither pretty nor ugly, the features of her round face plain and uninteresting, like the crockery in a cheap restaurant, made notable only through daily heavy doses of rouge and mascara and lipstick. Likewise, her short body was unexceptional, being neither slim nor fat and strangely free of curves. The only thing of beauty that Henry could acknowledge was her hair, which had a lovely natural wave and was the color—literally—of milk and honey. 'It was her strong point, she admitted to Henry at one of the 1:00 a.m. callings. That and her large breasts, which she referred to as "me jubblies." "Oh, the boys liked them," she said, pulling Willy's small pink mouth away from one wet nipple and fitting it to the other. "Boys always like them."

And the round heels, Henry thought sadly.

While Mary and the baby were unwanted, by the end of May, when Willy turned three months old, Henry had to admit that they were at worst a minor nuisance. In truth, their presence made no appreciable changes in his way of life, and other than the loss of sleep, which Henry compensated for with afternoon naps in the study, no major inconveniences.

During the day Mary kept to herself mostly, reading magazines and listening to the radio, leaving Henry to spend his days much as he had before they arrived, following a schedule made rigid by years of practice. In the mornings he would rise and bathe and eat his breakfast, then retire to his study to sit in the big leather easy chair with the morning paper and his first pipe of the day. The later hours of the morning would be devoted to house and yard chores—outside when the weather permitted and inside when it didn't.

As often as was practical, he would have lunch with Irene and, since her marriage, her husband Jeff. The two had met in college after Jeff had been medically discharged from the Marine Corps. They both wanted to be teachers, Irene English and Jeff, despite his prosthetic leg, PE. At first Henry had been wary of the young man, of his tremendous physical strength, and of the

221

wild and unfocused anger Henry could sometimes smell steeping beneath a thin veneer of quiet good manners. But with Irene he was as gentle as a lamb. When Henry had given her away at their wedding, he couldn't have been happier for her.

In the afternoons on all but the coldest days, Henry would travel down Centennial Drive to walk in the downtown parks and frequent the cafes and bookstores, visiting people he knew. Or he would drive east across the river to the university to pad quietly through the maze of stacks of books in the big library. Often in the late afternoon, he would meet his good friend Irwin Meyer, finally married and the father of twin girls, for a glass of beer at Otto's new tavern, which featured a juke box and a grill and a new clientele that made Henry and Irwin feel like the old men they were well on their way to becoming.

Then, back home and after dinner and the dishes, Henry would sit in the parlor puffing on his pipe and listening to the radio, or would retire to his study with a book and a glass of porter. Since Clara's death, Henry had, without any clear intent, become addicted to reading. At first his reading interests had echoed his pastimes—architecture, mechanics, and engineering—but he soon found himself drawn to art and the humanities, and finally to prose fiction. What was curiously absent from Henry's eclectic reading interests was anything relating to the broad social dimensions of life—politics and economics and history. Politics, and politicians especially, left him stone cold. It was politicians after all who had sent him to France as cannon fodder in the Great War, and politicians who had paved the way for the ruin of so many of his friends in the Great Depression.

But while it was true that Henry had no practical use for society at large, it was also true that he cherished human contact and loved deeply. So by the mid-1940s, when he finally realized that over the course of his everyday life he had slowly but surely become what most people would call a loner, it surprised him. In truth, though, he had become a loner the day Clara died. From that day onward he was alone, never got over being alone, and finally got used to being alone.

One area where Mary's presence was an issue, though, involved the whole business of Henry's livelihood, which was solely based on his long and successful counterfeiting operation. Henry made no apologies to himself for his profession and never lost a moment's sleep over it. To his mind he was forced into it by the Depression, printed only enough money to cover the reasonable needs of himself and those he loved, and, as long as he didn't get caught, never hurt anyone in the process.

The not getting caught part was the key, and Henry was very, very careful. Thus the secret room, designed initially to keep it a secret from young

222

Will. In those days Henry printed while Will was in school, and when Irene lived with him during the early years of World War II, he worked during the night while she was asleep, keeping himself sharp with black coffee and the lively music from his phonograph. With Mary's arrival, he'd gone back to the graveyard shift, stealing down to the basement every now and again after Willy had been fed and changed and Mary had fallen back to sleep. If in this way she occasionally deprived him of most of a night's rest, she compensated in her own way by pitching in with the house cleaning and cooking. And if he fell asleep in the big leather chair in the study, his head slumped to one side and his stockinged feet stretched out in front on the ottoman, she would remove his glasses from his head, cover him with a quilt, gently close the door and let him sleep until lunchtime. Around noon she'd reenter the study and nudge him awake. "Lunchtime, Dad," she'd say. "I've got something nice for you."

And usually it was. Henry had to admit that all in all she was a pretty good cook, even if she did like her fish and chips greasy and her vegetables cooked to a mush. She was an especially good baker, so that the kitchen and dining room always contained plates of cookies and pies and coffee cakes. By the fall of 1946, when she'd been with him for a year, Henry noted that his stomach had grown substantially and that his pants didn't fit as loosely as they had, and vowed to better resist Mary's constant temptations.

As for Mary, she was steadfast in her role of dutiful wife and dutiful, if somewhat inept, mother to Willy. She wrote Will regularly, and waited anxiously for the terse letters that came once a month and the telephone calls that came sometimes on the weekends, hoping always for the familial summons that never came and digesting as best she could the evolving litany of increasingly preposterous excuses for why she had to stay with Henry. The last straw came in December as Christmas approached, when a letter she'd written was returned by the post office, address unknown.

"Now look what he's gone and done," she said as Henry, from his desk in the study, examined the returned letter. "He's not even telling me where he lives."

When Henry looked up from the letter, he could see the deep hurt in her face, her mouth small and twisted and her wet eyes dark and defensive. He handed her a tissue from the box on his desk and she blew her nose and wiped her eyes, leaving black slashes of soggy mascara on the sides of her cheeks.

"What should I do?" she asked plaintively.

Henry thought for a moment, his fingers tapping absent-mindedly on the polished oak surface of his desk. "I think," he said finally, "that it's time for you and Willy to pay Will a visit."

Will's phone had been disconnected, so that it had taken Henry a couple of hours of working through the bureaucratic switchboards to get a message through to him. When Will had called back the next day, it had been very early in the morning, so that the terse conversation had been between father and son. Later in the day, Will had dutifully called his wife, and the details of the trip had been hastily arranged.

And so several days later, Henry drove Mary and Willy to the train station to begin their Christmas journey to Washington, D.C. The late afternoon was breathtakingly beautiful, with a clear sky and bright sunlight bouncing off several inches of new snow. Mary was all smiles and happy energy as she carried Willy across the platform to the Pullman car of the waiting train. Following behind, Henry lugged her two big suitcases loaded with clothes and diapers and gaily wrapped presents for Will and Willy. When her bags had been loaded into her compartment, Mary turned to Henry and gave him a long hug, then kissed him on the cheek.

"Bye, Dad," she said happily. "Who knows? Maybe I won't see you again until next Christmas."

She was overflowing with giddy optimism, her eyes sparkling and her mouth frozen in a wide smile. As the train pulled out, she waved to Henry from the long window of her Pullman compartment, then took Willy's little hand and waved it at him. Who knows? Henry thought, waving back until her smiling face disappeared behind the polished metal of the moving train. Who knows? What Mary knew was next to nothing. She didn't really know anything about what Will did for a living, or what he did on the evenings or the weekends, or why he had left his apartment for a hotel. And she didn't know that the reason why Will on the telephone had been so flattering and gracious and anxious for her to come out was because Henry had threatened to take the matter of his abandonment of his wife and child to Will's superiors.

Who knows? Henry thought as he directed the Buick slowly along its homeward path. Henry knew that of all the possible scenarios, Mary had chosen to believe in the most naive. She was neither smart nor savvy, and at this most critical juncture in her short life had no desire to be either. She believed, Henry knew, that the fast train speeding across the empty, snow-covered fields of middle America was taking her to her second honeymoon.

When he had the Buick parked in the garage, he went inside to find a bottle of porter and his pipe. Sitting in his leather chair in the stillness of the study, sipping from the tall glass of black porter and puffing on his pipe, Henry reflected on the sad outcome that his gut told him awaited Mary. His mind drifted back to his phone conversation with Will, and to the black vitriol that had ended the conversation. For better or worse, Will was now gone from him, Henry knew, just as if he had died. It was not to be reasoned or rationalized or avoided. It was just an outcome that had to be. After a moment the pain of it overwhelmed him, and he put down the pipe and glass, closed his eyes, and let the grief come.

Three days later, Mary called from her hotel in Washington, D.C. to let Henry know that she was coming home, and two days after that, on Christmas Eve, he fetched her and Willy from the train station. As they drove home, Mary sat next to him in the front seat of the Buick with the sleeping Willy in her arms. She looked to Henry to be exhausted, as if she hadn't slept in several days. Deep black bags surrounded both of her eyes, and when she spoke it was in half sentences, like someone whose mind was distracted. She lit a cigarette and smoked it mechanically, the unnoticed ash growing long and bent. Henry learned the excuse for Mary's early return: that Will was being sent overseas on a secret mission—where he would not say, not even the continent—that would keep him away and out of touch for at least a year. He'd arranged to have a hundred dollars sent to her automatically every month, so that she couldn't complain that he had abandoned her and the baby.

As they turned off Centennial Drive on to Summit, Mary finally unburdened herself. "We didn't have one meal together," she said in a pleading voice so small that Henry could hardly hear her. "And we stayed in separate rooms. He didn't even want to…" Her voice trailed off to nothing, and she raised her hand to bite on the knuckle of her thumb, spilling a long line of cigarette ash onto her lap.

When they got into the house, Mary hugged Henry hard, then went right to bed. The little baby was wide awake, though, so after changing his diaper, Henry carried him into the study and set him down on one of Sophie's quilts to let him wiggle and pitch happily, like a boat in the tide. He was, Henry had to admit, a remarkably good baby. He only cried for a good reason, when he was hungry or his diaper was dirty, and he was surprisingly sedate, sitting quietly, almost lethargically, for the longest periods without fuss.

Henry watched him on the quilt, his voice making small panting sounds, then sat down on the quilt next to him and offered the little boy his index finger. Willy reached out to touch the finger, but despite Henry's coaxing would not grab it. Who will he look like? Henry asked himself for the first time, leaning down to examine Willy's round little face. His hair, first light brown, had turned dark like his father's, and his eyes, which Henry had first taken to be blue like Mary's, had, he noticed, turned a black-speckled green. His mouth was long, with narrow pink lips that undulated out to upturned edges, as if he were amused.

And then, as Henry's gaze moved back and forth between the little boy's green eyes and his naturally smiling mouth, it hit him out of the blue and with full force. Involuntarily he moaned as his stomach tightened, and his memory flew back, back to the big bed in the early morning, back to Clara as she woke to Henry's stirring next to her. And there for a moment they were together again in the big bed, Clara's green eyes coming to life after heavy sleep, her long mouth first pursing, then opening to him for their first kiss of the day.

When, after several moments, his mind returned to the study, Henry sat in stunned silence beside the baby, drinking in the little boy's soft face. Finally he reached out to gently touch the face, then bent to kiss the small, smooth forehead. An hour later, when Willy was asleep in his crib next to his mother's bed, Henry left the house to travel downtown to buy last-minute Christmas presents for Mary and Willy.

Mary spent the cold months of January and February 1947 on the davenport in the parlor, smoking cigarettes and listening to the radio. After a year in the U.S., she'd finally developed a taste for coffee and drank it all day long—mornings and afternoons of coffee and cigarettes. Twice a day, like clockwork, she would get herself up from the davenport to fix first lunch and then dinner for herself and Henry. Henry observed the cheerless routine mostly from the safety of his study. Sometimes she'd want to talk, and occasionally she'd take Henry up on his offer of a card game or a movie, but mostly she sat alone wrapped in her thoughts. She lived, Henry thought, as if she were sick with an illness, as if she were fighting a parasite that consumed all of her energy. There was no grief and there was no joy; there was just getting through the day.

"Mary," Henry finally said one day, "your problem is that you're just sitting around waiting for that damned phone to ring," he said. "Why don't you get out? Volunteer someplace. Get a job if you like."

For a moment she stood silently digesting his statement, as if she were translating it from some foreign language. Then she brightened, and the corners of her mouth turned up into a small smile. "You know what?" she said. "I think I will."

After a couple of days of searching, Mary found a job at the downtown Woolworth's working as a waitress at the lunch counter. She worked from ten to four five days a week and one day on the weekend. It was exactly what she needed. The job occupied the long afternoons, she had her own money to spend, and as the months slipped by she began to make friends. One of the other waitresses—a divorced woman named Francine—began to invite her to play cards in the evening with a few other women. Sometimes they would all go out to a movie or to dinner, and occasionally they'd go out to a nightclub for drinks and dancing. When men would try to pick her up, Mary would show them her wedding ring and politely decline; she was, despite it all, still a faithful wife.

While Mary worked, Henry looked after Willy. She had at first been apologetic at sticking Henry with the little boy thirty-six hours a week. Willy was, after all, still a baby and required the constant monitoring that all babies demand. But Henry had quickly dismissed her reticence; he was more than willing. He didn't try to tell her why, he couldn't have been able to find the words for it: of the memories the little boy carried in his face, offered to him like jewels in the sand under clear water, just out of reach.

And so, beginning that summer and into the fall, Henry's routine changed to accommodate Willy. After dropping off Mary at work, Henry would return home with Willy for lunch. Then, after Willy had had a nap, the two of them would head out in the Buick much as Henry had done before, for the downtown or a park or the University library. The little boy was really no trouble at all, sitting quietly in his stroller while Henry talked to a friend or read in the library, making a fuss only when his diaper needed changing. And only after several months of this, as the weather turned cold and Thanksgiving approached, did it occur to Henry that Willy was perhaps a bit too quiet. His only experience with babies had been Will, but his sketchy memory suggested that at twenty-one months, Willy should be doing more than sitting contentedly in his stroller hour after hour. At that age, Will had been forming words into sentences and identifying colors and drawing complete pictures in crayon, none of which Willy could do.

He was alarmed enough to seek out books on child development, and after digesting what relevant material he could find, sought out an expert at the University. Then, on a day mid-week in early December, when Mary was at work at the lunch counter, Henry bundled up Willy and drove him to a red brick building on the edge of the university where a gentle, bearded young man put him through a series of tests, asking him to identify objects by name and fold a piece of paper and put a spoon in a cup and place bright red cubes into a box. After the test, they retreated to the young man's office where, as Willy slept in his stroller, the two men puffed on their pipes and talked. When he left an hour later, Henry resolved to keep his secret to himself, at least for the time being.

Christmas came and went with no word from Will: no phone call, no letter, no packages sent for Mary and Willy. When word finally came, on a cold, slate-gray day in January, a week before Willy's second birthday, the timing could not have been worse. It was Mary's day off, so Henry left the house early to help Jeff Mullins with a kitchen remodel he was doing. Jeff and Irene had both graduated from the university by then and had gotten jobs as teachers, Irene at one of the middle schools teaching English and Jeff at Central High teaching PE and coaching the wrestling team. The five-year-old Rachel, bright-eyed and precocious and full of energy, was in kindergarten. As Henry and Jeff banged away in the kitchen, Irene and Rachel played alphabet games at the dining room table, and drew pictures that Rachel would run into the kitchen with to show her father and grandfather.

With Henry gone, Mary was alone with Willy for the entire day, and on this particular day, as he had been progressively for the last couple of weeks, Willy was driving her crazy. He started the morning by throwing up his breakfast all across Mary's front, so that she had to clean him, clean the kitchen floor, and finally clean herself. An hour later, he fell out of his crib and bumped his head badly, setting him off for a half hour of nonstop crying. He was toddling, so if she tried to leave him alone for even a few minutes he'd be pulling things from tabletops and dressers. On this particular day, in the span of fifteen minutes, he claimed an ash tray that had been inadvertently left on a window sill in the dining room and a full cup of coffee that Mary had foolishly left on an end table in the parlor. Hearing the crash, Mary hurried into the parlor to find Willy standing over the broken cup, and over the dark and spreading stain on Henry's Persian rug.

Then Mary broke, her weariness and frustration cascading into wild and uncontrolled anger. She stooped to grab Willy by the arm and smacked him hard across his bottom. "You're a bad boy," she screamed, her voice loud and shrill. Then she smacked him again, and Willy started to cry.

"That's right," she yelled down to him, her face red and distorted. "Go ahead and cry some more, you little bastard!" Then her eyes filled with tears and she collapsed onto her knees and buried her head in her hands, her rhythmic sobbing eclipsing the high moans of the little boy next to her.

When Henry came home for lunch, he found Mary curled up on the davenport, smoking. The room was blue with the pungent smoke, and the ash tray on the end table next to Mary was overflowing. From far away Henry could hear Willy crying. He didn't need to ask what had happened; he'd seen it coming for weeks. "Where's Willy?" he asked.

Mary looked up to him, then quickly looked away. She took a long drag on her cigarette, then answered. "Upstairs in the bathroom," she said.

Henry left the parlor and quickly climbed the steps to the second floor. He found him naked from the waist down, his face red and wet from crying, his little pink bottom smeared with feces and an unwashed diaper floating in the toilet. Henry bent over offering Willy his open arms, and the little boy ran to him. "Gampa, Gampa," Willy said. It was the only word he knew.

After Henry had cleaned Willy and fed him, he put him to bed and sat with him until the little boy had fallen asleep, then rejoined Mary in the parlor. She lay curled up on the davenport, her head on a pillow, one of Sophie's quilts wrapped tightly around the contours or her body. Her open eyes stared straight ahead.

"What happened?" Henry asked.

For several moments Mary was silent. When she finally spoke, her voice was small and tired. "He doesn't learn," she said. "He just doesn't learn." Her head turned slowly to Henry. "I've been around babies, Dad," she said. "It's not supposed to be like this."

"Willy's retarded, Mary," Henry said.

Henry had thought that the words would shock and surprise Mary, but they didn't. She considered them in stride, as she might if she'd been told that she'd lost her job. "You had him tested, then?" she asked.

"Yes," Henry answered.

Mary lay silent for several moments, staring ahead at nothing. "Me brother's like that," she said finally. "Mentally retarded. IQ of fifty, they say. He's twenty-four, but he's a six-year-old." Her head turned again to Henry. "So how bad is it for Willy?" she asked.

"The same," Henry said.

Mary closed her eyes and lay still for several moments, trying, Henry knew, to find a way to shoulder this new load.

She was still on the davenport an hour later when the telegram arrived. It was sent to Mary Winkler from William Winkler. Henry handed Mary the thin brown envelope, then stood by the edge of the davenport while she sat up, hurriedly dug open the envelope, and read. When she had finished, she let the brown paper drop from her hand. She took a deep breath, then closed her eyes and bowed her head, pressing her fingers to her brow, as if she had a headache.

After a moment she picked up the telegram and handed it to Henry, who read the terse, cruel lines quickly:

"Returning to US in summer stop
prepare for divorce stop Will stop"

"He's a real bell-head, isn't he?" Mary said.

Henry hadn't heard the expression before, but didn't need to know exactly what it meant to know that it was true. "Yes," he said, "I'm afraid he is."

Mary shook her head slowly, her eyes hard, an odd hint of a smile on her pale lips. Henry knew that steely smile. He'd seen it years earlier on Ire-

229

ne, and before that on himself and his comrades in the infantry as they shipped out for the apocalypse in Europe. I've drawn the short straw, it said. The joke's on me.

Mary went to bed early that night and slept in late the next morning, leaving Henry to tend to Willy's modest needs. When she finally came down around noon, still dressed in her bathrobe, she called in to work sick, then headed to the kitchen cabinet for Henry's small bottle of medicinal whiskey. Henry, who was preparing Willy's lunch, watched as she poured several ounces over ice, took a sip, then quickly drained the glass. Refilling the glass and turning to leave the kitchen, she caught Henry's watchful eye.

"You blame me?" she asked.

"No," Henry replied.

Mary spent the afternoon on the davenport, smoking and drinking whiskey and listening to the hit parade on the radio. When she'd had all the whiskey she could handle, she fell asleep, leaving the long end of a freshly lit cigarette to burn down to nothing in the crowded ash tray next to her. Around four she got up, took three aspirin and a Bromo-seltzer, and climbed into the shower, where she stayed until the hot water ran out.

An hour later, dressed in a robe and slippers, she came back down the stairs and walked to the dining room, where she found Henry and Willy in the midst of their dinner. Henry looked up to her as she entered. "Have some dinner, Mary," he said. "You need to eat something."

She stood for a moment facing them, her eyes blank and tired, then moved to her seat and wearily spooned some of the stew Henry had made onto her plate. For several moments Henry considered her in silence. "Mary," Henry said finally, "you ever think about home? You ever miss it?"

"All the time," she said, her voice small, like a little girl. "I miss it so. Me mum and dad. Me friends."

"Then go home for a while," Henry said.

Like magic, Mary's eyes brightened with hope. "You think I could?" she asked.

"Why not?" Henry answered. "You can wait for him there as well as here."

"I don't have the money, Dad," she offered.

"I do," Henry countered.

And so it was agreed. The next few days were filled with the details of planning Mary's trip home. Domestic and transatlantic air service was by then well-established and she could have flown back to England, but Mary, afraid of the big flying contraptions, opted for the train and ship. So Henry spent the good part of a day researching train schedules and ship itineraries, and when he had the information he needed, he went to Mary. He found her in her bedroom sorting through her clothes, which she had arranged into stacks on the twin beds. She was fresh and animated and full of energy, and smiled over to Henry when he entered. Willy lay in his crib, napping.

"Got a schedule I think works," Henry said. He consulted a scrap of paper on which he'd made some notes. "There's a ship leaving New York City for Liverpool in four days. It leaves in the afternoon, and I can get you on an overnight Pullman that'll get you into New York City that morning."

"Sounds splendid," Mary said. "Are they going to charge for Willy?"

"No," Henry answered. "Willy goes free."

"Oh, good," Mary said, returning to her sorting. "You wouldn't think they'd charge extra for little blighters."

Henry folded the slip of paper, then folded it again and stuck in in his shirt pocket. For several moments he stood awkwardly watching her, struggling with his thoughts and feeling, of all things, ridiculously vulnerable. Ridiculous because he had never felt until that day—that very morning—that he had anything to lose by Mary's leaving. He didn't know how to say it, so in the end he just said it.

"You know," he said. "Willy could stay here with me."

Mary stopped sorting and looked over to him, her eyes questioning.

"I mean," Henry continued, "it's only a visit, right? I wouldn't mind, really. We get along fine, you know, Willy and me." He looked to her hopefully, encouragingly, like a salesman. "Maybe...maybe a couple of weeks of...you know...rest...not having the worry...maybe that'd be good for you." It was in fact a sales pitch, a most earnest sales pitch, even if Mary, and Henry himself, didn't quite realize it.

Mary, who had never considered it an option, was surprised by the offer. She was silent for a moment, her mind racing through the calculus of choice. It should have been a straightforward choice—yes for these reasons, no for these—but for reasons of her own, which she and Henry both at least suspected but dared not put into words, it wasn't.

"I'll think about it, Dad," she said finally. And think about it she did, all that day and long into the night.

Two days later, after breakfast, Henry drove Mary and Willy to the train station one last time. It was a raw, gray day, the sky overcast and the clouds low. After Mary had checked in her bags, the three of them sat on a hard wooden bench in the station house waiting for the train. Willy sat between the two adults, sucking his thumb and alternatively clinging with his free hand first to Mary, then to Henry. In place of conversation, the two adults smoked, Henry puffing on his pipe and Mary lighting one Lucky Strike from the butt end of another. When the train arrived, the three moved quickly to the platform.

231

"Have a good trip, Mary," Henry offered.

Mary turned to Henry, forcing herself to smile. "Thanks, Dad," she said. Then she hugged him, tightly and for a long time, then kissed his cheek. "You're a good man, Henry Winkler," she said. "Too bad I couldn't of married you."

She turned to Willy and crouched down to be even with him. "G'bye, Willy," she said, her voice cracking. "Mum'll be back real soon. Real soon," she repeated. She kissed the little boy and hugged him, then stood up quickly and breathed hard. She forced a smile one last time to Henry, then turned and moved quickly to the waiting train.

In the late spring of 1951, when Willy was five, the day finally came that Henry had been waiting for. Walking with Willy out the side kitchen door to the driveway, Henry popped Willy onto the back seat of the Indian motorcycle, climbed onto the front, and attempted to introduce the boy to the pleasures of motorcycle riding. Kicking the old motorcycle to life and pulling his riding goggles down over his eyes, Henry turned to the boy.

"Hold on to my waist, Willy," he said loudly, above the crack of the Indian's motor. He took the boy's thin arms and directed them to his sides. "Okay?" he asked.

Willy seemed to get the idea, and when the little white hands had gripped the fabric of his jacket, Henry turned around, slipped the Indian into gear, and goosed it forward. Willy's first ride lasted two feet. The immediate forward motion of the motorcycle unnerved the little boy, causing him to let loose of Henry's sides. He screamed, then slid off to the side, landing on his bottom on the driveway and badly skinning his elbow.

Needless to say, all subsequent attempts to get Willy back on the motorcycle were fruitless. He was so frightened of the machine that just the raw sound of it running would send him indoors to his hiding place underneath the dining room table. It was hopeless, and left Henry immensely disappointed and dispirited. Motorcycle riding was one of his few true joys in life, and he had hoped for a full agenda of riding with the boy, much as he had done with Will when he was Willy's age.

The answer was a simple one, and ironically was provided by Irwin Meyer, the man who had been responsible for Henry's acquisition of the Indian Scout so many years earlier. They were sitting on Henry's front porch having a beer, and Henry had just finished outlining the details of the woeful tale to Irwin.

"Get a sidecar," Irwin said.

"What?" Henry asked.

232

"Get a sidecar," Irwin repeated. "You can strap him in. Give him a teddy bear or something to hold. He'll feel safe."

So Henry did. After checking out the various models, Henry settled on a black 1951 Harley-Davidson with a squat, well-padded sidecar apparatus. And while Willy was understandably reticent, he did, teddy bear in hand, allow Henry to lift him into the sidecar and strap him in, and didn't cry when Henry kicked the motor to life and eased the gleaming machine down the driveway and onto Summit Avenue.

After one ride Willy was hooked, sitting low in the big seat, his round little face moving continuously from side to side taking in the wonder of the fast-moving world around him, his mouth open in a big ear-to-ear grin. And so they rode together and became a team, and came to be recognized in the gas stations and diners for a hundred miles in any direction. In early spring they would impatiently wait for the rain to stop and the temperature to rise, so that they could get back on the road. They would ride through the springs and summers all the way to October, when the cold rains would force the Harley into hibernation next to the old Indian Scout in the back of the garage.

They rode together through the 1950s, on the days and during the hours when Willy wasn't at his special school. It was during these years that Willy learned to dress and clean himself and to use the toilet, and to have his own bedroom—the little one in front next to the big one that nobody stayed in. They were the best of days for both of them. Willy was happy and healthy and secure, and Henry had found one more person to love.

In the years immediately following Mary's return to England and divorce from Will, she kept in steady touch. Every month or so Henry would get a letter from her chronicling the development of her new life, and every Christmas and birthday, gifts would arrive for Willy and Henry. Then in 1952, as Henry had hoped, Mary met a decent guy, fell in love, and quickly remarried. Henry sent a card and a wedding present and his best wishes. After that Mary's letters became more and more infrequent, and finally stopped.

Midway into the 1950s, Henry bought a television. It didn't turn out to interest him much, but Willy loved it, and they would sit together in the parlor in the early evening eating popcorn and watching silly shows like *Howdy Doody* and *Captain Kangaroo* and *Kukla, Fran and Ollie* that made Willy howl with glee.

It was during this time that Henry remodeled the kitchen, refinishing the counter tops with Formica and the floor with linoleum, and replacing the aged refrigerator and stove. And it was also during this time that Henry stopped printing five dollar bills and switched to tens. Constructing new

233

plates for his printing press of the quality he needed was a daunting and tedious task that took him the better part of a year, but the five dollar bill had fallen in value due to inflation, and the change was necessary. In the end his tens were as perfect as his fives, and if Mr. Owens, his former employer and teacher, would not have approved, Henry thought wryly, he would at least have been impressed.

In 1960, Rachel Mullins graduated from high school. She was as smart as a whip, and had run away with the academic awards at Central High. Her physical resemblance to Henry had become more and more clear as she grew, so that at age eighteen she was slim and lithe like her mother, but shorter and round-faced and dark haired like Henry, with small black eyes that burned and sparkled with youthful energy. She was Jeff's adopted daughter, but her blood relation to Henry was made clear to her from the beginning. Her birth father, she was told as soon as she was able to understand, was Henry's son, who had been killed in the war. This particular "inaccuracy," as Irene and Henry jokingly referred to it, was justified, they felt, on the basis of its clear figurative, if not literal, truth. Will was, they both knew, gone for good and as good as dead.

Henry, at age sixty-four, was showing all the signs of gracious maturity. His hair was almost totally white and had retreated straight down the middle of his head, his waistline had expanded slowly but surely, and his afternoon naps had become longer and more frequent. But while his body flirted with old age, his mind remained young and sharp on into the 1960s. His health was good, and he was happy on Summit Avenue in close proximity to the handful of people he loved. He was content with the small pleasures of day-to-day life, and, like most people in early old age, never allowed himself to dwell on the surety of the dark days that lay just around the corner.

Those days began for Henry on a cold afternoon in late autumn in 1967 when Irwin Meyer, his oldest and best friend, broke the news that he had leukemia. He'd known about it for some time, but didn't want to make a big deal about it until he had to. That winter and spring, Henry and Irwin drank a lot of beer together, and later Henry would smuggle beer to Irwin in the hospital, until he could no longer hold the glass.

The next February Willy turned twenty-two. A man in body only, Willy's mental age had capped at seven. He could speak reasonably well and could write his name in clumsy block letters, and could draw landscapes in crayon and build simple structures out of Lincoln Logs. He was short like Henry, pudgy from pizza and ice cream, and wore thick glasses held to his head with the help of a large rubber band. He was guileless and honest and innocent, and loved Henry with all of his heart. And he was learning how to contribute to the running of the household. There was a small market a couple of blocks down the hill on Centennial, and Henry had trained Willy to go shopping all by himself.

"Here, Willy," Henry would say, sticking a short shopping list and a ten dollar bill in Willy's shirt pocket. "I need you to go shopping for us."

"You bet, Grandpa," Willy would say. "You bet."

Together they would walk out the front door and down to the sidewalk.

"Now where are you going to go?" Henry would ask.

"Down there," Willy would say, pointing down the street toward Centennial Drive.

"But not where?" Henry would ask.

"Not into the street," Willy would say solemnly, shaking his head from side to side.

And so on. When the route had been carefully rehearsed, Willy would be on his way, and Henry would return to the front porch to wait for his return. The store owners, a young immigrant couple from India, liked Willy as much as everyone else and didn't mind having to fetch the items on Willy's shopping list from the shelves. They would fill his bag, stick the correct change in his pants pocket, and send him on his way with a treat from the freezer.

"Goodbye, Willy," they would say in their lilting, melodic Punjabi accents. "See you soon."

On an unusually hot day that June, Willy had completed his purchases and was returning from the store, making his way slowly up the hill and on to Summit Avenue, awkwardly holding the bag of groceries in one arm and losing a battle with the sun over the Fudgsicle he held in the other hand. When he got to within sight of the house, he was surprised to see the front porch empty. The porch was never empty; Henry was always there waiting for him. Discomfited, Willy hurried across the street and up the steps to the front porch. "Grandpa?" he asked. Entering through the front screen door, he stopped in the foyer. "Grandpa?" he asked again.

Then he saw him. He was in the parlor talking on the telephone. His voice, very soft, sounded strange to Willy. For several moments Willy stood watching him, brown drops from his melting Fudgsicle falling into pools on the polished wood floor. Finally Henry hung up and turned to him.

"Willy," he said, his voice soft and tired. "You're back."

"You bet," Willy said happily, smiling back.

Henry walked slowly to him, ran a hand through Willy's hair, and took the brown paper bag of groceries from him. "Let's put these away," he said.

They walked together through the dining room to the kitchen, Henry walking slowly, his shoulders bent forward into the beginning of a stoop.

Later that day, he would clean the puddle of Fudgsicle from the floor in the foyer, then take Willy downtown to buy him a new suit for the funeral.

At Irwin's funeral, Henry was asked to speak, and reluctantly, in a voice so soft that he could barely be heard in the back of the small church, he spoke of their time together overseas in the Great War and the long friendship that followed, and of his admiration of the man for his decency and kindness, and his envy for the happiness that had come so naturally to him. What he could not speak of—what he had no public words for—was the magnitude of the loss: how tired and daunted and lonely Irwin's death had left him, and how to a small but significant extent the world seemed less worthy of the effort of living.

In the late spring of 1972, Rachel Mullins made Irene and Jeff grandparents and Henry a great-grandfather with the birth of a baby girl. Rachel had won a full scholarship to Swarthmore College in Pennsylvania. She'd graduated from Swarthmore magna cum laude with degrees in philosophy and mathematics, then went on to Princeton for a Ph.D. in mathematics. There she fell in love with functional analysis, and with a long-haired, big-hearted, free spirit of a man with a penchant for number theory, whose name was Craig. They'd married in 1969 and moved out west to teaching jobs at a good university in Washington State. When their baby was born, they named the little girl Carole.

As soon as the school year was over, Irene and Jeff closed up their house and hurried out to Washington to spend a month pinching and cooing to their new granddaughter. When they returned in July, Henry picked them up at the airport. He stood inside the gate watching as Irene and Jeff left the airplane and walked across the tarmac toward him. Irene's face and arms were tanned and her hair lightened by the sun, and her eyes sparkled with energy.

When they were together, they hugged. "A good visit, it looks like," Henry said.

"More than good," Irene replied, flashing a toothy smile. "Terrific."

They collected their bags and Henry drove them home, listening all the while to their stories of the beautiful little baby girl and the happiness Rachel and her husband Craig had found in each other. They lived on a small farm outside of a little town and had goats, and when they weren't at the university doing mathematics, they milked goats and made goat cheese and hiked in the mountains to the east.

"So did you get to milk a goat?" Henry asked.

"Yes I did," Irene responded, nodding matter-of-factly. "Got pretty good at it, too."

She was as happy as Henry had ever seen her, sitting in the back seat with her arms draped lazily over Jeff's broad shoulders, her eyes drifting to the scenery passing by, her mouth half-open into a smile that wouldn't go away. She would remain that way for a little while longer, vital and full of life and undiminished by grief.

Rachel and Craig flew out the next Christmas, so Henry was able to spend some time with his great-grandchild. She was only six months old, so it was anybody's guess what she would turn out to look like. Jeff thought she looked like Craig and Irene thought she looked like herself, and Henry. Henry went on record as agreeing with Irene. Inside, though, he thought something else. And when Rachel and Craig visited again the next Christmas, when the little girl was eighteen months old, he was even more sure of it. The little girl, he thought, looked remarkably like Ellen. When he told them so, they were all in Jeff and Irene's parlor having drinks before Christmas dinner.

"You think so?" Irene asked. She'd seen Ellen's framed photograph many times in the northeast bedroom, but not for a while, so she didn't know whether or not to agree.

Craig had never ever seen the portrait, so after dinner they all filed over to the Winkler house and crowded in to Ellen's old bedroom to take a look at it.

"She's beautiful," Craig said.

"And sad," Rachel added. She turned to Henry. "Was she sad, Grandad?" she asked.

"Yes," Henry answered. "I'm afraid she was."

Irene, who was holding Carole, looked first to the portrait and then back to her. She had to agree with Henry; there were clear and unmistakable physical resemblances. But if she looked like Ellen, Irene thought, she acted like Rachel. The little girl squirmed happily in her arms, her eyes bright and challenging and inquisitive, her mouth open into a wide smile. No, she told herself. This is Rachel all over again.

"Well, this one won't be sad, I guarantee you," she said.

On their way out, Henry stopped everyone on the porch and hurried to his study for his camera. Back on the porch, he insisted on taking photos of everyone there in various combinations: Irene and Jeff and Carole, Rachel and Craig and their daughter, and finally himself holding the little girl.

The next summer Irene and Jeff once again closed up their house and headed for Washington State, this time for the whole summer. In addition to the joys of sharing their time with Rachel and Craig and their granddaughter, they'd begun to fall in love with the small towns and the quiet farm and the long and perfect summer days of the inland northwest, and with the mountains that rose fast and steep to the east.

Irene had been right about Carole: she was every bit her mother's child. At two she could climb stairs and button her dresses and name all the letters of the alphabet. And she was as happy a child as Irene had ever seen, her blue eyes always wide and probing, her little voice squealing with delight as she stumbled her way around the house and farm, feeding her senses from an endless menu of new discoveries.

They milked goats and did farm chores and hiked in the nearby mountains, and spent the long, cool evenings on the back porch, reading and talking and playing games with Craig's Australian Shepherd, whose name was Daisy. And before they knew it, it was August and time to go home.

The day before she and Jeff were to return, Irene got a phone call from her sister, informing her that Henry had gotten into an accident on his motorcycle and was in the hospital. Willy had been hurt, too, but not badly, and was being taken care of by Mrs. Schumacher, Henry's next-door neighbor. Irene had her sister give her the phone number for the hospital, and as soon as they were done talking, she got herself connected through to Henry's room.

"What happened?" she asked.

Henry, lying propped up in his hospital bed, his left leg heavily plastered and elevated, could only shrug. "I was pulling out onto Centennial and got whacked by a Volkswagen," he said. "I'm lucky it wasn't a Cadillac."

"How bad are you hurt?" she asked.

"Ah, hell, Henry answered. "I keep breakin' my damn legs." Irene had heard the story of his experience in the Great War, and knew what he was referring to. "This time it's only one leg, but it's broken in two places."

"But you'll be okay," Irene asked anxiously.

"I guess so," Henry responded glumly. "I'm pretty old to be breaking bones. They tell me I might limp. And they tell me I can't ride anymore, that's the worst of it."

Irene didn't think their flight would get them back to town in time for a visit the next day, but promised to come out and see him the day after. The next day everyone piled into Rachel and Craig's van for the short drive to the airport. The plan was to put Irene and Jeff on the plane for home, then Rachel and Craig and Carole would head west to Seattle, where the two mathematicians would be presenting papers at a conference later in the week. They had three days to get there, and planned a roundabout route that would take them into the Cascade mountains south of Mt. Rainier for two days of hiking and camping.

Their plane was on time, so the wait at the airport was short—shorter than Irene had counted on. Before she knew it, it was time to say goodbye for many months. After the hugs, Irene turned one last time to Carole. She was standing holding her mother's leg, and had hair clips holding her shoulder length, light brown hair out of her eyes. Her smooth skin was berry brown from the long summer days. Irene stooped to her.

"Goodbye, sweet thing," she said, giving the little girl a long kiss on the forehead.

"Bye, Grandma," Carole, smiling up to her.

A minute later Irene and Jeff were seated on the small plane, and as the plane accelerated down the runway past the terminal, Irene peered out of the small porthole window to her left, hoping for a last quick sight of them. But they were not to be seen.

"I'm gonna like this grandmother thing," Irene said, turning her head to Jeff and taking his hand.

"Gonna?" Jeff responded good-naturedly. "Like you haven't been?"

Irene smiled. She was fifty-one years old, but looked forty and at that moment felt thirty.

As Irene and Jeff headed back east at thirty thousand feet, Rachel and Craig headed west on the interstate. It was already getting hot when they left the airport, so they rode with the windows down. Craig drove and Carole sat in Rachel's lap, and they sang to her as the van moved swiftly across the fertile farm land of eastern Washington State.

At the Columbia River they turned south, then west again, climbing into the Cascades to a trail head they had discovered the year before. Their plan was to spend the next two days camped at the trail head taking short hikes in the daytime and spending the evenings at their campfire telling stories and roasting marshmallows.

When they finally pulled in to the trail head, it was late afternoon and still hot. The campground at the trail head was pleasant and spacious, with individual campsites nestled under the tall douglas firs. A stream bubbling down from the mountain above cut through the middle of the campground, then crossed under a bridge across the highway and on down through the forest to the south. There were trout in that stream, and Craig intended to catch a couple of them for their dinner.

After they'd set up their tent and fire ring, Craig grabbed his fishing pole and tackle box, and with Carole on his shoulders set off with Rachel along a neat path that followed the stream downhill. He found a good fishing hole a quarter mile or so from the campground, where large outcrops of rocks narrowed the waterway, slowing the water's flow and forming a series of inter-connected pools twenty to thirty feet wide.

Halfway down one of these pools, the shoreline flattened out into a small terrace of grass and sand. Here Craig unloaded the little girl from his shoulders, rigged a spinner onto the business end of his fishing line, and set off downstream in search of trout. Rachel stayed at the beach with Carole, wading with her in the cold mountain water along the pool's edge, looking for things to show her. She found a snail, then a bit later a group of tadpoles, then finally a bright piece of rock etched with the green mosaic she knew was serpentine. Plucking it from the water, she gave it to Carole.

"Here, honey," she said. "A present for you."

The little girl took the pretty stone, then squealed and laughed. They walked together back to the beach, then sat down on the sand. Carole examined the stone for a few moments, then dropped it on the ground.

"Here," Rachel said, picking up the stone and putting it into the Carole's pocket. "We'll save it."

Rachel could see Craig fifty yards or so down the stream, standing on a rock and fishing a shadowed hole. "Hey, hey!" she heard him exclaim as his rod bent. She watched as he skillfully landed the rainbow. Unhooking the spinner from the fish's mouth, he turned to Rachel and held it up proudly. It was a keeper; they were halfway to dinner. Rachel turned her gaze away from Craig, letting her eyes drink in the beauty of the green forest and glittering water. The air was fresh and clean and smelled faintly of juniper, and the only sound to be heard was the soft bubbling of the stream as the water made its way slowly down through the rocks, and the occasional sound of a bird. It was serene and lovely. It was heaven.

It was cool under the trees but hot in the open by the stream where the sun shone clear and hard. Rachel was sweating around her forehead and neck, and was sticky from the hot ride. The water was cold but not too cold, and the pool in front of her was deep and inviting.

"Mommy's gonna go for a swim," she told Carole, who had risen to investigate a clump of wild flowers growing at the water's edge. "Can you sit here and be okay for a minute?"

The little girl nodded, then plopped down in the shade of a Manzanita bush growing by the stream.

"Good girl," Rachel said.

Looking up and down the stream to make sure they were alone, Rachel quickly stripped down to her underwear, then waded slowly out into the cold water. When the water was up to her thighs she dove forward into the deep pool in front of her, swimming a few strokes along the surface, then bending inward under the water and diving to the bottom. A moment later her head broke the surface and she breathed in deeply, looking immediately to the shore for her daughter. She was fine, sitting where she had plopped and drawing pictures in the sand. Rachel called to her and waved, and Carole waved back, her tiny white teeth bright in the afternoon sun.

Rachel dove one more time, then surfaced and headed for the shore. The soft current had drifted her downstream a bit, so she had to labor back upstream to reach the beach. As she moved toward the shore, her feet found the bottom, then lost it, then found it again. She could swim or walk, but against the current she chose to walk, using her arms to help her forward. As she moved slowly and awkwardly upstream, the stream bottom gave way, so then once again she was floating. She pushed forward hard with her arms until her feet once again found the bottom. But when she tried to move forward her right foot slipped and then became stuck, wedged between something. She tried pulling it free but it wouldn't budge, and for a brief moment she felt panic and almost called for Craig. But she was a good swimmer and sure of herself in the water, and so she calmed herself down, took a deep breath and dove under the surface, bending herself down to her trapped foot. She found her foot trapped in a tangle of tree roots that had reached out from the shoreline deep into the stream. Rachel tugged at her foot, but it wouldn't quite let go. Running out of air, she surfaced, then dove again. She struggled for a moment, then a root let go. But it was the root under her foot, not alongside of it, so that instead of freeing her foot it pulled her several inches deeper into the mass of roots. And then Rachel's stomach turned and her heart leapt to her throat, because she knew, without a doubt and in just a split second, that her head could not reach the surface, and that unless she freed her foot she would drown.

Downstream Craig had just hooked another rainbow. Turning to the beach behind him, his broad smile quickly disappeared when Rachel was nowhere in sight. His eyes quickly scanned the shoreline, and when he couldn't find her, he dropped his rod and began to scramble back across the broken outcrops of rocks toward his daughter. As his alarm grew, he scrambled faster and still faster, his legs slipping and falling hard against the sharp rocks.

From twenty yards away he finally spotted Rachel motionless under the water, her arms loose at her sides, her shoulder-length chestnut hair streaming out with the current. Crying out, he threw himself into the water, his long, strong arms flailing against the current, pulling him quickly to her. When he reached her, he dove to her feet, his hands pulling, pulling against the pitiless roots. In a few moments he was out of air. But in those last frantic moments, there was no rational calculus to override the single-mindedness of his fury. There was no number theory, there was no farm, there was no Carole sitting quietly on the shore above him. There was only Rachel and him and a blinding white scream of rage and desperation.

And when his tortured lungs finally won over and he looked upward to the light of the stream's surface, his reluctant arms pushed to lift him. But it was too late. He was without strength, and his boots and pants had filled with water, holding him down as securely as the black roots that held Rachel. For a brief moment he struggled with all of the ebbing might of his young, strong body. Then, as the darkness came and consciousness slipped quietly away, he relaxed and was at peace, knowing that his life, too, was over.

Downstream, Craig's fishing pole lay where it had fallen in an outcrop of rock. The fish he had caught swam in slow circles in the deep pool, attached at the mouth to the barbed hook at the end of the bright red spinner that had seduced it minutes earlier. When the line went tight, the fish fought against the hook, writhing and twisting frantically against the hot pain of the barb. Finally the hook dislodged and the trout swam soundlessly away, deep and upstream, to a mass of tree roots where it could hide in the darkness, drinking its breath easily and languidly, resting.

A half-hour later a fisherman found the little girl sitting on the sandy beach crying. Soon he spotted Rachel and Craig, side by side and motionless in the clear water. By nightfall a fire service team had removed the bodies, and the little girl named Carole was in a police car on her way to Yakima, where the wife of a police lieutenant would feed her and bathe her and stay with her through the long night.

Irene never made it to the hospital the next day. They had gotten home around nine o'clock that night, jet lagged, and had just managed to drift off to sleep around midnight when the phone call came with the horrible news. The next day, and the day after that, Irene didn't leave the house. And on the third day, when Rachel and Craig were to have given their talks in Seattle, Jeff Mullins, his iron will mastering his own wrenching grief, shepherded Irene back onto a westbound plane for the worst of all her journeys.

Jeff had also been the one to break the news to Henry. When Henry, listening on the phone from his hospital bed, had heard the few words Jeff had to say, the color drained from his face and the telephone receiver fell from his hand. Outside the room in the hallway, a passing nurse, new to the ward, heard the long cry. Hurrying into the room, she found an old man in the narrow bed, his plastered leg elevated. The old man was in agony, holding his clenched fists to the back of his head, his eyes closed tight, his face red and contorted. One more time the old man cried out, blindly, to no one. A moment later the nurse hurried from the room to find help. Later that morning they found a doctor who examined Henry, and who, out of pity, gave him a shot that sent him into welcome darkness.

They kept Henry in the hospital for several more days, then sent him home to mend. Hobbling around on his crutches, he was able to provide slow but competent basic care for himself and Willy, and Mrs. Schumacher stopped in once a day at least to make sure everything was all right and to see if they needed anything from the market. And so Henry and Willy got by, Willy in happy ignorance laughing along with the TV, Henry in the bleak solitude of his study, smoking his pipe until the acrid smoke scorched his lips and tongue. For the fourth time in his life, he struggled with that most daunting of mortal tasks: to outlive someone you love.

The day he got home from the hospital, he was able to get through on the telephone to Jeff. He and Irene were at the farm and were trying to take care of the most demanding of the official paperwork that had to be done. They would be leaving for home in a couple of days, and would be bringing Carole and the dog Daisy home with them. Jeff gave the phone over to Irene and Henry talked with her only briefly. She was ill, Henry knew, physically ill, and had neither the energy nor the will to speak.

Three days later, and eight days after the accident, Irene and Jeff came home. It was a sweltering hot day, and Henry was on the front porch waiting when they arrived back on Summit Avenue. Irene's sister had picked them up at the airport, so it's understandable that Henry didn't recognize the car when it turned off Centennial and made its way west along Summit Avenue. He watched the foreign car as it approached slowly, idly surveying the vague forms of the passengers. From the distance he could recognize none of them. A woman was driving, and a white-haired woman sat next to her in the front seat. There appeared to be at least one person—vague and unidentifiable—in the back seat.

Henry's eyes disengaged from the occupants in the strange car, and for a moment became unfocused. As the car pulled up even with his house, the white-haired woman turned her face to the window and raised her hand in acknowledgment. And as Henry's surprised eyes again focused on the slowly passing car, his heart jumped, for the white-haired woman was Irene. Jeff, sitting in the back seat, also raised his hand as the car passed by. And next to him, seated in the back, Henry could see the dog, and the small face of his great-granddaughter Carole.

There was no way, at his age and in the terrific afternoon heat, that Henry could attempt to hobble over on his crutches to the Mullins', so he had to sit and wait until they came to him. This they did an hour or so later, when Jeff and Irene, holding to each other tightly, crossed the street to walk the short distance between the houses in the shade, the little girl staying at home

243

with Irene's sister, asleep after the long journey. After they'd all hugged, they sat in the parlor, the room darkened by the closed drapes protecting them from the westing sun, the heavy stillness broken only by the soft whirr of a floor fan.

"How are you?" Irene asked when they were seated.

"I'll mend, they tell me, even at my age," Henry replied.

Irene nodded. "How do you like my hair?" she asked. "You see I've become an old woman overnight."

Henry's mind searched for a response, but there was nothing he could find to say. Irene, in fact, looked old, and it wasn't just her hair. She was gaunt and drawn and had wrinkles around her eyes that Henry had never seen before. And she moved with the slow weariness of the old, her body still between each movement, as if she were resting for the next great effort. In the end, having nothing to say, Henry could only offer his big hands to her, which she took and squeezed tight.

Luckily for both Irene and Henry, Jeff Mullins was stronger than either of them. Jeff had come to love Rachel deeply and was equally devastated by the catastrophe, but he was just made of tougher stuff than the other two, and could more effectively deal with life's random treacheries. And while Henry's eyes had seen it in Irene's pained and wearied face, it was Jeff who saw it in Henry's. As they stood to leave and again hugged, Jeff looked into Henry's eyes, and deep down beyond the flat gray sadness of them, he saw that Henry, too, was defeated.

A month later, when the cast had been removed from Henry's leg and he could hobble along with a cane, Irene paid a visit to Henry alone. She found him at the big roll-top desk in his study, puffing on his pipe and making notes in a tablet of writing paper. She walked to him and put her hands on his shoulders. "What are you doing?" she asked.

"I'm making up my will," Henry answered.

"Ah," Irene responded.

"I wish I could make you and Jeff rich," Henry said, "but I don't have all that much, to tell the truth." He shrugged. "Unless you like old furniture."

"Jeff and I are fine," Irene said. She patted his shoulder lightly.

"And Willy...Willy'll need all the help I can give him," Henry offered.

"All the help *we* can give him, Henry," Irene added. "You know that, don't you?" she asked, looking hard into his eyes.

"Yes," he responded, taking her hand and squeezing it.

After a moment, she cleared her throat and caught his eyes. "I have a favor to ask of you," she said.

"Of course," Henry responded. "Anything."

244

She wavered for a moment, then spoke. "I want you to take me back to church. Back to Seventh Street," she said.

Irene had attended church with Henry on Sundays when she had lived with him during the early years of World War II, when he would go with the Kleins. She had stopped going after she and Jeff had married, and Henry had stopped going after Fred Klein died and Minnie moved away. They had both been away from the church for a long time.

For just a moment Henry looked to her quizzically, surprised by the request. But then he nodded, his soft eyes responding to his own question with the obvious answer. "Okay," he said. "When do you want to go?"

"Right now," Irene said.

So Irene went and got her car, helped Henry into the front seat, and drove down Centennial into the old part of town to Seventh Street, to the location of the old Evangelical and Reformed Church that had been their Sunday institution those many years ago. It had been remodeled and painted and now bore the name of a different faith, but it was still small and plain and welcoming.

Irene parked her car on the empty street and helped Henry from the front seat. They entered through the open front doors into the soft coolness of the shaded sanctuary, sunlight filtering through the kaleidoscope of stained glass filling the rows of tall, narrow windows running the length of the opposing walls. At the far end of the sanctuary, a young woman was cleaning wood with a cloth, while halfway up the row of pews, a young man was dusting with a feather duster. They both wore tank tops and cutoffs. The soft voice of a woman singing could be heard coming from a portable cassette deck. Rachel and Craig could have told them it was Joni Mitchell.

When the young man noticed Irene and Henry, he moved quickly to them. "Hello," he said. His brown hair was very long, and was tied behind his head into a pony tail.

"Hello," Irene responded. "My father and I used to go to church here. We were wondering if the minister was available."

"That'd be my wife," the young man said, smiling. He pointed down the aisle.

Irene and Henry were lucky in their choice of churches. The young minister, whose name was Laura, was both kind and intelligent, and when Irene had forced herself to recount the events that had brought her there, she took Irene and Henry by the elbows and directed them to seats in her office. And then she talked to them in roundabout ways about love and loss and bewilderment, slowly working up to the point.

"And why have you come back here?" she asked finally.

Irene wiped her eyes with a tissue, then set her jaw and focused for a moment. "I want God to explain himself," she whispered.

Laura raised her eyebrows and nodded in agreement. "How much time do you have?" she asked.

"All the time in the world," Irene answered.

"Good," Laura said. "If you're patient, you might very well get an answer. Once in a while someone does."

And so Irene and Henry returned to the little church. Jeff went along with them much as Henry had for Clara years earlier, and while Irene searched for her answer, he and Henry took comfort in the gentleness of the place and the company of the modest, decent people who congregated there.

It was after one of these Sunday services in late September, as they gathered for lunch around Henry's dining room table, that Irene broke the news to Henry.

"We're giving up Carole for adoption," she said.

Henry, who had been laying out paper napkins, froze. After a moment he turned to her. "Good God," he said. "You...why do you feel you have to?" he finally got out.

Irene sighed, looked over to Jeff, then back to Henry. "Because we're old, Henry," she said gently.

"I'm old," he said, his voice challenging, "but you're not. You're both young and vital still."

"I'm fifty-one," Irene said, her voice even, making the point that she and Jeff had agonized over for days on end. "Jeff's fifty-three. When she graduates from high school, we'll be close to your age, if we're even still around."

She was silent for a moment, letting her words sink in. She knew what he was thinking, he didn't have to say anything. She knew it as well as he did. Carole was all that was left of Rachel and Craig, and, along with Willy, all that was left of Henry.

"We want her to have a good life," Irene said finally.

"And you can't give her a good life?" Henry asked.

"Maybe a good life," Irene said, "but not a normal life. Not one with brothers and sisters and parents who aren't pretending to be young." She was quiet for a moment, then, looking Henry straight in the eyes, she ended it. "We think we've found a couple, Henry," she said.

A month later, the adoption paperwork was all done. On the day that Carole was to leave, Henry hobbled over on his cane to the Mullins' to say goodbye. He had a present for her. He'd taken the piece of serpentine they'd found in her pants pocket and that she'd carried back from Washington State and had a piece of it cut to fit the end of a gold necklace.

"Here, Carole," he said to her when he saw her. "I have a present for you."

When she came to him, he stooped to show her the necklace. "Remember the pretty rock you brought from home?" he asked.

The little girl nodded yes.

"Well this is a piece of it," he said. He placed the delicate gold chain around her thin neck and fitted the clasp. "It's for you to..." he stopped himself, then began again. "It's for you to have for all time," he said, bending to kiss her on the forehead.

When it was time to go, Jeff bundled Carole up and, carrying her small suitcase, walked her to the car. Irene and Henry stayed inside and watched from the parlor window as Jeff helped her onto the front seat, then got behind the wheel and backed the car down the driveway. Slowly the car pulled away, offering Irene and Henry one last sight of her, her small head staring straight ahead at the dashboard, her light brown shoulder-length hair pinned back behind her ears with barrettes. When she was out of sight, they stood by the window and Irene cried into Henry's shoulder until she was out of tears.

Henry Winkler, who was seventy-eight years old, would never recover, either physically or spiritually, from the disastrous events of the summer of 1974. His broken leg would not heal quite right, so that he would walk only with the aid of a cane. He would progressively eat less and sleep longer, and his heart would begin to bother him. Twice in the next year Irene would have to drive him to the emergency room at the hospital across the river where doctors would investigate his attacks of angina, giving him EKGs and monitoring him overnight before sending him home.

He was, quite simply, spent. Life for Henry in those last years was just something that had to be done; he had his responsibilities still. He viewed it with the same sense of patient discomfort he might have felt having to go for a long ride on a crowded bus. It was just something to be gotten through.

In the fall of 1976, Henry had a genuine heart attack. It happened in the basement where Henry was cleaning up after printing a supply of ten dollar bills. Luckily, the attack was mild enough that he didn't collapse. He was able to find Willy and send him running for Irene, who called an ambulance. Doctors discovered three clogged arteries and performed triple-bypass surgery. They kept him in the hospital for two weeks before sending him home to recover.

Henry's recovery was long and slow; his old body just didn't seem to want to heal. During those long weeks Irene was more a resident of Henry's house than she was of her own, cooking and cleaning and watching over Henry, giving him sponge baths and dressing him and helping him back and forth to the bathroom. When he was finally able to leave his bed, he would hobble down the stairway to his study, where he would sit and listen to his phonograph.

One day shortly after his return to his study, Irene found him there puffing on his pipe. "I thought the doctors told you to stop that," she said, waving her hand through the cloud of blue smoke.

"To hell with them," Henry said flatly.

Irene glared back a challenge, so Henry continued. "They should know better than to try and take away an old man's comfort," he said. "They think the point of it all is just to keep going."

Irene softened. "Do you want to die, Henry?" she asked.

Henry thought for several moments. "No, I don't think so. I..." He struggled to piece together the rush of conflicting feelings, and the words to express them. "I guess," he said finally, "I just don't have any interest in continuing this particular story."

Henry Winkler's long story ended in the spring of the next year, in April of 1977, less than a month after his eighty-first birthday. It was a lovely day in the early afternoon, and a morning shower had freshened the air before giving way to the sun. Henry was plopped on a chair on the front porch. It was warm on the porch, and Henry unbuttoned the cardigan sweater he had put on against the coolness of the rainy morning. The sweater had been Irene's Christmas gift. He was looking at the snapshots he'd taken of Carole the winter before Rachel and Craig had died.

After a moment Willy came hurrying through the screen door onto the porch. His face was filled with happy animation; it was time for his trip to the market. "Ready, Grandpa," he said.

"Good boy, Willy," Henry said, putting the snapshots back into a worn envelope and then into the pocket of his cardigan. "Got the list?"

Willy nodded, pulling the list from his jacket pocket. "You bet," he said.

"Got some money?" Henry asked.

Willy felt into the pockets of his blue jeans, then shook his head sadly.

Henry grunted, then twisted his body to extract his wallet from his back pocket. Opening it, he grunted again: he only had one ten dollar bill, and wanted to give Willy twenty dollars. Not feeling up to the long trip to the study, he enlisted Willy. "Willy," he said, showing him the bill. "You know where grandpa keeps his money? Like this? In the box in the big desk?"

Willy nodded enthusiastically. "You bet, Grandpa," he said.

"Get me the box, will you?" Henry asked.

So Willy went scampering off to the study. But Willy was easily distracted, and when he opened the side drawer where he knew the box to be, instead of focusing on the box, his eyes found the shiny nickel barrel of Etta

248

Mae Blumberg's Smith and Wesson pistol sticking out from a corner of the oiled rag in which Henry kept it hidden.

Henry had discovered the pistol shortly after his return to the house, and for reasons unclear even to himself had decided to keep it. Until that day Henry had kept the gun well-hidden, so that Willy had never seen a real gun before. But he'd seen plenty on television. The Lone Ranger had one, and so did the other cowboys and detectives and soldiers he watched in the evenings. No one had ever told Willy not to touch a real gun, so he didn't hesitate to take it out of the drawer and handle it. He stared into the barrel of the shiny pistol, then gripped the handle in his pudgy hand. He was shooting at imaginary bad guys. "Bam...bam, bam...!" he yelled happily.

Skipping out of the study, he headed for the front porch. "Grandpa," he said, charging through the screen door. "Look!"

When Henry saw the gun in Willy's hand, his stomach turned over and a sharp pain passed across his chest. "Willy...no," he managed to say.

Somehow he managed to stand and face Willy who, all smiles, was pretending to shoot him, like he was a bad guy. "Bam!" Willy said. "Bam...bam!"

When Henry saw that somehow Willy had managed to lock back the hammer of the pistol, the searing pain in his chest grew more severe. "Put it down, Willy!" Henry yelled. "Put it down!"

The gravity in Henry's voice caused Willy to stop in his tracks, his broad smile instantly wiped away, replaced by a look of anxious fear. The tone meant that something was bad. Really bad.

"Grandpa?" Willy asked tentatively.

"Put it down, Willy," Henry commanded, even as the pain in his chest exploded.

He couldn't hold himself against the pain, and collapsed against the wall behind him. His last vision was of Willy standing over him crying, the pistol hanging limp in his hand. Then his mortal senses left him. He didn't see it when Willy dropped the gun, didn't hear it when the gun went off when it hit the floor, and didn't feel it when the errant bullet tore into his chest.

Jeff Mullins, working in his yard, heard the gun go off. Hurrying as fast as his prosthetic leg would carry him, he found Henry sprawled against the porch's wall, a growing circle of red spreading out from the point on his chest where the bullet had entered his body. Air bubbles gurgled from the wound, and Henry, motionless, breathed lightly in and out, his unseeing eyes open, staring straight ahead.

Isolated from the senses of the world, Henry could feel his life leaving him. He had a sense of moving: not up or down or sideways, but inward, as if he were collapsing on himself. He became aware of a bright circle of light

249

surrounding him. For many moments the circle of light stayed with him, then slowly shrank as it appeared to move away, becoming smaller and smaller, quickly becoming just a pin prick of light in a vast darkness. But as it faded away, other points of light appeared, first two or three, then scores, then hundreds and thousands, until Henry imagined he was staring into the clearest night sky he had ever seen. Then one of the infinite points of light began to brighten and grow, warm and golden. When it was the size of the moon, Henry thought he could make out the vague outline of a person, like the man in the moon that had fascinated him as a child.

As the circle of light grew and moved rapidly toward him, the vague outline came into focus, and Henry's heart leapt with pure joy, for it was clear to him who the figure was, smiling and reaching out to him, offering herself to him forever.

Chapter Fourteen

On a Friday in early September, Carole finally went to court for Stella Phillips. The trial itself took half a day, with Carole presenting her impeccably prepared oral argument to the judge, followed by the incoherent rambling of Stella's backyard neighbor—the old man who was the respondent and who in the end had insisted on representing himself. When all was said and done, the judge took the evidence under submission, promising to issue a ruling within a couple of days.

"It was pathetic," Carole told Carlos, describing the old man's performance. It was the next day—Saturday—and they were driving north on the interstate, heading for the care facility where they would find Willy's ashes. It was a hot morning, and they had opted for Carole's car instead of Carlos's truck, to take advantage of the more comfortable ride and the functioning air conditioner. They were dressed down for the trip, Carlos in a tank top and cutoffs, Carole in shorts and an old Northwestern tee-shirt. As Carlos drove, sipping from a Styrofoam cup of coffee and slowly exhausting the contents of a bag of Skittles, Carole sat back in the passenger seat sipping a Diet Coke, her bare, pink toe nailed feet propped up against the dashboard.

"He was a joke," Carole continued. "He stood up there talking about 'freedom' and 'communists' and about how 'next they'll be takin' away all our rights to bear arms,'" Carole quoted, trying to mimic his bad grammar and cowboy drawl. "Judge Parker couldn't believe it," she said. "She kept looking over to me with these big eyes that said 'is this guy for real?'"

Carole sat for a moment thinking, her mouth open in an easy smile. "Oh, jees," she said suddenly, remembering something. "You won't believe what happened at the end."

"What?" Carlos asked, popping a Skittle into his mouth.

"Get this," Carole said. "When it's over, the old guy's leaving, and he walks by our side where Stella's sitting..." She was chuckling while she talked, her eyes beaming with humor. "...and they're glaring at each other, and then..." By then Carole was laughing hard, having a hard time finishing the story. "...and then...Carlos...he sticks his tongue out at her."

"What?" Carlos asked.

"He sticks his tongue out at her," Carole repeated, laughing so hard her face was red.

Carlos shook his head in amazement. "So what does Stella do?" he asked.

"She..." Carole said, laughing, "...she sticks her tongue out at him."

"No way," Carlos said flatly.

251

"I kid you not," Carole said. "Think of it, Carlos, two oldsters in their eighties, sticking their tongues out at each other like little kids."

"So what's the judge do?" Carlos asked.

"Nothing," Carole said, getting her laughter under control. "I looked over to her, and she's doing everything she can to keep from cracking up."

An hour later they'd reached their destination, and some minutes after that, following the street map Carlos had photocopied at the library, they found themselves in the driveway of Heritage House.

"Some heritage," Carlos grunted. Heritage House was in fact nothing more than a rather dilapidated and architecturally uninteresting two-story house dating, Carlos guessed, from the 1950s, and badly in need of a coat of paint. On the long covered porch and on the lawn, in the shade of a large sycamore tree, a half-dozen gray-haired men and women sat in lawn chairs staring passively back at the strangers parked in their driveway.

Carole had done her homework and knew why they were there. Heritage House contracted with the state to provide for the modest physical needs for a handful of citizens who had no particular physical limitations but who nevertheless found themselves wards of the state. That was to say they were mentally deficient, retarded or brain-damaged in some important way.

Carole sat for a moment surveying the array of featureless faces confronting them. "Sad, huh?" she asked.

Carlos's eyes moved quickly between the faces. "I guess," he said. "But maybe not," he added, trying to be upbeat. "Maybe they're happy here."

"Yeah?" Carole asked, turning her head to him and arching an eyebrow. "Well if I ever get that happy, promise me you'll tie a rock to me and throw me in the river."

At the door they were met by Mrs. Cooper, the woman who ran the place and with whom Carole had spoken on the telephone. She was a thin woman and quite tall, taller than Carole by several inches, and while she was clearly old—her hair white and her skin wrinkled and loose on her face and arms—her eyes were bright with vitality and her handshake was strong and surprisingly forceful. She led them into the parlor and made them sit while she went for iced tea and cookies. The furniture was old and worn and mismatched, and the house smelled of tobacco and frying meat. But the interior of the house was surprisingly cheerful, with flowers and plants everywhere, and with gay pictures clipped from magazines hanging on the walls in dollar store frames. Mrs. Cooper was an optimist.

When she returned with her tray of iced tea and cookies, Mrs. Cooper found Carlos and Carole at the long bookcase in the adjoining dining room. Carole had found the ashes. "That's them, honey," Mrs. Cooper said, putting the tray down on the long dining room table. "Our dear-departed. There's four of 'em now, since they stopped burying 'em. Your Willy was the last so far."

The four identical containers were displayed lengthwise along an eye-level shelf of the bookcase. Each container had the name of the deceased written across the lid in black indelible ink.

"Are those what I think they are?" Carlos whispered to Carole.

"Uh-huh," she whispered back. "Tupperware."

Behind each container Mrs. Cooper had taped to the back of the bookcase a snapshot of the person. There was Arlene Miller, laughing a toothless smile; a dour and frowning Herbert Clatt; a very old lady named Ida Bullard, who appeared to be trying to hide from the camera; and finally, at the end of the line, William Winkler Jr. He was younger than the rest, only middle-aged, his short-cropped hair showing only a hint of gray. And while his round face showed the clear signs of mental retardation, it was not without emotion. The eyes behind the thick glasses seemed to be staring intently into the camera, and his smile was wistful, as if he were enduring a sad memory. As Carole concentrated on the photograph, her hand sought out Carlos's, squeezing it tight. Here was her Uncle Willy, the last of them, a final Winkler she would never know.

When they finally sat for their iced tea and cookies, Carole was full of questions. "How long was he here?" she asked first.

"Oh, honey," Mrs. Cooper replied, "More'n twenty years, anyway. I've been here since seventy-five, and Willy came only a couple of years after that. He was real young, then. Maybe only thirty or so."

"Did he have any visitors?" Carole asked. "Anyone ever come to see him?"

"Oh, sure," Mrs. Cooper replied. "A nice lady. Old enough to be his mother, but she said she wasn't. A friend of the family, she said she was. She'd come every month or so for all those years, regular as clockwork. Don't remember her name or where she was from. Somewhere down south, I'm thinking."

"Hmmm," Carole grumbled softly, her mind clicking. "Any idea where he was before he came here?"

"Why he was in jail, honey," Mrs. Cooper said.

"Jail?" Carole asked, sitting up in her seat.

"You didn't know?" Mrs. Cooper asked.

Carole shook her head.

"Oh, dear," Mrs. Cooper said. "You're in for a shock then."

Carole looked quickly to Carlos, then back to Mrs. Cooper.

"Well," Mrs. Cooper continued uncomfortably, "you see, Willy got hold of a gun and...and accidently shot his own grandfather. It was an accident...they called it involuntary slaughter."

"Manslaughter," Carole whispered to herself.

Carlos watched Carole as she digested this latest surprise. For a second, her eyes closed and her face was still, then she reopened her eyes and looked first downward, then over to him. She looked to Carlos like she was going to throw up.

On the drive home they stopped for burgers and fries to go. As they drove south, Carole nibbled at the French fries, the Tupperware container holding Willy's ashes on the floorboard at her feet. Her initial shock over Henry's accidental shooting had given way to wry chagrin.

"Some family," she said, brushing the excess salt from a French fry. "Henry's a counterfeiter and Willy...poor Willy...is a murderer."

"A manslaughterer, you mean," Carlos offered.

"Manslaughterers are murderers, Carlos," Carole said, "because manslaughterer isn't a word." She popped the French fry into her mouth and reached for another. "Jees," she said after she swallowed, "this bunch makes your family look like stamp collectors."

Carlos smiled. Carole was almost always circumspect about the colorful and sometimes bizarre behavior of the Estrada clan, and comments like her last one almost never slipped out. "Wait a minute. What Winkler ever went fishing in the bathtub, eh?" he asked. He was referring to his great-uncle Juan, who had suffered from mild dementia in his later years and who had been the subject of several of Carlos's early cartoons. "And what Winkler ever sat naked on a Xerox machine?" he asked, referring to the antics of his sister Angelina.

"All right, all right," Carole said, holding up her hands in defeat. "You make a point. But wouldn't you like them to be more..." She went silent, searching for the right word.

"Like stamp collectors?" Carlos offered. "No," he said, answering his own question. "I like 'em weird. That way I look normal. It's a good approach. You should think about adopting it." Carlos winked, then reached for a French fry. "So what do you want to do with Willy?" he asked.

"I don't know," Carole said. "I don't suppose it's proper to bury him."

"You mean like in the back yard?" Carlos asked.

"No!" Carole responded firmly. "In the cemetery, along with everyone else."

"Well," Carlos said after a moment. "You wouldn't need much room. Maybe six inches. Get a post hole digger out there and..."

"Will you stop it?" Carole ordered, smiling despite herself. "I'm serious."

By the time they got home, they'd agreed to keep the ashes in some inconspicuous spot in the house, and had further agreed that the Tupperware container was inappropriate. And so after Carole had left for work the following Monday morning, Carlos went in search of a more suitable container to hold Willy's ashes. His search of first the kitchen cabinets and then the garage yielded nothing, and he was just about reconciled to a trip downtown to the hardware store when he resurrected a vague memory of having boxed away some metal containers that had been part of the flotsam of what had been left behind in the house. They were somewhere in the basement, then.

The boxes containing the miscellany of Henry Winkler's daily life were stacked neatly on shelves along the west wall of the basement. They were unlabeled, so it took Carlos a half hour or so of digging before he found what he was looking for. The box was an odd mixture of things, lumping together all the sundry items that didn't belong anywhere else. He found several old coffee cups and bunches of pens and pencils held together with rotting rubber bands, along with a pair of scissors and a magnifying glass and a random assortment of things you'd find in the drawer of a desk. And lying on top of what appeared to be an old sweater, Carlos found the metal cans he'd remembered. What they turned out to be were pipe tobacco cans: pound-sized metal cans with names like Prince Edward and Revelation and Old English. A few of the cans had been filled by Henry with business receipts—telephone and electric bills and so on—and one was still half filled with very stale tobacco, but Carlos was able to isolate a pristine Prince Edward can that was empty and was at least the appropriate size. He knew that he was probably kidding himself to think that Carole would actually approve the use of a tobacco can as the shrine for Willy's ashes, but decided to let her say no before he went to the trouble to search the stores for a more tasteful container.

Removing the empty Prince Edward can, Carlos closed the box, lifted it to its place on the shelf, and turned his back to the row of shelves. He'd taken a half dozen steps toward the stairway when he heard the thud of the box hitting the basement floor. Then, with a dismissive "humph," he returned to the box and once again lifted it to its spot on the shelf. But halfway into sliding it into its place he stopped, and his eyes narrowed.

"Wait a minute," he said, his eyes scanning the empty basement. "You trying to tell me something?"

Now smiling, Carlos moved the box to a workbench, reopened it, and began to carefully remove and reexamine the assorted contents. It was all a lot of nothing, though, and Carlos was about ready to conclude that the box had actually slid off the shelf all by itself. All that was left at the bottom of the box was the bulky piece of gray knit cotton that appeared to be a sweater. Removing and unfolding it, he saw that it was in fact a sweater. It was the type they call a cardigan, that buttoned up the front, and it was quite big—way too big for Carlos. It was Henry's, Carlos knew immediately. And then he saw the stain. It was brown, and traveled several inches down the left side of the sweater, where Henry's shirt pocket would have been. An ink stain, maybe, or a food stain, Carlos thought. Like when the ketchup dribbles out the back end of your burger, if you're not careful. But then he remembered about Willy and the gun, and his stomach tightened. "Madre de Dios," he whispered.

This, he resolved, he would not show to Carole, at least for a while—a good long while. It was a well-intentioned but ill-timed offering the house had made, he thought. "Thanks," he told the house, "but I don't think so. Not right now."

But as he was carefully folding it to put it back in the bottom of the box, he felt something bulky in one of the front pockets. And so lying the sweater back on the workbench, he reached into the pocket and found, finally, what the house was offering. It was a small envelope, and inside it were several black-and-white snapshots. There was one of an elderly man, round and mostly bald, holding a little girl. And another of the old man with a middle-aged couple, the woman very pretty and energetic, the man's face lean and chiseled, his upper body broad and strong, like a boxer. And finally, one of the little girl with a younger couple, the woman short with dark, shoulder-length hair, the man tall and bearded, with long hair held back in a ponytail.

As Carlos looked back and forth from one photo to the next, his mouth opened into a wide smile and his eyes sparkled with happiness. It was a gold mine. And while Carlos could not have known that next to his photographs of Clara these were the ones that had been dearest to Henry, he knew with certainty that they would be Carole's dearest. For there was no doubt, even to Carlos's incomplete understanding, of who these people were.

"Thank you!" he exclaimed to the cool walls of the basement. "Thank you so much!"

That afternoon the region was visited by a quickly moving rainstorm that swept in from the southwest, so that when Carole got home from work around six o'clock she had to hurry from her car to the side door to keep from being soaked. She found Carlos in the kitchen, making a salad for their dinner. "Hi," she said, waltzing to him.

"Hi honey," Carlos responded.

Plopping down onto the counter the six-pack of Sierra Nevada Pale Ale she'd bought on her way home, she moved to him for a kiss. "Brought you a present," she said.

"What's the occasion?" Carlos asked after the kiss, eying the beer.

"It is because I," Carole said, lapsing into her Southern Belle imitation, "have emerged from another battle of good versus evil, and the evil-doer has been vanquished."

"All right!" Carlos exclaimed. "Which case?"

"Stella Phillips's easement dispute," Carole said, her voice back to normal. "Got the ruling this afternoon. It was a slam-dunk." She searched in a drawer for a bottle opener, then popped the cap off one of the bottles of beer. "The old fart'll have to stick his tongue out at Stella from thirty feet away from now on."

She handed the beer to Carlos, then searched through the refrigerator for a bottle of the lemon-flavored bubbly water that had become her staple since her pregnancy. "Here's to stupid old men," she said, clinking glasses with Carlos. She was animated and happy, Carlos saw, her eyes wide and glowing, her synapses clicking along double-time. They were in for a fun night.

"We should celebrate," Carlos said. "Something better than a salad."

"Oh, yeah," Carole responded. "How about pizza?" Carole asked. "Right here. On the front porch."

"That's all you want?" Carlos asked.

"Well...all I want for dinner," Carole replied playfully.

The pizza arrived a half hour later, and Carlos and Carole arranged themselves on lawn chairs on the front porch, the pizza between them on a folding table. The heavy rain had diminished to a drizzle, the soft fingers of rain tap-tapping erratically on the porch roof above them, the damp, chill breeze turning their noses pink. Carole had changed out of her business suit into a sweat shirt and pants, and as she picked away at a slice of pepperoni pizza, she described to Carlos the judge's ruling.

"She gave us everything," she said, finishing up one slice of pizza and reaching for another. "We get title to all thirty feet of the easement, *plus*," she emphasized, "he has to pay to reseed the lawn and replant the flowers he destroyed, PLUS," she emphasized still more, her index finger wagging in the air, "he has to pay to rebuild Stella's fence and paint it on her side...the whole thing, not just the new part." She smiled sweetly over to Carlos, blinking her eyes. "That was my idea."

"Very good, counselor," Carlos said, reaching for another slice of pizza. Carole was starting her second slice and he was starting his fourth. They were right on pace.

"Stella's coming in tomorrow morning," Carole added. "I called and told her I had good news, but I didn't say how good."

"So then you'll be done with it," Carlos offered. "This is good. Now you can start billing again."

257

"I bill her," Carole responded in mock indignation. "Besides, she's going to teach me how to grow orchids. Quid pro quo." Carole sat silent for a moment, thinking. "I really like that old lady, Carlos," she said. "I'm going to get a photo of her tomorrow, the two of us, then I'm going to invite her over for dinner."

The mention of a photo jarred Carlos's memory: in the excitement of Carole's good news he'd completely forgotten about his own. "Oops," he said, rising from his chair. "Be right back."

Carlos hurried to the kitchen for a second bottle of Sierra Nevada Pale Ale, then to the study for his offerings. He returned to the front porch with his hands full. "First things first," he said, sitting back down. "Okay, how about this for Willy," he said, handing Carole the old Prince Edward tobacco can. "It's the best I could do."

He was sure she'd reject it immediately, perhaps even be mildly offended, and was surprised by her response. "It's perfect," she said, turning the elegantly printed tin box around in her hands.

She saw his look of disbelief. "No, really," she said, "it's great. You know...fitting. Something of Henry's."

"Okay," Carlos said, relieved.

"So what's in the envelope?" Carole asked, handing the Prince Edward tin back to Carlos.

"Something else of Henry's," Carlos answered, offering her the envelope. "Another gift from the house."

The tone in his voice correctly alerted her. It was tender and concerned, almost consoling. It told her to brace herself. Tentatively she reached out and accepted the envelope. Dusk was rapidly overtaking the space around them, so Carlos got up and switched on the porch light, then stood behind Carole, his hands on her shoulders. Slowly and carefully Carole opened the old envelope and extracted the half dozen photographs from inside.

One by one she considered them, her head bent to the task, her mouth closed and small. Except for Henry, whom she recognized from other pictures, the faces were all new to her: the beautiful, middle-aged woman and the husky, short-haired man with the chiseled face; the young couple, happy and intense, the man with long hair and a beard, like a hippie; and the little girl. She was in all of the photos, passed around proudly from parents to grandparents to great-grandparent. In only one of the photos was she caught looking directly into the camera, and this was the photo Carole kept going back to. Her hair was short and light brown and curled in wisps around the sides of her face. Her mouth was closed into a long, thin smile, and her eyes, wide open, stared out confidently, as if she were demanding an explanation for something.

For the longest time Carole considered the little girl in the photograph. When she finally looked back to Carlos, he saw that her eyes were full of tears. She raised a finger, as if she was about to speak, then lowered the finger and pressed it to her mouth. She was sad, yes, but happy too, happy to have them finally in at least two dimensions. But mostly she was bewildered. She raised her finger once more.

"How could they," she managed to say, then choked on her words.

How could they abandon me? Carlos thought, finishing her sentence. He bent forward and kissed her on the top of her head. "I wonder what happened," he said, asking the question Carole could not.

"Yeah," Carole responded, her voice high and soft and wavering. "What happened?"

Carlos gently took the photograph she was holding and considered it. "It's right here on the porch," he said after a moment.

"What?" Carole asked.

"Right here on the porch," he repeated. "Look." He handed the snapshot back to her and pointed out the west edge of the stained-glass trim on the front window that was captured at the edge of the photo. "Plus," he said, pointing to a spot on the picture, "You can see the porch rail."

Carole studied the photo. Right here, she thought. Right here in this very spot. How long ago? she asked herself. "Almost thirty years," she concluded, talking to herself. She looked up to Carlos. "All gone now," she said. "All gone."

Carlos leaned forward and again kissed her on the top of her head. He didn't say anything, though he wanted to. Because he wasn't so sure they were all gone. There was something about one of the people in the photos—the beautiful, middle-aged woman posed smiling with the baby and her husband—that looked vaguely familiar, tickling his memory, like a telltale itch in his foot.

They stayed on the porch together for a while longer, as the evening deepened and darkness descended on the streets and houses around them. They were interrupted finally by the ringing of the telephone. It was Carlos's mother calling from New York City for advice on a family conundrum. But instead of going inside with Carlos, Carole gathered a pillow and one of Sophie's quilts from the parlor and returned to the porch. Switching off the porch light and moving the chaise lounge to her best approximation of the exact spot where her mother and father had posed with her in the photograph, she stretched out on the tight webbing of the chair, tucked the quilt snugly around her legs and chest against the evening chill, and let herself drift.

Lying still, she could hear the soft tapping of errant raindrops against the porch roof and the sound of Carlos's voice on the telephone through the open front door, vague and distant. Soon her eyes closed, and very soon after that she fell asleep. And while she was asleep she had a dream. In the dream she was sitting in freshly-mowed grass, and a cool breeze was tickling her face. Barely audible was the sound of a man's voice, coming from an un-known place that was out of her sight. She was alone and frightened, and called out soundlessly to the voice, then called out again. And then, just as she was about to start to cry, she was lifted up from behind, so that her legs dangled free in the air. The hands holding her turned her around so that the man's face was square in front of her, so big that it was all she could see. The face was young and bearded, the mouth open into a wide, toothy smile, the eyes bright with energy and humor and intelligence. The man brought her face close and kissed her on the nose. Below her was the sound of a dog barking. She couldn't see the dog, but knew what it looked like. She was three colors—black, white, and brown—and her name was Daisy. She barked again, and then again, and Carole woke up.

The barking dog was somewhere several blocks away, and the barking continued for a few moments more, then abruptly ended. Carole lay still for several minutes, hoping to fall back to sleep and regain the dream. But it was not to be, so Carole rose from the chaise lounge and moved inside. Carlos was just finishing up his phone call; she could hear him saying his goodbyes to the half dozen or so Estrada clan members who would have insisted on getting in a few words to him.

Carole climbed the stairway to the second floor, entered the bathroom and began drawing water into the tub. She tested the temperature with her fingers, adjusting it until it was just right, then poured in a double-dose of bubble bath. Sitting on the edge of the tub watching it slowly fill, she felt serene and content, as if she had been relieved of a great fear. She didn't bother to question the feeling, choosing instead to simply enjoy it. But if she had wondered about the source of it, she might have been able to see it; after all, it was simple and straightforward and undisguised. Carole would never have long evening conversations with relatives back home, or family reun-ions, or birthdays to remember. She would always only have Carlos, and the family they could create together. Still, she was not, she knew, without her own distinctly peopled history. And now they were all there for her, too, their distance from her measured by a different metric, to be sure, but there for her nevertheless. They were inside of her, only waiting for the opportuni-ty to be reintroduced. When the tub was full, Carole turned off the water and left the bathroom to search for Carlos, to invite him up for a good soak.

The next morning, after Carole had left for work, Carlos worked for a couple of hours on his cartoons, then hopped into his truck and drove downtown to a hardware store for a can of varnish. With the advent of Carole's pregnancy, they'd decided against converting the small room adjoining their bedroom into a master bath, opting instead for a baby bedroom. So Carlos had gotten to work and cut a neat doorway through the plaster and lath between the two rooms, had framed it in oak, and had beveled the thin strips of trim to match the existing door trim throughout the house. All that was left to finish the job was to seal and varnish the trim, then mount it around the door frame with brads.

The late morning was perfect, the early autumn sun held to only warm by a gentle breeze, the air fresh and clean from the scrubbing of the day before. So instead of doing his varnishing in the basement, he set up his sawhorses on the front lawn and brought the job to the open air. The job was simple and fast, but the morning was so alluring that Carlos slowed it down as much as possible to enjoy the luxury of the fine day. Finally, though, he had to admit that he was done, and reluctantly tapped the cover onto the can of varnish and dropped his thin brush into a can of solvent. He stretched languidly, then ambled down the lawn to the sidewalk and looked lazily up and down the quiet street. No one was to be seen except the old lady with the walker slowly making her way toward him from the west. She's changed directions, he thought idly. Usually she comes from the east. He had to admire her conviction, he thought. In her eighties probably, out there every day doing her rounds, daring her old, worn-out body to fail her. He waited patiently for her to reach him.

"Hello," he said when she'd gotten even with him.

"Hello to you," the old lady said, stopping her walker and looking over to him. She had a natural wide-open smile, as if she were squinting against the sun, and Carlos was amazed at how white her teeth were.

"You amaze me," Carlos said. "I think you have more energy than I do."

The old lady chuckled. "It's do or die," she said. "I'm afraid if I let in, I'll start rusting up like one of those old hay balers you see out in the fields."

"I'm Carlos Estrada," Carlos said, offering his hand.

The old lady hesitated for a moment, then took his hand. "A pleasure to meet you finally, Mr. Estrada," she said.

Carlos considered the woman's hand. It was wrinkled and dotted with liver spots and showed early signs of arthritis. But the hand was delicately boned and the fingers long and sculpted. There was a time, Carlos knew, when her hands had been beautiful. "I'm sorry," Carlos said, "I missed the name."

The old lady again hesitated for a quick moment. "Mrs. Mullins," she said finally. Her eyes left Carlos and scanned the three stories of the shining Winkler home. "You've done a marvelous job with the house," she said. "For a while I was afraid he was a goner."

"Thanks," Carlos said smiling, "it's been a labor of love."

"Nice to know there's still people who care," she said.

"Say," Carlos offered, "I'm about to have a something to drink. Would you care to join me?" He was enjoying their conversation and wanted it to continue. He also had a couple of questions for her taking shape in the back of his mind.

"Well…that would be lovely, actually," she said, looking to him and offering up again those two rows of white teeth. And so Carlos arranged two lawn chairs on the grass in the shade of the dogwood tree, helped the old lady into one of them, then excused himself and hurried to the kitchen to prepare two tall glasses of Carole's lemon bubbly water.

While Carlos was pouring the drinks, Carole was just finishing up outlining to Stella Phillips the wonderful details of their court victory. Carole had her office windows open wide to the warm morning, and the soft breeze moved the ends of the drapes and cooled and refreshed the musty office air. The two women sat side by side in armchairs, sipping tea.

"So he's going to have to rebuild that fence," Stella said, her face beaming with sweet victory.

"No," Carole corrected. "He's going to have to pay to have it rebuilt by someone you hire. It's on your property, remember? And he's persona non grata, right?"

"That's right," Stella agreed heartily, taking a sip of her tea. "The old stinker," she added.

"Was he always such a poop?" Carole asked.

"No," Stella responded, her voice suddenly perplexed. "He was never what you'd call friendly—always to himself—but when Loretta was alive— that was his wife, Loretta—when Loretta was alive, he was at least part of things. Now…" she shrugged her shoulders and thought for a moment, "he just seems to hate everything."

Carole sat quietly, trying to imagine what it would be like to hate everything.

"Well he can hate me if he wants to, and I'm sorry about it, but I'm not going anyplace," Stella offered stubbornly. "It's my old house and my old memories, and I'm not leaving until I have to."

Carole took in the statement, then drifted away momentarily into her own thoughts. "My house is filled with memories, too," she said finally. "Old, old memories, but none of them are mine."

Stella looked over to Carole curiously. "You live in an old house, too?" she asked.

"Uh-huh," Carole said, nodding. "Up on Summit Avenue."

"You don't say," Stella responded. "My sister lives on Summit Avenue. Now which part do you live on?"

"Two blocks off of Centennial," Carole answered. She was smiling now, and animated. "It was a dump when we got it...boy, what a dump...you wouldn't believe...but my husband Carlos, he's a miracle worker with anything constructed, and he goes to work on it and..."

As Carole continued on with her story Stella sat still, her eyes locked on Carole's happy face, making a quick personal inventory of what she knew and remembered of Summit Avenue. After several moments of listening, she was finally able to get a word in. "You're not talking about the old Winkler place?" she asked.

"That's the one," Carole responded. "And get this," she continued, "I inherited it."

And at that, Stella's mouth fell open.

While Stella was trying to regroup her wits at the law office, Carlos sat on the front lawn with the old lady, sipping bubbly water and talking small talk. And unbeknownst to the woman sitting next to him, he was on the hunt and closing in. The possibility had presented itself to him when he was pouring their drinks, and what he had to do before taking the plunge was to get a good, long, hard look at her.

"I imagine you've lived on the street a long time," he said.

The old lady held her glass in both hands, lifting it carefully to her lips for a sip. "Oh, yes," she said finally, sitting her glass down and wiping her lips with a finger. "Most of my life, really."

"I gather the house had been empty since the late seventies," Carlos said.

"That'd be about right," the old lady said vaguely.

"What a shame," Carlos offered to the air around them. "Such a beautiful house, sitting here wasting away."

"Terrible!" she said heatedly, forgetting herself. "Just terrible! Broke my heart to see it, all those years." Then she caught herself. "I mean, as you say, such a waste," she said, lifting her glass to her lips.

"My wife Carole is related to the Winklers," Carlos threw out casually.

"Really?" the old lady responded.

"Yup," he said, "she inherited the house from Henry. We know about Henry and Willy, and we know a little about Ellen, and William, who we guess was Henry's son."

He was watching her closely, and noted happily that she was pulling away, withdrawing from him. He had her, and he knew it. So he took the plunge. "We have some holes, though," he continued, "that maybe someone like you can help us fill. Did you know any of them?"

"Oh," she said nervously, "there were some, but I...they were a close-knit bunch," she concluded, looking quickly down to her glass.

"Hmmm," Carlos said, disappointed. "So you didn't know any of them."

The old lady forced herself to look over to him. "He was a solitary man, Henry," she said. "Henry Winkler, I mean," she added.

For a moment Carlos sat considering the awkward statement and the equally awkward old lady next to him, trying, he knew, to hide the truth without lying. "Excuse me for a second," he said, getting up. It was time to end it.

Once inside the house, Carlos hurried to the study for the old envelope with the photographs taken on the porch. It ended up taking him several minutes of frenzied searching to find the envelope, which had managed to become hidden under a disorderly pile of loose paper on the bookshelf. "Hah!" he exclaimed when he found it. Grabbing the treasure, he headed quickly back through the house.

But when he had left the house onto the front porch, he stopped flat in his tracks. For to his surprise, before him on the lawn, stood Carole. In the few minutes he'd been inside, she'd arrived, her car parked in the driveway. The old lady had risen from her seat and stood facing her. Standing behind them and off to the side was another old lady whom Carlos presumed to be Carole's client, the woman named Stella.

Carlos watched as the two women considered each other. They were a contrast in age: the old lady frail and bent and much shorter, looking like the softest wind might blow her away; Carole straight and vital, her stomach showing the first signs of the great-grandchild growing inside of her, her blue eyes deep and bothered, her pink lips small and pursed, her arms hanging loose at her sides.

I was captured by the small piece of serpentine she wore on a gold chain around her neck, still a part of her after almost thirty years. Then, a moment later, I was captured again by the pathos that was so clearly to be seen in her face, and my obvious complicity in it. But now that I was finally face-to-face with her I couldn't help making the comparisons that were impossible when she was a vague portrait passing quickly by in an automobile or a distant figure on her knees in the garden. I wanted to see something of

264

Rachel in her, and I did: in her eyebrows, thin and arched high, like Roman bridges, and in her ears, which were small and round, like saucers, and in her skin, which was mottled lightly, almost imperceptibly, with freckles—like Rachel's, and like mine when I was young. I stood there meekly as she appraised me, very much afraid.

When Carole finally spoke, her voice was small, almost a whisper, and tentative, as if she were just learning to speak. "Hello," she said.

"Hello, Carole," I said.

"You're my grandmother," Carole said. It wasn't said as a question, or as a matter of fact. It was an accusation.

"Yes, honey," I said. "I'm your grandmother. Your grandmother Irene."

Carole was silent for a moment. Her lips trembled slightly, her eyes defensive. "What were their names?" she asked finally.

"Their names were Rachel and Craig," I said. "Rachel was my daughter, and Henry's granddaughter." I let my eyes drop to the stone around her neck. "That piece of serpentine was Henry's last gift to you."

Carole's hand went to her throat and covered the stone, as if protecting it. "How old was I?" she asked.

"You were a little more than two," I said. For a moment more I watched her, knowing full well the demons she was wrestling. "They loved you with all their hearts, honey," I said. "Don't ever think otherwise. But they died." Then my voice failed me.

For a moment Carole stood in silence, her lips pressed together, her eyes deep and sad and wet. "Why didn't you tell me?" she asked finally, her voice breaking.

"I didn't know if you'd want me," I answered.

We stood there for a moment longer, separated still. But then by some grace she moved to me, and I to her, and finally we were together, in each other's arms. She was lithe and strong and beautiful, and I could feel her shoulders shaking next to my face. Finally, we were all back together, Craig and Rachel and Henry and Willy and me, and my beloved Jeff, together again with Carole. And finally I had my answer, and could be at peace.

Carlos left the porch and walked to the two women, who stood close together on the lawn, holding each other. He reached out to touch Carole's back, then moved his hand downward until he found Irene's thin arms.

Behind them, the old house rose up on its hilltop perch, its front windows warm and twinkling, the long porch smiling happily, joyously, in the bright autumn sun.

Made in the USA
San Bernardino, CA
15 May 2017